A Woman of the Iron People

A Woman
of the Iron
People

Eleanor Arnason

© Copyright 1991 by Eleanor Arnason
First e-reads publication 1999
www.e-reads.com
ISBN 0-7592-2416-1

For the Members of the Aardvarks,
the oldest established SF-writing workshop
in Minneapolis and/or St. Paul

(We also do mysteries
and doctoral dissertations.)

The water says:
I remember.
I came first of all.
There was nothing before me.

In the time of rain
rain fell on the water.
In the time of dryness
the water reflected the sky.

I came first of all.
There was nothing before me.

Vapor rose.
It became
the tree of heaven.

Vapor rose.
It became
the bird of the sun.

A seed fell.
The earth began growing.
Animals sprang up.
The vegetation was thick.

Then came the people.
Then came the spirits
and the powerful demons
who live under the earth.

Let me tell you:
I will outlast them.

Even the demons
will disappear in time.

I have no shape.
No one can divide me.
No one can say
what I really am.

Acknowledgements

M y thanks to the following people who read this novel in manuscript and gave me advice on changes:

Ruth Berman, John Douglas, David G. Hartwell, Eric M. Heideman, Albert W. Kuhfeld, Mike Levy, Sandra Lindow, and Shoshona Pederson.

Al Kuhfeld designed the wonderful starship and read the novel with an eye for errors in science. The manuscript went through three revisions after he saw it, and he is in no way responsible for any new errors that may have been introduced. Susan Pederson helped me design the culture of the Iron People. Ruth Berman came up with my favorite name for the starship. P. C. Hodgell drew the map.

My special thanks to Bill Gober, who heard me talk about the novel years ago at Minicon. Every year since then he has come up to me at Minicon and loomed over me and said, "Have you finished the novel about the furry people yet?"

Here it is, Bill. I hope it's worth the wait.

Table of Contents

FROM: *The Committee on the First Contact Problem*
TO: *The Members of the First Interstellar Expedition*

The problem, as we see it, divides in three: (1) You may meet people who have a technology more advanced than ours; (2) You may meet people with an equal technology; (3) You may meet people with a less advanced technology.

(We will leave aside, for the time being, the problem of what is meant by "more" and "less" advanced. We will also leave aside the possibility that the aliens may have a technology so different from ours that there is no way to compare the two.)

We think you are most likely to encounter problem number three: the aliens with a less advanced technology. But we'll discuss all the possibilities, just in case.

The aliens with an equal technology present the least problem. We certainly cannot hurt them, not at a distance of 18.2 light-years. If their technology is more or less the same as ours, they won't be able to hurt us, either. There is the possibility of considerable gain for both cultures without much risk. You can probably go ahead with confidence.

If you meet aliens with a really advanced technology (with FTL travel, for example) you will have to stop and think.

According to current social theory, any species that is able to travel to the stars is also able to destroy itself, and any species that can destroy itself, will, unless it learns very quickly how to deal with its own less pleasant aspects.

We think it's unlikely that you will meet a star-faring species that is aggressive, violent, bigoted, or crazy with greed. But all our theories are based on a sample of one, and we may not be as nice as we think we are.

If you meet a species with a superior technology, be cautious. You may want to keep your distance, at least at first. You may not want to tell them where you come from.

If they are decent and peaceful, they will respect your caution. If they do not, remember that your ship has been provided with the means for self-destruction. If necessary, you can wipe the computer system clean and kill everyone onboard.

This capability has been provided with extreme reluctance. (See Appendix D.) It may be evidence that we, as a species, have not outgrown our own terrible past.

The problem when dealing with a more advanced species is self-protection.

(Remember, when we talk about advancement here, we are speaking only about technology.)

The problem when dealing with a less advanced species is karma. We don't want to hurt them. Our species has done a lot of hurting over time.

Be *very* careful if you encounter people whose technology is not equal to ours. Remember all the cultures destroyed over the past seven centuries. Remember all the millions of people who have died on Earth: entire tribes and nations, language groups, religions—vanished, murdered. Remember the other hominids who are no longer with us. Remember *Homo sapiens neanderthalensis.*

We think we understand the process now. We think we will not do these things again. But we are not certain.

Go very slowly. Think about what you are doing.

Lao Zi and Zhuang Zi remind us of the dangers of action.

The masters of Chan and Zen warn us that when we discriminate, when we divide "good" from "evil" and "high" from "low," we are moving away from true understanding.

Karl Marx tells us that action is inevitable and that we have to discriminate in order to understand.

You have your choices of sages.

However, remember that—according to Marx—the goal of socialism is *mindful* action, history made conscious, people who know what they are doing.

xiv

Remember, also, that categories are not fixed. "Good" and "evil" change their meaning. "High and "low" are relative. The distinctions—the discriminations—you take with you on your journey may not be useful when you arrive. Good luck.

Copies of this memo have been input to the Open Access Information System (OASIS), the Archives of the Alliance of Human Communities (ANKH), and the Archives of the Fifth, Sixth, and Eighth Internationals.

Appendix A: On the possible meaning(s) of "more" and "less" advanced.

Appendix B: Why we think you are more likely to meet people with a less advanced technology.

Appendix C: Minority report on the dangers of cultural chauvinism.

Appendix D: Minority report on the dangers of fear.

Appendix E: Minority report on the relevance of Daoist and Buddhist concepts.

Appendix F: Minority report on the relevance of Karl Marx.

Appendix G: *Dao De Jing.* (Complete)

Appendix H: *The German Ideology.* (Selections)

A Woman
of the Iron
People

Part One

Anasu

H er mother had been a metal worker, a follower of the Mistress of the Forge. But she died young, one spring in the mating season. This sometimes happened. A woman left the village and never returned.

The old crones said, "A crazy man got her. Hu! The lot of women is difficult!" In any case, Nia and her brother were alone. Suhai, who was one of her mother's sisters, took them in. She was a large gruff woman with a pelt so dark that it looked more black than brown.

Besides taking them, she took their mother's belongings: the tent, the cart, the six bowhorn geldings, and all the tools of iron, bronze, and stone.

"A just payment," Suhai told them. "You will cost me a lot in the winters to come. I have children of my own to care for, too."

Her brother Anasu, who was eight then, said, "You have always been a grasping person."

Suhai glowered. "Go outside. I don't want to look at you."

Anasu made the gesture of assent, then stood. The flap of the tent was up. She could see her brother clearly. He was slender and graceful. His pelt was reddish brown. It shone like copper in the sunlight. He wore that day—she thought she remembered later—a kilt of dark blue cloth, high boots, and a belt with a silver buckle.

Anasu left. Nia looked at Suhai, sitting hunched by the fire, which was out.

"Thank the Mother of Mothers I have no sons. Well, I intend to do that which is right. I'll raise him, though I don't expect to enjoy a moment. You, Nia, will be less trouble, I am sure. The women of our family have always been even-tempered."

Nia made no reply.

Things turned out as Suhai had expected. She got no pleasure from raising Anasu, though he was clever and dexterous. No lad his age did better embroidery. He was good with a bow. He was good-humored, too, except around Suhai. The two of them always quarreled.

Nia stayed out of the quarrels. She was, she discovered, a timid person. Good for little, she told herself. She could not help Anasu, though she felt closer to him than to anyone; and she could not stand up to Suhai. Always and always she did what her aunt wanted.

Like all the people in the world, her people followed the herds. In the spring they went north to the Summer Land: a wide, flat plain. There were many small lakes and shallow rivers. On days when Suhai let her go free, she and Anasu built fish traps out of the branches of a bush that grew at the edges of the rivers. The branches were thin and flexible. They could be woven around one another, then tied with pieces of stringbark.

They put the traps into a river. Then they sat on the bank and talked till a thrashing in the water told them a fish was caught.

When he was in a dreamy mood, Anasu talked of flying. The large clouds of summer looked habitable to him.

"Not the thunderclouds, of course, but the others. I don't think they'd be good for herding. They have too many hills. But I could take my bow up there. We know there is water. Maybe there are fish."

She listened, not saying much. Anasu was two years older than she was. He always had more to say.

In fall the village went south: the herd first, guided by the adult men. Then came the carts, the women and children, and the very old men. Hisu, the bow master, was one of these.

The Winter Land was a rolling plain dotted with trees. In the south were stony hills. Beyond the hills was an enormous body of water.

"Our salt comes from there," Anasu told her. "Some of the men, the really adventurous ones, stay here alone in the summer. Hisu told me this. He did it when he was young. He waited till the herd was gone, then crossed the hills. On the other side are smaller hills, made of sand, and then the water. It stretches to the horizon, Hisu said, like the plain in the Summer Land; and it

4

tastes salty. Anyway, he made pans out of wood. There is no wood nearby, he said. He had to bring it from the hills of stone. Hu! What a lot of work! Anyway, he filled the pans with water. When the water dried, there was salt in the pans." He looked at her, excited by this bit of information and wanting her to be excited, too.

Nia made the gesture that meant she heard and understood.

Anasu made the gesture that meant "if that's the way you feel about it." Then he said, "I think I'll gather salt when I'm a man."

There was something hard in her throat. She never liked to think of growing up.

The years went by. When she was ten, Suhai began to teach her how to work iron. This made her happy, she told Anasu.

"You ought to have started a year ago or maybe two years back. Suhai is always grudging and slow."

"Nonetheless, I am happy," Nia said. "Suhai is good at what she does."

"In the smithy, maybe. Elsewhere, no."

Anasu grew tall. His body began to thicken. Suhai really hated him now.

"I have never liked men. Even when I was full of the spring lust, I still thought they were awful. I'm tired of coming home and finding you in my tent."

Anasu, who was fourteen by this time, made the gesture of assent. He gathered his belongings—the kilts, the boots, the one long cloak for winter—and left. His bow was in its case over one shoulder, and his knife hung from his belt.

Nia stood up, shaking. "Enough is enough, old woman. I won't tolerate you any longer. I'm going, too."

"Very well." Suhai sat down by the fire. Dinner was cooking in a big pot. She pulled out a hunk of meat and ate it.

Nia began to pack.

She walked out of the tent, feeling proud. For the first time she could remember, she had done something important on her own. What next? She didn't know. She stopped and looked around. It was late summer. The day was hot and still. Smoke rose straight up from the village's cooking fires. In the distance the yellow plain shimmered. She had no idea at all of what to do.

"Nia?"

It was Ti-antai, her cousin: a plump woman with dark brown fur.

"Anasu told me he has left my mother."

Nia made the gesture of affirmation. "So have I."

"That terrible woman! She will end by driving everyone away. My grandmother told me once, Suhai ought to have been a man. She is too quarrelsome to be a woman. Come stay with me, for the time being anyway."

Nia made the gesture of agreement.

She stayed with Ti-antai on the trip south. Then, when they reached the Winter Land, she moved in with Hua, an ancient woman whose children had all died. Her tent was empty, and she needed help at her forge.

"A good exchange. You help. You keep me company. I will teach you the secrets of gold and silver. I know them, you know. There was a time when I was the best smith in the village. I'm not so bad these days, either. My hands have gotten a little stiff, of course, and my eyes aren't what they used to be. But what is, after all? In any case, I will teach you how to inlay silver into iron. And gold, too. Move in whenever you like."

Anasu traded his best piece of embroidery for two pieces of leather. From these he made a tent, a small one. He lived by himself at the edge of the village. That winter Nia saw him little.

In the spring, on the trip north, he rode near Hua's cart and helped with the bowhorns. One of them was a young male, strong but reluctant to pull.

By this time Anasu was full grown. He was quieter than he used to be, though still good-tempered.

One morning, midway through the trip, Nia woke a little earlier than usual. She got up and went outside. They were camped next to a river. Mist drifted on the water. The sun was just beginning to show above a range of hills in the east. She went to the cart. The back panel was fastened with hinges and chains. It could be let down, so that loading and unloading could be done more easily, and it could be fastened halfway down, making a flat place. Anasu slept on it. He had thrown off his cloak sometime in the night. He lay on his back, one arm over his face, shielding his eyes. All at once Nia saw her brother clearly. He was large and solid. He looked shaggy, rough, a little unfamiliar. The change was coming. She felt a terrible grief.

He woke and stretched. "Hu! Am I stiff!"

She thought of hugging him, but decided no. She would have to explain why she did it. Instead, she went to start the fire and make breakfast.

That summer Nia tried to spend more time with Anasu. But he was restless, silent. He liked to hunt and fish alone. When he was in the village, he worked at making arrows or on finishing a large piece of embroidery. It showed a man with large curving horns: the Master of the Herds. On either side of him were bowhorn does. Above him was the sun and a pair of birds.

"Don't bother him," Ti-antai said. "He is getting ready for the change. If you want to do something for him, work on his parting gifts."

Nia made the gesture of assent.

The summer was rainy and unusually short. The sun was still pretty far to the north when the birds began to leave.

6

"A bad winter," Hua said. "I'll ask the tanner what she wants in exchange for a good fur cloak. Now, we'd better start packing."

Just before they left the Summer Land, the sky cleared. For two days it was bright and warm. Anasu came to her then. "Let's go catch fish."

They made traps and set them in the river. Then they sat on the bank. Already the leaves on the bushes were starting to turn yellow. The sun was hot. A river lizard sat on a nearby rock. Head up, it watched them carefully. Under its chin was a bag of skin, orange in color. Once or twice, it inflated this and croaked.

Anasu picked up a twig and broke it into pieces. "I'm getting more and more irritable. There are days, Nia, when I can barely stand people. I think—the next one that comes near me I will hit."

The change, Nia thought.

"I decided to tell you this. I want you to know, if I leave suddenly or get violent, it is because I cannot keep control any longer."

"We all know this."

He made the gesture of disagreement suddenly, violently. "You cannot know. My bones are on fire. It's like a fire in a peat bog that never goes out. I have never felt worse than this, even when our mother died." He stood up. "I'm not going to stay here, Nia. Good-bye."

He walked away. Nia sat awhile looking at the river. A fish thrashed in the water where they had set one of their traps. She waded out to get it.

On the trip south she barely saw him. Once or twice, through the dust, she got a glimpse of a young man riding. It might have been him. One evening he came to their tent. His fur was rough and dull. His clothes were dirty. He sat down across from them and helped himself to dinner. Old Hua, who was usually talkative, said nothing.

At last Nia said, "How are you?"

He looked at her blankly. His eyes were not pure yellow, she noticed. There was orange around the pupils. She hadn't remembered that.

He made the gesture that meant neither good nor bad. Then he went back to eating. After he was done, he left.

"Finish up your gifts," old Hua said.

She did. The last one was a buckle made of iron, covered with silver. It showed a bowhorn fighting a killer of the mountains.

"Not bad," said Hua. "You will do me proud someday."

Nia made the gesture that meant a polite or modest refusal to agree.

"You have too little self-respect," Hua said.

The trip ended. The people set up their tents next to the Brown River. North of them there was a stone ridge. Its lower slopes were forested. To the south, across the river, was the plain: rolling, tree-dotted, late summer yellow. The herd was pastured there.

7

There was no sign of Anasu. Nia felt uneasy.

"He will come," Ti-antai said. "No man leaves without his parting gifts—unless, of course, the change drives him crazy. But that rarely happens."

"You are not always a comfort, cousin."

At first the weather was dry. Then it began to rain. Every day there were a few drops at least. Most days it rained or drizzled for hours. The air was cold. Hua said her bones ached. Nonetheless, she kept busy.

One afternoon they were both at the forge. Nia worked the bellows for Hua, who was making a long knife: a parting gift for Gersu, the tanner's son, who was a little younger than Anasu.

When the hammering was done and the blade was in cold water, Nia set down the bellows. She rubbed her neck.

"Nia." It was Anasu. His voice sounded hesitant.

Nia looked around. He stood nearby, holding his bowhorn's reins. He looked worse than ever: shaggy, muddy, confused.

"Anasu?"

"I—" He stopped for a moment. "I have come for the gifts. I am going across the river."

She made the gesture of acknowledgment, then the gesture of regret.

"You stay here," Hua said. "No one will bother you. We'll pack everything."

They went inside. Hua put wood on the fire, then set a pan of milk to heat.

Nia got out the new saddlebags the tanner had made, then the cloth she had gotten from Blind Angai, the weaver, in return for a new pot. She or Hua or Ti-antai had made most of the rest of the things. She laid them out one by one: the new knife, the kettle, the brass needles, the awl, and the long-handled comb, the kind that men used to comb the hair on their backs.

What else? She was having trouble thinking.

"The new belt, ninny!" Hua was packing food: dried meat, dried berries, bread.

At last they were done. Hua poured the milk into a cup. They took the saddlebags to Anasu. It had begun to rain a little. He was standing where they'd left him, looking nervous. His bowhorn, sensing the nervousness, kept moving, turning its head, flicking its ears, tugging at the reins.

Just as they reached Anasu, he yanked the reins and shouted, "Keep still, you!"

The bowhorn bellowed and reared. Anasu pulled it down. He grabbed the saddlebags from Nia. A moment later he was astride the bowhorn. He bent and slapped the beast on one shoulder. The bowhorn began to run.

"Anasu!" Nia cried.

He was gone.

"Men!" said Hua. "They always make a spectacle. And here I am with this cup of milk. I meant to give it to him. Well, it will do me as much good." She took a swallow.

Nia made a groaning sound, then doubled her hand and began to beat one thigh.

"That is right. Get the grief out of you."

Nia kept hitting her thigh.

As Hua had predicted, it was a bad winter. It was cold, and there was a lot of snow. Nia wondered how Anasu was doing. She prayed to the Master of the Herds, asking him to protect her brother.

At the time of the solstice Gersu went crazy and had to be driven out of the village. Afterward, his mother took his gifts across the river. She hung them from the branches of a big tree. Maybe he would find them and take them. Most likely, not.

"He always had a bad look in his eyes," said Hua.

Nia made the gesture of agreement.

Spring came early. The plain turned pale blue. The bushes along the river put out yellow blossoms. Nia felt almost happy.

"You see," said Hua. "We get over everything."

"No. I don't believe that."

"You will see."

The mating season came. Ti-antai, who had just finished weaning her last child, felt the spring lust and left. Nia moved into her tent and took care of the children.

Ten days later Ti-antai returned. She looked rumpled and relaxed. "Well, that's over." She stretched and yawned.

"Did you see Anasu?"

"Of course not. Nia, what's wrong with you? He must be far to the south with the other young men. I didn't get down there." Ti-antai rolled a blanket into a pillow, then lay down. She yawned again. "I got a big fellow, half a day's ride from here. He does good carving. He gave me a salt horn full of salt. Hu! Do I need to sleep!"

None of the women had met Anasu, but none of them had gotten very far south. They had all mated with older men, who had their territories close to the village.

"Don't worry," said Hua. "In a year or two or three someone will meet him and tell you."

Nia made the gesture that meant she understood. As she made the gesture, she thought—there was something wrong. Something out of balance. Why were people so often lonely?

9

They went north to the Summer Land. Once settled there Nia looked around for new friends. She had spent too much time with Anasu. She had relied on him too much.

She picked the younger Angai to be her friend. Angai was the daughter of the shamaness. She was a thin, clever girl, often sarcastic. But she knew many interesting things: the uses of plants, the meaning of flights of birds. Like Nia, she was lonely.

"I have many skills," she told Nia. "But not the skill of friendship. How terrible!"

Nia looked at her. Was she being sarcastic? Yes. Her mouth was twisted down at one corner, a sign that she didn't really mean what she had said.

At midsummer, at the festival, they got drunk together and fell asleep in one another's arms.

In the late summer Nia made a necklace for Angai. Every link was a bird made of silver.

"Wonderful!" Angai said. She hugged Nia, then put the necklace on. "Everyone in the village will envy me!"

"You think too much of other people's opinions."

Angai looked irritated, then said, "That may be."

For a day or two after that Angai was standoffish. Then she came to Hua's forge and brought a gift. It was a salve that made any burn stop hurting.

"It's my mother's own recipe. I made it this time. My mother says it's good."

Nia took the jar. "Thank you."

"Can we stop fighting now?"

Nia laughed. "Yes."

The fall was dry, and the trip south was easy, almost pleasant. Nia and Angai kept together. Sometimes Angai rode in Hua's cart. Sometimes Nia rode beside the cart of the shamaness. She never got into it, of course. It was full of magic.

One day they rode off, away from the caravan. They let their bowhorns run. When the beasts began to tire, they stopped. The land was flat and empty. They saw nothing except the yellow plain and the blue-green sky. Somewhere close by a groundbird sang: *whistle-click-whistle.*

"Hu!" said Nia. She rubbed her bowhorn's neck.

"There are times," Angai said, "when I get tired of people. I think, I would like to be a man and live by myself."

"You have a lot of strange ideas."

Angai made the gesture of agreement. "It comes of living with my mother. Let's spend the night out here, away from everyone."

"Why?"

Angai made the gesture of uncertainty.

"That is not much of a reason," Nia said. "And I have no desire to do the things that men do."

10

Late in the afternoon they rode back to the caravan. It was still moving. The carts and the animals threw up clouds of dust. As they came near Nia could hear the sound of voices: women and children shouting. For a moment the noise made her angry. She wanted to turn back, into the silence of the plain.

She didn't. Instead, she rode on, looking for Hua's cart.

When they reached the Winter Land, Ti-antai fell sick. Blood came out of her, and she miscarried. The shamaness held a ceremony of purification and a ceremony to avert any further bad occurrences. After that Ti-antai grew better, but very slowly. She was sick well into the winter.

Nothing else important happened, except that Nia found she could get along with Suhai. They took to visiting each other—not often, but once in a while. Suhai was getting old. There were gray hairs in her pelt. Her broad shoulders sagged. She complained of the winter cold and her children's ingratitude.

"They never visit me. After all the years of care they leave me alone. Is this in balance? Is this usual and right?"

Nia said nothing.

"Well?" Suhai asked.

"I will not criticize their behavior. The proverbs say, don't speak badly of kinfolk or anyone else you travel with. The proverbs also say, don't intervene in other people's quarrels."

"Hu! I raised a wise woman, did I?"

Nia didn't answer.

Suhai got up, moving stiffly. "I'm not going to listen to a child spit out wisdom like the fish in the old story that spit out pieces of gold. It's unnatural. Good-bye."

"Good-bye, foster mother. I will visit you in a day or two."

Spring came. It was early again. Nia began to feel restless. At night she was troubled by dreams. Often, in the dreams, she saw her brother or other young men, even crazy Gersu.

When she was up, she was usually tired. She found it difficult to concentrate on anything. She began to make mistakes at the forge.

"Can't you do anything the right way?" Hua asked.

Nia stared at her, bemused.

"Well, that's an answer of a kind. But not a good kind," Hua said.

Finally she picked up a knife blade that was still hot. She burnt her hand badly. Hua took care of the burn, then said, "Enough. Get out. Don't come back until you are able to work."

Angai gave her a potion that reduced the pain. She slept a lot. Her dreams were fragmentary, unclear, disturbing. Always, it seemed, Anasu was in them.

1 1

At length her hand stopped hurting. Now, though, it seemed her body was full of eerie sensations: itches and tingles. Often she felt hot, though it was still early spring. The weather wasn't especially warm.

She went to visit Ti-antai.

"The spring lust," her cousin said. "I can see it in your face. Well, you're old enough. Pack your bag now. Food and a gift for the man. Something useful. Cloth or a knife. You'll be ready to go in a day or two."

She packed. That night she didn't sleep at all. Her body itched and burned. In the morning she went out. The touch of the wind made her shiver. Time to go, she thought. She got her favorite bowhorn and saddled it. After that she went to get her saddlebag.

"Take care," Hua said.

For a moment she didn't realize who the old woman was. Then she remembered. "Yes." She went out, mounted, and rode away.

She forded the river. The water was shallow. There was a little mist. On the far side was a tree. A couple of rags hung from the branches. There was a knife driven into the wood. The blade and hilt were rusted. She glanced at all this, then forgot it and rode onto the plain.

At midafternoon she came to the edge of the herd. The first animal she saw was a huge male. One horn was broken. The long shaggy hair that covered his neck and chest was silver-brown. He bellowed, then lowered his head, as if about to charge. Then he lifted his head and shook it. A moment later he trotted away.

Good, she thought. She was in no mood for a confrontation.

She rode on. Soon she came upon other animals: yearlings and two-year-olds. They were too old to be mothered and too young to stand their ground against the big males, the guardians of the herd. This time of year they stayed at the edges of the herd, well away from the does and their new fawns. They didn't like it at the edges. Often the yearlings would try to go in and find their mothers. But the big males would drive them away.

Nia stopped at dusk. She found a tree and tethered her bowhorn. Then she built a fire. The night was cold. She had forgotten her cloak. She stayed up and kept the fire going.

In the morning, at sunrise, the man appeared, He looked to be thirty or thirty-five, broad-shouldered, heavy. His pelt was dark brown. He wore a yellow tunic, high boots, a necklace of silver and bronze.

He reined his bowhorn and looked at her a moment. His gaze was steady and calculating. Then he dismounted. She stepped back, all at once uneasy.

"I thought you looked pretty young," he said. "Is this going to be a lot of trouble?"

"I don't know."

12

His fur was thick and glossy. He had an interesting scar: a streak of white that went down his right arm from the shoulder to the inside of the elbow.

"Who are you?" Nia asked.

He looked irritated. "Inani. Do you mind not talking? Talking makes me edgy."

She made the gesture of assent. He moved closer, then reached out and touched her. She shivered. Gently he put one arm around her. What happened next was not entirely clear to her.

When they were done, Nia got up and rebuilt the fire. She heated milk. Inani dozed with his back against the tree. From time to time he started awake. He glanced around, then relaxed and dozed off again. At last he woke completely. Nia gave him a cup. They sat on opposite sides of the fire and drank.

Inani said, "Who are you?"

"Nia. Suhai's foster daughter. Have you met my brother Anasu?"

"No. I know the men whose territories are next to mine. I keep away from them as much as I can, but during the migrations things get mixed up. People get too close together. Sometimes I think it would be better to go away entirely."

"Who is your mother?"

"The tentmaker. Enwa. Is she alive?"

"Yes."

"Good." Inani stood up. "Stay here, will you?" He mounted his bowhorn. "You're less trouble than I expected. I'll return in the evening."

He rode off. She slept most of the day. In the evening Inani returned. They mated again. He made camp a short distance away. Nia watched his campfire for a while, then went to sleep.

The next day he left again and came back in the late afternoon. They mated. He returned to his camp. The night was cloudy. There were gusts of cold wind. Nia huddled close to her fire and shivered. After a while she looked up and saw Inani. He stood at the edge of the firelight, just barely visible.

"Yes? What is it?"

He stepped forward and held something out. A cloak. It fluttered in the wind.

Nia got up. "Thank you."

She took the cloak. Inani stayed where he was. For a moment Nia thought he was going to speak. He didn't. Instead, he made the gesture that meant "oh, well." He turned and walked into the darkness.

Strange! She wrapped the cloak around her, then lay down.

The next morning he rode off again. Nia stayed by the tree. She was getting restless, but she didn't dare go riding. She didn't know where Inani's ter-

13

ritory ended. If she strayed into another man's territory, he would claim her. Inani might follow her. Then there would be an argument. She had heard about such things. Usually, the two men threatened each other until one of them gave up and went away. But sometimes they fought. Old Hua had seen a man die, a knife blade in his chest. How terrible! But also interesting. What would it be like to watch a fight that was really serious?

Inani came back in the evening. They mated. This time he stayed after. He sat on the far side of the fire and asked questions. How was Enwa? And his sisters? Was old Niri still alive?

"No."

Inani scratched his head. "Well, he was old. He taught me carving. Can I stay here tonight?" Nia made the gesture of assent.

She woke at sunrise. The air was cold and still. Inani was gone. She sat up, stretching and groaning. The fire was out. Beside its ashes lay two objects.

"What?" she said out loud. She went over and examined them: a bag full of salt and a box. The box was made of dark wood and inlaid with pieces of shell. She turned it over, admiring the work. He was a fine craftsman, Inani.

After a moment or two she realized the meaning of the objects. They were mating gifts. Such things were given when the time for mating was over. Inani was done with her.

This soon? She felt embarrassed and insulted. Had she done something wrong? Or had Inani found another woman in his territory? Someone he found more attractive.

Nia sighed, then packed the box and the bag of salt. She laid out her gifts for Inani: a knife, a belt, and a piece of blue cloth. He would come back and find them. She saddled her bowhorn. She felt tired and a little disappointed. But the lust was gone. That was good. She mounted and rode home.

When all the women had returned to the village, Nia asked if anyone had seen Anasu. No one had.

"Don't worry," Hua said. "He will turn up. He isn't one of the unlucky ones." Nia made the gesture of acknowledgment.

The trip north was difficult. There was rain. The herd, traveling ahead of the village, churned up the wet earth, turning it into mud. Time and time again the carts got mired. Tempers grew short. Several of the old men saddled their bowhorns and took off.

Hisu, the bow master, was too old to go. He sat in his cart and cursed fate.

Nia, riding close, heard him say, "I should have died years ago." He was talking loudly to no one she could see. "In my prime, alone. The proper way. Now . . . O Master of the Herds, what an end! To live surrounded by women!"

In truth, he looked miserable. He was huddled in a cloak. A wide leather rain hat sheltered his face. His fur, she noticed, was completely gray.

14

She waved. He cursed. She rode on.

At last they reached the Summer Land. Most of the old men returned and settled down as usual at the edge of the camp. But two never came back.

"Two fools!" said Hua. "Why did they go? They were old. They could behave in a reasonable fashion. Did they? No! They ran off like crazy boys. And now something has gotten them."

Nia said nothing.

The rain stopped. The summer was cool and dry. It became evident to her that she wasn't pregnant.

"Don't worry," said Ti-antai. "This often happens. You will have a child next year or the year after."

Nia made the gesture of acknowledgment. She hadn't been worried. She was happy as she was. In the day she worked at the forge. In the late afternoon she and Angai went riding or sat by the river and talked. Angai did most of the talking. She was very observant and had sharp things to say about the people in the village. Because of the dry weather, there were only a few bugs in the air. It was pleasant to sit and listen while the sky changed color.

Her friend was certainly clever, Nia thought. Almost as clever as Anasu.

That summer there was a scandal in the village. It concerned the bronze smith Nuha and her son.

He was sixteen; and everyone could see that he had gone through the change. His fur was coarse, his body thick and wide. He acted restless. But he didn't leave the village. Instead, he stayed inside his mother's tent or worked with her at her forge.

The old women grimaced and muttered. Hua said, "This is what happens when a woman has no daughters. She cannot let go of her sons. Look at the way she treats him! She doesn't send him to learn archery or something else that will be useful to him. She lets him work the bellows and even pour the bronze. Aiya! This is terrible."

Nia said nothing. She had always liked Enshi. As a child he had been friendly and talkative, always telling stories and making jokes. Even now he was always polite. He never lost his temper, which was strange in a boy—or a man—of his age.

He was a poor archer, though. Anasu had told her that.

"He rides badly, too," her brother had said. "He won't last on the plain alone."

Fall came. The village made ready to move. Enshi rode off one morning.

"At last!" Hua said. "Now I can talk to his mother again."

He was gone five days. Then he rode back in, looking tired and dirty. The villagers glared. Enshi ignored them. He rode to his mother's tent and dismounted.

Nuha, who was short and fat, ran out and hugged her son.

15

"Disgusting," Suhai said. "May the Mother of Mothers teach that woman shame."

"Are you cursing the woman?" Nia asked. "If so, I'm going to make the gesture that averts. Who can tell what spirit will hear a curse? Or what it will do about it?"

"Are you planning to become a shamaness, my foster daughter?"

"No."

Suhai glowered, then made the gesture that averts.

"Good," said Nia.

The next morning, early, the old women went to the shamaness. They stood at the entrance to her tent and complained. Nia heard their shrill voices and went out. The day was bright. The air smelled of wood smoke and leather and the dry summer plain.

Nia watched the shamaness walk across the village. She wore a robe covered with red embroidery and a big necklace made of bronze. Hu! What an impressive woman!

The old crones hobbled after her. Nia watched.

They all stopped at the tent of Nuha.

"Enshi!" the shamaness cried.

After a moment Enshi came out. Nia couldn't see his expression.

"Have you no sense of what is right?" the shamaness asked loudly.

Enshi looked down, then up. He mumbled something that Nia couldn't hear.

"It's time you left," the shamaness said.

Enshi made the gesture of assent. His shoulders were sagging now. He looked discouraged.

"Go today. And don't come back. You have become an embarrassment."

Enshi made the gesture of assent a second time. Then he turned and went into his mother's tent.

The shamaness left. But the old women sat down and waited.

Nia went to the forge and worked alone. Late in the afternoon Hua came.

"He is gone," she said. "We told him we would curse him if he ever came back."

"Is that so?" Nia said. She straightened up and rubbed her neck. "How I ache today."

The village went south. The weather remained dry. The herd kicked up a cloud of dust that went most of the way to the sky. Day after day they saw the cloud in front of them. It was dark brown in color. Nia thought, Anasu is there, riding in the dust. And Enshi, too, the poor buffoon.

They reached the Winter Land. Usually they camped to the north of the herd. But this year they went south and east to the Great Rush Lake. Now they were at the eastern edge of their pasturage. Across the lake was the land

16

of the Amber People. They pitched their tents. The shamaness went to visit the Amber People. Angai went with her, also nine other women. They all led pack animals, laden with gifts.

They were gone thirty days. The weather remained dry, though Hua kept saying that rain was coming. She could feel it in her bones.

When they returned, they brought gifts from the Amber People: amber, of course, colored shells, and copper.

"Hu! What an experience," Angai said. "We had to go around the lake. On the far side are marshes. Beyond the marshes is a river. It is wide and deep. We had to cross it. That was dangerous. Animals live in it. They are like river lizards. But larger. Much larger. They will eat anything, my mother says."

"Hu!" said Nia. "Tell me more."

"We made rafts. That's how we got across the river. I didn't see any of the animals. They are called divers or killers of the deep water."

"Aiya!" said Nia.

"On the far side of the river is the land of the Amber People." Angai paused and frowned. "They are the same height as we are, but broader; and a lot of them are fat. Their fur is dark. Their shamaness is huge. She wears a hat made of feathers. I could barely understand them. They talk so strangely. They are very hospitable, though. And they drink a kind of beer I've never had before. Nia, I heard a story there I don't believe. But they swear it is true."

Angai paused to drink a little milk. Nia waited.

"They say to the east of them are a people who stay in one place. They never move."

Nia made the gesture of astonishment.

"They live in houses made of wood. The houses can't be folded or taken apart. They are solid like boxes.

"They live next to a forest, the Amber People say. And their men live in the forest. They don't herd animals the way men ought to. Instead they hunt and catch fish. The women don't think much of them. They say, all men are savage and nasty."

"The Amber People say this?"

"No! No! The people who never move. In fact, the Amber People say, some of the women refuse to mate with men."

Nia scratched her head. "How can that be?"

"When the spring lust comes, they go out in pairs, two women together. They mate with one another."

For a moment Nia sat quietly and stared at the fire. "How do they produce children?"

17

"The usual way. The Amber People say, few of the women mate only with women. Most of them want children. They mate with men until they have as many children as they want."

Nia scratched her head again. "This is a very strange story."

"Yes. I'd like to go and visit those people."

"They are perverts!" Hua said. "And the Amber People are liars. No such people exist. Houses of wood! What a crazy idea!"

Angai looked angry.

"I don't want to talk about this anymore," Nia said. "This story makes me uneasy."

The winter was cold. At night, in the northern sky, lights shone. They were green and white and yellow.

"The winter fire," said Hua. "Up north it fills the sky. We don't often see it down here."

Ti-antai said, "It is bad luck."

Snow fell. There was a coughing sickness in the village. A number of people died. Most were old women or very young children.

Suhai got the sickness. For a while, in the dark time after the solstice, everyone thought she would die. In the end she recovered, though slowly. All the rest of the winter she stayed in her tent. Nia and Ti-antai looked after her. It was hard for Nia to go and see her, hunched by the fire. Her fur was more gray than brown. She looked bony and unhappy.

Why, Nia wondered, did her throat contract at the sight of the old woman? She didn't even like her foster mother.

Spring came at last. It was cold and rainy. Hua's hands became so stiff that she could not work at the forge. "This place is full of bad luck," she cried.

"I think you are right," Nia said.

The trees put out leaves, pale blue in color. Among the dry reeds in the lake, flowers blossomed. They were yellow and orange. Other flowers, tiny and white, appeared at the edge of the plain. Nia began to feel restless. The spring lust, she thought. She began to assemble supplies.

"Why don't I feel the lust?" asked Angai.

"You are younger than I am." Nia crouched and stared at the things she had made in the winter: long knives and needles, brooches, files and awls. What was the right gift?

"I'm half a year younger," Angai said. "That isn't much."

"Why do you ask me? What do I know? Ask your mother."

Angai left. She was angry, Nia realized. Too bad. She reached out and picked up a knife. It had a good blade, made of iron that had been folded and refolded. That would do, she thought. And needles and a brooch, also—maybe—leather from the tanner.

18

She stood up. Now, food for the trip.

That night she dreamt of Anasu and of riding on the plain. She woke, feeling more restless than before. She pulled up the tent flap and fastened it. Sunlight came in. The air was still and mild. It smelled of the new vegetation. She thought, I will go today, before the lust gets any stronger. I will ride until I forget this terrible winter. She turned and looked at Hua.

"I know," the old woman said. "I sometimes wish I still felt the lust. Then I think, I must be crazy to want a thing like that. In any case, go."

She packed her saddlebags and went to find her favorite bowhorn. By noon she was on her way. Her bowhorn was restless and wanted to run. She let it. After a while it slowed, then stopped. Nia looked around. She was alone. On every side, the plain rolled to the horizon. She took a deep breath, then let it out. Her bowhorn flicked its ears.

Where did she want to go? Not west, she decided. The herd was there and the full-grown men. No. She would go south, toward the hills where the young men were. She glanced at the sun and then at her shadow. Then she turned her bowhorn south.

She traveled for three days. The weather remained clear. She met no people, nor anything, except for birds and the small animals that lived on the plain. Slowly the lust grew stronger. It felt almost pleasant. She began to wonder what kind of man she would meet this year.

The fourth day was cloudy and windy. At noon she reached the southern hills. They were low, with many outcroppings of stone. There were trees on the hills. One kind was in blossom. Here and there on the blue slopes were patches of yellow. She found an animal trail that went along a stream. It led east into the hills. She followed the trail, feeling a bit uneasy. She wasn't used to places where the sky was narrow.

"O Mother of Mothers, take care of me," she whispered.

Overhead the branches moved. Leaves rustled—a loud noise, unlike the soft *whish* of vegetation moving on the plain.

She prayed to the Mistress of the Forge. "Bring me safely home, o holy one."

Late in the afternoon she met a man. He was on top of a small hill, sitting on a boulder. There were no trees nearby, only bushes with small blue-green leaves. His bowhorn grazed on one of these.

Nia reined her animal. Her heart began to beat quickly.

"I thought I saw a woman. What a surprise! Nia, is it you?"

She looked at him. He was dark brown, and his eyes were gray. A very strange color. "Enshi?" His tunic was ragged, she noticed. He looked thin.

"How is my mother? And what are you doing here? The women never get this far south."

19

She opened her mouth to answer. Enshi stood up, then jumped off the boulder. "Let's talk later. There is a scent coming from you, Nia. I can't tell you what it does to me." He held out a hand. "Come on."

His dark fur gleamed in the sunlight. She realized, all at once, that he was handsome. She dismounted and tethered her bowhorn, then got her cloak.

They went into the bushes and mated there. The ground was stony. The leaves had a fresh spring smell. As for Enshi, he was a little awkward, but perfectly adequate.

When they were done, he rolled over on his back. "Is that what it's like? I expected more. Still . . ." He looked at her. His gray eyes were half-shut. He reached out and touched her gently. "What soft fur!" He made a low *rub* noise in the back of his throat, then shut his eyes completely and went to sleep.

Nia pulled the cloak up so it covered both of them. She looked at the bowhorns, then at the sky. The sun was gone, but the clouds were still shining, white and pale gold. She felt drowsy and happy.

Enshi the Joker! She had never imagined mating with him. For one thing she'd thought he was dead. Who would have thought he could have survived the bitter winter?

Enshi woke at twilight. He glanced at her. "It wasn't a dream. If the spirits are responsible for this, I thank them." He grabbed her. They mated again. Afterward they went down into the nearest valley and made camp. The night was windy and cold. Ragged clouds filled the sky. The fire flickered. Enshi talked.

"What are you doing this far south? Why didn't one of the big men get you, before you got to Enshi?"

She thought for a moment. "I wanted to get down here. I wanted to find my brother Anasu." She stopped, feeling surprised. Was that right? Had she come to find Anasu?

"You did?" Enshi stared at her. "Why?"

Nia scratched her head. "I don't know. Do you know where he is?"

Enshi made the gesture of affirmation. "I get my salt from him. I used to, anyway. The winter was hard, and I don't think I have anything left to give him."

Nia opened her mouth.

Enshi looked at her. His eyes were half-closed. He looked thoughtful, almost clever. "You want me to tell you where he is. I won't. If you came this far to see him, then you're likely to go farther and leave me here alone, feeling stupid. I don't intend to let go of you, Nia. Not until the time for mating is over."

"You certainly are talkative," Nia said.

Enshi made the gesture of agreement. "Remember, I've had no one to talk to all winter."

"Will you tell me where Anasu is when the time for mating is over?"

"Yes."

Nia made the gesture that meant "so be it."

"Now," Enshi said, "tell me about my mother. Is she well? Does she still grieve for me?"

She spent eight days with Enshi. The weather remained cold and windy. Now and then rain fell. It wasn't heavy. The trees above their camp protected them; and they kept a good fire going. They mated often.

Every morning Enshi went out hunting. In the afternoon he came back with leaves and roots and the tender shoots of spring plants. Twice he brought back game: a winter-thin groundbird and a builder of mounds. The builder of mounds was small, but fat. Or at least it was not thin.

"He did better than I did this winter," Enshi said.

Nia skinned the animal, gutted and spitted it. They sat side by side and watched it cook.

"Hu! What a smell! I used to dream about the smell of cooking meat. I'd wake up and find nothing except snow. What a disappointment! There were times when the weather was bad, and I couldn't travel. I'd begin to look at my bowhorn and think about him as a roast. But I thought, no, Enshi. You'll die without an animal to ride. Then I prayed to the spirits; and the weather would break. I'd go down to the edge of the herd and look for a bowhorn that was too weak to run from me and kill it. The meat was always stringy, with no fat at all. Well, those days are over. Why think about them?"

Nia turned the spit. While the other side of the animal was cooking, they mated.

The next day Nia made a fish trap and set it in the stream at the bottom of the valley. That evening they ate fish stuffed with herbs.

"What a fine cook you are," Enshi said. "Almost as good as my mother."

Nia felt irritated. It seemed to her that Enshi was always talking about his mother. It wasn't right. A boy who was properly brought up talked about himself or about the old men who taught him how to be a man. He didn't go on and on about his mother.

"What is Anasu like these days?" she asked.

Enshi made the gesture that meant "who can say?" "I've met him two times. The first time I tried to talk with him, he said, 'I don't want a conversation, Enshi. What do you have that you are willing to give me?' He wouldn't say anything else. I got out one of my mother's bronze cups and set it on the ground. He got out a bag of salt, then waved me back. When I was far enough away, he came and took the cup, then put down his bag. That was it. He left.

21

I picked up the salt. The second time I met him, he said nothing at all." Enshi paused a moment, then went on. "He's friendlier than the other men. He never makes faces or waves weapons at me."

This sounded bad. Would Anasu be willing to talk with her? She didn't know.

The time for mating ended. Nia gave Enshi her gifts. He looked uncomfortable. "The winter was hard. I lost most of my parting gifts. First a killer of the forest found my cache and tore it apart. Then I lost most of the rest this spring while crossing a river.

"But I make poems. Can I give them to you?"

"Yes."

He recited nine or ten. Afterward she remembered only one. It was about a tree he had seen a few days before.

"All the branches were bare, and the bark was peeling off. Nonetheless, there were shoots all around the tree, growing from the base of it. They were as long as my arm. They bore leaves and flowers. I thought this must be significant. And I made a poem. It goes:

"If you don't give up,
old tree—

"Then I won't
either."

"That one I like," Nia said.

He recited it again. "Is that enough? Have we made a fair exchange?"

"Where is Anasu?"

"Oh, yes. Follow the trail until it forks. Then go south. You will come to a big stone with markings on it. The stone is magical, and no one ever claims that it is in his territory. People go there to exchange gifts. Wait by the stone. If Anasu is anywhere around, he will come."

"Thank you. We've made a fair exchange."

They said good-bye. Nia saddled her bowhorn, then mounted and rode away. The day was sunny. A light wind blew. Birds whistled. She felt content.

At twilight she came to the stone. It was tall and narrow with lines cut into it. She could barely make them out; and she didn't know what they meant. Had people done this? No one she knew cut lines in stone.

She tethered her bowhorn and made a fire. The night was cloudless. She lay on her back. Above her the Great Moon rose. It was three-quarters full. She watched it for a while, then went to sleep.

In the morning she looked at the stone. The lines represented animals: bowhorns, mostly. But there was another animal that she didn't recognize. It had a thick body and short horns. What was it? Nia scratched her head. There were hunters on the stone: men with bows. They made a circle around the animals. Off to one side was a man by himself. He was bigger than the others, and he had horns. They were short, like the horns on the unfamiliar animal. Who was he? A spirit of some kind, apparently. But no spirit she knew. The Master of the Herds had long curved horns. The Sky Spirit was hornless. She scratched her head again. Then she made breakfast.

At noon Anasu appeared. He rode down the trail into the clearing where the stone was. He reined his bowhorn.

Nia stood up. "Brother!"

He was bigger than she remembered and very broad through the chest. His fur was coarse and dark. He wore a red kilt, a wide belt, high boots, a knife with a silver pommel. "Nia?" he said after a moment. He stared at her. "You are past the lust." His voice sounded harsh and disappointed. "Someone else got to you."

"What kind of thing is that to say? Can men think of nothing except sex?"

He laughed. It was not entirely a friendly sound. "This time of year I think of little else. I think—if I were brave, I'd go north. Then I think, I'm not old enough to confront those men. What are you doing here?"

She made the gesture of uncertainty.

"You have never known your own mind." He dismounted. "Do you want salt? I have it."

"No. I want to talk. How are you?" She took a step toward him.

He held up a hand. "Stay where you are. I'm not used to people."

She stopped.

After a moment Anasu said, "I am fine. Is there nothing you want to give me in exchange for salt?"

She took off her belt. "Do you want this? I made the buckle. It's gold mixed with silver."

He hesitated. "All right." He turned toward his saddlebag.

"I don't want salt. I want a conversation."

He turned back and stared at her. "Why?"

"Brother, when I think of you, I feel lonely."

Anasu scratched the back of his neck. Then he made the gesture that meant "so be it" or "these things happen."

"Is there no way we can talk?"

For a long while he was silent. She waited. At last he said, "I do not think that what you want is words. I could give you words, though it would not be easy. I'm no longer used to talking much or saying what is on my mind. But I think you want something else. I think you are like the woman in the old story, whose children turned into birds. She left her tent and wandered on the plain, trying to find them. But she never did; and in the end she died and became a spirit—a bad one, a hungry one." He paused and frowned.

Nia opened her mouth.

He held up his hand. "No. Wait. I want to follow the track of my own thought." She waited. At last he said, "I think you want something that is gone."

"No."

"I know you, sister. I think I am right. In any case, I don't want to talk anymore." He mounted his bowhorn. "Whatever you are trying to do, I don't want to be a part of it." He made the gesture of farewell, then turned his animal and rode away.

Nia doubled one hand into a fist and hit the magic stone. Aiya! How that hurt! She groaned, opened her hand, and felt it. As far as she could tell, no bones were broken. But the skin was scraped along the side of her hand where there was no fur. She licked the scrape, then sat down and rocked and groaned. It did no good. Her hand kept hurting and grief stayed in her, as solid as a stone.

Toward evening she got up and built a fire. All night she sat watching the flames and thinking about her childhood.

In the morning she put out the fire and saddled her bowhorn. There was no point in staying. Anasu wouldn't come back. He had always been stubborn. She rode north. The sky was cloudy. A cold wind blew. Flower petals drifted down onto the trail. They were yellow or greenish white.

In the afternoon it began to rain. She stopped and made camp under an overhang. She went to sleep early. Sometime in the night she woke.

Her fire was still burning. On the other side of it was Enshi. He was plucking a bird.

She lifted her head. He made the gesture of greeting, then held up the bird. It was large and fat.

"I found it on a nest. I have the eggs, if they haven't broken. How was Anasu?"

"He wouldn't talk to me. What are you doing here?"

"You're in my territory; and I thought you might be hungry. Also, I thought I would like to talk some more."

"Why are you so different from other men?"

"I don't know." He looked embarrassed for a moment. Then he went back to plucking the bird.

Nia went to sleep.

In the morning they cooked the bird with its own eggs stuffed inside it. They ate, then Nia got ready to go.

"Can I go with you?" Enshi asked.

"What do you mean?"

"I want to visit my mother. I thought you could show me the way to the village."

"But the old women will curse you."

"Not if you tell me where my mother's tent is, and I sneak in at night. The old women will never know."

"This is wrong."

"Maybe. But I have lost all my parting gifts. I won't last through another winter with what I have. I intend to live, if I possibly can. And I don't care if I do a few things that are shameful. Who knows what the spirits of the dead feel? I'd sooner be alive and a little embarrassed."

Nia looked at him a moment. He was certainly thin, and his tunic was very ragged. She rubbed her hand, which still hurt. Then she sighed. "All right. I'll help you. I expect I'm going to regret this, though."

Enshi saddled his bowhorn. They rode north together.

Lixia

E ight of us were set down, each one alone: three on the big continent, which sprawled around the south pole of the planet, many-fissured and many-lobed. The center of the continent was ice. The coasts were green, blue-green, and yellow: prairie and forest and desert, according to the people who analyzed the holograms.

Another four went to the small continent, which lay north of the equator. It had no ice worth mentioning and almost no desert, but plenty of vegetation. There were mountains: a range in the west along the coast and other lesser ranges in the east and south. Nothing impressive, nothing like the Rockies or the Himalayas. But two of the ranges were volcanic, according to the planetologists. One was active. The other might be.

The final person was set down on one of the many islands in the archipelago that stretched in a curve from the big continent past the equator, almost reaching the little continent.

Other islands dotted the rest of the planet-ocean. They were tiny and widely spaced. Interesting to the biologists, of course. There is nothing like an island for studying evolution. But not, we decided, the place for us to begin.

I went to the northeast coast of the northern continent. I was equipped with a denim jacket and a light cotton shirt. My boots were plastic, tough and flexible. In my right forearm, under the skin, was a row of capsules that provided me with vitamins not available on this planet. In my gut were five new kinds of bacteria, designed to break down the local proteins, turning them into amino acids that I could digest.

I had a pack that contained a radio, a medical kit, a poncho, another shirt—exactly like the first one—and a change of underwear. One big compartment was full of trinkets. The trinkets were made from native materials. We didn't want to introduce anything alien except ourselves.

Finally, I had a medallion on a gray metal chain. The medallion was metal, flat and dark, inset with pieces of glass. It was an AV recorder and almost indestructible, I was told. No matter what happened to me, it would survive.

I landed on a beach, next to a row of dunes. They were high and bare, orange-pink in color.

The boat that had brought me turned and started back toward the plane. I went inland, scrambling up a dune. When I reached the top, I heard a roar and glanced around. The plane was moving across the water. Spray flew up, then smoke. It was in the air. Wings shone in the sunlight. The plane kept rising. After a minute or two it was gone.

I looked at the empty sky and felt suddenly very lonely. Then I started down the far side of the dune.

At the bottom I found a trail. It wasn't much to look at. Narrow and sandy, it wound away from the dunes toward a stand of trees.

Had it been made by people? By some kind of intelligent life? We knew the planet was inhabited. Satellite pictures had shown villages and herds whose migrations—the zoologists had told us—were too orderly to be entirely natural.

In any case, I was faced with a trail. I decided to follow it. It led me through the trees and into hills. Often the tops of the hills were bare except for patches of a plant that looked something like tall yellow grass. The leaves or blades were stiff and had saw-tooth edges. It wasn't a pleasant-looking organism. Was this planet friendly?

In the hollows between the hills there were more trees. They were small and twisted with little dark leaves. Thorns stuck out of the trunks. The thorns were long and narrow, needlelike. Another unpleasant-looking organism. I began to remember horrifying science fiction stories. Why had I read that stuff? The senior members of my family had warned me: no good would come of science fiction.

There was no point in getting nervous, nor in thinking about the past. I was in a new place, and I had no good idea of what it was like. My job—for the time being—was observation. Later, when I had some information, I could think and remember and compare.

After a kilometer or so I came to an artifact. It was in a hollow at the center of a clearing. The slopes around it were covered with trees. I stopped. The thing was three meters high and made of long narrow pieces of wood. It reminded me of a jungle gym or else of the ritual structures made by the aborigines of southern California. I'd spent time with them. Between my breasts and on my upper arms were the scars of their initiation ceremony. I had never been able to figure out why I had gone through with it. But I kept the scars. I had earned them, and they reminded me—every time I took a shower—not to get too involved with other people's value systems.

I looked the structure over. Now I saw the remains of a fire underneath it. Three gray things hung from one of the lower bars. I knelt and examined them. Fish or something a lot like fish. I rocked back on my heels and felt satisfied. A fish-smoking rack. Someone intelligent had made it. I was the first Earth person to see an alien artifact close up—on this planet, anyway, and as far as I knew.

I stayed where I was for several minutes, contemplating the pieces of wood. They were knobby and twisted. Was there no better wood in the area? I glanced around. All the trees in sight had twisted branches. The structure was tied together with strips of fiber. I broke off a piece and rolled it between my fingers. It felt like some kind of vegetable product. Maybe bark.

Something made a noise in back of me. I got up slowly and turned, holding my hands out, the palms forward. The gesture meant "You see? I carry no weapons."

Something stood at the edge of the clearing, maybe twenty meters away. A biped. It was about my height, stocky and covered with fur. The fur was dark brown, almost black. The creature had two arms, a head, and a face. I was too far away to make out the features. It or he or she wore a kilt and carried—in one hand—a knife.

"I am extremely peaceful." I kept my hands out and my voice low and even. "I mean no harm."

The creature said something, which I, of course, could not understand. But I didn't like the tone. It was loud and had a rasping quality.

"I mean no harm."

The creature raised the knife and took a step forward. I stepped back.

"Can't we discuss this?" I concentrated on keeping my tone soft and placating. I didn't meet the creature's eyes. In many species, including my own, a direct stare was a challenge.

The creature took another step toward me. I decided to leave.

"Okay. You win. Good-bye."

I backed across the clearing. The creature followed me halfway, then stopped beside the rack. When I reached the edge of the clearing, I stopped. "Are you sure about this?"

The creature raised the knife higher and shouted something. I turned and walked quickly away. The skin on my back was prickling. I kept imagining a knife blade going in.

When I reached the top of the next hill, I looked back. The trail was empty. Nothing was following me.

Okay. What next?

Maybe the creature I met was a hermit. Surely there ought to be other members of the species who were friendly or curious.

I walked on, still going inland. I began to notice noises: a low buzz that came, I imagined, from pseudo-insects hidden in the trees. Things like birds flew from branch to branch. When they were at rest, they moaned or whistled. I realized, for the first time, that the day was bright and mild. A light wind blew. Alto-cumuli moved across the sky, which was deep blue-green. The air smelled of salt water.

I thought about my childhood in the Free State of Hawaii, on the island of Kauai. I had lived in a big house, five minutes from the ocean. Nine parents had cared for me, and there had been a dozen siblings to play with. It should have been a happy time. I remembered sunlight, flowers, kind faces, a white beach, blue water, and no undertow. But I had been a sullen kid, always anxious to get away.

By afternoon I was walking through a boggy forest. Here the trees were tall and straight. Their dark foliage shut out sunlight. The air was still and cool and had a new aroma: the scent of the forest. It was strong and distinctive and like nothing I had ever smelled before.

I thought I'd recognize it if I ever smelled it again, though I was not entirely positive of this. It was a lot easier to remember something if it had a name and a description. For the time being, I would call the aroma "different" and "pleasant."

Late in the afternoon I came to a village. First I smelled wood smoke, then saw houses ahead of me among the trees. I couldn't see them clearly. The forest was too full of shadows. Here and there firelight shone through a doorway or a window.

I stopped and considered what to do. There was no point in sneaking around. If they caught me spying, I'd be in real trouble. The best thing— the thing I had done in southern California and New Jersey—was to walk right in.

The technique hadn't worked in New Jersey, of course. The people there had tried to sacrifice me to their god, the Destroyer of Cities. I decided not to think about that incident. I spent another minute or two gathering courage. Then I entered the village.

At the edge were small huts, built of wood. They were widely scattered, as if the people who lived in them were none too friendly. Farther in, the buildings were large and long, set close together. Children, naked except for their fur, ran in the streets. A trio saw me, stopped and stared, their mouths open. They were close enough so I could see their faces: round and flat and covered with fur. Each one had a mouth, a nose, and a pair of yellow eyes.

"Hello," I said gently.

The children screamed and ran.

I went on, between the houses. Several times I passed large people. Adults. They stared at me, but said nothing. They made no threatening gestures.

This was hopeful. I came to an empty place that seemed to be more or less at the center of the village. A square. I hunkered down and waited. By this time the sun was gone. The sky was darkening. People gathered, talking softly, at the edges of the square. I was sweating. If I'd made a mistake, if they were unfriendly, I was going to die here.

Someone walked toward me: a tall, thin person. He or she wore a robe and many necklaces. Someone important. A shaman or a chief.

I was, of course, using labels from Earth.

I stood up slowly, then held out my hands. "I come in peace."

The person looked me over. At last the person spread his or her hands, duplicating my gesture.

Now what? Let the native decide. I waited. He or she took off a necklace and offered it to me. I took it. The beads were copper, little cylinders. There was a pendant: a piece of shell carved in the shape of a fish.

This was almost certainly a friendly act.

"Thank you." I put the necklace on. Now I would have to reciprocate. I let my pack slide off my shoulders, then bent and opened it.

"Here." I straightened, holding out a necklace made of shell. This particular kind of shell—dark blue and lustrous—was found in the planet's northern ocean, around a little archipelago we named the Empty Islands. Harrison Yee and I had gathered the shells and carved them, using techniques that Harrison had learned at Beijing University, in the School of Anthropology.

The person took my gift, then gestured to me, turned, and walked away. I followed. We went past a crowd of people who stared. My shirt was wet with sweat.

We reached a house. The person gestured again. I walked in and found myself in a large long room. A fire burned in the center. By its ruddy light I saw log walls and log rafters. The floor was dirt or clay.

I looked around. No furniture. But there were piles of fur in the corners. Along the walls I saw pots. Some were a meter tall. Black and highly polished, they gleamed in the firelight. The air smelled of wood smoke and something else: a spicy aroma. I looked up. Bunches of plants hung from the rafters. Herbs, I thought. Were they wild or cultivated? Did these people farm? Did they have the potter's wheel? What metals did they work, other than copper?

My host followed me in. I looked at him or her. Now, in the firelight, I saw bent shoulders, bony hands, and graying fur. This was an old person, I was almost certain. Orange eyes regarded me. The lids were heavy. The pupils were vertical slits.

After a moment the person spoke.

"I'm sorry. I don't know your language."

My host reached out and very gently touched my face. There was no fur on the inside of the hand. His or her skin felt hard and dry.

"Hu!"

I had my hair pulled back and fastened at the nape of my neck. The person touched the side of my head, feeling the hair there, then touched the hair that flowed down between my shoulder blades.

"Tsa!"

I reached back and took the clip off my hair, shaking my head. The hair flew out.

My host started. He or she took hold of several strands and tugged.

For a moment I stood the pain, then I said, "Hey," and touched—very lightly—the furry hand.

The person let go. He or she spoke again—was it an apology?—and waved me toward the fire.

Other people appeared, wearing kilts or tunics. I saw more necklaces made of copper and belts with metal buckles. The metal was yellow, either brass or bronze.

The new people spread furs on the floor. My host and I sat down. Someone brought a bowl full of liquid. My host drank, then offered the bowl to me. It was fired clay, black like the pots and polished. A geometric pattern was incised on the outside, below the rim. The liquid within looked dark and smelled pungent.

I remembered what the biochemists told me. I could probably eat what the natives ate.

"There's a lot you won't be able to metabolize, of course, even with the bugs we've given you. If you stay there any period of time, you will develop a lot of deficiencies. But we don't think you'll be poisoned."

I raised the bowl and drank.

The liquid was sour as well as pungent. Rather tasty. I'd consumed things that were a lot worse, in New Jersey.

I said, "Thank you," and handed the bowl to my host.

31

He or she moved one hand quickly and definitely. The gesture meant something. The other people said "ya" and "hu." It seemed to me that they were more relaxed than before.

In any case, they spread more furs. More people sat down till I was surrounded. The air was full of their dusty, furry aroma.

Food came. I wasn't sure what anything was. I ate slowly and carefully and as little as possible. But I did eat. In most of the societies I knew about, it was rude to refuse food. An anthropologist had to have the digestion of a goat.

The people around me began to talk softly. Often they glanced at me. Only my host kept quiet. He or she kept handing me new dishes, watching to make sure I ate.

One dish was made of fish, I was almost certain. Another reminded me of pickled green tomatoes. A third had the texture of kasha and no taste that I could distinguish.

The people around me belched and made little cooing noises. "Hu" and "ya." I did the same.

The meal continued. I began to feel light-headed. Something I had ingested was having a narcotic effect. The people around me grew noisier. Several reached over and touched my clothes or hands or face.

Someone got out an instrument like a flute. Someone else began to beat two hollow sticks together. *Tock-whistle, tock-whistle,* the music went. I leaned back on one elbow and watched the flute player. He or she wore a yellow tunic and a pair of wide copper bracelets. The bracelets flashed as the flute player swayed, keeping time with the music. I had no trouble hearing the beat. It was almost always regular: a heart with a slight arrhythmia.

The music stopped. My host stood up, and I glanced around.

There was a new person in the room, just inside the open door. Like my host, this one wore a robe. A sign of importance? Or age? Gender or occupation? The person wore a hat, the first one I'd seen. It was tall and pointed, decorated with shells.

I got up, swaying a little. It took me a moment to focus my eyes.

The new person looked grim. I saw trouble in the stiff, upright posture, in the shoulders held back and up, in the narrow, almost-shut eyes that stared at me directly. He or she carried a staff. Feathers hung from the top of it and fluttered—but not in the wind. The person was shaking. I could not tell if the motion was deliberate.

The person said something. It sounded angry.

My host replied curtly.

The people around me began to rise and move back. This was some kind of power conflict. I had a feeling that I was in the middle of it.

The person with the staff spoke some more. My host clenched one hand into a fist and waved it, then pointed at the door. That was clear enough. "You so-and-so, get out!"

The person with the staff glared and departed. One by one the other people followed until there were only three left: my host, the flute player, and a person with red-brown fur that gleamed like copper in the firelight.

"Hu!" my host said.

The others made gestures that probably meant agreement.

I felt tired and dizzy. I'd had too much of something, most likely the liquid. I would have to be careful about drinking it in the future. I rubbed my face.

My host looked at me, then gestured. I picked up my pack. He or she led me to one end of the room. There was a pile of furs there. My host gestured again. I lay down.

"Nice party. Good night."

My host left. I moved my pack so it was between me and the wall, and went to sleep.

I woke with a headache and a feeling of disorientation, sat up and looked around and found I was in a large interior space. Light came through a hole above me and through an open door. It was yellow, the color of sunlight in the late afternoon. But I was almost positive that it was morning.

A voice spoke nearby. I looked toward the sound. It was the old person, my host. He or she wore a dark orange robe and wide belt made of copper. One hand held a staff of wood inlaid with pieces of shell. The other hand was held out to me, palm up. I decided this was a greeting. By this time I had remembered my current location.

The old person came closer and sat down. He or she spoke again, softly and courteously.

I laid one hand on my chest and said my name. "Lixia."

After a moment my host said, "Li-sa," and pointed at me.

"Lixia," I repeated.

My host laid a bony hand on his or her chest. "Nahusai."

I pointed. "Nahusai."

The answer was a gesture, a quick flick of one hand. On a hunch it meant "yes."

Well, then. I knew a word. It referred to my host. But what did it mean? Was it a name or a title or a generic term such as "human being"?

Time would tell.

A person came in: the flute player. He or she wore the same tunic as the night before and the same copper bracelets.

"Yohai," my host said and pointed.

The flute player looked at us.

33

It was a name. I was almost certain.

Yohai made breakfast: a gray-brown mush. It had a sour flavor. I learned the name of it: *atsua*. When we were done eating, Yohai went to the door and gestured. I got my pack, following him or her around the house. There was an open space in back, where vegetation grew. Most of it was blue with a few white or yellow flowers.

Was it a garden? I didn't think so. The plants grew helter-skelter, and they had a ragged look. This was a patch of weeds.

In the middle of the open space was a building about the size of a walk-in closet. As soon as I got close to it, I knew what it was. A privy. It stank to high heaven. I considered for a moment. Then I used the thing. Afterward I asked what it was called.

"*Hana*," Yohai said. Or maybe *bna*. I wasn't certain I was hearing a vowel in the first syllable.

He or she gestured again. I followed. We went through the village. The streets were full of children. We met only a few adults. The children stopped playing and stared at me. The adults pretended I wasn't there. I had a feeling that Yohai was uneasy. I felt a little uneasy, too. But the day was lovely, sunny and mild. A light erratic wind blew. It carried the smell of the forest and—very faintly—of the ocean. This wasn't a day to worry. I tried not to.

We reached the edge of the village. There were gardens there: long, narrow, rectangular plots that lay between the houses and the forest. Each was surrounded by a fence made of wood, low enough to see over. Inside the fences people worked, one or two in each garden. They moved between rows of plants. Some weeded. Some picked. Some poured water out of jugs that looked like amphorae.

That answered one of my questions. The society was—to some extent, at least—agricultural.

We entered a garden. At one end was a tree. Yohai led me into the shade and pointed at the ground. I sat down.

My companion began to work. I glanced around. Off to the east were ragged cumuli. A storm tonight. In the next garden over was a baby, tiny and furry, sitting under a plant. As I watched, it reached up, trying to grab hold of one of the leaves. But the leaf was too high.

A short distance away an adult was pouring water. He or she emptied the pot, then set it down, straightened, and turned. Under her tunic I saw the bulge of breasts. Two breasts. She was the first person I had seen who wasn't flat-chested. Clearly she was a nursing mother.

The woman looked at me, then made a gesture: a vertical slash. I had a feeling it was hostile. I looked away.

At noon Yohai came over to me. We sat together and ate bread. The bread was flat and sour. Afterward Yohai taught me several words: "bread," "sky," "tree."

We went back to the house. My host was there. Yohai left. I sat down and learned more words. Late in the afternoon I heard the roll of thunder. Rain began to fall—first a sprinkle, then a downpour. My host and I ate dinner. It was the same as breakfast: *atsua*. Gray mush. I didn't eat a lot.

Afterward we sat without talking. The sun was down. The rain glistened, lit by firelight, a silver curtain at the door. I leaned against a post. My host was by the fire. He or she was hunched over, huddled in the orange robe. One hand moved now or then. It twisted a bracelet or tapped on the ground. This was a person with a serious problem, and I had a feeling the problem was me. Yohai had given me the impression of nervous valor, of someone making a point that he or she did not want to make. "See what we have here. See our guest. See the person we are not ashamed of." That had been the message given when he or she took me to the garden. What exactly was going on? I decided not to speculate. I had too little information, and I could not be sure that I understood anything about these people.

There was more rain the next day. My host and I worked on vocabulary: household objects mostly and some common verbs. In the afternoon Yohai got down a small loom that had been hanging on the wall. He or she began to weave a strip of cloth. The yarn was white and blue. I watched. Yohai worked quickly. Soon I made out a pattern. It was geometric, full of sharp angles. It looked hostile to me and far too intricate. What did it mean? Was this culture byzantine? Or was I paranoid?

I stood and began to do yoga exercises. My host looked at me, eyes opened wide.

I stopped. "This is nothing harmful or malevolent," I said gently. "I do this to keep my back from hurting and to keep my mind reasonably tranquil."

I continued my exercises. My host watched. The rain lightened. It was a drizzle now.

"Excuse me." I took my pack and went to the privy. It smelled as bad as ever. I went in and sat down, then got out my radio and called the ship.

"Yeah?" the radio said. The voice was deep and a little hoarse. I was talking to Edward Antoine Whirlwind, Ph.D., author of *Native American Society on the Reservation* and *Patterns of Survival in the Late Twentieth Century*, formerly the Bellecourt Distinguished Professor at the University of Duluth—he resigned the position when he left Earth—and for many years my colleague in the Department of Cross-cultural Studies.

"This is Lixia," I told him. "I'm calling from an outhouse, so I'm going to be quick."

35

Eddie laughed.

"I needed someplace private."

"Okay," Eddie said.

I rested the radio on my knees, then took my medallion off its chain and put it in a slot in the radio.

The little computer in the medallion spoke to the slightly larger computer in the radio. That computer spoke to a computer onboard the ship. It only took a minute. The radio beeped and I pulled the medallion out. Everything the medallion had recorded—everything that had happened to me in the past two days—was now in the information system on the ship.

Directory: First Interstellar Expedition

Subdirectory: Sigma Draconis II

Sub-subdirectory: Field Reports—Soc. Sci.

File Name: Li Lixia

The radio asked. "Is there anything else?"

"No."

"Okay. Three other people have made contact. No trouble so far. But take care and call again as soon as possible. I ought to have some real information in a couple of days."

I shut off the radio, packed it, and went out. The rain was coming down hard. I ran to the house.

The next day was clear. Yohai and I went to the garden. The ground was still wet. Drops of water sparkled on the leaves. Yohai taught me to weed. We worked all morning. At noon we rested under the tree. In the other gardens people moved around, talking to one another. But no one came to visit us. Interesting. Once again I had a sense that a point was being made, and Yohai did not want to make it. I bit into a yellow vegetable. It was juicy and bittersweet.

In the evening I sat with Nahusai. Yohai went out, I didn't know where. I learned more verbs and a lot of prepositions: the curse of every language, but they held all information together. To. From. At. Of. Between.

The next day was my fifth on the planet. The sky was clear again. Yohai and I worked in the garden. I learned the names of various plants. Yohai told me that she was a woman. She wasn't a mother, though. When she told me this, she seemed unhappy.

"Nahusai?" I asked.

She made the gesture that meant "yes." "Mother," she said, then put her hand on her chest. "Mother me."

Aha. A kinship relationship. My first one. I began to feel I was getting somewhere.

The day after that Yohai took me to the river. It ran between the gardens and the forest. This time of year—midsummer—it was low. The water ran around yellow stones. Yohai waded in and turned over a stone, then grabbed something. "Tsa!"

She handed the thing to me. It was maybe ten centimeters long, green and hard, with eight legs. I held it gingerly. The legs moved. At one end were two long stalks. Were they eyes? Or antennae? They flicked back and forth.

"We eat," said Yohai.

"Oh, yeah?" I made the gesture that meant uncertainty or confusion.

"You see." Yohai took the creature and tossed it into a pot. "You here." She beckoned.

I took off my boots, rolled up my pants, and waded in. She had another creature. It went into the pot. "You."

I reached into the water and rolled over a rock. Something scurried past my fingertips. I grabbed and missed.

"Damnation." I found another rock and tried again.

We spent all morning in the river. Yohai caught twenty or so of the creatures. I caught two.

At last she waded out of the river. She stared at me, looking puzzled.

"What am I good for?" I said in English. "An interesting question. I'm *very* good at learning languages and pretty good at figuring out how other people think. Though I can't always explain how I know what I know. Is that any help?"

Yohai picked up the pot. The green things were still alive. They crawled over one another, trying to get out.

"Come." She beckoned.

I picked up my boots. We walked downstream. After a few minutes the gardens were gone, and there were trees all around us. The air smelled of whatever-it-was: the forest aroma, sharp and distinctive, for which I had no name.

There were rapids in the river. Nothing important. The water rippled down over a series of little drops. Here and there I saw a little foam. At the bottom of the last drop was a pool. The water was quiet, deep, and green.

My companion put down the pot she carried. She kicked off her sandals and pulled her tunic over her head. Her body was lovely, dark and sleek. It reminded me of otters and bears and of my own species as well. She was remarkably humanoid. The only striking difference was the fur. The eyes were a bit unusual, of course. The pupils were vertical slits. The irises, which were pale yellow, filled the eyes. I could see no white. Her hands had three fingers and a thumb. Her feet had four toes. Except for this and her flat chest, she looked like our senior pilot, Ivanova.

She pointed at me. "You. Li-sha."

I undressed.

"Tsa!" She touched my bare shoulder. "What?"

I kept still. She walked around in back of me. "Hu!" I felt the touch of her hand very lightly on one shoulder blade. I shivered. She came around in front and stared at my chest. For a human woman I was pretty flat. Still, my breasts were far more noticeable than hers.

"Mother? You?" she asked.

"No."

She looked me straight in the eyes. She was frowning. "What you?"

I answered her in English. "I can't explain, Yohai. Not yet. I don't know how you say 'world' or 'star' or 'friend.' But there's nothing wrong with me. I'm not dangerous. I mean no harm."

Yohai stared at me for another minute, then turned and dove into the pool. She was a terrific swimmer. I saw her glide through the green water as gracefully as a seal.

I dove after her. My foot slipped on the bank, and my dive turned into a belly flop. I came up, coughing and embarrassed. Yohai made a barking noise. A laugh?

I swam to the middle of the river, turned over and floated. The water was cool. There was hardly any current. Far above me a bird soared across the sky. Ah!

After a while I swam to shore. I climbed out and washed my clothes, using a couple of stones—I had learned the technique in California from the aborigines—then hung the clothes on a bush to dry.

Yohai joined me, brushing the water out of her fur. We sat together on the riverbank. Her eyes were half-closed, and her fur glistened in the sunlight. She looked so comfortable! Why couldn't I relax like that? Maybe I should take another course in yoga.

Yohai roused herself and told me the name of the creatures in the pot.

That evening I learned how to kill and shell the creatures. I didn't enjoy this. But I did it. Yohai boiled the remains. The result was delicious. I ate too much. Afterward I sat in the doorway. Children played in the street. They seemed to be playing tag. I watched and felt more or less contented, though I could have used an after-dinner drink. Something light and dry. A white wine maybe.

The next morning I paid another long visit to the privy. I called the ship and got Eddie again.

"I have news for you," he said. "But first, transmit your information."

I put the medallion into the radio and waited. There were half a dozen bugs in the privy. A couple buzzed around my head. I waved them away. The radio beeped. I pulled the medallion out.

"Anything else?"

38

"Yes. I'm staying with two people. Nahusai and Yohai. No one visits them. When Yohai and I work in the garden, no one talks to us. I think the problem is me."

There was a pause. "Do you think the situation is dangerous? Do you want to get out?"

"No. Not yet."

Another pause. "Your instincts are usually excellent. Okay. But I want you to call in more often."

"I'll try. It won't be easy. There isn't much privacy here."

"Do what you can. Now, for your information—Harrison Yee got driven out of his village. They were polite, but firm. It happened after he took a bath. We think he violated a nudity taboo or a taboo against washing in running water or maybe just in that particular river. Try and find out how your people bathe before you take a bath."

"I've already taken one, Eddie."

"Yeah? Where?"

"In the nearest river."

"Alone?"

"With Yohai. The daughter of my host. She looked a little surprised when she saw me naked. Apparently she hadn't realized that I had no fur on me anywhere. Well, almost no fur. In any case, nothing happened."

"That's interesting. Of course, Harrison was nowhere close to you. However, the language you are learning is similar to the one he was learning, before he took his bath."

"He's on the other side of the continent."

"Uh-huh. And your language is almost identical to the one Derek is learning. He's down the coast from you."

A bug landed on my face. I swatted and missed. The radio began to slide off my knees. "Damnation!" I grabbed it before it could go into the hole below me.

"Lixia?"

"Nothing. What does all of this mean?"

"We don't know. But there are theories. You may be learning a trade language, something like pidgin English. Or maybe all the people contacted so far are closely related, part of a recent migration."

"How likely is that?"

"Not very. The trade language is a distinct possibility—or so we think at the moment."

I signed off and left the privy. Outside, a couple of meters away, a person waited. He or she wore a robe and a tall hat. The robe was covered with embroidery. The hat was decorated with shells. After a moment I recognized him or her. It was the person who had broken up Nahusai's party.

"Yes?" I said in the native language.

He or she made a gesture—a vertical slash—then turned and walked away.

I went back to the house feeling a bit nervous. The person had radi-ated hostility. Who was he or she? I couldn't ask. I didn't know the right words.

For the next half-dozen days the sky remained clear. The weather was hot. Yohai and I worked in the garden. Mostly, we brought water from the river: pot after heavy pot. We poured the water out on the dry ground. Then we returned to the river. We refilled our pots. We went back to the garden.

My arms hurt. My shoulders hurt. There was a terrible ache in the small of my back. I tried to remember how I had gotten into this situation. It had something to do with the romance of interstellar travel. Or was it the quest for knowledge?

In the afternoon we went to the house and rested. In the evening Yohai went out—back to the garden or maybe somewhere else. I stayed with Nahusai. She taught me more of the language. I began to understand complete sentences.

I was never left alone, except when I was in the privy. I wasn't sure why. Did Nahusai and Yohai fear me? Or were they afraid that someone might try to harm me?

I didn't feel especially safe, even in the privy. People might be watching. The person in the hat certainly had been. People might notice if I spent a long time inside. They might decide to creep up on me and listen. They wouldn't understand my conversation, but they would know that I was talking to some-one who was not present.

I ended by calling from the house on a night when my companions went to sleep early.

"Where in hell have you been?" asked Eddie.

I turned the volume down and explained.

"Lixia, you have to keep in touch. We've been getting worried. Ivanova has been talking about coming after you. Can you imagine what that would be like? She'd go in like the Seventh Cavalry, and we'd have to figure out how to fix the mess that she made."

"Okay," I said and turned the volume down further. On the other side of the house Yohai and Nahusai snored. They sounded almost entirely human.

Eddie told me the news. Harrison Yee was back on the ship, as was Antonio Nybo. Tony had been in the archipelago. He'd found a number of ceremonial sites—rocks arranged in circles and cliffs with pictographs—but no people. His island was empty.

"Of archaeological interest only," Eddie said. "We pulled him out."

40

There were five other people from Earth still on the planet. Four of them were in villages more or less like mine. The fifth—Gregory—was staying with an extended family in the western mountains.

"They keep flocks and do fantastic weaving, or so Gregory tells me."

"Uh-huh."

"There don't seem to be any large population centers. We don't know why as yet. We don't even have any theories."

"A desperate situation," I said.

Eddie laughed.

Yohai groaned and rolled over.

I said, "I have to go."

On the fourteenth day of my stay in the village I decided I had to call again. I waited till after dark, then went to the privy. The planet's one big moon was rising. It hung over the rooftops, bright orange, three-quarters full. I left the door of the privy open. Moonlight shone in. I could see well enough to operate my radio.

This evening Eddie had a new and interesting piece of news.

"Yvonne says there are no mature males in her village. There are a few old men. They live at the edge of the village, she says, each one alone. And there are boys—male children. But in between, nothing."

I thought for a moment. "I know the word for 'boy,' and I've seen boys play in the street. The younger children wear no clothing. Gender is obvious and an interesting example of parallel evolution. But I don't know the word for 'man.'" I chewed on my lip for a moment or two. "Let me check into this."

"Okay," said Eddie.

I signed off and slung the radio over my shoulder, then stepped out of the privy. The moon was directly above me. It was smaller than Luna, but closer to its primary, with a much higher albedo. It lit the area around me: the weed patch, the privy, and half a dozen houses.

I started toward the house of Nahusai. Something moved in the shadow along the wall.

"Yes?" I called. "What is it?"

Something else moved to the right of me, near one of the neighboring houses. I turned. A person stood in the moonlight. He or she wore a robe.

"What is it?" I asked.

"I am Hakht," a voice said harshly. Or maybe the voice said "Akht." I was not certain about the initial aspirate.

Other figures emerged from the shadows. There were half a dozen. Two had sticks. They formed a circle around me—at a good distance. Nonetheless, they blocked my way out of the yard.

41

"We heard you. You go there." The figure in the robe pointed at the privy. "You talk. You do . . ." he or she said something I didn't understand. It sounded like an accusation.

"I do nothing bad," I said.

The person made a gesture that meant—I was pretty sure—"no" or "I disagree." "You are a something-something. I tell you, go!"

"I do not understand," I said.

"Go!" the person shouted.

I looked around. No one was coming close. What was I supposed to be? An evil spirit? I walked forward. The people in front of me moved to either side.

"Thank you," I said in English.

Behind me the person in the robe shouted, "Something! Go!"

I walked around the house to the front and then inside. Nahusai had gone to bed. Yohai sat by the fire. She was weaving, using the little handloom. She looked up.

"A bad thing," I said. "A person named Hakht or Akht."

"Tsa!" Yohai scrambled upright. "What?"

"I was in the privy. I came out. Hakht was there. Hakht said, 'Go.'"

"Hu!" Yohai ran to her mother and shook the old lady awake. They talked softly and rapidly. I bit my thumbnail.

"Nahusai!" a voice said behind me. It was Hakht, of course. He or she stood in the doorway. One hand held a staff. The other hand held a rattle. The rattle was painted white. Black feathers dangled from the handle.

"What is this?" asked Nahusai.

I glanced at the old lady. She was standing now. Yohai held a belt made of silver. The old lady smoothed her robe, then took the belt and put it on. After that she opened a box and pulled out half a dozen necklaces. They were silver, copper, bronze, and shell. She put them on. Yohai handed her a staff. She walked toward us slowly, with dignity, leaning on her staff.

"It is night, daughter of my sister," she said to Hakht. She spoke slowly and clearly. I had an idea that she wanted me to understand. "Why are you here?"

Hakht waved the rattle at me. It made a buzzing sound. "This one will go."

"No," Nahusai answered.

"She is a something!" Hakht said.

"No. What did I teach you, daughter of my sister? How do we know a something?" Nahusai held up a finger. "They do not like to eat." She held up a second finger. "They never sleep." She held up a third finger. "They do not go in the water. Is this not so?"

Hakht frowned, then made the gesture that meant "yes."

Nahusai waved at me. "This one sleeps. She eats—" My host made a wide gesture, indicating that I ate plenty. "She uses the privy. She has been in the water. Yohai saw this. She is not a something. You say a bad thing, daughter of my sister. It is not true."

Hakht frowned. She opened her mouth to answer.

Nahusai pointed at the door. "I will not talk in the night. Go!"

After a moment Hakht turned. She left slowly, with obvious reluctance. Her back looked rigid. The hand that held the rattle moved slightly. I heard a soft erratic buzz.

When she was gone, Yohai began to moan.

"Tsa!" the old lady said.

I discovered I was shaking. I sat down, almost falling as I folded myself up. Nahusai and Yohai began talking. Their voices were full of strain. I couldn't understand a word of the conversation.

What had happened, anyway? Hakht had accused me of being some kind of supernatural creature. A monster, an evil spirit, a ghost. Nahusai had said I didn't have the distinguishing characteristics of whatever it was. She had sounded like a doctor, discussing the symptoms of a disease. She must be a magician or a priestess, and Hakht must be one, too. A rival specialist. In any case Hakht had withdrawn, foiled for the moment. But I was pretty sure that this quarrel wasn't over. Should I ask Eddie to pull me out? I bit a fingernail. Not yet.

My host spoke, her voice calm and definite. Whatever she said sounded final. Yohai made a gesture I didn't entirely understand. But I thought it meant "so be it."

Nahusai sighed. She leaned her staff against the wall, then took off her jewelry. She looked exhausted.

"Li-sha." It was Yohai.

"Yes?"

"Sleep." Yohai pointed at my pile of furs.

I went there, but I didn't get to sleep for hours.

Yohai shook me at dawn. "Wake you. Eat."

I sat up. The fire was burning brightly. A pot hung over it, and my host sat nearby.

"Come," said Yohai. "Now."

I went to the privy first. It was cold outside. There was dew on the ground, and the sky was an indeterminate early morning color. Why was I up at this hour? More trouble, I decided. I used the privy and went back to the house. There was water in a big basin next to the door. I washed and went inside.

Breakfast was mush. It seemed to be their favorite food. When we were done eating, my host looked at me. Her expression was grave. "Li-sha." She paused and frowned. "Hakht says bad things. People listen. They say, 'Yes. Li-sha is a something. She is bad.'" She paused again and stared at the fire, then

43

looked back at me. "I am old. They know I go—" She patted the floor. Underground, that gesture meant. "I talk. They do not listen. Go with Yohai."

"Where?"

"A good place. Go."

I packed, then slung my pack over my shoulders. Yohai put on a plain brown tunic and a leather belt. A sheath hung from the belt, and there was a knife in the sheath. It had a handle made of brass and horn.

"Come," Yohai said.

I stopped in front of Nahusai. I didn't know the word for "thank you," but there was a gesture. I touched my chest, then turned my hand so the palm was toward Nahusai.

She returned the gesture.

I held out a gift: a box. It was made of wood from one of the Empty Islands, inset with pieces of shell. They were iridescent pink and green, lovelier than abalone or mother-of-pearl.

Nahusai took the box.

"Good-bye," I said in English. I followed Yohai out the door.

The sun was just appearing. Looking to the east I saw it: a line of orange light above a rooftop. The sky was clear. The street was empty, except for a yellow *ki*—a domestic bird, something like a crane. It was hunting for bugs in the weeds along a house wall. We startled it. It stalked away, and we hurried off in the opposite direction.

By the time the sun was fully up we were in the forest. Trunks rose up on every side of us like pillars in an old-time cathedral. Way above us were the branches. Their dark leaves hid the sun. Now and then we came to a clearing, full of sunlight and flying bugs. There must have been a hatch. Or was I seeing a migration? In any case, the bugs were all the same. Their bodies were electric blue. Their wings were transparent and colorless, except for two large red spots.

There was one clearing where the bugs were especially numerous. They floated around us. One landed on my arm. I stopped, enchanted. It fanned its wings. I counted eight legs and two antennae.

"Come," said Yohai.

I hurried on. The bug flew away.

At noon we came to a building standing in a larger-than-usual clearing. Weeds grew around it, and a stream ran in the back. I heard the rushing water.

"This is the place," my companion told me.

The building was small and old. A log propped up one wall. The roof was leather. I was pretty sure that it wasn't the original roof, but rather a makeshift repair, done by someone who was no carpenter. Off to one side was a second structure. A lean-to. Smoke came out of it. What was it? I got my answer a moment later: the sound of a hammer. A smithy.

44

My companion walked toward the sound. I followed. We stopped at the entrance to the lean-to and looked in. A fire burned in a stone forge. A person bent over an anvil made of iron. There was metal on the anvil, glowing bright yellow. The person lifted a hammer, then brought it down, lifted it and brought it down again.

Yohai raised one hand in warning. "Wait" that gesture meant. I waited.

After a while the person put down the hammer. He or she straightened up, stretched, groaned, then turned and saw us. "Hu!"

Yohai said something I didn't understand.

The smith made a gesture.

Yohai talked some more. I studied the smith. He or she wore a leather apron and sandals. Nothing more. I got a good look at him or her: broad shoulders, a deep chest, and powerful-looking arms. This was a formidable creature. The fur that covered him or her was reddish brown. An unusual color. Hadn't there been someone like this at the party on the night I arrived?

Yohai stopped talking.

The smith made another gesture, then looked at me. "I am Nia. You will stay here."

I made the gesture of assent.

Yohai said something to me. Was it good-bye? She turned and walked away, moving quickly. In a minute or two she was gone.

"Sit down," said Nia. "I—" He or she waved at the fire.

"I understand."

I settled in a corner. Nia added charcoal to the fire, then began to pump the bellows: a large bag, made of leather, with a stick attached to it. Nia raised and lowered the stick. The bag filled and emptied. The fire brightened. After a while Nia picked up tongs and laid the metal in the fire.

"What is that?" I asked and pointed.

Nia told me the word for iron, then went back to work. He or she beat the piece of iron till it was flat, then heated it and folded it, then beat it flat again. This was done over and over. I got tired watching.

Sometime in the afternoon Nia stopped working. He or she sighed and stretched. "Food."

"Yes." I stood up.

We went to the other building. Inside it was empty except for a pile of furs and a couple of jars. Nia took off the apron, then rummaged among the furs and found a tunic. She put it on.

"Here." She pulled bread out of one jar. The other jar was full of a liquid: the pungent narcotic I'd drunk at the party.

We sat down in the doorway and ate and drank.

45

"Where are you from?" asked Nia. Her mouth was full of food. I didn't understand her, and she had to repeat the question.

"Not around here," I answered.

"I am of the Iron People," she said. "They are far away. There." She pointed toward the sun. "You?"

I waved in the opposite direction, eastward.

"Ya." She drank more of the liquid. "These people are hard to understand." She got up and went to the smithy.

I stayed where I was until I heard the sound of Nia's hammer. Then I got out my radio and called Eddie.

After he heard what had happened, he said, "I ought to pull you out."

"No."

"Why not?"

"I don't think I'm in any danger, and if I am . . . Eddie, we all knew how dangerous this might be. We could have sent down robots. We sent down people because we wanted whatever it is that people bring to a situation. The human perspective. We voted to take the risk. It got a clear majority."

Eddie was silent.

"I want to stay. That's *my* human perspective. This is the reason I left Earth—not to sit in a room in the goddamn ship. I'm finally able to carry on a conversation, and I'm starting to learn how the natives work iron. You know I'm interested in technology."

There was more silence, then a sigh. "I opposed using robots because I thought they'd be more disruptive than people. Okay. Stay. But I think you're wrong."

"About what? The situation?"

"No. Technology. It's a typical Western bias. You think a tool is more important than a dream because a tool can be measured and a dream cannot."

I made a noncommittal noise.

"The Greeks are to blame," he said.

"What?"

"They were the ones who decided that reality was mathematical. A crazy idea! An ethical value isn't like a triangle. A religious vision can't be reduced to a formula. Yet both are real. Both are important."

"You have no fight with me. I don't know enough about Western philosophy to defend it. And I have to get off the air."

"Give me a call tomorrow."

"Okay."

At twilight Nia came back. She divided her pile of furs in two. "You sleep there." She pointed at one pile.

I woke at sunrise. Nia was up and putting on her apron. "Yohai says you can learn. Come."

46

We went to the smithy. Nia got the fire going, then taught me how to work the bellows. That morning she made the blade for a hoe. The blade was pointed and had two barbs at the back—for weeding, I decided, though it looked as if it could be used as a weapon.

I had not seen any real weapons. No swords. No pikes. No battleaxes or battle clubs. Nothing that was clearly designed to harm another person.

That was interesting. Maybe the men—wherever they were—had the tools for killing.

At noon we stopped and ate. I asked Nia the names of several things: the hoe blade, the hammer, and so on. She frowned and told me. I had a feeling that she wasn't going to be a very good teacher. She seemed laconic by nature.

We went back to work. My arms started to ache, then my back, and finally my legs. The smoke was bothering my eyes, and I wasn't too crazy about the clouds of steam produced when Nia dropped the glowing blade into a bucket of water. She did this twice. Finally she took the blade outside. She examined it in the sunlight, then made the gesture that meant "yes."

"Is it good?" I asked.

"Yes. I will make another one."

Damn her. She did. By the time she was finished, I was exhausted. I went outside and lay on the ground, while she banked the fire and put her tools away. She was meticulously neat in her work. Her house was a shambles, though. The day—I noticed for the first time—was bright and cool. A lovely day, now almost over. I decided not to call Eddie. It was too much effort. Instead I went to bed.

The next day Nia made wire. I worked the bellows and learned a new phrase. "Pump evenly, you idiot."

In the evening we sat in Nia's house and drank the pungent liquid. We both got a little drunk. Nia began chanting to herself, slapping one hand against her thigh to keep time. Her eyes were half-shut. She looked dreamy.

I leaned against the wall and watched smoke rise from the fire. This was a change for the better, I decided. Nia was taciturn and short-tempered, but she wasn't melancholy. Nahusai had spent a lot of time sitting and brooding, and Yohai had almost always been busy. I found that unrestful.

Nia stopped chanting. I looked at her. She was lying down. A minute later she began to snore. A very restful companion, I told myself.

Nothing much happened in the next ten days. I helped Nia in the smithy. At night I talked to Eddie.

"There's no question about your language," he said one evening. "It's pidgin, which explains why it's so easy to learn.

47

"The big continent has a trade language, too—a different one, in no way related to yours. Yvonne and Santha are learning it. Meiling is learning something else. A local language, horrifying in its complexity."

"And Gregory?" I asked.

"Another local language, but less difficult. Oh, an interesting thing happened to Gregory . . ."

I waited expectantly. Eddie, I had learned, tended to save the really important information till the end of a conversation.

"His people found out he was male. They told him to leave. He asked why? The question was a stunner, apparently. They couldn't believe he was asking it. But in the end they told him. In their society the men live alone, up in the high mountains. They take care of the flocks, and they never come to the houses where the women live. The idea is shameful. Gregory says, he couldn't think of a polite way to ask about procreation."

"Did they throw him out?"

"No. He told them he didn't know how to stay alive alone in the mountains. They had a long argument, then decided to let him stay in one of the outbuildings—a barn of some kind. And there he remains. *J'y suis, j'y reste,* he says."

"The men live entirely alone?"

"According to Gregory, yes. The women say the men are bad-tempered. They don't like company."

"Oh, yeah? It explains what happened to Harrison."

"Uh-huh. I warned Derek and Santha. Yvonne is going to talk to her hostess. She's the ideal informant: a tribal historian who never stops talking."

I made the gesture of agreement, then grinned and said, "Yes."

"You talk to Nia. Ask her about the men in her society."

I said I would, but I didn't. Nia was never easy to talk with. Often she would stop in the middle of a sentence and stare off into space or else change the subject. I got the impression she had lived alone for a long time. She had forgotten how to carry on a conversation. I concentrated on prying information about grammar out of her. Questions about folkways could wait until later.

One morning Nia reached into the rafters of her house. She pulled down two axes.

"Come," she told me. "We are going to get wood."

We spent all morning in the forest. Nia felled a tree, maybe ten meters tall. The trunk was straight. The branches were bare, except for a few shriveled leaves. The tree was obviously dead and had been for some time.

When it was down, Nia said, "Make it into pieces."

"I'll do my best."

I started chopping. Nia went off. When I paused to rub my hands, I heard her axe a short distance away. She was felling another tree.

At noon we rested.

"What is this for?" I asked.

"Charcoal." She chewed on a piece of bread. "This wood is dry already. Tomorrow we put it underground. It will burn for nine days, ten days, slowly, underground. Then it will be charcoal." She got up, stretched, and rubbed her palms along her thighs. "Time to work."

I groaned and got my axe.

A few minutes later the blister on my right hand broke. I put down my axe and looked at the blister. There was blood. I was going to have to spray it. I walked back to Nia's house and opened my pack. Should I wash the wound? I decided not to. It looked clean, and I didn't know what kind of microbe lived in the streams, especially the streams close to a village. In theory, nothing on this planet could live off me. Our genetic material was too different. No local virusoid could use my DNA for replication. No local bacteroid could use my cells for food. Still and all—

I got out the bandage can and sprayed on a small thin bandage. It stung. That would be the disinfectant. I sat down and waited for the bandage to dry. It was shiny and dark brown: flesh-colored, according to the label on the can, and made in the South African Confederation.

"Nia!" a voice cried.

I looked up. Yohai came out of the forest, walking quickly.

"Where is Nia?"

"There." I pointed. "You can hear the sound of her axe."

"Bad news! I must tell her." Yohai ran off.

I thought about following her, but decided no, put the can of bandages away and did a little housework. The mess was beginning to drive me crazy. I hung up Nia's clothes and arranged the furs we slept on in two neat piles. When I was done, I went outside. I couldn't hear the sound of chopping or anything except the rustle of leaves. The sun blazed overhead, almost as bright as Sol. The air was hot. I sat down in the shadow of a wall and waited. After half an hour Nia and Yohai came.

"It is time to tell you what is going on," Nia said.

"I would like that."

They squatted down. Nia laid her two axes on the ground, then scratched her nose. "Nahusai lies in bed. She cannot get up. She cannot eat. Hakht says, you have done this. Hakht says, you must be driven away. If not, Nahusai will die and then other people. You will make songs. The songs will do harm. They will steal breath out of the mouth. They will make the blood in the belly get hard like a stone." Nia glanced at Yohai. "This is what you said."

Yohai made the gesture of agreement. "I think Hakht made the songs. She is the one doing harm. My mother is old. She cannot defend herself. I have no power. The people who are no longer here do not talk to me. I cannot defend my mother."

Well, this was pretty clear. Nahusai was ill. Hakht was accusing me of putting a spell on the old lady. I was a witch—according to Hakht, anyway.

"Why is Hakht doing this?"

Nia answered me. "She cannot wait. She wants to be the most important woman in the village. She will be, when Nahusai goes . . ." Nia paused, then patted the ground. "Nahusai taught her. Nahusai said, this is the one who will come after me. But she cannot wait." Nia frowned. After a moment she said, "There are people like this."

I made the gesture of agreement.

"She tries to put herself in the middle of everything. If Nahusai says 'yes' to anything, this woman says 'no.' Nahusai made you welcome. Because of this, Hakht says you are a demon."

"This is true," Yohai said.

"What do we do?" I asked.

"I can think of only one thing," Nia said. "We must wait. If Nahusai gets better, she will make Hakht be quiet. If she does not—" Nia made a gesture I did not recognize.

"What does that mean?"

"Who can say?"

I was going to repeat my question, then I realized Nia had answered it. The gesture—the hand held out, then tilted from side to side—meant "who can say?"

Nia stood. "Yohai, you go home. Li-sa and I will be careful. Thank you for the warning."

Yohai made the gesture of acknowledgment. She left. I waited till she was out of sight, then looked at Nia. "Do you think she is right?"

"In what way?"

"Did Hakht make this happen? Did she harm Nahusai?"

Nia frowned. "I do not know if songs do anything. Or if the people who are no longer here listen to anyone. But a woman like Hakht knows things to put in food. This is a bad situation." She clenched one hand and hit the wall above me. "I hate this place! I am tired of the dark trees. I am tired of the people. They are always telling stories about one another. They are always making plans to do one another harm." She bent and grabbed an axe, then walked away. A bit later I heard the sound of the axe. Nia was chopping down another tree.

I thought of calling Eddie, then decided no. Ten to one, he'd want to pull me back up to the ship. I didn't think the situation was dangerous, and I wanted to see what would happen next.

I went to the bank of the stream and did my yoga exercises. Then I meditated, watching the rushing water. At twilight bugs appeared—little ones, like gnats. They didn't sting, but they got in my nose and eyes. I got up and went back to the house, feeling relaxed. My mind, usually busy and a bit anxious, seemed as empty and clear as the sky above me. I stopped outside the door and looked up. There was a moon above the forest: a narrow sickle, less than a quarter full. It was pale yellow, bright with the light of vanished sun. All at once I was full of an intense joy. At any moment things were going to make sense. I would see the pattern in—or beyond—observable phenomena. I would understand the mystery of life, the secret of the universe.

Then the feeling was gone. The moon was only a moon. I shrugged. Once again I hadn't gotten through. To what, anyway? I wasn't really sure these moments of almost revelation meant anything.

I went inside and found Nia making dinner: a thin gruel with berries mixed in. Her movements were abrupt, and her body looked tense. She was still angry. I decided to keep quiet. We ate and went to sleep.

I woke, hearing a noise: a soft *tum-ta-tum*. It came from outside. A drum.

"Nia?" I called.

She scrambled out of bed. A moment later she was at the door, pulling it open. Gray light shone in. Nia stood in the doorway. She was naked, and she held an axe.

I got up and moved in back of her.

It was a little before sunrise. There was light in the east. In the clearing in front of the house five torches burned. They looked impressive, streaming in the wind, but they didn't do much in the way of illumination. I saw dark shapes and knew they had to be people. But I didn't know who they were or even how many stood there. Twenty-five? Thirty? Maybe more.

Nia muttered something and stepped through the door. I followed. A person came toward us. She held a rattle, and she kept it moving continuously. It made a noise like a rattlesnake gone nuts.

"Stop that noise," Nia said. She sounded angry.

"Very well." The noise stopped. "We have come for the demon." I recognized the voice. Loud, harsh, and arrogant, it belonged to Hakht.

Nia glanced around. "What does this mean? Is Nahusai dead?"

"She died last night. I was in my house, making a song to drive away bad luck. I heard Yohai shout. I knew the old woman was gone."

"And Yohai?" Nia asked. "Is Yohai here?"

The sky was getting brighter. I saw the gesture that the sorceress made. It meant "no."

"There are ceremonies that must be performed. She has begun them." Hakht raised her voice. She sounded triumphant. "She will not help you. I told her, she has caused bad luck. She has caused anger among the people who are no longer here. I have said, this must stop. She listened, î woman of the Iron People. She will do what I say. Now—" Hakht raised a hand and pointed. "The demon. Give her to me."

"No."

Hakht took a step forward. Nia lifted up the axe. "Listen to me, sorceress. I have no respect for you. I do not fear your power." Nia paused. Usually her shoulders were rounded. But now she drew herself upright. "All of you, listen! I have done something that few women ever do. I have killed a person."

The villagers shifted around a little. No one spoke.

"West of here, on the plain, are the bones of a person who made me angry. I did not even bury him." She glanced around. "I am willing to do this again."

Hakht opened her mouth.

"Be quiet! Let me finish!"

Hakht closed her mouth. She was frowning.

Nia went on. "I do not want to stay here. I am tired of the darkness under the trees. I want to see the sky again. I will go and take the demon with me. There will be no one left to stand up to you, Hakht. You can be happy then." The contempt in her voice was obvious. "Give me one day, o sorceress. Go away and come back tomorrow morning. I will be gone with the demon, and no one will be hurt."

There was a long silence. Nia kept her pose, standing very straight, her axe raised. Hakht stared at her and frowned. At last Hakht said, "Very well. We will come back tomorrow." She turned and walked away. The rest of the villagers followed. In a minute or two they were gone—out of sight in the forest.

Nia sighed. Her shoulders went down. She took a step back and leaned against the wall of the house.

"Did you really kill a person?"

She made the gesture of assent. "I was very angry." She looked out at the forest. "I would like to kill Hakht, but I am not angry enough." She dropped the axe. "Go in. Get ready to leave. I will come in as soon as I stop trembling."

I went inside and packed. After a while Nia came in. She reheated the remains of dinner. We ate.

"Maybe this is good," she said. "I might have stayed here till I was an old woman. Now I will see the plain again." She got up and pulled a bag out of the rafters. "I'll have to leave my anvil and most of my tools. Aiya!"

She went to the smithy. I went to the stream to wash. When I got back, she was dressing. The bag lay at her feet. It was half-full and lumpy.

"What did you pack?"

"As little as possible. And nothing really big. The kinds of tools I use are not light. The bag is going to seem very heavy, after I carry it for a while." She paused, then made the gesture that meant "so be it." "I am not willing to leave everything behind."

She finished dressing and folded up a cloak made of leather. It went into the bag, followed by all the bread in the house. Ten pieces. "Let's go. Hakht might change her mind." She handed me one of the axes, then picked up the other and slung the bag over her shoulder. I put on my backpack. We left the house.

The sun was up. The sky was cloudless. A strong wind blew.

"A good day," Nia said.

"What will happen to Yohai?" I asked.

"She will listen to Hakht. It will be hard for a while. Then she will get used to it. And Hakht will become friendly when she sees that Yohai does nothing against her wishes. In the end they will get along. The fight was never between the two of them. It was between Hakht and Nahusai. This is my opinion, anyway."

We took the path that went toward the village, walking quickly, and reached the river before noon. I looked around. On the far side of the river was a fence, a low one made of wood. Beyond it was a garden. Blue leaves glistened in the sunlight. I saw no gardener. That was odd. The people of the village seemed to spend a good part of every morning in their gardens.

In the distance something honked. A musical instrument. Maybe a horn. I heard voices, wailing and shrieking.

"The ceremonies," Nia said. "They are going around the outside of the village, making noise to drive Nahusai away, into the far land." Nia frowned. "My people are not like this. We do not fear the dead—only death, which is unlucky. There must be ceremonies, of course . . ."

The horn honked again. It sounded closer. Nia paused and listened, then went on.

"The ceremonies drive away bad luck. They make the village clean. But we do not fear our friends and relations simply because this bad thing had happened to them. They are—they must be—the same people they were before." She resettled her bag on her shoulder, then walked off.

I thought of asking her for more information about the funeral ceremonies, but she was moving quickly. I had to hurry to catch up, and I had no breath to spare.

Enshi

We followed a new path that went upstream along the river. The sun went on ahead of us—or seemed to, anyway. We were traveling west.

Midway through the afternoon we turned onto another trail. It led north into an area of low hills. The soil was sandy. The trees were small and scrubby. Here and there we came upon outcroppings of a sandy rock, yellow or dull orange. The trail was barely visible: a faint line that wound among the rocks and trees. It led finally—in the late afternoon—to a shack, made of long branches leaning against rock. Skins were stretched over the branches. Smoke came out of a hole. What a sad little dwelling place!

Nia stopped. "We bring gifts," she called.

A deep voice answered, "Go away."

"I am Nia, the iron smith. Do you want a knife? It has a sharp blade. The handle is bone. Very handsome, I think."

There was a long silence. "What gift do you want?"

"I need food. Smoked fish, if you have it."

"Yes." There was another long silence. "Put the knife down. Go away. When the sun is out of sight, come back."

54

"Yes," said Nia. She rummaged in her bag and pulled out a knife, which she laid on the ground. Then she turned and walked off. I followed.

We went only a short distance. Nia put down her bag. "This is far enough. He can't see us here."

I sat down. "Who was that?"

"I don't know his name."

"It is a—" I paused. I didn't know the word for man. "It is what a boy becomes?"

"A man. Yes. Who else would live out here alone? I have met him before. He is friendlier than most men."

"You call that friendly?"

"Yes. The men around here have no manners. Their mothers raise them badly, and the old men who ought to teach them to behave when they leave the village—the old men are surly and mean. They lack self-respect. This is my opinion, anyway."

"Why do the men leave the village?"

Nia stared at me. "What kind of question is that?"

"Do all men leave the village?"

"Yes. Of course." Nia frowned. "What kind of person are you? Why do you ask something like that?"

I thought for a moment. "I come from a long distance away. My people are different from yours. How different, I don't know. Maybe the differences are small—things on the surface, like the fur that you have and I don't. Maybe the differences are big. In any case, among my people men and women live together."

Nia frowned again. "How can that be? After the change no man can bear to be with other people—except at the time of mating, of course, and except for Enshi."

"Enshi?" I asked.

Nia stared at the sky. "The sun is almost gone. We can go back."

We returned to the shack. Firelight shone through gaps between the skins. I didn't see anyone, either inside or out. The knife was gone. In its place was a basket, full of smoked fish.

"This is good!" Nia said. "Now we won't starve."

The basket had a top. She put it on and fastened it, then put the whole thing in her bag. "Come on. We'll go back toward the river and find a place to camp. This fellow won't like it if we stay here."

"That is true," the deep voice said. "It is a good knife, Nia."

Nia glanced at the shack. "The fish smells good. Thank you."

We walked off. The sky darkened and stars appeared along with a moon: a point of light that moved rapidly up from the eastern horizon. We stopped in a hollow. Nia made a fire, and we ate a couple of pieces of fish. It was bony and oily with a strong smoky taste. I did not especially like it.

55

"Who is Enshi?" I asked.

Nia stared at the fire. There was a brooding expression on her face. At length she glanced up. "I made up a poem about Enshi after I had been in this place a year. It goes like this:

> "I am in this dark place,
> this forest.
>
> "He is in that dark place,
> that grave."

"He is dead?"

Nia made the gesture of affirmation. "I will not talk about him. Do your men really live with the women?"

"Yes."

"That's very strange. Is it right?"

The word she used had several meanings: "usual," "well made," "moral."

"We think so. We've always lived this way."

Nia made a barking noise. "If Hakht knew this, she would be certain that you are a demon. Of course, her people do many things that are not right."

"What?" I asked.

Nia frowned, then scratched her nose. "They do not like men, not even their sons. 'A son is a mouth,' they say. They mean a son is something that eats food and makes noise and does nothing useful."

"Hu!" I said.

Nia made the gesture of agreement. "It is very badly done. There is something else . . ." She paused. "They do not like to mate with men. Often in the spring they go out, two women together. They stay in the forest. They do things with their hands." Nia shivered. "Do your people do anything like this?"

"Some of us do. I don't."

"Do you think it's right?"

I thought for a moment. "It is common. I don't think that it is wrong." I used a word that meant "unusual," "immoral," "badly made," or "done in a seriously inept fashion."

Nia shivered again. "I did it once. Yohai kept asking me. One spring I went with her. I do not know why. I didn't like it. I felt ashamed. Aiya!" She paused for a moment. "I wish we had something to drink."

The next day we went back to the river. We continued west along it. The land was flat and covered with forest. The sky was cloudless, and the river shone. Birdlike creatures glided from tree to tree, and other things—invisible to me—moved through the underbrush. I saw one as it crossed our path: a bronze shell about half a meter long with many quick-moving little feet beneath it. Two huge faceted eyes stuck out on top.

"What?" I asked as the animal vanished.

"It's called a *wahakh*," Nia said. "It can live in water and out of it. The people here say that it carries messages from the spirits, and sometimes it acts as a guide for women who go on spirit-journeys. They never eat it, though it is delicious when roasted." She paused. "We'll leave it alone."

Toward evening we came to a lake. The water was clear and dark green. Rushes grew at the edges.

Nia looked around. "I have been here before—when I came east, after I left my people. I remember this place reminded me of a lake in my country. The Great Rush Lake. This is smaller, of course. Aiya! How the years go by!"

We made camp. Nia spent the evening staring into the fire. I went off and called Eddie and told him what had happened in the last few days.

"You take chances, don't you?" he said.

"A few. Not many."

"That crazy shamaness might have decided to kill you."

"I don't think that's likely. I get the impression these people aren't violent."

"Uh-huh. Tell that to Derek."

"What happened?"

"He decided he had to tell the people in his village that he was a man— to see what would happen. He is, as you remember, extremely curious. They tried to stone him. He grabbed his radio and ran."

"Is he all right?"

"Yes. But what would've happened to someone else, someone who couldn't run the way he can?"

I thought about that for a while. Derek was a tall blond from southern California, an aborigine who'd spent his childhood traveling on foot in the desert. When he was fifteen, there had been a drought. He walked up to a trading station on the coast and said, "I'm tired of living like this. Teach me something else."

They sent him to school, and he took up running as a sport. Over short distances he was good. Over long distances he was unbeatable.

"Where is he? On the ship?"

"No. He's traveling west. The country is pleasant, he says. Rolling hills, forest, and some prairie. There's a lot of game, much more than in California. He is going to make a bow."

A bug flitted past me. I batted at it and missed. "How is Gregory?"

"Fine. But he says his people are treating him differently. They talk to him slowly and firmly, and they give a lot of orders. Very simple orders. He thinks they've decided he is not very bright. What other explanation is there? He doesn't know the right behavior, and he can't take care of himself."

I grinned.

"One other thing," Eddie said.

Aha, I thought. The zinger for today. "What is it?"

"Gregory says there must be gold in the mountains. His people wear a lot of jewelry, and most of it is gold."

"What's so interesting about that?"

"The planetologists think it may be significant. The planet is denser than Earth, and there's plenty of evidence of volcanic activity. There's a good chance, they say, of finding metal close to the surface. Not just gold—silver, copper, platinum, tin, iridium, chromium, you name it." His voice sounded peculiar: flat and careful.

"What's going on?"

"People up here are getting interested. Members of the crew, mostly. I don't think they have enough to do. They are talking about possibilities. If the metal is here, and if it's high quality, and if it's close to the surface, maybe even on the surface, then it could be mined."

I rocked back on my heels and looked at the radio. I couldn't really see it, of course. The night was too dark. "A mining colony? Eighteen light-years from home? Do they have any idea of the transportation costs?"

"They are thinking of a manufacturing center. A colony to build ships."

"No one is ever going to build a ship at the bottom of a gravity well, unless you are talking about the kind of ship that goes through water, and I don't think you are."

"Final assembly would be done in space."

"Huh," I said.

"There are problems," Eddie said. "Everyone admits there are a lot of problems, but they won't stop talking. They are absolutely fascinated by the idea of all that metal."

Hardly surprising. Our ancestors had done a job on Earth. Most of the metal and coal and oil that was easy to reach was gone, along with other resources. Much of the water. Much of the soil. Hundreds—no, thousands— of species of plants and animals.

Eddie went on. "I've been thinking about Cortez and what happened when he found gold in Mexico."

"You worry too much."

"Uh-huh. I'll bet that's what Montezuma said to his councilors."

I rubbed my eyes and tried to think. I was exhausted. "Eddie, I have to sleep."

"Is it night down there? I guess it is. Sweet dreams, Lixia."

58

I went back to camp and lay down. Above me the stars shone. Somewhere up there was a relay satellite and a long way to the south—over the middle of the ocean—was the I.S.S. *Number-One.* I imagined it, turning in the light of this system's primary, gleaming just a little: an enormous hunk of lithium hydride, shaped like a cigar. The surface was pitted and discolored. More than half the mass was gone. The lithium hydride had been our fuel as well as our main protection against radiation.

At one end of the cigar was a series of metal and ceramic coils. These were the magnets that contained and controlled the fusion reaction that drove the ship. The other end was bare. When we left Earth there had been an umbrella made of cermet, additional protection against the tiny amount of matter between the stars. We had dropped the umbrella at turnaround. From that point on, the engine acted as protection, burning whatever bits of space debris might lie ahead of us into ionic vapors, which the magnets guided away.

That was it: a dirty white cigar and a series of rings, black and tan and gray. The living quarters were invisible, hidden in the middle of the cigar: a cylinder made of ceramic, encased in salt.

That was the part of the ship I knew: the rooms and corridors lined with tile. They gave the ship one of its many nicknames—my favorite, the China Clipper.

It had no sails, of course. That idea had been abandoned early on. And there wasn't a lot of porcelain onboard. The wall material reminded me of earthenware. It was dull and a bit rough, light orange in color. In places it was glazed, usually white or blue.

It was a lovely material: light and hard and durable, immune to corrosion, resistant to heat, excellent insulation. Eddie was nuts. We hadn't gone to the stars in a tin can. We had gone in something made of clay and salt. There was plenty of both where we came from. We didn't need the metal on this planet.

For the next three days Nia and I continued west. The land rose. We entered a canyon. At the bottom was a narrow shallow stream. In the spring it must have been an impressive river, for it ran through the middle of a wide bed. Even now the water moved quickly. Here and there it was streaked with foam.

Cliffs rose on either side of us. They were dark gray and flecked with something that glittered in the sunlight. Mica?

I saw a new kind of animal. It was tiny and dark gray, the color of the cliffs. Its skin—or shell—glittered as if it were flecked with mica. In most parts of the canyon the animal seemed to be uncommon. But one section had hundreds of the little things. Motionless, they were invisible. I saw them when they moved, flashing out from under my feet, running up a rock away from me. It seemed as if pieces of stone were coming alive, changing into—what? Lizards? Not exactly. For one thing, they had six legs. On Earth that would have made them insects. But they didn't look like bugs, and the bugs on this planet seemed to have at least eight legs.

"I don't know what they are," said Nia. "And I don't know why there are so many of them. This isn't my country. Ask me questions when we come out onto the plain."

I made the gesture of acknowledgment.

Late on the third day she said, "A person is following us."

"What?" I looked back.

The canyon was shadowy, and I couldn't see far, but as far as I could see, the trail was empty.

Nia grabbed my arm and tugged. "Keep going. Don't let him know that we know."

We trudged on.

"I saw him twice today, this morning and a short time ago. If he means to do harm, he'll do it tonight."

"Harm?" I said.

"There are men who go crazy. They become violent. They attack other people."

"Why?"

"I don't know. But some men—when they go through the change—become like animals. They cannot control themselves. And there are other men who are fine till they get old. They grow weak. They cannot get women. This makes them angry. I have met one like that. They do not attack large groups of women, but if a person travels alone or in a small group, a twosome or a threesome—that is asking for trouble!" She glanced at me. "We have to find a place to camp."

We kept going until we came to a place where the canyon floor was wider than usual. The stream spread out. On the far side the canyon wall was broken. There were fissures and huge black boulders. A waterfall tumbled down between the rocks and there was vegetation, bushes, and a few small trees.

"We'll camp on the other side of the river," Nia said, took off her sandals and picked them up.

I followed her to the edge of the stream. Casually she glanced back. "He's close now. He thinks the dark will hide him. But I have good eyes."

She waded in. I followed. As promised by the people in supply, my boots were waterproof.

Halfway across the water deepened. Nia went up to her knees. I stopped and considered what to do. I couldn't take off my boots where I was, and I didn't like the idea of going back the way I had come. The sun was gone. It was twilight in the canyon. Somewhere in the shadows was the man. I had no wish to meet him, especially alone. I waded on. My boots filled with water.

By this time Nia was on the far bank. She bent and brushed the fur on her legs, then stamped her feet. I climbed up beside her and took off my boots, turning them over. Water poured out.

Nia jumped. "Not on me, you idiot! I just dried my fur!"

"I'm sorry." I took off my socks and squeezed them. "What now?"

"We'll make camp there." She waved at the tumbled boulders. "The man will have to come close in order to see us. I intend to be waiting."

There was a hollow—an empty space—among the rocks. We set our baggage down. In the last light of day we gathered wood.

"Now," said Nia softly. "You build the fire. But do not light it until I speak."

As I worked I heard her moving close to me, invisible in the shadows among the rocks. The noise she made stopped. I listened. A bird whistled, and I could hear the stream. Nothing else.

In back of me a voice spoke: "Light the fire."

I got out my lighter. The dry leaves caught at once. Yellow flames licked up around the branches. I was able to see. On the other side of the hollow was Nia's bag and something that looked like a person lying full length on the ground, wrapped in a cloak or a blanket. But Nia had spoken from in back of me. I was sure of that. Whatever was under the cloak, it was not my companion.

"Going to sleep already?" I said. "All right. Good night." I put another branch on the fire. I was thirsty but afraid to go to the stream. I thought about eating. The bread was dry, and the fish was salty. If I ate either one I'd get even thirstier. Anyway, my stomach was queasy.

The fire dimmed. I added more branches. I had the feeling that someone was watching me. The skin on my back prickled, and I was beginning to sweat. I stood up and stretched, then casually looked around. There was nothing visible except a heap of rocks. I sat down. A pebble rattled. I stood again. What had that been? I listened but heard nothing.

I sat back down. After a moment I began to do my breathing exercises. I inhaled and thought the syllable *so*. I exhaled and thought the syllable *hum*. Gradually I relaxed. It was, I realized, a pleasant night. The air was cool and dry. The sky was clear. Stars shone brightly. A moon was rising over the canyon's rim: a reddish point of light. I kept on breathing slowly and deeply. *So. Hum. So. Hum.*

A scream! I scrambled to my feet, looking around. Something moved behind a boulder. I grabbed my axe and ran.

Two bodies struggled in the shadows. They were both dark, both furry. I couldn't tell them apart. They rolled out of shadow into firelight. A hand went

61

up, holding a knife. Around the wrist was a wide copper bracelet. Nia wore no jewelry. I turned the axe and swung it, bringing the flat side down against the fellow's arm. There was a groan. The hand opened. The knife fell. I stepped back.

They rolled again—almost into the fire. Nia was on top. She had a hammer in one hand. Her other hand reached for the fellow's throat. He grabbed her tunic with both hands. Then he arched his back and heaved. Nia went up. She was in midair. I couldn't believe it. How could he be that strong? She came down in the fire. Sparks flew. Burning branches scattered across the ground. Nia screamed.

The man scrambled upright and grabbed a branch. It was burning from one end to the other. How could he hold it? Was he crazy? He started for me. He certainly looked crazy. His eyes stared and his mouth was wide open. He was howling.

I raised my axe. He swung. I blocked the blow. I could feel the shock along my arm from the wrist to the shoulder. He stepped back and raised the branch again. It was still burning. He was still howling.

The branch came down. I blocked it again. He let go. The branch fell blazing, and he grabbed the handle of my axe, twisting and yanking. I lost my grip.

He turned the axe around—it was a single rapid motion—and raised it over his head. He was making a noise like an evacuation signal, a high even scream.

There was no time to get out. He had reached the top of his swing. The axe blade glinted. I tasted bile.

The screaming stopped, and the man grunted, then looked surprised and fell. Nia stood on the other side of him: a silhouette against the light of the scattered fire. She was still holding the hammer.

I took a deep breath.

She asked, "How is he? I hit as hard as I could."

I knelt and felt his throat. There was no pulse. Was that normal? I had no idea. I put my hand over his mouth. There was no breath. "Where did you hit him?"

"The head. With this." She lifted the hammer.

I felt the back of his head and found a spot where the skull went in. I pulled my hand away. There was blood on my fingers and something else as well: an object, stuck to the tip of my middle finger. It was hard and triangular. The edges felt rough. I couldn't see the color, but I was pretty certain I knew what the object was. A piece of bone. I wiped my hand on the man's kilt, then looked at Nia. "I think you killed him."

"Aiya! Another one." She dropped the hammer and rubbed her face. "I have to sit down."

I stood up, holding out a hand. She tumbled toward me. I caught her, but she was too heavy. I couldn't keep her upright. I fell, landing on the dead man, and Nia came down on top of me.

Damn!

"Nia?" She didn't answer. I pushed and wriggled out from between the two furry bodies, stood up and rolled Nia over. It wasn't easy. She was limp. A dead weight.

I felt her throat. Ah! There was a pulse, strong and regular, maybe a little rapid. I couldn't be sure. I went to the fire and found a branch that was still burning and carried it back. What was wrong? Her tunic was torn, and one of the torn edges was smoldering. But I saw no other evidence of burning. I crouched and looked at her hands. One palm was puffy. Maybe that was a burn. I touched the palm. Nia winced and groaned.

"Are you awake?"

She blinked.

"Where does it hurt?"

She frowned. "My hand and my leg."

I felt along her legs. There was no blood. I found no wounds.

"The ankle," she told me.

I touched her left ankle. She winced again. I pressed in. Nia groaned. Something was wrong there. But what? How could I tell if anything was broken or out of place? I didn't know how an ankle was supposed to feel. Not on this planet. Not an ankle belonging to an alien. I thought for a moment. There was always bilateral symmetry. I checked her right ankle, then went back and rechecked the left.

"They feel the same."

Nia frowned. "To you. Not to me. What am I lying on?"

"The man."

"Aiya!" She got up on one elbow. "Help me."

"I don't want you to move."

"I will not lie on a corpse."

I frowned, trying to remember my first aid. Would it be okay to move her? I was having trouble concentrating, maybe because I had just helped to kill someone and the body was right in front of me.

Nia struggled into a sitting position. I laid down my torch and helped her off the dead man. "Is your back all right?" I asked. "Are you hurt anywhere else? Do you feel any other pain?"

"I told you. My hand and my leg. Nothing else. I think I will lie down."

I eased her onto the ground. She lay full length next to the dead man. I got up and grabbed hold of his arms. He was heavy, much heavier than Nia, and entirely limp. I managed to pull him a meter or so, then gave up and let go. His arms hit the ground with a thump. "That's it. He stays here."

"I do not feel good," said Nia.

I didn't think her leg was broken, but I wasn't positive. I'd better put on a splint. And get cold water for the hand. And get a cloak. She might well be in shock.

"I am going to need your cooking pot."

"Take it. What a strong man! I made a mistake. I thought he'd be old or very young. I am not as clever as I think I am."

I got her cloak and covered her, then took the cooking pot to the stream, filled it with water, and brought it back. "Put your hand in. It will help the burn. I'm going to rebuild the fire."

She made the gesture of assent. I went to gather wood. When the fire was burning brightly, I made a splint. I had an elastic bandage in my first-aid kit. For padding I used my undershirt and a spare pair of socks.

"I hope this is temporary," I said. "I need those socks. How is the hand?"

"Better, but now my shoulder hurts."

I pulled the cloak down. The fur on one shoulder was matted. I touched it and looked at my hand. The fingers were red. "Another wound. He did a good job on you."

"I knew when I saw him I was in trouble. But it was too late to change the plan. Is the wound bad?"

I got a piece of gauze and wiped the blood away. "It's a nick. He must have got you with the point of his knife." I looked at the contents of my medical kit. What was safe to use? She wasn't human. I had no idea of how she would react to any human medication.

I had brief, horrible fantasies about allergic reactions, toxic reactions, shock, and death.

But the wound ought to be covered. I didn't think any harm could come from a bandage.

I got out the can. "This is going to sting just a little." I hit the button.

"Aiya!" Nia said.

The wound vanished. In its place was a small dark patch of plastic. The patch was lumpy, and clumps of hair stuck out of it, coated with plastic. Idiot! I told myself. I should have shaved the area around the wound. Well, I hadn't and the best thing to do now was leave the wound alone. I rocked back on my heels. "Anything else?"

"No." She took her hand out of the pot, then grimaced. "This still hurts."

"I'll get more water."

I went to the stream and filled the pot again and brought it back. Nia put her hand in. Her eyes were almost shut. I had the impression she was exhausted. I tucked the cloak around her.

"Thank you." Her voice was drowsy. She closed her eyes.

64

I put more wood on the fire, then got the poncho out of my pack. It was light and waterproof with a removable thermal lining. I did not remove the lining. Instead I wrapped the poncho around me, lay down, and went to sleep.

I woke later, feeling cold. The fire was almost out. I got up and laid branches on the coals. Flames appeared. How silent the canyon was! I could hear water, but nothing else. Above me stars shone. I recognized the Big Dipper. It looked the way I remembered it—maybe a little brighter. That would be the air in the canyon. It was dry and extremely clear.

I went over to Nia. Her hand was still in the pot. On her face was an expression of pain. But she was sleeping, breathing slowly and evenly.

I checked her leg. It had stopped swelling. The bandage wasn't tight. She groaned when I touched her, but she didn't wake. I went to my pack and got out the radio.

This time I got Antonio Nybo. Another North American. There were a lot of them on the sociology team, maybe because there were so many different societies in North America. Tony was from somewhere in the Confederation of Spanish States. I couldn't—at the moment—remember exactly where. Not Florida. Texas maybe. Or Chicago. Most of his work had been done in southern California, studying the Hispanic farmers who were moving back into the California desert and interacting—not always easily—with the aborigines.

"Lixia! How are you?" His voice was light and pleasant with a slight accent.

"I had an interesting day . . ." I told him about it, then said, "Now for the problem. I don't think the leg is broken, but I'm not sure. Is there any way to tell without doing a scan?"

"I'll ask the medical team. Is it okay to call you back?"

"Yes."

He signed off. I got up and stretched, then touched my toes five times. My stomach gurgled and I remembered that I hadn't eaten dinner. I got a piece of bread. It was stale. I enjoyed it, anyway.

The radio rang. I turned it on.

"First of all they say they need more information." I could hear amusement in Antonio's voice. "They also say there ought to be more hemorrhaging with a fracture—than with a sprain, I mean. And hemorrhaging produces bruises—usually. Or did they say often? Anyway, if her foot turns black and blue in the next three days, she may have a fracture. But a bad sprain could produce bruising, too."

"What are you telling me?"

"The only way to be certain is to do a scan. The medical people suggest that they come down with the necessary equipment."

"Oh."

65

"They think," Tony said gently, "they ought to. And they would love— absolutely love—to get hold of a native. It is interesting what one finds out when one asks an apparently simple question. The aliens are not alien enough."

"What?"

"I don't mean at the cellular level. There—we have to assume—they are like the rest of the life on the planet. The biologists say there is no question that the organisms they have examined are alien and belong to a different evolutionary line. That is why they can say—so confidently—that we can't catch the local diseases. Nor can we spread our own diseases to anything on the planet." Antonio paused. "You might be interested in knowing that Eddie asked the medical team to double-check this fact."

"Why?"

"A native died shortly after you arrived at your village."

"I told Eddie what the woman died of. Old age, poison, or magic. There was nothing unnatural about her death."

Antonio laughed. "Eddie was worried about the bugs in your gut. The ones that were designed to metabolize the local food. The biology team said absolutely not. The bugs can't live outside a human. The biology team became offended and spoke about people moving outside their areas of expertise, especially people in the social sciences—which, as everyone knows, are not *real* sciences like biology and chemistry."

"Ouch."

"The problem is not at the cellular level. It's the fact that the natives look like us. They shouldn't, according to all the best theories. We ought to be dealing with intelligent lobsters or talking trees.

"According to the biology team, the natives are an example of parallel evolution—like the marsupial saber-toothed tiger of South America. But no one is really comfortable with this explanation. We need more information. The medical team wants some tissue samples, and they want to know what goes on the intermediate levels—between the entire organism, which looks like us, and the biochemistry, which is almost certainly alien. What are the organs like? The muscles and the skeleton? The endocrine system? The chemistry of the brain? They want—in sum—to get into a native and take a really good look around. I'm going to refer this to the committee for day-to-day administration."

"Okay."

"In the meantime, the medical people say to treat the injury like a fracture."

"Okay." I turned the radio off.

"Li-sa?"

It was Nia. I glanced at her. She was up on one elbow, staring at me. Her eyes reflected the firelight. They shone like gold.

"Yes."

"Is there a demon in the box?"

I tapped the radio. "This?"

Nia made the gesture of affirmation.

"No."

"Then how can it speak?"

"A good question." I thought for a while. "It's a way for people to talk when they're far away from one another. My friend has a box like this. When he speaks into it, his voice comes out here." I touched the radio again. "I can answer by talking into my box."

Nia frowned. "Among the Copper People—the people of Nahusai—there are songs of calling. When Nahusai wanted something, rain or sunshine or a ghost, she would draw a design that represented the thing she wanted. Then she sang to the design. The thing she wanted would hear her song and come. This is what she told me, anyway."

I made the gesture of disagreement. "This isn't a ceremony. It's a tool, like your hammer."

"Hakht would not believe that."

"What does she know?"

Nia barked. "That is true. Well, then, the box is a tool—though it's a kind of tool I've never seen before. I've never even heard of a tool like that." She paused. "It sounds useful. I am going back to sleep."

I woke in the morning before Nia did. The sky was clear and there was sunlight on the rim of the canyon. I went in among the rocks and relieved myself, then went to the stream and washed. On the way back I passed the dead man. He lay on his back, his arms stretched above his head. He was large—not tall, but wide and muscular with shaggy fur. His kilt was brown with orange embroidery, and his belt had a copper buckle.

His mouth was open. I could see his teeth, which were yellow, and his tongue, which was thick and dark. His eyes—open also—had orange irises.

I was going to have to bury him, I realized. The bugs were gathering already. Damn it. I had no shovel. I glanced at Nia. Still asleep. I bent and grabbed a rock and laid it next to the body. It—he—stank of urine. Poor sucker. What a way to go. Was there a good way? I went to get more stones.

Bugs hummed around me. Clouds drifted across the narrow sky. They were small and round like balls of cotton. My back started hurting. I scraped one hand on the rough edge of a rock. The injury wasn't serious. It didn't even bleed, but it stung.

Finally the man was out of sight, hidden by pieces of rock. Enough. I didn't have to make him a tumulus. I straightened. By this time the clouds were gone. Sunlight slanted into the canyon. Nia was sitting up.

67

"Good," she said. "His ghost should have a home. Otherwise, the wind will take him and blow him across the sky. That is no fate for anyone."

"Is there any ceremony that ought to be performed?"

"No. If a shamaness were here, she would sing. That would avert bad luck. I do not know the right words nor what to burn in the fire." She frowned and scratched her nose. "I ought to do something. I will give him a knife. A parting gift."

"All right," I said.

We ate breakfast. I bandaged Nia's hand. We didn't talk much. Nia looked tired, and I found myself thinking about the dead man under his heap of stones.

Midway through the morning my radio rang.

"Your box," Nia said. "It wants to talk with you."

I turned the radio on. "Yes?"

"Lixia? This is Antonio. I talked to the day-to-day committee."

"Uh-huh?"

"They voted 'no.' And then they decided this was not an administrative problem. It was a question of policy. I wasn't at the meeting, but there must have been someone on the committee who got upset with the vote and raised the question of policy in order to get another chance."

I nodded agreement to the radio.

"So the question was referred to the all-ship committee. We had the meeting. An emergency session, but a good turnout nonetheless."

"What happened?" I asked.

"Eddie—of course—is against any kind of intervention. You know his arguments. I won't repeat them. Ivanova went along."

"She did?"

"According to her, we decided not to reveal ourselves to the people here until we knew more about them. There are good reasons for our decision: our own security and the fear of endangering the native culture through ignorance. How do we know what kinds of information they can handle?

"Now—according to Ivanova—we are asked to abandon a carefully thought out, democratically decided, historically important course of action. Because of a hairline fracture. A possible hairline fracture.

"She would have a different opinion if one of our people was in danger. But the person with the injury is a native, and the injury is not in the least bit dangerous."

"Huh," I said.

"As for our friends from the Chinese Republic," Antonio paused for effect. "Yes?"

"They said this never would have happened if the members of the survey team had been properly trained."

68

"What does that mean?"

"You ought to have gotten a course in socialist medicine. Acupuncture, herbal lore, and Marxist ideology. As far as I can figure out, you are supposed to stick your companion full of needles and read selected passages from the *Communist Manifesto* to her."

"Who came up with this wonderful line of reasoning?"

"Who do you think? It's a perfectly preserved ancient Chinese argument. It came from a perfectly preserved ancient Chinese. Mr. Fang."

The Chinese had said it was hard to go to the stars without children and crazy to go without people of age and experience. The rest of us had remained firm re children. There were none on the ship. But we had taken a number of people over sixty and a few over seventy. Mr. Fang was close to eighty, a thin man with long white hair and thick gray eyebrows. He was from Zhendu in Sichuan, a master wicker worker and a master gardener, in charge of the main room in the ship's garden. Bamboo grew there, a dozen or more varieties. Along the walls were trellises covered with climbing palms. These were the raw materials for furniture. Most of the furniture on the ship was bamboo or rattan. Mr. Fang repaired it when it broke and made new furniture when needed.

I liked him. I had spent hours in his shop watching him work. From time to time we talked about philosophy. He especially liked the ancient Daoists and Karl Marx.

"They respected—at least in theory—the wisdom of the people. That is what matters, Lixia. A philosopher who fears or despises the people will come up with monstrous ideas."

"How did the vote come out?" I asked Tony.

"What do you expect? We talked for hours and ended up where we started. For the time being we will stick to our original decision. We won't go down to the planet—except maybe to help our own people. You are on your own. The medical team is not happy."

"Ah, well." I scratched my head. "What do I do now?"

"Continue to treat the injury as if it were a fracture. Keep it in a splint. Keep your friend off that foot. Time heals all wounds."

"Wonderful. If that's all the advice you have to offer, I'm going to sign off."

"Good luck."

I turned the radio off, then glanced at Nia.

"What did your box say?"

"You're supposed to stay put till the ankle heals."

She grimaced. "How can I do that? We are almost out of food, and there's nothing to eat here. We have to get to a village."

"Is there one nearby?"

69

"Yes. A day from here. Less than a day. The Copper People of the Plain live there." Nia clenched one hand into a fist. "What bad luck!" She hit her thigh, then winced. "I could walk a short distance if I had a stick to lean on. But I will not be able to walk to the village. And there is climbing. The path goes up in the place where the water falls." She frowned. "You go, Li-sa. Tell the people of the village what has happened. Ask their shamaness to come and bring medicine. I will give her a fine gift. Tell her I am a smith. A good one, from the Iron People. I can make a knife that will cut anything except stone." She thought a moment. "It won't cut iron, either. But anything else."

"Okay."

"What?" she asked.

"I'll go."

"What is that word? Ok . . .?"

"Okay. It means 'yes' or 'I agree.'"

"Okay," Nia said. "Go now. If you walk quickly, you'll be at the village before dark. Come back tomorrow. I'll be all right till then."

I got my pack and left. On the other side of the river I stopped to dry my feet. I couldn't see Nia, but I saw smoke rising from our fire, and I saw the grave of the crazy man. I thought I saw it. Maybe it was some other heap of stones.

I put on my socks and boots. Then I turned and walked away.

A curious thing about the canyon. From a distance the walls looked bare, and the canyon floor was stone gray. But close up I saw flowers and brightly colored bugs. The six-legged animals had vanished. Now I saw creatures that looked like birds or maybe tiny dinosaurs. They stood on their hind legs, and they were covered with feathers. But they had arms instead of wings. I saw one catch a bug. It grabbed the bug with little clawed hands and opened its mouth. I saw rows of teeth. A moment later—crunch! The bug was gone.

The hunter tilted its head and looked at me. I returned the gaze. The creature had blue feathers except on its belly and throat. The belly was white. The throat was sulfur-yellow.

The creature hissed at me.

"Oh, yeah?" I said.

The creature ran away.

At noon I stopped and ate. Above me birds soared on the wind. A fish jumped in the river. I rested for a while, then went on. The river got more turbulent. The trail began to go up and down, twisting around great rough lumps of a grayish-black stone. Ahead of me I saw the end of the canyon: a wall of stone, badly broken, full of crevices. Water ran down through the crevices, appearing and disappearing. At the top the water was in sunlight. It glittered like silver. Farther down, in shadow, it was gray. At the bottom of the cliff was a pool, half-hidden by mist.

Even at a distance I could hear the sound of the water. It was a continuous low roar.

I kept going. The trail went along one side of the pool. The canyon wall was next to me. Designs had been cut in the rock: spirals and triangles and the figures of animals.

Aha! I thought. A sacred place. But sacred to what? The spirals might represent the sun. Back on Earth the triangle was often a symbol of fertility or female sexuality. The animals were local species, or so I assumed. A quadruped with horns. A biped with a neck like an ostrich and long narrow arms. Were they worshipped or hunted? Or both?

The wind blew spray toward me from the waterfall. The trail became slippery. I decided to concentrate on my footing.

The trail went around a tall rock covered with pictographs. On the other side was a man. No question about his gender. He was naked, and his male member was large enough to be conspicuous. He was dancing, hopping from one foot to the other. He carried a pole. On top was a pair of metal horns, green with corrosion. Copper, almost certainly. The man spun and waved the pole, then spun back so he was facing me. He wore one thing, I realized now. A string of large, round, bright blue beads. They reminded me of faience beads from Egypt.

He stopped dancing and stared at me. I stood without moving, looking back. He was my size, maybe a little wider. His fur was dark brown and shaggy. His eyes were large and pale yellow.

He said something I didn't understand.

"I do not know that language," I said.

"You speak the language of gifts," he said. "You must be a stranger. I thought you were a demon, but a demon would have understood me." He frowned. "I suppose you might be a demon from far away. A demon from far away might not know the language of my people. Are you one?"

"A demon? No. I'm a person. My name is Lixia. Who are you?"

He looked surprised. "The Voice of the Waterfall. Haven't you heard of me?"

"No."

"You must be from very far away."

"Yes."

"I speak for the spirit of the waterfall. It is powerful and knows almost everything." The man sang:

> "It knows
> what the fish say
> in the water.

71

"It knows
what the birds say
on the wind.

"It knows
what the demons say
deep underground—

"The movers,
the shakers,
the ones who send up fire—

"It knows
what they say
to one another.

"People ask me questions. I tell them what I hear in the sound of the water." He hopped on one foot and turned, still hopping. Then he staggered and came down on both feet. "What do you want? Why are you here?"

"I've been traveling with one of your people. She is hurt, and I'm looking for help."

The man frowned. He waved the pole and shouted:

"O waterfall,
tell me,
tell me what to make of this."

He tilted his head and listened. I listened too, but heard nothing except the roar of the water.

"The waterfall says you are probably telling the truth. In any case, the waterfall says, it is bad luck to give trouble to travelers or people who ask for help. Therefore I will help you. Come along." He turned and walked up the trail. I hesitated a moment, then followed. It was never a good idea to argue with an oracle, especially one from a society you didn't understand. Soon we were a good distance above the pool. I looked down and saw churning water. Part of a rainbow shone faintly in the mist.

The trail entered a crevice. We walked between black walls of stone. Water trickled down. There were patches of shaggy orange vegetation on the rock. A creature walked between the patches. It was level with my shoulder and moving slowly, Earth-sky-blue with at least a dozen legs. Two antennae stuck out in front of it, waving gently. Two more antennae stuck out behind. They also waved gently. I couldn't see a mouth or eyes.

I assumed that the animal was traveling forward, but I had no way of telling. I thought of picking it up. Maybe there were organs visible on the underside. But I had never liked animals with more than eight legs.

My guide was moving quickly. I followed him, slipping now and then on the wet stone.

We were coming to the end of the passage. The walls were only a couple of meters tall. On top of them plants grew. I saw leaves and stalks and flowers.

The height of the walls decreased further. I could see over them and over the vegetation. We were coming out onto a plain.

Off to one side was a bluff—a low one, dotted with trees. In every other direction the land was flat and covered by a plant with long, narrow, flexible leaves. The plant was about a meter tall. Its color varied: green and blue-green, yellow-green and a silvery blue-green-gray. I couldn't tell what the differences in color meant. Was there more than one kind of plant growing on the plain? Or did the color represent variations within a species?

"There." The man pointed at the bluff. "The river is there. The trail goes along it. Follow the trail. At nightfall you will come to a village. Ask for the shamaness and say you have a message from the Voice of the Waterfall. Tell her the waterfall says give this person what she asks for. Say there is no harm in this. I know. The waterfall has told me.

"Do not disbelieve me,
O you people.
I know what the river knows.

"I know the secrets
discovered
by the rain."

He waved his pole and danced sideways, then spun and pointed down the trail. "Go!"

I went. When I got to the top of the bluff, I looked back. I could see the trail, winding through the pseudo-grass, but I couldn't see the man. He must have returned to the canyon and the waterfall.

I scrambled down the slope toward the river, which was wide and shallow here, shaded by trees with dark blue leaves.

In the middle of the river was a gravel bar. Half a dozen creatures rested there: large hairless quadrupeds with tails. One lifted its head and stared at me, then croaked a warning. They all got up and lumbered into the water.

Lizards, maybe? The name seemed appropriate, and it gave me a label. Though I would have to remember that these creatures were not real lizards.

I reached the village at sunset. It stood on top of the river bluff, and all I could see at first was a wall made of logs. Smoke rose from behind the wall. Cooking fires. A lot of them. On the wall were standards like the one the oracle had carried: long poles that ended in metal horns. The horns gleamed red in the sunlight. Polished copper, I told myself.

I climbed the trail up to the gate. A woman was standing there, watching the sun as it went down. She was dark like the two men in the canyon and dressed in a bright blue tunic.

"Make me welcome," I said.

The woman turned.

"Who are you?"

"A traveler. The Voice of the Waterfall told me to come here."

"Did he? Come in. You got here just in time."

We entered. She closed the gate and put a bar across it. "There!" She brushed off her hands. "Come with me. I'll take you to the shamaness."

I followed her along a narrow street that wound back and forth between houses. The houses were octagonal, built of logs. The chinks between the logs had been filled with a fuzzy yellow plant that seemed to be alive and growing. The roofs were slanted, going up from the edges to the center, where there was a smoke hole. I couldn't see the holes, but the smoke was obvious, rising from almost every house. The roofs were covered with dirt—an excellent form of insulation—and plants grew in the dirt. They were small and dark. I reached up and picked a leaf. It was round and thick and waxy. I squeezed. Water squirted out. A succulent or something very like. Chances were it would not burn, which was all to the good. Sparks would float out of the smoke hole. If they landed on a dry plant, these people would have a prairie fire going over their heads. What was the plant for? Was it edible? Was it decoration?

The woman stopped in front of an especially large house. "O shamaness, come out!"

The door opened. A woman came out, short and fat, wearing a long robe covered with stains. The robe was off-white, and the stains were easy to see. A poor choice for an obvious slob. She had on at least a dozen necklaces. Some were ordinary strings of beads. Others were elaborate with chains and bells and pendant animals. Everything was copper, and everything was tangled up. I didn't think there was any way she could have taken off just one necklace.

"This very strange person has come, o holy one. She says she has a message from the Voice of the Waterfall."

74

The shamaness peered at me. "Where is your fur? Have you been sick?"

"No. I come from far away. My people don't have fur."

"Aiya! This is strange indeed. What is your message?"

"The Voice of the Waterfall says he wants you to help me."

"No."

"What?"

"That man could not have said that. He has no wants. He has no opinions. He is the Voice of the Waterfall. When he speaks, it is the waterfall speaking. Therefore, what you said was wrong. It is not that man who wants me to help you. It is the waterfall who wants me to help you."

The other woman made the gesture of agreement.

"What do you need?" the shamaness asked.

"I have a friend who has been injured. She is a day from here—to the east, in the canyon. Will you go for her?"

The shamaness frowned and scratched her chin. Then she made the gesture of assent. "Tomorrow." She turned and went back in the house. The door closed.

"Aiya!" said the other woman. "This is something she never does. She never goes to people. They must go to her. But everyone listens to the Voice of the Waterfall. And that man used to be her son. She used to be fond of him. Come with me."

I followed her to another house. Inside was a single large room. Large pillars held up the roof. They had been carved and painted red, white, black, and brown. The patterns were intricate, made up of curving lines. They seemed to represent animals. Here and there I saw faces and hands with claws. The faces had copper eyes and copper tongues that curled right off the pillar.

In the center of the house was a fire burning in a pit. Three people sat close to it. They were children, about half-grown. They played a game. One threw a bunch of sticks. Another bent and looked at the pattern. "Aiya! What luck you are having!"

The third one looked at us. "What is this?"

"A person. Be courteous. Bring us food to eat."

We sat down. The woman said, "I am Eshtanabai, the go-between. It's fortunate that I was at the gate instead of some ordinary woman."

"You are a what?"

The children brought bowls of mush and a jug full of liquid. The liquid was sour. The mush was close to tasteless. We ate and drank. Eshtanabai explained.

"People get angry with one another. They do not talk. They sit in their houses and sulk. I go to each person. I listen to what they say. I say, This argument is no good. Is there no way to end it? What do you want? What resolution will satisfy you?' Then I go back and forth, back and forth until everyone agrees on what ought to be done. It's hard work. I get headaches a lot."

"I can imagine."

"Someone must do it. The shamaness is too holy. The Voice of the Waterfall doesn't always make sense. And how could a man—even that man—ever settle a quarrel?"

I had no answer for that question. We finished eating, and I lay down, using my pack as a pillow. One of the children put more wood on the fire. Another child began to play a flute. The tune was soft and melancholy. I closed my eyes and listened. After a while I went to sleep.

I woke in the middle of the night with a terrible crick in my neck. The fire was almost out. Around me in the dark house I heard the sound of breathing. My companions were asleep. I sat up and rubbed my neck, then lay down. This time I didn't use my pack as a pillow. When I woke again it was morning. Sunlight shone through the open door. Eshtanabai was sitting by the fire. The children were gone.

"The shamaness has left the village," she told me. "People have gone with her. They will bring your friend back."

"Good. When?"

"Tomorrow or the next day."

I ate breakfast—more mush—then went outside. The sky was cloudless, and the air was warm. It smelled of midden heaps. I decided to take another look at the plain. I found the village gate and went through it.

A trail led around the village. I followed it. The plain stretched south and east, almost perfectly flat. There were animals in the distance: black dots that moved from time to time. I shaded my eyes, but I couldn't make them out.

On the north side of the village were gardens that looked exactly like the gardens in the village of Nahusai. I stopped by one.

A woman looked up. "You are the stranger."

"Yes."

"You certainly are strange."

I pointed at the animals on the plain. "What are those?"

Her eyes widened. "You don't know?"

I made the gesture that meant "no."

"How can anyone be that ignorant?"

I said nothing. After a moment she said, "They are bowhorns. Most of the herd is in the north. In the fall the men will bring them back. The whole plain will be black then."

"Where are the men now?"

She frowned. "Don't you know anything? They are with the herd. Where else would they be?"

"Thank you." I wandered on.

76

The next day was overcast. I went down to the river, taking my pack with me. I settled at the foot of a tree and got out my radio.

Eddie was back. "How's your friend?" he asked.

"I don't know. I went to get help, and the help has gone to get Nia. I'll find out how she is sometime today."

"Where are you?"

I described the location of the village and told him about my meeting with the Voice of the Waterfall.

"Now that sounds fascinating." He was silent for a minute or two. Then he said, "I don't know much about oracles. They were big in Greece, weren't they?"

"Yes."

"Maybe I ought to do some reading. What is the village like?"

I described the village. "As far as I can tell all the adults are women. The men are up north, taking care of a herd of animals. They're migratory. The women stay put. How is the ship?"

"Pretty much the same. We got a message from Earth."

"Oh, yeah?" I felt the usual excitement. "Anything interesting?"

"There's a new space colony, and the Ukrainians are beginning to settle the wilderness around what used to be Kiev. And someone has come up with a practical faster-than-light radio. They have sent us the plans."

I rocked back on my heels. We wouldn't be isolated any longer. We wouldn't have to wait forty years for the answer to a question.

"How long will it take to build the thing?"

Eddie laughed. "We can build the receiver. The engineers are almost sure of that. But in order to send messages, we have to be able to generate a very strange new particle, and the machine that does that is *big*."

"Shit."

"My thought exactly. The particle—you might be interested in knowing—is called *fred*. Not in honor of Friedrich Engels. The message was very clear about that." Eddie's voice had the tone he used when describing obvious lunacy. "It was found—no, theorized—by two people more or less simultaneously. Everything about this particle happens in sets of two, according to the message. The person in Beijing wanted to call it a *guanyon* in honor of the Chinese goddess of mercy Guan Yin. Apparently the goddess came to her in a dream, standing on a lotus flower and holding the crucial equation written on a fan.

"The person in Santiago wanted to call the particle a *pablon* in honor of the poet Pablo Neruda. I don't know why. Maybe he got an equation in a dream. Neither person was willing to back down. So the particle is being called a *fred*. It always comes as one of a pair. The other particle is named *frieda*."

"I suppose this is another example of the terrible whimsy of physicists," I said.

"Uh-huh."

"Why did they send the plans if we can't use them?"

"For our information and just in case we ran into a lot of metal and a lot of silica and a modern industrial society. Always be prepared, as somebody said. Friedrich Engels maybe."

I scratched my nose. "What is bothering you?"

"Aside from the *fred?* Derek has found a lump of copper. It's a meter across, and as far as he can tell, it's pure. It was lying on the edge of a river. Just lying there in plain sight. People are saying, maybe we can find the resources to build the new transmitter. You people are finding too much. Why don't you shut up?"

"Come on, Eddie. We can't do that. Secrecy is the enemy of democracy. Is there any other news?"

"Derek's moving north as well as west. He's only a hundred kilometers from you. He'd like to join with you. Do you think your friend would object to traveling with a man?"

"Yes."

"I was afraid of that."

Something moved at the edge of my vision. "I have to go." I turned off the radio and shoved it into my pack, then looked around and saw a bipedal animal something like the one I had seen in the canyon. This was a new variety, however, as tall as I was, with a dark blue back. Its belly was cream-white, and it had a crest: a bunch of long feathers that shone bright blue in the sunlight. The animal was feeding off a tree covered with berries, reaching up its long arms and pulling the berries off, handful after handful. It crammed the berries into its mouth, then swallowed and reached for more. I got up. It twisted its long neck and stared at me, then went back to eating. There was something oddly human about its motions. It couldn't be intelligent. Its crested head was tiny. Still and all—I watched till it finished eating and wandered off. Then I walked back to the village.

In the evening the shamaness returned. I saw her enter the village. She was wearing a blue robe and a hat made of feathers. Five women followed her. Two of them carried a litter. Nia was on it. Her eyes were closed. She seemed to be asleep.

"Don't worry," Eshtanabai said. "Our shamaness will cure your friend."

"I hope so."

The shamaness said, "Take the woman to my house. I will go and gather herbs."

Eshtanabai touched my arm. "Come with me. The shamaness will not want visitors, except for the holy spirits. And you wouldn't want to meet them. It isn't safe."

"All right."

I spent the evening in the house of Eshtanabai. I felt restless and uneasy. What was happening to Nia? I bit my fingernails and watched the fire.

Eshtanabai played with her children. After a while I went outside. The village was quiet except for the sound of a drum. Was that the shamaness? I didn't know. I looked up. The sky was clear, and the stars shone brightly. A cool wind blew in off the plain. It was a lovely planet: pure and clean and almost empty. We had been working on our own planet for over a century when the ship left and the work had continued. Two centuries so far. There were still scars everywhere: stripped mountains, poisoned marshes, wide stretches where the land was useless, at least to humans—eroded, full of salt or dry, the water gone, pumped up and used in the twentieth century.

What had they been thinking of, those people then? They had left their descendants almost no water and great mountains of uranium. What kind of inheritance was that? How did they think we were going to survive?

We had managed with not much help from them. It was amazing how many people we had been able to save. When I thought of Earth, I thought of crowds. Only the ocean was really empty and the polar ice caps and the ruined lands.

Looking up at the starry sky I felt a terrible sense of loss.

Not that I objected to my society. It was sane, decent, humane, the best society that Earth had ever known. But it was enormously complex. Nothing was easy. Nothing was straightforward. For the first time history was a conscious process. For the first time people were shaping their lives deliberately, knowing what they did.

We argued every point. We voted. We compromised. We formed factions and coalitions. We thought—always—about justice and fairness, about the consequences of what we did, about the future.

The drum stopped. The breeze shifted. Now I could smell the cooking fires and the outhouses. I decided to go in.

In the morning I went to the house of the shamaness.

Eshtanabai led me. "O holy one," she cried. "The hairless person has come to visit."

The door opened. The shamaness peered out. "Your friend is sick. She burns. I can feel the heat in the places where her fur is thin. And she is weak. But I will cure her. Do not fear."

"Can I come in?"

The shamaness frowned, then made the gesture of assent and opened the door farther.

The fire was out. The only light came in through the smoke hole: a golden beam that slanted down and lit an old basket, faded and bent out of shape. Everything else in the house was hidden by shadows. I saw heaps of stuff, but I couldn't tell what it was.

"Nia?" I looked around.

79

One of the heaps moved and raised a hand. I went over. It was Nia, lying wrapped in a blanket.

"How are you?"

"I feel terrible. Sit down. Keep me company."

I glanced at the shamaness. She made the gesture of assent. I sat down.

Nia closed her eyes. For a while she said nothing. Then she said, "Is the shamaness good? Do you know?"

"They seem to think well of her."

"Good. Maybe I will live." She opened her eyes. "Enshi came to me last night. It's bad luck to dream about dead people. But he didn't threaten me. He joked and told me what it is like to live in the sky. Not bad, he said, though he goes hungry from time to time. He was always a bad hunter. Even when the animals come to him, as they do in that land, he still misses the shot. What a useless man! But he told good stories, and his temper was wonderful. He never got angry." She closed her eyes. I waited. She opened her eyes. "We did a shameful thing."

I glanced around. The shamaness was at the door, talking to Eshtanabai. She was too far away to hear.

Nia lifted her head and looked at the two women. Then she lay back down. "I won't tell you about it. Not here. I am not crazy. I'm tired. I want to sleep."

I left her and spent the day wandering through the village, watching children as they played in the streets and talking with mothers and grandmothers. They were courteous, friendly people. A coppersmith showed me how she worked the metal. An old woman told me how the world was created out of a seed let fall by the bird who lives in the tree of the sun. In the evening I ate dinner with Eshtanabai.

"Your friend will be fine. The shamaness told me. The shamaness says your friend is a smith. She has promised her a knife."

I made the gesture of affirmation, followed by the one for agreement.

"She is from the Iron People?"

"Yes."

"They live to the west of us, beyond the Amber People. They are fierce, we hear."

"I don't know."

"The Amber People say they quarrel a lot and when they give a gift, they always make sure the gift they get in return is just as good."

I made the gesture that meant "maybe" or "if you say so."

The next day I saw Nia again. A fire burned in the fire pit, and the house of the shamaness was full of aromatic smoke. My friend was sitting up, her back against a pole. I sat down. The shamaness left, closing the door behind her.

"I asked her to," said Nia. "I had another dream. I saw Hua, the woman who raised me. She died before anyone knew what I had done. But now she knows. She is angry. She spoke sharp words. Aiya! How they cut!

"I told her it was none of her business what I did. And anyway, what I did was nothing bad. She said, 'Everyone will agree with me. It was bad.' I said, 'I will tell the story to Li-sa. She is from far away. She knows how things are done in different places. Let her decide whether or not the thing I did was bad.' Then I woke up." Nia looked at me. I found it hard to read the expression on her face. But I thought she looked tired and unhappy.

I said, "Tell me your story, if you want to."

Nia frowned and scratched her nose. Then she began. Up till then, I had thought she was the strong silent type. She had never said a lot. But now she spoke fluently. She must have practiced the story. I imagined her telling it—to herself, most likely. She must have gone over it again and again, trying to make sense of what had happened.

"The first mistake was this: I helped Enshi meet his mother. I don't know why. He was always good at talking. He could always make the thing he wanted seem reasonable and right.

"I led him into the village—at night, of course, and waited outside the tent. He and his mother talked. She gave him gifts. He had lost the gifts that she had given him before. That was typical of him. When he was done, I went with him to the edge of the village. Now came the next mistake." Nia clenched one hand and struck the ground. "He wanted to come again. He was lonely on the plain. He would die out there in the emptiness, he said, unless he had something to look forward to. The warm fire in his mother's tent, good food, and new clothing. What a talker he was! I agreed to help him." Nia rubbed her face. "What a fool I was!

"His mother began to complain about her neighbors. She said there was too much noise in the village. She was tired of the smell of her neighbors' cooking. There was too much garbage. There were too many bugs. She began to pitch her tent away from all the others. They had planned this together. Now it was easy for him to find her tent, and people were not as likely to see him.

"But they still needed someone to carry messages in and out of the village. They needed someone to keep watch when he came. I did it all summer and through autumn. In the winter he could not come into the village. People would have seen the tracks in the snow. I went out to find him, taking food and a new cloak, a thick one made of fur. In the spring we met and mated. That was in the hills. The young men stay there. He had the worst possible territory. It was all stone, going up and down. There was nothing to eat there. Nonetheless, I went to him." She hit the ground a second time. "Maybe Hua is right. Maybe I am a pervert."

I said nothing. Nia went on. "He had nothing worth giving. He picked things up—feathers out of a bush or stones that glittered in the sunlight. He made up poetry. What kind of gift is that? He was a useless man!" She stopped for a moment. She looked puzzled. "When I was with him, I felt—I do not know what to call the feeling. I felt as if I had found a new relative, a sister or a mother. Someone to sit with in the evening, someone to gossip with. I felt contented. When the time of the lust was over, I stayed on. I liked being there. I stayed another ten days. Then I went home, and people asked me what had happened. I said my bowhorn went lame. I had to walk most of the way back, I told them. Now I was a liar." She frowned. "What happened next? We went north and pitched our tents in the summer country. Old Hua hurt herself. She got a burn working at her forge. The burn did not heal. Her leg began to rot. In the end she died.

"Everyone said she died the way a woman ought to—without complaining or making a lot of noise. The spirits were pleased with her. That is what people said. I found it hard to bear.

"After she was in the ground, the shamaness performed ceremonies of purification and ceremonies to drive away bad luck."

"Why?" I asked.

Nia looked surprised. "Every death is unlucky, and Hua had died unexpectedly. She was old but strong, and she had gotten burned many times before. The burns had always healed."

I made the gesture that meant "I understand" or "I see."

"The bad luck stayed," said Nia. "It did not seem that way at first. The summer was good. There was just enough rain. The rivers were full of fish, and the bushes had so many berries that their branches bent down till they touched the ground. We had plenty to eat.

"At the end of the summer people came to the village out of the west. They brought tin and white fur. One of them got sick. That one died. Then our shamaness died. I got sick and so did Nuha. She was Enshi's mother. She went crazy and cried out, 'Enshi! Enshi!' Then she asked the spirits to forgive her. She said it was my fault. Her son would never have done anything wrong. I had made him behave in a shameful fashion. I had made the spirits angry. She promised everyone if she died, she wouldn't go away. Her ghost would stay in the village and find ways to get even with me.

"She died. I got well, though I thought for a while that I would die, too. When I was able to get up and move about, the old women of the village asked me to leave.

"Aiya! That was difficult! I asked them to let me stay. I pleaded with them. But they said, 'Go.'

"I went to find Enshi, and the two of us went south until we came to the Hills of Iron. They are midway between the land of summer and the winter home. The soil is red there. The streams and rivers are as brown as rust. Every year certain women go there and mine iron. They stay till fall, digging out iron and smelting it into bars. Then they rejoin the village. By the time we got to the hills, the women were packing. We hid in the bushes. They loaded their wagons. At last they were gone.

"We found a shelter at the entrance to a mine. It was built of wood and stone, and the woman who'd built it had left some of her tools behind. We found an axe and a pick and shovel. There was an anvil as well—a big one, too heavy to carry.

"We stayed the winter there. We almost starved. There was a child in me, but it died and came out as blood. Enshi thought his mother was responsible. He begged her to go away, and then he told her, 'Hurt me! Hurt me! I am the one who acted shamefully.'"

Nia stopped talking. I shifted position and rubbed my legs. They were getting numb.

"In the spring we moved farther into the hills. The women came back. We stole from them. Enshi was good at this. Or at least better than I was.

"We found a river full of fish—far back in the hills, away from everyone else. There was a cliff nearby red with iron. I made traps to catch the fish. Enshi learned how to dig out iron. We built a shelter, and I set up a forge. Nuha left us alone." Nia frowned. "I did not feel especially ashamed. On some days it seemed to me that what we did was right. What was wrong with me?"

I made the gesture that meant "no comment."

"That winter we had plenty of food. At the end of the winter I had a child. I gave her the name Hua. Enshi liked her. He held her and talked with her. At times she made him angry, but he didn't yell or strike out. He put her down and went for a walk. He was crazy, without a doubt."

I turned my hand, telling her "maybe yes and maybe no."

"My throat is dry. Will you get me a drink?" She pointed. I went and got a jar of water. She took a big swallow. "Aiya! That is good! What was I saying?"

"You had a child."

"Two. The other was a boy. Anasu. He was born in the third winter that we were in the hills. By then I was used to being alone, except for Enshi and the children. I liked it. I still do. There is too much talk in a village. Too much gossip. Too many arguments. But not in the hills. There it is quiet. Once in a while Enshi got restless and went off by himself. Sometimes I did the same thing. I liked those times the best, I think. I went up till there was nothing above me except the sky. Below me were red cliffs and deep red ravines. There

83

were trees as well, tall ones with leaves the same color as the sky. I was above everything. I sat and listened to the wind. Then I felt contented.

"Afterward I had to go down and help Enshi with the children.

"This went on five winters. Then—in the spring—the crazy man came. He rode up one morning. His bowhorn was so thin that I could count every rib. As for the man, he was ragged and gray. One eye was gone. He looked terrible.

"I was in the forge, beating out a piece of iron for a pick. Enshi was hunting. And the children—I don't remember where they were. Near me, I guess.

"I heard a voice. It was deep and harsh. 'Are you ready, woman?'

"I looked up. He dismounted and came toward me. 'Is it time?' he asked.

"'No,' I said. 'What are you doing here?'

"He stopped and tilted his head to one side. I remember that and the look in his one eye. He was crazy. This happens to old men. They lose their territories. The younger men drive them away. But they won't give up. They refuse to go to the village. Instead they wander by themselves. They have no place. They forget the rules and customs. They are dangerous.

"I took a tight grip on my hammer.

"He said, 'Soon. Another day or so. I can tell. I used to have five women—six women—in a season. Aiya! The gifts they brought and the smell of their bodies.'

"'Go away,' I said. 'I don't want you here.'

"'I can wait,' he said. 'I have waited a long time already. I will stay.'

"Then I saw Enshi behind the man, his bow in his hand. 'No,' he said. 'This woman is mine. Get out.'

"The old man turned. 'You scrawny little thing! Do you think you can confront me? I've met men twice your size. They were the ones to lower their gazes. They were the ones to turn away.'

"Enshi lifted his bow. There was an arrow ready, fitted to the string. He began to draw the bow. 'I will kill you, old man. I will put an arrow through your gut.'

"The old man said, 'This is outrageous. Don't you know how these things are done? No true man ever uses an arrow on another man. A knife is the proper weapon. A club is all right, too. But nothing that kills at a distance. A true confrontation is up close.'

"Enshi spoke in reply. He said, 'I don't care what the rules are. This woman is mine. I will do what I must to keep her.'"

Nia paused for a moment. Her face looked thoughtful. "I lifted up my hammer and said, 'I don't care for the rules, either. If you come close to me, I will kill you, old man. Believe me. I tell the truth.'

"What else is there to say? The old man backed down and went away. A day later the lust began. Enshi and I were together for three days. I think that is right. Maybe four days. One morning I woke. Light came in the door of our shelter. Enshi was close to me. The old man was above him. I saw him drive his knife into Enshi's throat. Anasu cried out. I got up. But it was too late. The old man was completely crazy and strong the way that crazy people sometimes are. He was much stronger than I was, and I am not weak. He pushed me down and stuck his penis into me. I tried to get free. He hit me. The knife he was holding cut my shoulder. I still have the scar. The children were crying. Both of them. The old man made grunting noises. I bit him. He hit me again." Nia frowned. "I dream about that sometimes. There is blood in my mouth. There is blood on the ground. I feel the old man on top of me and inside me. I hear the children cry. I know—in my dream—that Enshi is dead. After a while I wake.

"But then I did not wake. The old man stayed until the lust was over. That was five or six days. We mated again and again." She clenched her hands. "When we were not mating, he kept me tied. He was not stupid, even though he was crazy. He knew I would have taken the children and run. He said I was the crazy one. No ordinary woman would have told him to go away. No ordinary woman would have tried to fight him off.

"The children got hungry. They cried. He untied me then, so I could feed them. But he would not let me bury Enshi. He dragged Enshi out of the shelter and left him to lie in the bare place outside the door. The weather was hot. Enshi swelled up. He began to stink. Bugs came and birds. When the shelter door was open, I was able to see them feeding. Hua kept saying, 'What is wrong? What has happened to Enshi?'

"I told her to keep quiet. She would make the old man angry.

"What else could I say? Two men had met at the time of mating. One killed the other. This did not happen often, but it wasn't wrong. Why did I think it was wrong? Why did I hate the old man? He had the right to mate with me. He had won, though maybe not entirely fairly.

"It was wrong that Enshi was unburied. It was wrong that the children were there. It was wrong that he tied me up. But it was not wrong that he lay on top of me and stuck his penis in me. Why did I hate him for that? It was not wrong."

Nia stopped talking. I waited. There was a sour taste in my mouth, and I couldn't think of anything to say.

"The lust ended and he left. I buried Enshi. I fed my children and cleaned them and comforted them. Then I saddled our animals.

"I took the children with me. I could do nothing else. Anasu I held. Hua rode on Enshi's bowhorn. I had to tie her into the saddle. We followed the old man's trail. It took two days.

85

"I found him at the foot of the hills, at the edge of the plain. He had built his fire in the last grove of trees before the plain began. Aiya! I remember how it felt when I saw his smoke twisting up into the sky!

"I tethered the bowhorns. I put the children on the ground and told Hua to watch her brother. I told them not to cry—I would be back soon—and went down the hill. I had a weapon now. A bow. It was the one that had belonged to Enshi. I remember the time of day. Just after sunset. The western sky was orange. The old man's fire shone among the trees. I crept up. I saw him hunched next to the fire." Nia paused. "I shot him in the back. He cried out and fell over. I shot him again.

"What else is there to say? I made sure he was dead. Then I put out his fire and went back to my children. They had kept quiet—hidden in a bush, like a pair of bowhorn fawns. Aiya! How good they had been! I praised them and fed them.

"Later I went north to the village. I left the children with Angai. By this time she was the shamaness. She told me she would raise them the right way. I could not. I went east and ended up where you met me—in the village of Nahusai."

Nia leaned back and closed her eyes. She must have lost weight in the last few days. Her face looked thinner than usual, and the bones were easy to make out, even under the fur. Her jaw was heavy. Her forehead was round and low. She had thick cheekbones, and there was no indentation where her nose met her forehead. It went straight up, wide and flat all the way. She opened her eyes and blinked. "Decide between us. Is Hua right? Am I a pervert?"

I glanced up, seeking inspiration. The smoke hole was dark. Something was up there, blocking the light.

What on earth? I stood.

The thing moved. Sunlight came in. I could see the sky. "I'll be back," I said to Nia. I went out and turned.

Like all the roofs in the village this one was covered with vegetation. The small round leaves shone in the sunlight, and there were orange flowers. Bugs fluttered over the flowers. They had yellow wings. Midway down the roof the shamaness stood. Her robe was kilted up, and I could see her legs. They were bony and hairy with big knees.

"You listened at the smoke hole. You heard what Nia said."

"My eyes are bad, but my ears are the best in the village. Aiya! What a disgusting narration! I ought to make you leave today." She went to the edge of the roof and sat down. "Help me."

I reached up. She dropped into my arms. She was light and she stank. It was a mixture of aromas, I decided as I set her down. Fur, musk, and bad breath. The old lady needed a dentist. I took a step back.

86

"The Voice of the Waterfall said help you. So I must. That crazy man! Why didn't he grow up the right way and go out to join his brothers? Not him, the lunatic! He had to hear voices and see things in his dreams. I go and talk with him. He dances around and jabbers. Naked, too. He'll catch a bad cold some winter and die. Let me tell you, it's hard to be a mother. Now, go away! The woman in there is weak. She needs to rest."

I opened my mouth.

"I won't tell her what I heard. Go! Get out!"

I turned and walked away. Behind me the shamaness was muttering. I heard the word "perversion" and the word "disgusting." Then she said in a loud voice, "Why do these things happen to me?"

I kept going till I reached the house of Eshtanabai. She was sitting in the doorway, leaning against the door frame, looking sleepy and contented.

I stopped. She looked up. "How is your friend?"

"Better. Tell me, what is the shamaness like?"

"Old and strange. Many people say her mind isn't what it used to be. But she still remembers the ceremonies. She talks about the past. Old women always do. And she worries about her children. Not the daughters. They are in the village. She knows how they are getting on. She worries about the sons. She had five, and they all lived long enough to go through the change. Four are up north, if they haven't died by now. The fifth—the youngest—you know about. He came from her last mating, when she was already getting old. Maybe that's why he became an oracle. Old women have strange children. That is well known. Why do you ask?"

I made the gesture that can mean anything or nothing, the gesture of uncertainty.

"That isn't much of an answer." Eshtanabai got up. "Come in. I have some *bara*."

This was the native alcohol. Or—at least—the native intoxicant in a liquid form.

"We'll get drunk. I have nothing else to do today." She led the way into her house.

I followed. Why not? We sat down near the fire. It was a heap of coals. I saw a tiny red glow at the bottom of the heap. A wisp of smoke drifted up, twisting and coiling in the beam of light which shone through the smoke hole. Eshtanabai filled two bowls and gave one to me. I drank. The liquid was bitter, and it burned in my mouth. I coughed, then swallowed.

"Drink more," she said. She drained her cup, then refilled it. "Listen." She leaned forward. "I think you are worried about the shamaness. She is a good woman. Old and strange, but good. But not everything that comes out of her mouth is holy. Only an oracle is holy all the time, and it's a terrible strain.

87

Most oracles die young. Drink some more. It will do you good. It is hard to sit and wait for someone you love to get better."

I drank the rest of the *bara*.

Eshtanabai poured out more. "The shamaness is often holy. But at times she is a foolish old woman, who talks about her sons. We try to be polite. It isn't easy. Last year we sent a boy out, and she got drunk. She didn't sing the proper songs, the songs that tell the boy, 'Be brave! You are doing what is expected!' She sang about the woman who mated with the wind. That song is not appropriate."

"What is it about?"

"You don't know? It's a very old story. It took place long ago, when we lived like the Amber People. Our houses were tents. We followed the herd. There was a woman who went out at the time of mating. There was a terrible storm that year. The bowhorns stampeded, and the men went after them. As a result this woman did not find a man. Her lust ended. She returned to the village. After a while it became evident that she was pregnant. Late in the winter she had a child. It was a child of the wind. No one could see the baby, and she was hard to get hold of. When she was hungry, she would go to her mother to nurse. Then the mother learned—by touching her—that the baby was a girl and covered with soft fur. But most of the time the baby was restless. She ran in her mother's tent. She ran through the village. One day she ran out onto the plain. She never returned. Her mother knew this would happen. She made a song for the child before she left. It goes like this:

> "Hola!
> my little one.
> Hola!
> my child of the wind.
>
> "Now you whirl
> in my tent.
> Now you make
> the hangings flutter.
>
> "Soon you will be gone
> on the wide plain
> forever.

"This is the song the old woman sang when we sent the boy out of the village. Everyone was angry, especially the mother of the boy. A woman has many rituals in her life. A man has one: the ceremony of parting. And the old

88

woman had ruined it. She made it a sad occasion. But what can we do? A good shamaness is hard to find. This one is excellent. She can cure almost any kind of illness. And the spirits send rain for our gardens when she asks them to. Have more to drink."

We drank. Eshtanabai told me about the old shamaness, the one before the one they had now. She had been greedy.

"Aiya! She had a house full of things. The older she got the more she wanted. She asked for more than the ceremonies were worth. We gave it. We had to. No one wants bad luck or the anger of the spirits. But the spirits got angry, anyway. The ceremonies didn't work."

"Why?"

Eshtanabai frowned. "Because we gave too much. Look. I fill your cup. I'm generous. I fill it to the brim. That is a proper giving. You have enough. It makes you happy. I know you will give me something in return. That makes me happy. But if I keep pouring and the *bara* goes over the brim, if it gets your hand wet and spills on your clothing or the floor, that isn't a proper giving. That is an insult and a mess.

"A giving is a binding. But only a fool ties a strong rope to a piece of string. You must tie like to like, otherwise the knot will slip or break."

"Are you sure?"

Eshtanabai blinked. "I know the spirits did not listen to that woman. Her rituals got us nothing. We found a new shamaness—one who takes what is right and gives what is right, even though she is half-crazy and talks about her sons. Here. Let me show you again." She poured out more of the liquid. "To the brim and no more. What will you give me, o hairless one?"

I went to my pack and got out a necklace and gave it to her. She gave me more *bara*. I gave her a bracelet carved out of a native wood and inlaid with the teeth of a kind of native fish. Derek had made the bracelet. He was a wonderful craftsman. By this time it was dusk. The western sky was orange-pink. One of the moons was up: a brilliant point of light. Too much was happening, I thought, and I wasn't in control. Oh, well. I went to the back of the house and passed out on a heap of furs.

In the morning I went back to the house of the shamaness. Nia was sitting up, eating a bowl of mush. "Why are you having trouble walking?" she asked me.

"I did a stupid thing. Oh, my head!" I sat down.

"You did not come back yesterday."

"The shamaness told me you needed rest." Nia looked blurry. I rubbed my eyes.

"You didn't give me an answer." Nia set down her bowl. There was a blob of mush in the bottom. She picked it up with one finger and put it in her mouth. "Am I right? Or is Hua right?"

"What?"

"Am I a pervert?"

I rubbed the back of my neck. "How do I know? I can tell you this: People have different customs. There are places where men and women live together the way you and Enshi did. There are places where the people would say what the old man did to you was terrible."

"Hu!" said Nia. "Where are these places?"

"A long way from here."

"Maybe someday I will go to a place like that."

I said nothing. My headache was getting worse, and I was having trouble concentrating.

Nia scratched her nose. "But maybe I wouldn't like a place like that."

"Maybe not."

In the evening I went to the river. It was hot and muggy there. The air was full of bugs. I made a call to Eddie and told him the story of Enshi.

"Interesting. They seem to have invented monogamy. Nia and Enshi, I mean."

"And the old man invented rape."

"Uh-huh." He didn't say anything for a minute or two. Rape was a subject that made most men nervous. Finally he said, "We've done another satellite survey. There are no cities. Not one. According to Tony, this makes sense. The men can't survive in an urban area. And the men have to be close to the women. Otherwise mating would be difficult, maybe impossible. The whole species is stuck in a pre-urban stage of development. They always will be."

A bug flew up my nose. I snorted and coughed. A second bug flew in my mouth. I spat it out. "Eddie, I can't stay here. There are bugs all over."

"Okay. Harrison says to ask about warfare. He doesn't think it exists on this planet."

"Okay." I ran to the village. The gate was shut. I had to yell and bang on the wood till someone came along and let me in.

The next day I talked to Eshtanabai. She had never heard of organized violence. "How could such a thing happen? Sometimes, when two men meet, they both refuse to back down. Then they fight. And there are crazy women who quarrel with their neighbors. But no one will side with a quarrelsome woman. And no one will ever side with a man."

Hm, I thought. I was on a planet without war or cities or sexual love. Was this good or bad? I didn't know.

Eshtanabai held out a bowl. "Have *bara*. Let's drink and talk about something that makes sense."

After a while I asked, "Why do you have walls around your village?"

"There are animals on the plain. Killers. They follow the herd. And when the herd comes south, they prowl around. They look for anything that can be eaten. Garbage. Children. The wall is to keep them out."

"Aiya!"

"Also, we like walls. We feel more comfortable when we look around and see we are enclosed."

That made sense to me. I had grown up on an island. The wide ocean did not bother me, but I had never been entirely happy with the middle-American plain. There was too much of it. I did not feel comfortable standing on a piece of land that went on—apparently—forever.

We talked about other things. I stayed more or less sober. Eshtanabai got obviously fuzzy. Did she have a problem with the intoxicant? If so, why? The strain of being a go-between? Or was there some other problem, psychological or physical, about which I knew nothing?

We slept. I woke to sunshine. Nia came to visit me, limping and leaning on a staff.

"I am ready to go," she said. "This place is making me restless, and the shamaness is giving me some very odd looks."

"You're barely able to walk," I said.

"I know what to do about that. Don't plan on staying here much longer."

She limped away. I went to the house next door. There was an old lady there who knew everything there was to know about kinship. Or so my host had told me.

Late in the afternoon Nia came back. I was sitting outside, next to the old lady. She was explaining the obligations between sisters and the children of sisters.

Nia stopped and leaned on her staff, a rough piece of wood. The bark was still on it, and a twig stuck out near the top. "We go tomorrow. I gave my tools to the coppersmith. She gave me two bowhorns. We can ride."

The old lady frowned. "You are interrupting me. I was about to explain who gives gifts to a boy when he is ready to leave the village. This person without hair is amazing. She knows nothing about anything. But she is willing to listen, and she doesn't interrupt."

Nia made a barking noise. "I will go. But be ready, Li-sa. I want to leave at dawn." She limped away.

The old lady finished her explanation. I gave her a necklace made of wooden beads. The wood came from an island in the western ocean, a cold and rainy place that reminded me of Ecotopia in North America. It—the wood, not Ecotopia—was red and had a fine grain, full of twists and coils. The polished surface glimmered.

"Aiya!" the old lady said. "This will impress everyone." She put the necklace on.

I went back to the house of Eshtanabai. My host was out—working on her garden, I decided. I sat down. In time she returned.

"You are leaving."

I made the gesture of assent.

"Good."

"What?"

"The shamaness is angry. If you stay, there will be a quarrel—a bad one. There is nothing worse than an angry shamaness."

"I suppose you're right." I thought for a moment. "What happened to the old shamaness? The greedy one? She must have been angry when you found someone to replace her."

"She was furious. But she had no power. The spirits had stopped listening to her. She went off onto the plain. Most likely she died. Or found another village." Eshtanabai sounded completely uninterested.

They were a cool people. Was it because they did not love the way we did? Then I remembered Hakht and Nia. Neither one was cool.

"Tonight we will eat well," said Eshtanabai. "Fish from the river and a fat bird. Tomorrow I will give you food for the trip."

"Thank you."

We did eat well. The fish were stuffed with vegetables and roasted. The bird was made into a stew. We drank plenty of *bara*. People came to visit and stare at me. The old lady from next door showed off her necklace. One of Eshtanabai's children played a flute. Another beat on a drum. All at once Eshtanabai jumped up. She grabbed a branch from the fire and whirled it around her head. Then she ran out of the house. The rest of us followed. Out in the street my host was dancing, turning, and waving her torch. The other women shouted, "Hola!" The two children kept playing flute and drum. Eshtanabai sang in her language, which I did not understand. She strutted back and forth. The other women made gestures of agreement and affirmation.

What was going on? I looked around. Nia was leaning against the wall of a house. Her arms were folded, and she was frowning.

"What is this?" I asked.

"I can't tell you the words, but I know what they mean. She is bragging. She is saying, 'I am wise. I am prudent. I can settle every quarrel.' She is telling them, 'I am generous. You have eaten my food. I have found a way to get rid of these strange people, who have made everyone uneasy. You see all the good that I do for you.' This is what she is saying."

It was a political speech. I watched with interest. More torches appeared. Everyone was dancing now, except for me and Nia. Children climbed up on top of the houses. They leaped amid the foliage and shouted. Eshtanabai kept up her chant.

After a while Nia said, "The Copper People are always the same. They always make too much noise. I am going to bed." She limped off.

The party broke up an hour or so later. All the food and drink was gone. Eshtanabai had said everything she had to say. We all went to bed. At dawn Nia came and shook me awake. I groaned and rolled over.

"Come on," said Nia.

I stumbled off to the privy. When I got back, Eshtanabai was up. I gathered my belongings. She gave me a bag of food.

"Good-bye, hairless one."

I answered with the gesture of parting, followed by the gesture of gratitude. Nia said, "Come on."

I followed her out. At the moment the air was cool, but it had the feel of a summer morning in Minnesota or Wisconsin. The day would be hot. Nia led me through the village. She didn't have the staff, and she was having trouble walking. In the end I helped her. We reached the gate. She opened it. We went out. Off to the east the sun was rising, hidden by the village. Its light filled the sky. There were two animals tethered by the gate: quadrupeds—and herbivores, I was almost certain. They had long legs and wide chests. Their tails were deerlike. Their horns were narrow and curved like the horns of antelopes. One jerked its head and snorted. The other stamped a foot.

"These are bowhorns," Nia said. "They are in good enough shape, though one is getting old. I can't say much about the saddles. They ought to last until we get wherever we are going."

She untied one animal and mounted. I hesitated, then untied the other animal. It moved.

"Wait a minute," I said. I put a foot in the stirrup, grabbed onto the saddle, and pulled myself up. The animal moved again, taking a step and tossing its head. Somehow I managed to get into the saddle, but I dropped the bag of food.

"You don't know how to ride," said Nia.

"Not well."

She swung her leg over the saddle and stepped down, as easily and casually as if she were stepping off a curb. As she reached the ground, she winced and groaned. She muttered to herself and reached for the bag. A moment later she was back on top of her animal. "This is going to be a long trip," she told me.

Derek

W
e forded the river. On the other side Nia found a trail. We followed it up the bluff and over, onto the plain. In front of us the
trail led toward the western horizon.

"Who made it?" I asked.

"Women. The ones who take gifts to the Amber People and bring gifts
back." Nia slapped the reins. Her animal started forward. My beast followed,
and I shifted position, trying to get comfortable.

The day came through on its promise of heat. Our animals ambled west.
Nia was quiet and I spent my time looking. There wasn't much to see. The
plain was almost featureless. The sky was clear. I saw no animals except bugs.

At noon we stopped and dismounted. I did stretching exercises, then
drank from Nia's water bag. The water was warm and had a funny taste.

"How are you?" Nia asked.

"Sore. But I can keep going."

"That's good." She drank and wiped her mouth with the back of her hand.
"I hurt, too. I have not ridden for years. We'll stop early tonight."

Late in the afternoon we stopped by a low mound. I dismounted and
stretched and groaned.

"I will take care of the animals," Nia said.

"Are you sure?"

Nia made the gesture of affirmation. "It's evident that you know nothing about bowhorns."

I made the gesture of agreement and went up on the mound. Above me a single bird moved in a great slow circle. I did my exercises, then meditated. I was so stiff that I could barely get into a half-lotus position.

Nia finished with the animals and wandered off. She came back with her arms full of stuff. It was round and gray and crumbly.

"Dung," she told me. "It's left from the spring, when the herds came through."

She built a fire, using the dung as fuel. We ate dinner: bread and a piece of meat that looked and tasted like leather. When we had finished we sat and watched the fire.

I asked her about her ankle.

"It hurts. So do my other injuries." She paused. "I have felt worse. I will survive." The word she used meant "last," "keep," "remain usable," "not wear out."

"Good." I glanced at the mound. It seemed unnatural to me. Artificial. What was it doing all by itself in the middle of the plain? "Where did that come from?" I pointed.

"I don't know. It was not built by animals. It's too big. Maybe by women. Or demons. The spirits do not build." She sounded uninterested. Did her people lack a sense of history? Or was she tired?

"Where are we going?" I asked.

Nia frowned. "Is there a place you want to go?"

"Another village. I want to learn more words and customs."

"The people to the west of here all travel, and their villages are in the north right now. But if we keep going we ought to be able to meet the Iron People when they come south." She paused. "It has come to me that I would like to see my children."

"Those people drove you off. Aren't they likely to do that again?"

"They might, if I came to them alone. But you are a stranger. Who could possibly be more strange? And they know—better than the Copper People do—what is owed to strangers."

"What?" I asked.

She looked surprised. "Food. A place to sleep. Help, if help is needed. Stories and gifts. It is never right to drive a stranger off, unless he is violent."

"But it's all right to drive off a member of the village?"

"Yes. What harm can be done by someone who is passing through? If a traveler has unusual ideas, that is to be expected. If she behaves oddly, she'll be gone soon enough. But if a villager is perverted or quarrelsome or crazy . . . Hu! That is a serious problem!"

95

Wonderful reasoning. I grinned.

"You are showing your teeth," said Nia. "Are you angry?"

"No. My people show their teeth when they are happy."

"Aiya! The Iron People will certainly let us in!"

The next day was like the first one, and the third day like the second. The weather remained hot and clear. The plain continued flat and covered with pseudo-grass, which had not changed either. It remained about a meter tall, green and blue-green and yellow. The dominant form of animal life was bugs. They fluttered and whirred all around us.

What was the story?

A bishop asked a biologist, "What have your studies taught you about the Creator?"

The biologist replied, "He has an inordinate love of bugs."

After four days we came to a new kind of vegetation: a bright green plant that looked like grass or pseudo-grass, except that it was five meters tall. It formed a wall that went north and south as far as we could see.

"There's water here," said Nia. "This stuff grows at the edge of rivers."

We rode north along the barrier. There was no way through. The stalks grew too close together, and the leaves had rough edges.

"They cut," said Nia. "This is what I wanted." She reined her animal and pointed. "A path."

We dismounted. I groaned as usual, but the pain was getting less. Nia went down the path. I followed, leading my animal. It crowded me. It must have smelled water. "Stop that!" I slapped the creature's nose. It snorted.

"Be quiet," said Nia. "You can never tell what is waiting for you at a river."

The vegetation ended. We were on the riverbank. In front of us a narrow trickle wandered over a wide sandy bed. On the far side was more of the monster grass. Downstream was a pool.

"Aiya!" said Nia.

A man stood in the pool. He was naked, and he had no fur. His skin was brown. His long hair was blond. On his back was a tattoo: a complex geometric pattern. It represented the cosmic forces in and around the Gray Whale. It—the whale or rather the pattern of the whale—was the totem of his lodge. Maybe I ought to use his terminology. It was the mandala of his eco-niche.

He had a fishing rod, and he was casting with all his usual skill.

"I have a question for you," said Nia. "Do you know what that is?"

"A person. A friend of mine."

He glanced around and pulled in his line, then waded to shore. His beard and his pubic hair were reddish brown. On his chest and arms were initiation scars. The rod he carried was handmade. It was long—extremely long, and it didn't have any reel.

96

"How is it?" I asked in English.

"The fishing rod? Not good." He grinned. "But I have fish." He laid the rod down. "You are Nia," he said in the language of gifts. "I am Derek. My tribe is the Angelinos. The house I belong to is the house of—" He paused for a moment. "The big fish. The name I got for myself is He Who Fights in the Sea. And I had better tell you, I am a man."

"I thought you might be," Nia said. "Though it is hard to be certain about anything when dealing with people who are so different. Are you holy? Like the Voice of the Waterfall? Is that why you are naked?"

"No. I'll be back." He went off along the river, moving quickly, out of sight in a minute.

Nia looked at me. "I didn't really believe there were other people like you. I thought you were something peculiar, like the young our does have now and then. They have five legs or two heads. We kill them, and the shamaness performs ceremonies to avert bad luck."

Derek returned wearing jeans. His hair was pulled back and fastened at the nape of his neck. He had on a necklace made of shells and pieces of bone and a metal pendant. It was the same kind I wore, an AV recorder.

As usual, he looked graceful and barbarous. He had a Ph.D. in anthropology, and he was a full professor at the University of San Francisco, on leave at the moment, of course. A rather lengthy leave. He wouldn't be back for another 120 years, at the earliest.

"Now for the fish." He went to the river and pulled out a stringer. There were six fish on it: long, narrow, and silver-gray. He held them up. They twisted and flapped their tails. "You take care of your animals. I'll take care of mine."

"Good," said Nia.

By the time we got back, Derek was cutting the last fish open. A fire burned next to him. The rest of the fish lay on a rock in a neat row, gutted.

"We have two choices," he said. "We can put them on sticks and roast them or wrap them in wet leaves and bake them in the coals."

"Which is faster?"

He grinned. "Roasting. Go cut the sticks."

We turned and walked back to the monster grass.

"He gives a lot of orders," Nia said. "Who does he think he is? A shamaness?"

"He has tenure," I said. "It gives him confidence." I felt a twinge of envy. My own academic history was far less distinguished. The job I had left had been untenured.

"What is that? The word you said?"

"Tenure. It means that what he has, he is able to hold on to."

97

"He is like the big men among my people," Nia said. "They hold their territories, and no one can make them back down—until they get old."

"I guess that's right."

We got our sticks and went back to the fire. Derek cooked the fish. We
ate. Afterward I said, "You aren't supposed to be here."

"I got lonely and from what Eddie told me about Nia, I thought she could
tolerate a man."

"That may be," Nia said. "But you are nothing like Enshi, and he was the
only man I ever spent time around."

I looked at Nia. She began to lick the inside of her hand, getting the last
of the fish oil. "If you mind him, I'll tell him to go."

She glanced up. "No. I want to learn how he catches fish. Now I am going
to wash myself." She stood up and undid her belt. Then she pulled off her
tunic. Naked, she walked to the river. She knelt and undid her sandals. Her
fur shone like copper, and she moved as easily as Derek. No. I was wrong. Her
movements were more powerful and less graceful. She stood, kicked off her
sandals, and waded into the water.

My companion rubbed his nose, which was peeling a little. "I thought,
from what she said before, that nudity wasn't entirely proper. Or does that
apply to men only? Or maybe it is appropriate to undress in order to bathe,
no matter who is around."

"When in doubt, ask."

"A good idea." He got up. "I imagined her as a tough old lady. A Mother
Courage. She's beautiful." He followed her to the edge of the river.

Oh, no, I thought. Derek was notorious. The Don Juan of San Francisco.
The Interstellar Lover. He had gone through the ship like a devouring
flame. There were even rumors about him and Ivanova, though I found that
combination highly unlikely. He wouldn't say if the rumors were true, and I
certainly didn't have the nerve to ask her.

I asked him why he was promiscuous, one evening after we had finished
making love. Guilt, he told me.

"Among my people, we marry young. I had a wife. She was maybe thirteen, thin like a reed with long brown hair. Her eyes were blue. I left her when
I left my people. I will never betray her. I will never settle down with a woman
from outside."

Nia was waist-deep in the water and splashing her arms. He called to her.
I couldn't make out what he said. She answered. They began to talk. She
moved closer to the shore. Thank heaven it was the middle of summer. The
time for mating was past. Nia couldn't possibly be interested in Derek.
Nonetheless, I decided to join them. I heard Nia say, "My people think it's
shameful to go without clothes. But the women in the village of Nahusai like

98

to swim. They wash often. They say the only shame is being naked when a man is there. Or even a boy, for they grow up to be men. But I do things my own way." She said this defiantly. "I do not pay attention to the opinions of old women. I do what I think is right."

Derek grinned, then made the gesture of agreement. Nia waded farther out and began to wash her back.

Late in the afternoon he showed her how to use a fishing pole. She caught nothing. We ate dried meat for dinner. Night came. There were shooting stars.

"They come this time of year," said Nia. "We call them the Arrows of Summer."

Derek put more wood on the fire. I went to sleep and dreamt of him. We were in one of the recreation cabins on the ship. The walls were glazed yellowish white. Derek was naked and laughing. His penis was erect. He reached for me. I woke. Off to my right Nia was snoring, and Derek was on the other side of the fire. I could hear his deep, slow breathing. I lay for a while watching the night sky. Then I went back to sleep.

In the morning Derek went fishing. For bait he used a local bug. It looked like a caterpillar: fat and green with a lot of legs. There were hundreds of the creatures along the river. They fed on the monster grass. The fish fed on them. We fed on the fish.

"And thus we understand the great chain of being," Derek said as he finished the last piece of fish.

Nia looked puzzled. He had spoken in English.

"Nature red in tooth and claw," he went on. "That's a line from Tennyson. He also said that we rise on the stepping stones of our dead selves to higher things." He grinned at me. "I used to be fascinated by the history of the West, especially the history of industrial societies. That was when I first left my people. I thought—there is a secret here, in Marx and Tennyson and in the big machines. Later I decided my people were right. It is better to be close to the gray whale and the peyote cactus. But by that time I was used to being comfortable. What do we do now, Lixia?"

"Travel west. There are people on the plain. Nomads. Nia says she can find them for us. I mean to do as much fieldwork as possible. I want my name all over the preliminary report."

He grinned. "Is this ambition in little Lixia?"

"I know what I am. A first-rate collector of facts. But I've never been good at the academic bullshit. The analysis. The playing with theory. If I am ever going to get anywhere, it's going to be on the basis of what I do here in the field."

"Maybe. There's no question about your ability to collect facts. You can learn a language faster than anyone I know."

"Except Gregory."

He made the gesture that acknowledged that I might be right. "But listen to the way you talk. You say 'academic bullshit' and 'playing with theory.' This shows a bias. The refusal to theorize is—in itself—a theoretical position, my love. Unfortunately for you, it is not a popular position. Where would we be without our systems, our hierarchies of information, our analyses? Our points and our morals?"

He got up and stretched. "Those animals of yours don't look any faster than horses. I can keep up." He kicked dirt on the fire. Then he collected his belongings: his pack and fishing line, wound in a coil, a bow and half a dozen arrows.

"You made the bow?"

"Of course." He looked down at his feet. "I can't run like this." He took off his boots and socks. "Here." He gave them to me.

Nia said, "If you are going to travel without shoes, keep to the trail or—if you are off it—watch where you put your feet. There are plants that sting on the plain. Don't step on anything that looks unusual."

"Always good advice," said Derek. He made the gesture of gratitude.

We saddled up. I tied my belongings and Derek's on my animal. Nia and I mounted. We splashed through the river. On the other side we found a trail that wound through the monster grass. Soon we were back on the plain. It stretched to the west and north and south without interruption.

At first Derek tried to walk beside us, but the trail was too narrow. He loped ahead. His hair was untied and flapped in the wind. So did the tail of his shirt. He moved easily, confidently. He looked happy and relaxed.

"This man is strange," said Nia. She glanced at me. I made the gesture of agreement.

"Is this the way your men are?"

"No. He is something special. He makes most of us uneasy."

"Hu!"

The land changed. Now it was rolling. Often, in the distance, I saw clumps of monster grass: tall and brilliant green, like a stand of trees. Late in the afternoon we made camp in a hollow. Derek and Nia went to gather dung. I took care of the animals. They were restless—thirsty, I decided. When Nia came back I said, "Why don't we go into one of those groves? You told me they grow near water."

"There is an animal. The killer of the plain. It lies in wait near water. Bowhorns come to drink. It jumps on them."

"Oh." I thought for a moment. "That's why you were uneasy when we came to the river."

Nia made the gesture of agreement. "I knew there was no way around the river. We had to cross it. But I am afraid of that animal."

After dinner I called the ship. Eddie answered.

"Why is Derek here?"

Eddie laughed. "He made it, eh? Three reasons, Lixia. He is a first-rate field worker, and he was being wasted off by himself." He paused for a moment. "Nia is our most unusual informant. We wanted a second evaluation of her and her information. That is reason number two. Finally, you don't call in often enough. Derek is there to keep tabs on you and Nia."

"Oh, yeah?"

"Uh-huh. You lack social responsibility. If I were Chinese, I'd be upset with you."

I bit the edge of my thumb. "Is that so?"

"Uh-huh. Speaking of our comrades from East Asia, there are a lot of posters going up along Democracy Wall."

There was a main corridor that went through the living quarters. The Chinese had lined part of it with corkboard and named it Democracy Wall. They said it was necessary for the proper expression of the mass will.

What was wrong with computers? the rest of us asked.

Computers isolated people, each one in front of a little screen. The wall brought people together. They could discuss what they read. They could look around and see how their neighbors were reacting. They could tell who was listening.

Computers emphasized linear thinking and logic. The wall, like the Chinese ideogram, used linear *and* nonlinear ways of organizing information: pattern as well as sequence, space as well as time. When one looked at the wall, one used the entire human brain.

Besides, it was traditional. Human beings had always written and drawn on walls.

It was hard to argue with that, and the wall had a certain disheveled charm. There was no telling what people would put up: a clever drawing, a stupid limerick, a papier-mâché mask. "Wanted—a partner for chess." And a lot of political arguments. It was a way of getting at the people who would never think of entering any of the political discussion networks.

Eddie went on. "Lu Jiang, the plumber, has a theory, which she has posted. It goes as follows: if the information we have now is right, all the native societies are stuck at a pre-urban stage. As far as we know, it is impossible to develop an advanced technology outside of cities. Without an advanced technology, there can be no proletariat. Without a proletariat, there can be no socialist revolution. Therefore, she argues, the unfortunate inhabitants of this planet can never achieve a socialist society. She has, of course, been criticized for undervaluing the role of the peasantry in achieving socialism."

"It sounds wonderful."

101

"It's dangerous, Lixia. People are beginning to say if Jiang is right, then maybe we ought to make contact with the natives of the planet—formal contact, telling them who we are. Maybe we have to offer them our technology. If we don't, we condemn them to an existence without the possibility of progress. They will remain as they are forever."

I rubbed my nose.

He went on. "What I see happening is an alliance between the altruists and the technologists. The lovers of the people and the lovers of machinery. They will both decide that we have to open up the planet."

"Eddie, you are borrowing trouble."

"Listen to me. My grandfather was a medicine man. He saw things before other people did. And I tell you, right now I have his ability. I can see it like a vision: the mines and the refineries and the furry proletarians, punching the clock every morning."

I decided to stop talking. Eddie was getting angry, and I didn't want any part of one of his rages.

"I'm going to turn this thing off. I want to do my exercises."

"Okay. Tell Derek to call in. No. On second thought don't bother. He always remembers."

I turned off the radio and did my exercises. After that I meditated, fixing my gaze on the eastern horizon. The sky there was a transparent deep blue with a tinge of green. Farther up—where the blue grew lighter and a bit more green—a point of light shone. A planet. I concentrated on my breathing. In. Out. *So. Hum.*

Behind me Derek spoke. "Achieving oneness with the universe?"

I twitched, then looked around. He was standing about a meter away. He had come up soundlessly. He grinned. "Do you want any peyote? I brought some down."

"It seems to me we agreed, no narcotics on the surface of the planet. Unless, of course, they were provided by the natives."

"First of all, peyote is a hallucinogen. And second, it is necessary for the practice of my religion."

"The committee agreed with you?"

"Which one? The ship is full of committees."

I opened my mouth. He raised a hand. "You're right. I didn't get permission."

"What is this? Some kind of infantile rebellion?"

"I get tired of rules. I take it you don't want any peyote."

"No."

"How about sex? I've been noticing, you look very good down here. I think it's something to do with the sunlight. Nothing looks right on the ship. But here." He waved a hand at the darkening sky.

102

I thought for a moment. "Okay."

He sat down next to me, putting an arm around me.

He was, as I had remembered, very good. Not fast. Derek came from a hunting and gathering society. He knew the value of patience and slow, careful work. He knew how to use his hands. He knew what to say and when. Is there any pleasure equal to seeing—or hearing—or feeling—a really good craftsperson at work?

We ended naked in the prickly pseudo-grass. He was on top of me and in me.

Nia said, "What are you doing? Don't you realize it is the middle of summer? No one mates this time of year."

Derek said, "Go away, Nia. We'll explain later."

"Very well. But you people are strange."

Derek lifted his head. "She's gone. Now, where was I?"

I laughed.

Afterward we lay awhile in the vegetation. I felt wonderful. I had been alone too long. How many days? Forty-seven? Forty-eight? I would have to ask Eddie. I had lost count.

Derek got up and started dressing. I followed his example. A meteor fell. We walked to the camp. Nia sat next to the fire, which was dim and had a peculiar aroma. Dung did not burn the same way as wood. She looked up. "Are you through with your mating?"

"Yes."

"You are perverted."

"That may be." Derek sat down.

Nia looked at the fire. "I am unlucky. Everywhere I go, I meet people who do things the wrong way."

Derek grinned. "What do you mean by that? What is the wrong way? Is it what the old women say is wrong? You told us you did not care about their opinions."

"That is true. But everyone knows people feel lust in the spring. Only sick people feel lust at any other time."

"We are not ordinary people, Nia. You must understand that. We are stranger than you can know. But we are not bad. And there is nothing wrong with our health."

"You make me uneasy. I am going to take a walk." She got up and limped away. In a minute she was gone, out of sight in the darkness.

I sat down. He frowned. "How upset is she?"

I made the gesture of uncertainty.

"That's a lot of help."

We waited up for an hour or so. Nia did not return. At last I went to sleep. I woke at dawn. Nia was close to me, lying down, her cloak around her, snoring softly.

We rose at sunrise and continued west. The weather stayed the same: hot and bright. The land continued rolling. To the north of us was a range of low, round hills. Clouds floated above them.

"That is the land of smoke," Nia told us. "It is a holy place. The water there bubbles like the water in a cooking pot. Smoke rises out of cracks in the rock."

"Oh, yes?"

Nia made the gesture of affirmation.

A little past noon Derek stopped. He was on top of a rise. We rode up to him.

"There is someone behind us," he said.

"A man," said Nia. "No woman travels alone." She barked. "No. I do not tell the truth. I have traveled alone. But usually women go together." She glanced back. "I do not see him. You must have good eyes."

"Yes."

Nia shaded her eyes and looked again. "I will believe you. Someone will have to stay awake at night. If the man has decided to come close, he will do it then."

We kept on. By this time there were clouds all across the sky. They were small and fluffy, arranged in rows. The land was dappled with shadows. Here and there I saw outcroppings of dark rock. Basalt? I wondered. According to the planetologists, the rocks here were virtually identical to those on Earth.

The hills to the north were closer than before. Nia kept glancing at them. "I do not like the land of smoke. There are demons there."

"Oh."

In the evening we made camp near the top of a hill, under a huge mass of rock. It was black and rough. Volcanic. Below us was a valley full of bushes. Their leaves were yellowish green. We went down and found dry wood. Nia built a fire. It lit the dark face of the rock and the bodies of my companions: Derek—lean and smooth and brown, Nia—broad and furry.

We ate. Derek stood. "I'll take the first watch." He glanced around. "There ought to be a good view up there." He walked to the rock and began to climb, going up quickly with no hesitation.

Nia watched him. "Can he do everything well?"

"There are times when I think so."

"You do not like him."

"Not much."

"Why not?"

"Because he does everything well. For me nothing is easy. I envy him."

Nia frowned and looked at the fire. "I had a brother like that. Anasu. He did everything that was expected, and he did it better than most. By this time he is a big man. I am sure of it. He wasn't the kind to stay in the hills with the young men, with the men like Enshi. By this time he must have a territory close to the village and many women in the season for mating." Nia scratched her nose. "There was another one. Angai. A friend of mine. She was hard to get along with when she was young. People didn't like her. But she turned out well. She is the shamaness in my village. She has my children." She looked up. I was staring right into her orange eyes. "I do not understand what has happened to me. But I know this. It is wrong to feel envy. Hakht did. It burned in her like fire under the ground. It made her into something disgusting. I will not envy other people." She got up and went to get her cloak. "Now I am going to sleep."

She lay down. I stayed up. The big moon was visible in the west: high up and half-full, a bright lemon yellow. It lit new clouds. They were large and billowing. A new weather system? I grew drowsy. My mind wandered from subject to subject: envy, then Nia's brother. What was he like? What was it like to have a brother in her culture? I remembered the junior members of my family. Leon. Clarissa. Charlie. Maia. Mark. Fumiko.

Fumiko was the youngest by far. At the time I left she had been finishing college, getting ready for her wander year or years. I had gone early, at the age of twenty. I'd quit school and gone to the Big Island to cut sugarcane. Then I'd worked my way to Asia on one of the new freighters. I cooked and learned to operate the computer that controlled the sails. That was easy. The computer damn near ran itself. But I nearly went crazy, trying to cook in the tiny galley while everything around me moved.

Well, that was long ago and on another planet. I got my poncho and settled down to sleep.

I was awakened by an ululating scream: high-pitched, eerie, inhuman. A moment later I was upright. I didn't remember how I'd gotten into that position. On the other side of the fire was Nia. She was standing, too. Her eyes were wide open, and her knife was in her hand.

"What was that?" I asked.

"I don't know."

I realized I knew and that I had been wrong. The sound wasn't inhuman. It was the battle cry of a California aborigine. I looked around. "Derek?"

Out of the darkness came another sound, a cry of fear in the language of gifts. "Help! Help! A demon!"

I turned and ran downhill. Nia followed. We scrambled through the pseudo-grass. Below us the voice repeated, "Help! Help!"

Derek shouted, "Stop fighting me!"

I saw them, a thrashing mass, barely visible in the moonlight. I stopped. Two bodies rolled back and forth. Derek was on top. I saw his blond hair flipping. The person on the bottom cried, "Help me!"

Nia said, "If you are peaceful, stop struggling. The other person will not harm you. He is not a demon."

"No?" The body on the bottom stopped moving. "Are you sure?"

Derek climbed off the other person and pulled him or her up.

"Aiya! What a thing to happen! Are you absolutely certain that this being is not a demon?"

"Yes," said Nia. "Who are you?"

"I am the Voice of the Waterfall."

"You cannot be! I know about him. He spends his whole life next to the waterfall. When he dies and the people find his body, they throw it into the river. His bones lie among the rocks at the bottom of the waterfall."

"That is true. Can't we talk by the fire? I am afraid to be out here in the dark. And can't this being with the strong hands let go of me?"

"Lixia?" asked Derek.

"It's okay. Let go of him."

We walked up the hill. When we got close to the fire I looked at the oracle. This time he had clothing on: a ragged kilt. I couldn't make out the color. Gray or brown. Around his neck was a necklace: gold beads and big, uneven lumps of turquoise. The turquoise was blue and blue-green. The necklace was magnificent. The man rubbed his arms. "Hu! What a grip that being has!" He looked at Derek. "Another hairless one! What is happening to the world?"

"Why are you here?" asked Derek.

"Can't we sit down? I'm tired. I have walked for days. My feet hurt, and I am so thirsty that I can barely talk."

Nia got her water bag. He drank and then sat down. "Aiya! That is better. Do you have anything to eat?"

Nia gave him a piece of bread. He ate it.

Derek asked, "Why have you been following us?"

"That is a long story. Sit down. All of you. But not too close. I am not used to people."

We sat down. The man took another drink of water. Then he stared at me. "You are the one I met."

"Yes."

"You went to the village. After that my mother came with other women. She—my mother—brought food and a new blanket, a fine, thick, soft one. She told me I wasn't taking care of myself. I would freeze in the winter. I told her, 'Old woman, you are as crazy as I am. Don't worry about me. I belong to the waterfall. The waterfall will take care of me.' She gave me a medicine that is good for a sore throat and for a feeling of thickness in the chest. Then she went on. She came back with that one." He pointed at Nia. "After everyone was gone I had a dream. The Spirit of the Waterfall came to me. It was like a person, except that it was gray like silver, and I couldn't tell if it was male or female. It told me, 'Something important is going on, and it concerns the per-

106

son without hair. Follow that person. Watch that person. Listen to what that person says.'

"I tried to argue. 'I belong here. The Voice of the Waterfall never leaves this place.' The spirit began to look angry. 'You are *my* voice. Don't talk back to me.' Then I began to shake. The spirit went on. 'I do not belong to any one place, though I like this canyon and this waterfall. As for you, you belong where I tell you to be. Now go! And don't argue. Remember whose voice you are.'

"I woke up. What could I do? Only what the spirit told me. I went to the village. You"—he pointed at me—"were inside. I waited. I ate whatever I could find. When people came near I hid in the bushes. Finally you came out, and I followed you onto the plain.

"What a journey! It took—how many days? Five or six. I wasn't able to keep you in sight. But I knew you would follow the trail. After a day or so one of my sandals broke. I threw both of them away. My feet began to hurt and I was hungry. I dug up the root of the spiny *rukha* plant. It gave me food and water, but I stung my fingers on the spines.

"After four days I came to a river. Hu! What a pleasure! I drank water and gathered bugs. I made a fire and roasted them. How sweet! How delicious! I ate until I was sick, then rested and then crossed the river.

"The next night was terrible." He stopped for a moment and shivered. "I was lying on the plain—alone, with no cloak to cover me. An animal came. I heard the sound of its breath. Oo-ha! Oo-ha! I could smell it. It stank of rotten meat. It prowled around me. It sniffed and made a humming noise. I thought, I know what this is. A killer of the plain, and it is going to eat me. I didn't move. I was too frightened.

"The creature went around me a second time, humming all the while. I felt it. Aiya!" He shivered and blinked. "I felt it take one of my legs between its teeth. It lifted up my leg, then it let go. I let my leg fall as if I were dead already. The spirit must have guided me. The spirit must have told me what to do."

Nia leaned forward. "I have heard of this. They attack if you move. Or if they smell blood. But if a person remains motionless, they will leave her alone."

The oracle frowned. "This is my story. Let me finish it."

"Okay," said Nia.

"What?"

"Go on."

"After that the animal went away. I stayed where I was and thanked the spirit. In the morning I looked at my leg. There was no blood. The animal hadn't broken the skin. Aiya! What luck!"

Derek made the gesture of agreement.

107

"I got up and went on. What else could I do? I hurried. I was afraid of spending another night alone on the plain. The sun went down. I saw your fire shining in the darkness. I came near and that person"—he pointed at Derek—"jumped on me. I thought, I have met up with a demon. I am going to die, and I only hope the Spirit of the Waterfall is happy with this turn of events.

"But I didn't die and here I am. This is the end of my story."

Derek spoke in English. "Who is this?"

"He's an oracle. I met him after Nia was injured. His mother is the shamaness of the Copper People of the Plain. I think he's a little crazy, though I'm not sure. How does one judge insanity in an alien culture?"

"And how does one tell the difference between craziness and holiness?" Derek changed to the language of gifts. "What next? Do you want to travel with us?"

"Yes. Of course. That is the will of the spirit. I am going to sleep now. You can discuss whether or not you want me as a companion. But I warn you—no matter what you decide, I will follow you." He got up and moved away from the fire to the edge of the darkness. He lay down, his back to the plain, and curled up in a fetal position. After a moment he moved one arm, so it covered his face.

Nia said, "Truly, the world is changing. I meet people who mate in summer, and a holy man now appears, who is willing to leave his holy location and travel with ordinary folk. No." She looked at me and Derek. "I don't mean ordinary folk. I mean, people who aren't holy."

"Well," said Derek in English. "Does he travel with us?"

"Why not?" I looked at Nia and spoke in the language of gifts. "What do you think about him?"

"We can't leave him alone on the plain. He's as helpless as a child or an old woman. Moreover, he is holy. If we abandon him, the spirits will be angry. There is no question about it. He must come with us."

Derek nodded and got up. "I'm going back up to watch. Get some sleep, Lixia. I'll wake you later."

He woke me after midnight, and I kept watch. It was cool and still except for the noise the bugs made in the pseudo-grass. Toward morning I woke Nia. She got up, and I went back to sleep.

In the morning we went on. Nia and the oracle rode. I joined Derek on the ground. The trail wound among hills. There was plenty of rock here: cliffs and outcroppings and boulders, all black and rough. The valleys were grassy. Now and then we saw a flock of bipeds: the pseudo-dinosaurs. Most were about a meter tall and bright turquoise-blue.

"It's a beautiful planet," Derek said as he walked next to me.

"Yes."

"What's the line from Donne? 'O my America, my newfound land!' Of course, he was talking about a woman. A new mistress.

"License my roving hands, and let them go,
Before, behind, between, above, below.
O my America! My newfound land,
My kingdom, safest when with one man manned.
My mine of precious stones, my empirie.
How blest am I in thus discovering thee."

"Derek, how do you manage to be so literate?"
He glanced over, grinning. "Hard work, my love. And a very high intelligence."
"Oh. Okay."
He laughed. "Anyway, I feel the way Columbus must have. Or stout Cortez, silent on his peak in Darien. What a discovery! What a planet!" He swept out one hand, waving at the hills and the blue-green sky. A pseudo-dinosaur screamed and ran away.
Nia looked back. "What is it?"
"Nothing. Derek likes this country."
"I don't."
"Why not?"
She stopped and glanced around. "I don't remember it. I have taken a wrong turn somewhere. This isn't the trail I wanted."
The oracle made the gesture that meant "don't worry." "The spirit will guide us."
"That may be."
In the afternoon the sky got cloudy. Toward evening rain began to fall: a light drizzle. We made camp in a grove of trees. Derek shot a pseudo-dinosaur. Nia cleaned it. The Voice of the Waterfall and I went looking for wood.
After dinner I called the ship. A computer answered. It had a cool, pleasant female voice with a very slight Russian accent.
"No humans are available at present," it said. "You may report to me."
I did.
The computer thanked me and said the information would be relayed to the appropriate people. "I am a level-six program," it explained. "My intelligence is a construct and—do I mean or?—an illusion. I am therefore not a person, according to the current definition of the term."
"Do you mind?" I asked.
"That is not a meaningful question, at least when addressed to me. I neither think nor feel. I do what I am told to do."

109

I thought I heard sarcasm in the courteous even voice. But that was hardly likely. Why would anyone write sarcasm into a level-six program?

I turned the radio off, lay down, and listened to the rain pattering on the leaves above me.

The morning was overcast. Nia said, "You ride today, Li-sa. I want to find out how my ankle is doing."

"My feet still hurt," the oracle said. "They are covered with blisters."

Derek laughed. "Don't worry. You can have the other bowhorn."

Rain began to fall, and mist hid the distances. We traveled through grayness, up a long slope. Sometime around noon we reached the top. There was a level area, then a drop-off. We were on the rim of a valley. I reined my animal. The valley floor was visible in spite of the mist. The ground was bare and bright orange.

Derek sniffed. "Rotten eggs or sulfur. I think we can assume geothermal activity." He spoke a mixture of English and the language of gifts. I could understand everything, but our companions looked puzzled.

After a moment Nia said, "I don't know what kind of activity you are talking about. But I don't like the look of this valley. Or the smell for that matter."

Derek glanced to the side. "Don't worry. We aren't going down. The trail goes along the rim."

We followed the trail. The rain stopped. The clouds lifted. I could see the valley clearly. It was shallow and more or less circular. The entire floor was brightly colored: orange, orange-red, and yellow. Here and there plumes of white rose. Steam. The plumes moved, blown by the wind. In the middle of the valley was a lake: round and dark. Derek kept looking at it.

"Something isn't right. The lake is peculiar."

"I can believe that," Nia said. "This land is peculiar." She used the same word Derek had. It meant "unusual," "unexpected," "wrong." After a moment she went on. "I don't remember any of this. I am certain we're on the wrong trail, though I don't know how that is possible. I have a good memory and a good sense of direction. I never get lost."

I twisted in the saddle. She was trudging next to me. Her feet were muddy, and her fur was wet. Her tunic clung to her body. "What shall we do?"

Nia made the gesture of uncertainty.

"Keep going," the oracle said from behind me. "The Spirit of the Waterfall will see to it that we arrive in the right place."

"What a comfort!" Derek said.

We came finally to a place where the valley wall was low. A slope led down toward the orange and yellow floor. At the top the slope was covered with vegetation: little bushes and a lot of pseudo-grass. Farther down the ground was bare. A dark line wound across it: another trail, narrower than ours, less well used, going into the valley.

Derek stopped. I reined my animal.

The oracle rode up beside me. "What is it?" he asked.

"I think we ought to make camp."

"Here?" I asked.

Derek made the gesture of affirmation.

I looked around. On one side of me was the slope. On the other side was an outcropping of rock, black and massive. The trail—the main trail—led past it. There was nothing else. No wood except the little bushes and no evidence of water. "Why?" I asked.

"We aren't going to make it down off the rim before night, and I haven't seen any places that are better than this."

"He's right," said Nia. "That rock has an overhang. It ought to protect us, if it rains, and there is forage for the animals. I admit I would like some fresh water. The water in our bags is getting stale. But when a person travels without her village, she must take what she can get."

"And be grateful for it," said the oracle.

Nia made the gesture of agreement.

I dismounted. The oracle did the same. I stretched up as high as I was able, then bent over. I could barely touch the ground. I brushed it with my finger-tips and straightened up, breathing in at the same time. More exercise! This expedition was no excuse for getting lazy.

The oracle said, "He wants to go into the valley."

I looked at Derek. He was staring at the view. The sky was clearing. Sunlight edged the clouds, and the colors of the valley were even more brilliant than before. "Why?" I asked.

He turned. I knew that expression, the lifted eyebrows and the twisted grin. Derek was planning something that was either frivolous or dangerous. And he wanted my approval. The charm had gone on. I had no idea how he did it, but it was as dramatic as a light rod beginning to glow. His smile widened.

"Derek, stop it! Turn it off!"

"What?"

"The masculine beauty, the charm, the sexiness." I had switched to English. Nia began to frown.

"I want to take a look at that lake," Derek said. He was speaking the language of gifts. His voice was low and even. A reasonable voice. The voice of sanity. "I think I can make it there and back before the light is entirely gone."

"I doubt it, and I think you're crazy to try. That is a very active area down there. The ground is probably hot, and it may not be reliable. It may be a crust over something ugly. You could go through. You could end up in the soup, and I am being more literal than metaphoric."

"Speak our language," Nia said. "I am interested in this argument."

111

"Okay. I'm telling Derek not to go into the valley."

"You won't change his mind," the oracle said.

Derek laughed. "He's right. Give in, Lixia. There is no point in talking. I'm going to go."

I made the gesture that meant "so be it." "Take your boots."

"Why? I move more quickly with bare feet."

"I told you. I think the ground is hot." I bent to the side, raising one arm. With the other arm I reached down toward my ankle, then closed my eyes, concentrating on my breathing. In. Out. *So. Hum.* O jewel of the lotus.

I straightened up and opened my eyes. Derek was on his way: a small dark figure scrambling through the pseudo-grass, a good distance off already. Beyond him and below him was the valley.

Nia unsaddled the bowhorns. We built a fire under the overhang. Dinner was the last of the pseudo-dinosaur.

"Why did he go?" Nia asked.

"I have no idea. He does these things. Not often." I paused. I wanted to say, most of the time he plays by the rules. But I didn't know the native word for "play." I said, "Most of the time, he does what is expected."

Nia finished a piece of meat. She tossed the bone into the fire. "All men are crazy in one way or another."

The oracle made the gesture of agreement.

I stared out at the evening sky. The Great Moon was up. It was more than half-full now, and it looked to be—what?—three quarters the size of Luna when Luna was seen from the Skyline Drive in Duluth on a midsummer night.

Why didn't I know the word for "play"? I looked at Nia. "What is the word for what children do when they throw a ball?"

"It is called 'fooling around.'"

Well, yes. That made sense. That was one meaning of "play." But it had other meanings, too. I thought of *Hamlet* and the triple play, though I wasn't entirely sure what the triple play was. And swordplay. Hamlet and Laertes, for example. And musicians playing their instruments. What I needed was the O.E.D. Eddie had access to the language computers. I reached for the radio, turning it on.

I got a computer again. The same program as before. I recognized the accent and the tone of distant courtesy. There was more static than usual. The cool voice came through a constant faint crackling, like fire.

I asked for a definition of "play."

"Just a moment," the computer said.

I heard the usual noises that computers made when working: a beep, followed by a series of chirps, and then by a bell-like tone. A new voice—another program—told me what "play" meant in English.

This voice was male and had a Chinese accent.

When it finished I thanked it and turned the radio off.

"What is that thing?" asked the oracle.

Nia leaned forward. "Li-sa told me about it. It is a way to talk to people who are beyond the horizon."

"Oh. I thought it might be a musical instrument. It makes a lot of different kinds of noise, and some of them are pleasant."

"What do you do with a musical instrument?" I asked.

The oracle frowned. "What do you mean?"

"What is the word for using it. For making it make a noise."

"Oh. *Nakhtu.*"

"That is in his language," said Nia. "In the language of gifts, it is *nahu.*"

"Is that like fooling around?" I asked.

"No. Of course not. Children fool around. Grown-up people are sensible. Or—if they are not sensible—they are crazy, which is different from being a fool."

"Oh." I looked at the fire, then at the moon. The aliens had musical instruments. They had ceremonies. They danced. I knew they were capable of competition. Think of Hakht and Nahusai. But did they play as we did? Ritual aggression and competition were absolutely central to the Western cultures. The East Asians had opera and kabuki and all the martial arts. Everyone had soccer. Did these people need to play as much as we did? There was so much tension in human society, so much frustrated aggression. Even now, when the old society—the society of greed and deprivation—was gone.

Wait a minute. Not every human society was full of tension. I remembered the California aborigines. They were mellow, consciously and deliberately. Mellowness was central to their religion. It was a sign of enlightenment. The ideal aborigine was mellow and in touch. He or she kept a low profile, close to Mother Earth.

I thought about Derek. He could be mellow, but it was an act. Under the surface he was like a bull walrus. He knew what he wanted, and he would fight to get it. Had he known what he was like as a kid? Was that why he'd left his people? He would have been a failure, frustrated and angry, among people who could sit for hours watching a condor in the sky and be happy.

"That's where it's at," one of them told me, a witch wearing a loincloth and a lot of tattoos. "Mother Earth and Father Sky, the things that live—the plants and animals. All the old mysteries that the prophets spoke about. Black Elk and the Buddha. Jesus and Mother Charity. They all tell us the same thing. No matter how much you struggle and strive, you'll never get out of this world alive. So why struggle? And why strive? Do what you have to. Take what you need. Be thankful and be mellow."

Okay, I told that old memory. I closed my eyes and saw her: lined face and long flat breasts. There was—there had been—a crescent moon on her forehead. Between her breasts was a pendant, a double axe carved out of shell. A wise old lady. Had Derek known her? Not likely. Her tribe was different. They were mountain people, the Bernadinos.

I ate another piece of meat, then went to sleep, waking in the middle of the night. The moon was gone. The sky was full of stars. I sat up. The fire was a heap of coals that still glowed a little. I looked around. Nia was next to me, snoring. Farther off I saw another body. That must be the oracle.

On the far side of the fire was a third person standing upright, tall and pale. "Derek?"

"I just got back." His voice was low. "You were right. The ground is hot. I could feel it through the boots."

"Any trouble?"

"No. Except, a funny thing. When I was coming back, the moon was setting. Just as it went out of sight, I saw a flare. I think the moon is erupting."

I thought for a moment. "That's possible, isn't it? The planetologists said there was evidence that it had been active recently."

"The eruption has to be huge," Derek said. "Really huge, if I can see it."

"You're right." I thought for a moment. Could that be why I hadn't reached Eddie? No one in their right mind would want to miss seeing a major eruption. "More trouble for the planetologists."

"Uh-huh." He laughed. "The poor fools. It serves 'em right. They worked out all their theories on the basis of one system."

"They used what they had, Derek."

He said, "I want to go to sleep. I'll tell you the rest tomorrow."

"Okay." I lay back down. The wind had shifted. It blew out of the valley, bringing the smell of sulfur. I thought about the moon, which had an atmosphere. There was a lot of sulfur in it, as I remembered. It must really stink up there now.

The planetologists had not been happy when they saw the first long-distance holograms. The moon was too big, they told us. All the best theories said that Earth was an anomaly. Small planets didn't have moons. Or if they did, the moons were tiny: pieces of captured space junk.

The ship got closer in. The planetologists discovered the surface of the moon was comparatively smooth.

The system was full of junk. The planet had twelve other moons, all of them clearly captured planetoids. The big moon should have been covered with impact craters. Instead there were wide plains of volcanic origin and some fairly impressive mountains, also of volcanic origin.

The moon was active, and the best theories said that small planets did not have active moons.

114

Which meant the planetologists had to start working on new theories. I'd heard a couple. One involved tidal pull. The other assumed a really odd composition for the body in question. They were too far outside my area of expertise for me to have an opinion. I simply enjoyed the strangeness of the moon.

I woke at dawn, got up, and went to find a place to pee. Then I did my exercises, ending with the solar salute. I timed it perfectly. When I finished the sun was fully up, round and crimson, right above the eastern wall of the valley.

Nia woke, and the oracle. Derek was the last person up. He stretched and groaned, then climbed to his feet. We ate. Nia went to saddle the bowhorns. The oracle followed after her.

Derek yawned. "Coffee. That's what I need."

"What did you find?"

"The lake is mud. Hot mud. Boiling. It's an interesting sight. Bubbles appear on the surface. They get bigger and bigger, then—pssht. They're gone. Exploded." He yawned again. "The smell of sulfur is really offensive. And there are poles along the edge."

"What?"

"Wooden poles. Maybe ten centimeters thick. About three meters high. They're decorated with feathers and pieces of cloth. Some of them have horns on top made of copper. Really badly corroded. The gases from the lake must do that.

"I assume the lake has some kind of religious meaning. Wouldn't you think? I found this on the edge in the mud." He rolled up one sleeve. There was a bracelet on his arm. He pulled it off and handed it to me. It was gold, wide and heavy. I turned it and saw a design, repeated four times: a bowhorn with another animal attacking it, digging in with its claws and biting. What was it? The body was sleek like the body of a panther. The head was long and narrow with huge ears, and the tail ended in a tuft. "Nia?"

She came over.

"What is this?"

She took the bracelet. "Hu! This is good! One of my people made it. No one else can do work of this quality."

"What is the animal? The one on top?"

"A killer of the plain." She tilted the bracelet so the design was more visible. "A killer of the mountains is smaller and has scales as well as fur. I wonder how this got here? Where did you find it?"

"Derek found it in the valley, by the lake."

"Then it is an offering. A gift to the demons of fire. You should not have taken it." She handed the bracelet to Derek.

"Oh, no?" He put the bracelet on.

115

"I see you are going to keep the thing." Nia made the gesture that meant "so be it." "I think you are making a mistake." She turned and walked away.

Derek grinned, then rolled his sleeve down and fastened it.

"There are times when I think you are crazy," I said.

"No. Only badly alienated. Anyway, I don't believe in demons of fire." He glanced at the valley. "It's a good thing I don't. My own protection is too far away. The Gray Whale can't help me here."

The trail turned south, leaving the rim of the valley. Once again we traveled among hills. The day was overcast, and the sun was a bright white disk. In the diffuse light there were no shadows. I was pretty certain that we were traveling west, but I would not have bet on it. I thought—as well—that we were climbing, but I would not have bet on that, either. The trail wound up and down.

Gradually the slopes of the hills grew gentler. The valleys grew wider and more shallow. The bushes and trees—those few there had been— were gone.

"Nuh," said Nia, sounding satisfied. "We are coming to the plain."

We entered a new valley. A stream ran through the middle of it, and a flock of animals fed along the bank. They were bipeds, a new species, larger and heavier than any I had seen before. Only two were standing on their hind legs. Lookouts maybe. The rest had their front legs on the ground and their heads down, feeding.

Derek said, "They must be more efficient than our dinosaurs. They have competition from mammalian browsers. Or do I mean mammaloid? I don't understand how they manage to survive."

"There are—or were—a lot of odd birds on Earth. Ostriches. Emus. Cassowaries. How about the moa and the great auk? They survived into the age of mammals. In fact, I think they evolved in the age of mammals."

He shook his head. "They evolved from ordinary birds to fill specific ecological niches—on islands, in at least two cases. The moa lived in New Zealand. The great auk nested in Iceland. These creatures are all over. They are obviously competing successfully. And I don't think their ancestors were birds. They look reptilian, if that word has any meaning here."

"They have feathers, and I'm willing to bet they're warm-blooded."

"So were the dinosaurs. Warm-blooded, I mean."

One of the upright animals let out a bellow. The others reared onto their hind legs and moved away up the valley along the stream. They had a funny gait, a lumbering run. As awkward as it seemed, they covered a lot of ground. By the time we reached the bottom of the valley, they were gone.

Midway through the afternoon I looked around and realized the hills had ended. We were on a rolling plain, covered with pseudo-grass. It rippled in

116

the wind, changing color as the leaves turned over: green, blue-green, tan, and gray.

Something rose above the horizon in the north. I shaded my eyes and stared. The thing was almost the same color as the sky and so distant that it was barely visible. A cone, wide at the base. The top of the cone—the point—was missing. Instead there was a horizontal line. The rim of a crater.

I turned and waited for Nia, who was riding some distance behind me. The oracle was behind her, also riding. "What is that?" I asked. I pointed.

She glanced, then reined her animal.

"I have not seen it before. But I have heard. That is Hani Akhar. The Great Mountain. The home of the Mistress of the Forge."

The oracle came up beside us. He looked north. "Yes. That is the one. I can feel it even at this distance. It is a very holy place. Also dangerous. She is not always friendly, that spirit."

"This is definitely the wrong trail," Nia said. "We are way north of where I want to be."

"We will end up in the right place," the oracle said. "The route we take doesn't matter."

Nia scratched her nose. "There is no way to argue with a holy person. They are always certain they know more than we do. And if we say, 'No,' they say, 'The spirits have spoken.'"

I moved on ahead. I didn't like to be on the ground near the bowhorns. They were too big, and Nia's mount was sometimes restless and even nasty. I certainly did not want to follow the animals. It was a hassle to have to keep watching for dung.

That evening we camped by a little marshy lake. Derek and Nia went hunting. They came back at nightfall, empty-handed. We ate stale bread and drank water from the lake. It had a funny flavor.

"Swamp water," said Derek. "I've drunk worse in California."

"In the desert?" I asked.

"Mostly. But also in Berkeley. A couple of the people in my department had really lousy taste in wine. And they were important people. I had to go to their parties."

"What are you talking about?" asked Nia.

"A drink like *bara*," I said.

"Is it nasty-tasting?"

"Sometimes," Derek said.

He wandered off, taking his radio. I stayed with the two natives by the fire.

The big moon was up and more than half-full. I looked at it, trying to see evidence of a volcanic eruption, but the clouds veiled it and blurred its edges.

I looked at the natives. "Does anything unusual ever happen to the big moon?"

"What do you mean?" asked Nia.

I thought for a moment, trying to figure out how to describe something I had not seen. "Do bright spots ever appear on it? Do things ever appear on the rim, like a wisp of steam rising or like a tongue of flame licking out?"

Nia made the gesture of affirmation. "But that isn't unusual."

"What does it mean?" I asked.

"Nothing that I know of." She frowned, thinking. "There are people in the west who have found a way to look at the sun without harming their eyes. According to them, the sun is not flawless and untarnished the way we think it is. They say it is spotted. The spots are black. They crawl around like bugs. When the spots appear—a lot of them—it means the weather is going to get bad."

"I've never heard that story," said the oracle. "But I know what it means when a spot appears on the moon."

I made the gesture of inquiry.

"It means the Mother of Mothers has not been watching her pot."

"What?" I asked.

"The old women say the big moon is a cooking pot. It belongs to the Mother of Mothers. Sometimes she forgets to watch it, and it boils over. Then we see what you have described. The old women say it means the winter will be hungry." He paused. "My mother says the old women are wrong. She has kept a moon string for many years. Every time something happens up there, she ties a knot. And she has other strings that she uses to keep track of the weather. Rain. Snow. A big wind. Drought. She has a string for every kind of weather. There is no connection between what happens on the moon and what happens on the plain. That is her opinion. I think she is right."

"Huh," said Nia. "I have never heard the story about the moon. If it isn't true, I won't repeat it."

"The part about the cooking pot is most likely true," the oracle said. "My mother said nothing about that. Not everything that happens in the world of the spirits has an effect on our world here."

Nia made the gesture of agreement.

Derek came back. I glanced at him. "Did you get through to Eddie?"

"Yes. Why shouldn't I?"

"There was static last night, and I've been talking to computers the past couple of days."

"Eddie didn't mention anything about static." He sat down, folding himself neatly. "Or about computers. But he has been spending time in one of the big holovision rooms. The moon *is* erupting. And the eruption is big. We are missing one heck of a sight."

118

"What are you talking about?" asked Nia.

"The moon," I said. "It is boiling over."

She looked at the sky. "It's too bad the sky is cloudy."

The next day Nia said she wanted to walk.

"I am feeling restless again. If my ankle begins to bother me, I'll ask you to dismount."

"All right," I said.

The oracle, as always, rode. Now and then we passed little marshes or half-dry lakes. The sky was hazy. Hani Akhar remained just barely visible.

Late in the afternoon we reached the top of a rise. Below us was a lake. It was much larger than the others we had seen, irregular in shape and full of tiny islands. The edges were marshy. Monster grass grew in bunches on the shore.

Nia said, "I know this place, though I haven't been to it before. This is the Lake of Bugs and Stones. We are in the land of the Amber People. They come here in the fall on their way south. They fish and hunt for birds, and they perform ceremonies in honor of the mountain."

The oracle made the gesture of agreement. "Another holy place."

We descended. The sky was clear in the west. The sun was low. The water glittered, and I could barely see. We passed a grove of monster grass. The lake was only a few meters away. Reeds moved in the wind. The water flashed. Something bellowed. It was right in front of me, crashing out of the reeds, rearing up. My God! It was three meters tall! The mouth was open. The forearms reached toward me, claws spread. Another bellow! The animal I rode jerked its head. The reins whipped through my hands. The bowhorn bucked, and I kicked free of the stirrups. A moment later I slammed against the ground. The jolt went through me. I yelled. Then I was standing upright.

"Back off," said Derek. "Slowly. Don't frighten it."

I took a step back. Derek was next to me. I couldn't see Nia or the oracle or my bowhorn. The pseudo-dinosaur bellowed again. But it didn't move. Now, for the first time, I saw it clearly. Three meters tall. Hell! It was more like four. It had a bright pink belly and a crest of yellow feathers. Its arms and shoulders were dark blue-gray.

I took another step. The creature hissed. The open mouth was full of teeth. Blunt teeth. It was an herbivore. But the claws were long and sharp. For digging? Did it fight? The head tilted. A tiny bright eye stared at me.

"Keep moving," Derek said. His voice was low and even. "One step at a time."

I saw Nia on the other side of me, a knife in her hand. A useless weapon against this monster. It made another sound. A moan. What did that mean?

Something was moving behind it, coming up from the lake. Another monster. I blinked, trying to see against the sun. It was smaller than the beast confronting us and went on four feet. Its back was gray.

119

"The female," Derek said.

It turned its head and bit off a reed. Then it went on, chewing, making a loud crunching sound. Pieces of reed hung from its mouth. Three other animals came after it. These were small, about the size of a Saint Bernard. Two were quadrupeds. They waddled after the mother. The third hopped awkwardly.

"Well, what do you know?" said Derek.

We kept moving back, away from the angry male. Where was the oracle? I couldn't see him.

Mother waddled on. The children followed. At last they were out of sight, hidden by a grove of monster grass. The male hissed, then turned and bounded after his family. My shoulder began to hurt. My knees gave out. I sat down.

"Very interesting," said Derek. "They care for their young. That helps explain how they are able to survive in competition with the pseudo-mammals. The mammaloids. We need a whole new vocabulary. O Holy Unity! I thought I was going to piss in my pants."

Nia said, "Hu!" She put her knife away. "I hope the crazy man is all right. His bowhorn took off. The last I saw of it he was still holding on."

"Oh, my God, Derek. Our equipment. The radios."

He laughed. "On the bowhorns. Out there." He waved at the plain. "Are you all right?"

"My shoulder hurts like hell, and I bit my tongue. I don't know when."

He checked me over. "Your shoulder isn't dislocated. Your tongue is still there. I think you'll be okay." He turned and stared at the plain. "I'm going after our equipment. I used to chase horses back in California. Bowhorns aren't any faster. I'll catch up with them." He glanced at me. "You make camp around here somewhere. I'll find you."

"Derek—" I began.

He loped away.

"Derek!" I shouted.

He didn't look back.

"He is very strange," said Nia.

"Yes." I watched till he was out of sight, then I glanced at Nia. "Well, let's go find a place to camp."

Inahooli

We followed the trail along the shore until we came to a grove of monster grass. Nia cut branches and wove them into baskets: traps for fish. "This may not work. It is easier to catch fish in a river." She put the traps in the water.

After that we explored the grove. Nia found a patch of plants growing at the eastern edge. Their roots were edible. I gathered firewood. We baked the roots. They were crunchy and almost flavorless.

"They are good in a stew with meat," said Nia. "Alone—" She made the gesture that meant "the rest is obvious."

"Better than nothing."

She made the gesture of agreement.

Night came. The wind shifted, blowing off the lake. All at once the grove was full of bugs.

"Biters!" said Nia.

I slapped my neck. "You're right."

We crouched by the fire. The smoke protected us to some extent. I got bit a second time, on the wrist. Nia got bit once, on the palm of her hand, where she had no fur.

"Hu!" She clapped her hands together. "Well, I got the creature. It will not bother another person. How can you bear it, Li-sa? You have no fur. They can bite you anywhere."

Smoke had gotten into my eyes and they were watering. The places where the bugs got me were itching. "I am not fond of situations like this." I scratched one of the bites. "But what can I do about it? I can't grow fur. And anyway, I've been through a lot worse. I used to live in Minnesota."

"Where?" said Nia.

"A land with many lakes and many bugs." I paused and listened. The bugs hummed around my ears. There were a lot of them. They ought to be biting more. Maybe I didn't smell right. Maybe it was only the brave bugs—or the stupid ones—that decided to give me a try.

"Aiya!" Nia hit her forehead. "Another one!"

I waved the smoke out of my face. "They can bite through your fur?"

"Only in a few places, where it is thin. Around the eyes or in the crook of the elbow."

The wind shifted again and blew the bugs away. We lay down. We had nothing to cover us. Nia's cloak was with the rest of our baggage out on the plain. So was my poncho. But the night was mild, and I was exhausted. I curled up and went straight to sleep.

I woke early. The clouds were gone, and the sky above me was brilliant blue-green. Birds made noises in the foliage. Nia snored by the ashes of the fire.

I got up, groaning. My entire body was stiff, and my shoulder felt especially bad. I rubbed it, looking around. There was no wind. The lake was still. Out on the open water beyond the reeds a canoe glided.

"Nia!"

She scrambled to her feet. I pointed. She yelled and waved her arms. The canoe turned in. A moment later it was gone—out of sight among the reeds. We hurried to the shore.

"Who can it be?" I asked.

"I don't know. A woman. One of the Amber People."

The prow pushed through the reeds. A dugout, roughly made. It slid toward us. The woman in the back lifted her paddle from the water, then raised a hand and shaded her eyes. "Am I seeing things? Is one of you hairless?"

"Yes," I said.

The canoe hit shore. The woman climbed out. She was taller than I was and lanky with dark brown fur. Her face was wide and flat. Her eyes were dark orange, almost red. She wore a pale yellow tunic decorated with bands of embroidery. The pattern was intricate and geometric, done in various shades

of blue. Her belt was blue, and she had a long knife in a sheath of blue leather.
"Were you born like that?" she asked. "Or have you been ill?"

"This is the natural way for me to be." I used the word that meant "usual"
or "proper."

She looked me up and down. "Natural, eh? And you?" She turned to Nia.
"Who are you? And why do you travel with a freak?"

"I am a woman of the Iron People. Nia, the smith."

The new woman frowned. "There is something familiar about that name."

"It's common enough," said Nia.

The woman kept frowning.

Nia went on. "What is your name?"

"Toohala Inahooli. I belong to the Amber People and to the Clan of the
Ropemaker. Right now, I have a position of high prestige. I am the guardian
of the clan tower."

Nia made the gesture of acknowledgment.

I said, "What is a clan tower?"

She glared at me. "Where do you come from? Don't you know—among
the Amber People, every clan builds a tower in honor of its First Ancestor?
We make each tower as tall as possible. We cover it with decorations and perform ceremonies in front of it in order to impress the other clans and make
them feel envious and small."

A new kind of artifact! I thought for a moment. "Can I see the tower?"

"Yes. Of course. What use is a clan tower if people aren't impressed by it?
And how can people be impressed unless they come and see? But I warn
you—our magic is powerful. If there is anything demonic about you, you will
come to harm."

"No. I'm not demonic."

"We can't go," Nia said. "Deragu—" She paused. "I cannot say the name."

"Derek," I said.

"Derag told us to wait."

The woman frowned. "Who is this person? The name sounds male to me."

"The person is a woman," Nia said. "She comes from the same place as Li-
sa. They speak a language that is nothing like the languages on the plain. The
endings are different."

Inahooli made the gesture that meant she understood what was being said.

Nia went on. "Our bowhorns ran away. She—this person Derag—has
gone after them."

Inahooli repeated the gesture of comprehension.

"You stay here," I said. "If Derek comes, tell her where I am. She'll understand."

Nia made the gesture that meant "no."

"Why not?"

Nia scratched the back of her neck. Maybe she had gotten bitten there, though—as I remembered—the fur was pretty thick.

"Listen," Inahooli said. "I will go away. You two can argue. Maybe that one"—she pointed at Nia—"has something bad to say about me." She walked down the shore.

"Okay," I said. "What is the problem? Do you think the woman is dangerous?"

"No. But I think she has heard about me. When my people found out about me and Enshi, it made a big noise. The Amber People could have heard the noise. They trade with us."

"I want to see the tower. Have you heard about things like that?"

"Yes. The Amber People aren't like my folk. We are related to the People of Fur and Tin. We know that. We call them 'kinswoman.' And I think we may be related to the Copper Folk. Their language is not hard to learn. But the Amber People . . . Their language is difficult and their customs are peculiar. They boast a lot. Every clan tries to outdo the others in building towers and dancing. I don't understand it."

"I'm going," I said. "I ought to be back this evening."

Nia made the gesture that meant "so be it." "Don't tell her that we are traveling with men. I don't think she would understand."

"Okay." I waved at Inahooli. She came back. "I'm going with you."

"Good. This will be a remarkable event. No guardian has ever shown our tower to a person without hair."

We pushed the canoe out from shore and climbed in. Inahooli began to paddle. In a minute or so Nia was gone, hidden by the plants that I called reeds. They swayed above us, tall and dull blue-gray. Most of the stalks ended in a cluster of leaves, but here and there I saw a round, dark, shaggy head. The flower of the plant? I didn't know.

We slid out into open water. Ahead of us were islands. They were small, only a few meters across, and made of a soft volcanic stone that had weathered into very odd shapes. One looked like a mushroom. Another—tall and narrow—reminded me of a human woman in a robe. A third island was an arch. A fourth was a miniature cathedral. Late Gothic, I decided. The cathedral had a lot of spires.

We glided among the islands. I looked down. The water was clear. A fish flashed into sight, then turned sideways and vanished. What a planet! All at once I felt horrified at the idea of going home.

Stop it, I told myself. Don't think about Earth. Concentrate on the present. Enjoy what you have now.

I looked ahead. There was another island in sight: long and low, surrounded by reeds. At one end was a construction, twenty meters tall, I estimated, made of rough latticework. Banners hung from it, limp at present. As

124

we drew nearer I saw other kinds of decoration: bunches of feathers and long strings of shells.

"The tower of the Ropemaker," Inahooli said.

We rounded the island. On the far side was a beach. We landed and pulled the canoe up on the gravel. Inahooli led me toward the tower. The island was rocky and mostly bare with scattered patches of vegetation: orange pseudo-mosses and brown pseudo-lichens and a leafy gray plant that came up to the middle of my calf. There were only two objects of any size: the tower and a tent of dark brown fabric.

"That is my home," said Inahooli. "Every spring we come here. The clan rebuilds the tower and performs ceremonies to make it holy. Then we throw dice, and one of us is picked to be the guardian. All summer that woman stays by the tower. She watches it and makes certain that nothing happens to it. In the fall the tribe comes back. The clan invites everyone to a big dance. We eat. We make music. We brag about our ancestors. If everything goes well, the other clans are embarrassed. After that we all go south to the Winter Land. The Groundbird Clan give their dance there. Usually they do badly. For some reason they have never been good at bragging. And anyway, what do they have to brag about? Their ancestor is a miserable groundbird who did only one thing of importance."

"What?"

"She stole fire from the Spirit of the Sky and gave it to the people of the world. That is all well and good. We feel grateful in the middle of winter, when the snow is deep and the wind blows and so on. But our ancestor saved all living things."

"Oh, yes?"

We reached the tent. The tower was only ten meters away. Close to the bottom there was a row of masks hanging on the latticework. They were oval with round eyeholes. Each one was painted a solid color: red, yellow, black, white.

I pointed. "Who do they represent?"

"The black one is the Ropemaker. Yellow is the Trickster. Red is the Mistress of the Forge. And white is the Old Woman in the North."

"Tell me about them."

She looked me up and down. It was a calculating look, the look of a storyteller who has gotten an opening. "All right. But I can't use the masks. They have to stay where they are until the big dance. Sit down. I will make the story plain and as short as possible."

I sat down in front of the tent. Inahooli sat down facing me. Overhead a bird whistled, soaring over the lake.

"This is the story of the ivory comb," she told me in a loud voice.

125

"In the far north there is an old woman. Her tent is in the sky. The walls of the tent are made of light, hanging in folds from the tent poles, which are made from the bones of the original worldmonster. How they got in the sky is another story, which I don't have time to tell. The old woman has a comb, which is made from one of the monster's teeth. It is ivory, as white as snow. She uses it to comb her fur. When she does this, she pulls creatures out. They fall to the floor and vanish, going through the floor into the world. All the animals in the world come into existence this way.

"When the old woman combs the left side of her body, the animals that come out are good and useful: the bowhorns we herd, the birds we hunt and eat. When she combs the right side of her body, the animals that come out are harmful: lizards with venomous bites and bugs that sting. The people of the world sing to the old woman, praising her and asking her for help. This is one of the songs:

> "Grandmother, be generous.
> Comb the left side of your body.
> Then we will be prosperous.
> Then we will be happy.
> Our children will be fat
> In our tents by the fire.

> "Grandmother, be compassionate.
> Don't comb the right side of your body.
> Leave the lizards where they are.
> Don't send us
> the bugs that bite and sting.

"In the far south there is a young man. He is tall and handsome. His eyes are as yellow as fire. No one is certain who his mother is. Some people say it is the Great Spirit, the Mother of Mothers. Other people say it is a demon of fire.

"The young man is called the Trickster. He is the one who comes to men in the winter, when they guard the herd. Each man sits alone under a tent that is made by stretching a cloak over the branches of a bush or tree. Snow comes down on him. The fire in front of him is low. The man sits and shivers, holding his arms close to his body. Then the Trickster comes. His voice is like the wind. He says, 'Why are you doing this? Why do you suffer for the ungrateful women of the village? Forget your mother. Forget your sisters. Forget the sons and daughters you may have. Go off into the hills and live like an animal without obligations, pleasing yourself alone.'

126

"Most men ignore the voice. But some listen. They go crazy and leave the herd, wandering into the hills. No one sees them after that.

"The Trickster is the same one who goes to meet women in the spring, when it is mating time. He looks like the best kind of man, large and strong and self-confident. He establishes his territory close to the village. No other man dares to confront him. When the women come out full of lust, they meet him. Some of them meet him, anyway. Each woman who mates with him thinks, What an excellent father! My child will be hardy and resourceful. Good-looking, too.

"But the mating produces no children. Or if children are born, they are sickly and bad-tempered. They cause nothing but trouble.

"This is usually so. But the Trickster is never reliable, even in the evil he does. Once in a while a woman mates with him, and the child who comes out is like her father, large and strong and self-confident: a true heroine.

"One of these was my ancestor, the Ropemaker. But first I must tell how the Trickster stole the ivory comb.

"He was in the far north, cold and hungry. There was nothing around except the wide plain covered with snow. After a while he came to the tent of the old woman. It shone above him, white and yellow and green. He took off his snowshoes and stuck them in a bank of snow. Then he climbed up into the sky. He entered the tent. The old woman was there, sitting in the middle of the floor. Her fur was gray with age. She was combing it with the ivory comb.

"The Trickster sat down. He watched greedily. The old woman was pulling the comb through the fur on her left forearm. Out came animals. They were little and dark. The old woman shook her comb. The animals tumbled down. When they reached the floor, they vanished. They were going into the world, into the deep burrows of the builders of mounds.

"'Grandmother,' the Trickster said. 'Give me some of your animals. I am hungry, and they look delicious.'

"The old woman stared at him. 'I know who you are. The Trickster, the One Who Tells Lies.' She gave the comb a shake, then she caught one of the animals in midair. It sat up on her hand. Its tiny nose twitched. Its whiskers quivered. It looked at the Trickster with bright dark eyes. 'These animals are part of me. I give them to people who treat them with respect. But you—O Evil One—you misuse everything you get hold of. There is no respect in you. I will give you nothing.' She turned her hand over. The animal fell to the floor. It was gone.

"The Trickster ground his teeth. 'Grandmother, have pity.'

"'No,' the old woman said. 'You can starve for all I care. And let it be a lesson to you.' She turned around so her back was to the Trickster.

"He leaped up. 'You will regret this, you old biddy!' He ran from the tent. He climbed down out of the sky and sat next to his snowshoes in a heap of snow. There he waited till the old woman went to sleep. The sound of her snoring filled the plain. The Trickster climbed back up. He crept into the tent. The walls shone as brightly as ever, and the tent was full of a pale flickering light. He saw the old woman stretched out on her back. Next to her was the ivory comb. He picked it up.

"'But where am I going to hide?' he asked himself. 'When the spirits hear that this is gone, they will search the whole world. What place is safe?'

"Then he had an idea. He made himself small—and the comb as well— and crawled into the old woman's vagina. She groaned and scratched herself, but she did not wake.

"'This is not the most pleasant place that I have ever been,' the Trickster said. 'I'd like more light and a bit less moisture. But no one will think of looking here.'

"The old woman woke and reached for her comb. It wasn't there. She let out a scream. All over the world the spirits leaped up. 'What is it?' they cried. 'What is going on?'

"Then the search began. Up and down, back and forth, in and out. The spirits searched everywhere. But they didn't find the comb.

"'What will I do?' the old woman said. 'The comb is irreplaceable. There is none like it, and without it I cannot comb my fur.'

"The spirits had no answer.

"Spring came. Vegetation appeared. The hills and the plain turned blue. The people of the world noticed that something was wrong. In every village they went to the shamaness.

"'What is going on?' they asked. 'Fish thrash in the river as they do every year. But no one has seen any fingerlings. The birds build nests as usual. The nests are empty. As for the little animals, the builders of mounds, they puff up the sacks in their necks. They scream and moan and carry on. But they produce no young.'

"The shamanesses ate narcotic plants. They danced and had visions. They said, 'The Trickster has stolen the ivory comb. Without it, no more animals will come into existence. We will all starve because of that malevolent person.'

"All the people cried out. They beat their chests and thighs. They prayed to the spirits. But what could the spirits do?

"Now the story turns to the Ropemaker. She was a woman of the Amber People. She was large with glossy fur. Her eyes were as yellow as fire. Her arms were strong, and her fingers were nimble. Most people believed she was a child of the Trickster. She had the look.

"Her craft was making rope out of leather. She was very skillful at this. Her ropes were narrow and flexible. They did not stretch. They were hard to break, and they lasted for years.

"In any case, the time for mating came. The women of the Amber People felt the spring lust grow in them. But this year they were unwilling to go out onto the plain. 'What is the point of leaving the village?' they said. 'Why should we bother to go and find a man? The children we conceive will die of starvation.'

But the lust grew stronger. Each woman packed the gifts she had made during the winter. Each woman saddled a bowhorn and rode out onto the plain. The Ropemaker was among them. In her saddlebag was a fine long rope. It was her mating gift.

"Now the story turns back to the Trickster. By this time he was getting restless. There was nothing to do in the old woman's vagina. He knew it was spring. He wanted to go out into the world and play a mean trick on someone. He waited till the old woman was asleep and crept out. He left the comb behind. Off he went toward the south. After a while he came to the land of the Amber People. He found a territory close to the village. There was a man there already: a big man with many scars. The Trickster went up to him and said, 'You'd better leave.'

"'Are you crazy?' the big man said. 'I got here first. And anyway, I'm bigger than you.'

"The Trickster stretched himself till he was taller than the big man. He glared down. His yellow eyes shone like fire.

"'Well,' said the big man. 'If you put it that way.' He mounted his bowhorn and rode off.

"The Trickster shouted insults at his back. The big man did not turn.

"After that the Trickster settled down and waited. A day passed and then another. On the third day a woman rode into sight. It was the Ropemaker. The Trickster felt satisfied. This was an impressive woman. This was a person worth misleading.

"As for the Ropemaker, she liked what she saw: a big wide man. He was standing on the plain with his feet apart and his shoulders back. His fur was thick and glossy. He wore a fine tunic, covered with embroidery. On his arms were silver bracelets. They were wide and bright.

"When she got close, she noticed that he had a peculiar aroma. 'Well, no one is perfect,' she told herself.

"When she reached the man, she dismounted. They lay on the ground and mated. Afterward she said, 'I have some bad news.'

"'Oh, yes?' said the Trickster.

"'The Old Woman of the North has lost her comb. Because of this, she cannot comb her fur, and no more animals will come into the world.'

"'So what?'

"'If we have a child, it will die of starvation.'

129

"'So what? It's no concern of mine. As long as I am able to mate, I'm satisfied. Who cares what comes of the thing we do together?'

"'I care. And anyway, if this situation continues, we'll all die. For how can we live without the bowhorns and the birds in the air and the fish in the rivers?'

"'If you want to die, then go ahead and do it. I'm not worried. I intend to go on living, no matter what happens to the rest of the world.' The Trickster rolled over and went to sleep.

"The Ropemaker looked at him. His fur shone like copper, and there was a glow around his body. This was no ordinary man, she realized. It was a spirit. A nasty spirit. The Trickster.

"She got her rope and tied him up. Then she waited. He woke and tried to stretch. He could not. 'What is this?' he cried.

"'You are caught,' said the Ropemaker. 'And I will not let you go until you give me the ivory comb.'

"The Trickster ground his teeth. He thrashed and rolled. One heel struck the land and made a hole. Water rushed up and made a lake. The lake is still there. It is wide and shallow and full of stones and reeds. It is called the Trickster's Lake or the Lake of Bugs and Stones.

"The rope did not break. The Trickster continued to struggle. He rolled away from the Ropemaker. He beat on the earth with his bound hands. He made another hole, deeper than the first. Hot mud rushed up. It seethed around the Trickster. He was boiling like a bird in a pot. His magic was powerful. He took no harm. The rope, however, could not survive the heat and moisture. It began to stretch. The Trickster pulled free. He jumped up. He shouted:

"'I am the Trickster,
oh, you foolish woman!
I cannot be held.
I know no obligation.

"'I am the Trickster,
oh, you foolish woman!
No one can hold me.
No one can make me stop.'

"After that he ran off across the plain. He went north, back to his hiding place. The Ropemaker watched him go. She bit her lip and clenched her hands. 'He is a great spirit, and he may be a relative of mine. But I won't let him get away with this.'

130

"She mounted her bowhorn and rode north. For a long time she traveled, and she had many adventures. But I don't have the time to tell you about them.

"At last she came to the place where the old woman lived. It was midsummer. The plain was yellow. The rivers were low. The Ropemaker dismounted. She tethered her animal. Then she climbed into the sky.

"'Grandmother,' she called. 'Will you let me in? I have come a long way in order to see you.'

"'Come in,' the old woman said. 'But I can't help you. I have lost my comb. I have nothing to give.'

"The Ropemaker entered the tent. The old woman was there, sitting in the middle of the floor. She was naked and scratching her belly with both hands. 'I am going crazy,' she said. 'My fur is full of animals, and I can't get them out. I can feel them crawling in the folds of my belly. I can feel them in my armpits. I can feel them on my back. Granddaughter, I beg you. Be kind to me! Scratch me between the shoulder blades.'

"The Ropemaker scratched her back. The old woman kept on complaining. 'I can even feel them in my vagina, though I have no fur there. They stir from time to time and tickle me. Oh! This is terrible!'

"The Ropemaker frowned. She remembered the way the Trickster had smelled. All at once she knew his hiding place. 'But how will I get him out?' she asked herself. 'And how will I catch him and hold him, once he is out?'

"She decided to go to sleep. She lay down and closed her eyes. The old woman sat next to her, scratching. Soon the Ropemaker began to dream. Three spirits came to her. One was a woman of middle age with a big belly and noticeable breasts. She wore a long robe, covered with embroidery.

"The next spirit was a man. His fur was blue-green, and he had wings instead of arms. He wore a kilt of the same color as his fur. His belt buckle was round and made of gold. It glittered brilliantly.

"The third spirit was a young woman. She was large and muscular. She carried a hammer, and she wore a leather apron. Her eyes were orange-red.

"The Ropemaker knew them. The first was the Mother of Mothers. The second was the Spirit of the Sky. And the third was the Mistress of the Forge, who lives in Hani Akhar, the great volcano.

"'O holy ones,' the Ropemaker said. 'Help me out! I know where the Trickster is. But I need a way to get him out of his hiding place. And once he is out, he will try to run away. I need a way to catch him.'

"The Spirit of the Sky spoke first. 'I will keep watch. If he tries to run away, I will see where he goes. He won't be able to find a new hiding place.'

"The Mistress of the Forge spoke next. 'I will make a rope out of iron, forged with magic so it will never break. It will be self-fastening and able to move. The Trickster won't escape from it.'

131

"The Mother of Mothers spoke last. 'I know how to get the Trickster out of his hiding place.' She leaned forward and whispered into the Ropemaker's ear.

"In the morning the Ropemaker woke. There was a rope lying next to her in a coil. It was dull gray in color, and it had a peculiar texture, like the scales of a lizard. The Ropemaker took a close look at it. It was made of many tiny links of iron fastened together.

"'Good morning, grandmother,' she said to the Old Woman of the North. 'I've had an idea. You said that your vagina tickled, even though it has no fur.'

"The old woman made the gesture of agreement.

"'I don't think there's an animal in there. I think you need sex.'

"'You're crazy!' the old woman cried. 'It's the wrong time of year. And any-way, I'm too old to feel lust.'

"'Remember,' the Ropemaker said. 'A woman doesn't grow old easily. The feeling of lust doesn't vanish all at once. Often a woman becomes irritable and uncertain. Her behavior changes from day to day. She feels lust at the wrong time. At the right time, in the spring, she feels nothing at all. She cannot understand what is going on—any more than a young girl can when she becomes a woman. I think this is what has happened to you.'

"'No!' cried the old woman.

"'In any case, try sex. I will go and find a young man for you. If I'm right, and you are feeling lust—a bit late, I will admit—then the young man will respond to you. And maybe you will feel better afterward.'

"The Ropemaker got up and left the tent. She took the iron rope with her.

"The Trickster heard all this. He became uneasy. 'If that crazy woman can find a man willing to mate with this old biddy—well, my position will not be comfortable. I am likely to take a terrible beating. I'd better get out of here.'

"He waited till it was night, and the old woman was snoring. Then he crept out. The comb was in his hand. He stole to the door. Out he stepped. The Ropemaker was waiting there. The Great Moon was up. It lit the sky and the plain. It lit the man as he came through the doorway.

"'This is it, you nasty spirit!' the woman cried. She threw the iron rope.

"It twisted in midair. It wrapped itself around him. He stumbled and fell. The comb flew out of his hand. The Ropemaker caught it. As for the Trickster, he fell out of the sky and landed on the plain. He rolled back and forth. He yelled. He struggled. But the rope would not break. After a while he gave up. He lay still, breathing heavily.

"Three spirits appeared around him. He looked up at them. 'I can tell that you are responsible for this.'

"'Yes,' said the Mother of Mothers. 'This is the end of all your malevolent tricks. We are going to take you far from here and drop you in the ocean. You'll cause no further trouble.'

132

"'Don't be sure,' the Trickster said.

"They picked him up and carried him through the air. In the middle of the ocean they let go of him. He splashed into the water. Down and down he sank. At last he hit the bottom. Aiya! It was dark and cold! Deep-sea fish nibbled on his toes. He twisted and tried to yell. Instead he swallowed water. But he could not drown. His life was everlasting. He stayed there for more years than we can count. He gave his nature to the ocean. It became changeable and unreliable, impossible to trust. In the end he broke free. But that is another story.

"As for the Ropemaker, she went back into the tent. She woke the old woman and gave her the comb.

"'Oh! This is wonderful!' the old woman cried. She began to comb her fur. Animals came out, hundreds of them. They tumbled out of the sky and filled the world. All the people rejoiced."

Inahooli stopped talking. I unfolded my legs and stood. By this time it was noon. Sunlight poured down. The air was still and hot. I was sweating.

"Well," said Inahooli. "Are you impressed? Do you think my ancestor is great?"

"Yes." I turned and looked at the tower. A trickster god, like Anansi the Spider and Coyote and B'rer Rabbit. There were other odd similarities. The Old Woman in the North reminded me of a character out of Inuit mythology. Was there such a thing as a universal archetype? Would we find the same characters on planet after planet? I imagined a collective unconscious that extended across—or maybe under—the galaxy. What an idea! But I was moving too fast. I didn't have the data. I stretched. "I have to go."

"No! Don't leave. I have other stories."

I made the gesture of polite refusal, followed by the gesture of extreme regret. "Nia is waiting."

She stood up, frowning. "There is something about that name . . ." Her eyes widened. "I remember! Nia the Smith. The woman who loved a man." She used the word that meant familial affection, the love between sisters or between a mother and her daughters. "They told us about her, the Iron Folk. They said the man died. But she was still out on the plain. A big woman with the look of bad luck. They warned us about her. They said, 'If she comes to your village, let her stay only as long as is decent. Then tell her to move on. If you let her move in, she'll sour the milk in your pots. She'll make your fires go out.'"

"Nia does no harm," I said. I kept my voice low and even. A confident voice. The voice of sanity.

Inahooli was silent, still frowning, obviously thinking. "She hasn't given up her old behavior. When she mentioned your friend she wasn't using an ending from your language. You said the name differently. I heard. I didn't under-

133

stand. She gave the name an ending from her own language or from the language of gifts. In either case it is a male ending. Your friend is a man."

I opened my mouth. What could I say? I didn't like to lie, and I didn't think Inahooli would believe any lie I told. "I'd better go."

She stared at me, her eyes narrow. "What are you? Why do you travel with a woman like that? And with a man?"

"I told you, I am ordinary. Among my own people, anyway."

She made the gesture of disagreement, moving her hand emphatically. "I have met the Iron People and the Copper People and the People of Fur and Tin. No one is really different. Not about things that are important. I think you are a demon."

How does one reason with a religious fanatic? I thought for a moment. "Remember what you said before I came here. The tower is magical. If I am a demon, why hasn't it harmed me?"

She turned, staring at the latticework. At the top a couple of banners moved languidly. A couple of feathers fluttered. A wind must be rising, though I couldn't feel it.

Inahooli made the gesture of agreement. "I did say that."

"And I am fine."

There was a pause. Then Inahooli spoke. Her voice was slow at first. She was obviously thinking out loud. "You are right. The tower should have harmed you. It hasn't." She turned back toward me. "You have overcome our magic. The tower is something."

I didn't know the word, but I could guess the meaning. The tower was polluted, desanctified. It had lost its power.

"I brought you here," said Inahooli. "I am the guardian. This will destroy my reputation." She pulled out her knife.

"Listen to me," I said.

She grabbed my arm and raised the knife. I twisted and kicked, hitting her in the crotch. It was a good solid kick. She staggered back. I ran.

I made it to the canoe, but she was close behind me. There wasn't time to get the damn thing into the water. I grabbed a paddle and turned to face her. "Can't we talk?"

"No!" She lunged at me. I brought the paddle down on her shoulder. She yelled and dropped the knife.

"Listen to me! I mean no harm!"

She grabbed up the knife with her other hand. "How can we use the tower? The masks are ruined. The magic is gone."

She ducked to the left. My left. I turned and raised the paddle. The knife flashed. I swung. Inahooli jumped back.

"I got you, demon!" she cried.

134

"What?"

"Don't you see the blood on the ground?"

I glanced down and saw only the rocky beach. No blood. Something moved at the edge of my vision. Inahooli. She was coming at me, her knife raised again. I jerked the paddle up and out. It hit her in the gut. She grunted and bent double. I brought the paddle down on the back of her head.

She fell. I picked up the knife and threw it out into the reeds, then looked back at her. She lay facedown, motionless.

I knelt and felt her neck, then ran my hand over the back of her head. Her pulse was strong and regular. Her head felt rock solid. Good! But I wasn't going to stick around and nurse her. She was too likely to make another attempt to kill me. I pushed the canoe into the water, jumped in, and paddled away from the island. The things I did in order to get a myth!

After I was well out past the reeds, I noticed something was wrong with my left arm. I pulled in the paddle and took a look. My shirt was slit from the elbow to the wrist. Blood dripped onto the dark wood of the canoe and onto my jeans. "Goddammit." I took off the shirt and twisted my arm, trying to see the cut. There was a twinge of pain in my shoulder. Funny. I had forgotten how stiff the shoulder was. The cut was long and shallow. A scratch. Nothing to worry about. It was bleeding well, which ought to reduce the risk of infection. Not that infection was likely, unless from something that I had brought with me. I wrapped my shirt around the arm and tied the sleeves together. Then I went back to paddling.

A wind blew, light and fitful. Waves splashed against the canoe. My arm began to ache. My shoulder also. I concentrated on my breathing: in and out, keeping time with the motion of my arms as I lifted the paddle and brought it forward, drove it into the water and pulled it back.

Ahead of me was the shore. Where could I land? I shaded my eyes. There was a figure on the bank above the reeds. No. Two figures. They waved at me. I turned the canoe and paddled toward them. In a moment they were out of sight. The reeds leaned over me, their shaggy heads swaying, and I had no room to move. I stuck the paddle down, hit bottom, and pushed. The canoe went forward through the vegetation into an area of clear water. Nia and Derek waded out and pulled me to shore.

"Where is Inahooli?" Nia asked.

I stood. The canoe shifted under me. Derek grabbed my arm.

"No!"

He let go. "What is this?" He held out his hand. The palm was red.

"Blood." I stepped onto dry land, sat down, and fainted.

When I came to, I was on my back, looking up at foliage, the long narrow leaves of monster grass. They shone, edged with sunlight.

135

Derek said, "Can you understand me?"

"Yes. Of course." I turned my head. He sat cross-legged on the ground. His upper body was naked, and I could see the bracelet on his arm. The wide band of gold. It kept going in and out of focus.

"What happened?"

"The woman. Inahooli."

"Nia told me about her. What did she do?"

"She thought I was a demon. I was bad luck for her"—I paused, trying to think of the right word—"artifact. The one she was guarding. She came after me with a knife. I hit her. Derek, she's alive. What if she comes after me?"

He smiled briefly. "I'll worry about that. You rest."

"Okay." I closed my eyes, then opened them. "The bowhorns."

"I found one. The Voice of the Waterfall managed to stay on. I don't know how. He let it run till it was exhausted. He had no choice, he told me. In the end it had to stop. He calmed it and let it rest. Then he turned back. I met him at sundown. We camped on the plain. And in the morning—" He made a gesture I didn't recognize.

"What was that?"

"What?"

"The gesture. The wave."

He grinned. "It's a human gesture, Lixia. It means—approximately—'skip it' or 'why bother' or 'you can imagine the rest.'"

"Oh," I said.

"We got here at midmorning, after you left."

"Oh." I closed my eyes, then remembered something else. "The radios."

Derek laughed. "They're on the other bowhorn. The one I didn't find."

"Shit."

"Uh-huh. I thought I ought to make sure the Voice of the Waterfall got back to the lake. Nia will go out tomorrow on the animal we have. She's a better rider than I am, and this is her planet. With any luck she'll find the radios. And I will make sure what's-her-name—the woman who cut you up—"

"Inahooli."

"I'll make sure she doesn't cause any more trouble."

"What does that mean?"

He grinned. "Nothing dramatic. I'll stay here and keep my eyes open. Now, go to sleep."

Derek left. I worried. What if Nia couldn't find the other animal? We'd be alone for the first time. Really alone on an alien planet. It might be days before the people on the ship realized that something was wrong. Then what would they do? How would they find us? I tried to think of signals. A huge fire. That would be best. But could we make one that was big enough? And would they know it was made by us?

I dozed and had bad dreams. Inahooli was after me. I ran down a long corridor between ceramic walls. Then the corridor was gone. I was on a plain. I turned and saw a wall of flame advancing toward me. A grass fire! I ran. But it was so difficult. The grass was tall and thick. I kept tripping. The fire was gaining.

I fell, rolled over, and opened my eyes. Smoke drifted above me. I sat up, terrified.

Oh, yes. The campfire. It burned three meters away. My companions sat around it. Beyond them was the lake and the low sun. It was late afternoon. My arm hurt, my head ached, and my throat was dry. "Is there anything to drink?"

They looked at me.

"Are you all right?" said Nia.

"I'm thirsty."

Nia brought me a green sphere with a hole punched in the top: something like a gourd or maybe a coconut. Where had she found it? I took it and drank. The liquid inside was cool and had a sharp flavor. Like what? A citrus fruit? Not quite. I drank again.

"Can you talk now?" asked Derek. "What was the woman guarding? And why did she decide you were a demon?"

I looked at Nia, who was squatting next to me. "You were right. Your people have talked about you. Inahooli remembered. Nia the Smith. The woman who loved a man."

Nia frowned. "There are times I think my people talk too much. Don't they have anything better to do?"

"And she figured out that Derek was a man."

"Because I used the male ending on his name."

"Yes."

She stood up and clenched her hand into a fist, then hit her thigh. "I am just like my relatives. My tongue goes up and down like a banner in the wind, and I do not think." She opened her hand and made the gesture that meant "so be it."

"One of us ought to stay up tonight and keep watch. That woman is probably a little crazy. She has been alone too long, and she has been too close to something that is holy. She may come after Li-sa."

Derek made the gesture of agreement.

"I hit her pretty hard," I said. "For all I know, she is still"—I paused and tried to think of the right word in the language of gifts—"asleep. Or maybe dead."

Derek looked out at the water. "Maybe. I don't intend to go and check. The island is holy. She's made it very clear that she doesn't want us on it. And as a rule, I don't interfere with other people's karma. She chose to invite you to the island, and she chose to try and kill you. If those choices end in her death—well." He paused, then used the same gesture that Nia had used a minute or so before. "That is the way it is," the gesture said.

The oracle leaned forward. "I don't know what you did in the past, Nia, and I don't know why your people tell stories about you. But this situation is not your fault."

"Why not?"

The oracle pointed at Derek. "He went into the valley of demons. He took the bracelet. Now, the demons are angry. They are causing all this trouble— the *shuwahara* and the angry woman."

Shuwahara? Was that the name of the animal that had frightened our bowhorns?

The oracle stood up. He held out his hand. "Give me the bracelet."

Derek frowned.

"Do it," I said in English. "We're in enough trouble already."

Derek pulled off the bracelet. The oracle took it and slid it onto his arm. "What are you going to do with it?" I asked.

"The spirit will tell me." The oracle pulled off his tunic. He was naked except for the bracelet and his necklace. His dark fur shone. The jewelry glistened. Taken all in all, he was impressive. He tossed the tunic on the ground. "I am going off by myself. I will dance and sing until I am in a frenzy. Then— maybe—the spirit will come to me." He walked away toward the lake.

"Do you think I'll get it back?" asked Derek.

"No."

"Goddammit." He laughed and shrugged. "Oh, well."

Nia fixed dinner: fresh fish, gutted and stuffed with herbs, then wrapped in leaves and roasted in the coals. It was delicious, but I was too tired to be hungry. I ate half a fish and lay down. The sun had set. Clouds were moving in. They were high and hazy, golden in the last light of day. My companions talked quietly. The birds made little evening noises. I closed my eyes.

When I woke, the sun was up again. Who had guarded the camp? Had Derek remembered? I climbed to my feet, groaning. A body—dark and furry—sprawled by the fire. The oracle. Asleep. There was no sign of Nia or Derek or the bowhorn. I walked through the grove. The animal was definitely gone. Nia must have left as soon as there was any light. I looked out on the plain, shading my eyes against the sun. Nothing. I went back through the grove. The oracle had rolled over on his back. His arm was over his face. He was snoring.

Down to the lake. Birds flapped in the reeds. On the shore were two canoes. I stopped, terrified. I was in no condition to fight Inahooli. Had she done something to Derek? I needed a weapon. A paddle had worked before. I went to the canoes.

Inahooli was in one of them, on her back. She was naked. Her feet were tied with a strip of yellow cloth, and she was gagged with another piece of yellow fabric. Her hands were behind her. I couldn't see how they were tied. She glared at me.

I laughed, relieved. I hadn't killed her. "You must have met Derek."

She grunted.

"I don't think I'll take out the gag. I'd like to know where he is. But I don't suppose you'd tell me, even if you knew."

Inahooli growled and twisted. Was there any chance that she could get free? Of course not. Derek had tied her. I wondered if he would ever make a serious mistake.

"I have to go. I'll be back later."

Inahooli growled a second time.

I found Derek farther along the shore, on a beach of black gravel. There was a break in the reeds. A channel—two or three meters wide—led out into the lake. A bird floated in the channel. It was perfectly ordinary looking.

"It has teeth," said Derek.

His long hair was wet, and there were patches of dampness on his shirt. He tucked the shirt into his jeans, then grinned at me.

"A morning swim?" I asked.

"Uh-huh." He fastened one of his sleeves. I saw a glint just before he sealed the fabric. He had something metallic on his arm.

"I found Inahooli. What happened?"

"Nia went to sleep, and I went off to watch the oracle. I figured, never pass up a ritual. He did exactly what he said he would do. Danced and sang and waved a branch around, all under a moon that was three-quarters full and clearly erupting. You can see the plume above the rim. It starts in sunlight and then curves over the part of the moon that is still in shadow. A heck of a sight.

"I couldn't understand what he was saying. He wasn't using the language of gifts. But I got it all on my recorder."

"What did he do with the bracelet?"

"Tossed it into the lake. That was the end of the ceremony. He went back to camp. I wandered around and kept my eyes open. I figured he would be tired after all that jumping around. You were injured, and Nia had to get up early. That left me to keep watch, and I wanted to keep looking at the moon." He closed the front of his shirt.

139

"The woman came two hours later. No. More like three. The moon was still up. She came in the second canoe. I guess that's obvious. I didn't see her land—or hear her. She is a very quiet lady. But she woke up a bird, coming in through the reeds, and it whistled.

"I waited in the shadows. The fire—our fire—was burning. She moved toward it. I knew she would. When she came into the grove, I jumped her." He grinned. "She's strong as well as quiet. But I had the advantage of surprise. After she was unconscious, I dragged her back to the canoe and tied her up. I didn't have any rope. I cut up her tunic and used it. I'm hungry. Let's go back to camp."

We walked along the shore. Derek continued. "Nia left at dawn. I didn't tell her about what's-her-name. It was something else to worry about, and she looked moody enough. Nia, I mean. I guess she isn't a morning person."

"What are we going to do with Inahooli?"

"Hold her until Nia gets back, then let her go, but only when we're ready to leave. She won't follow us. She has her tower to guard."

"I wonder if we're driving her crazy."

"What?" He stopped and stared at me.

"She struck me as a vulnerable person, though it's hard to judge a person from another culture. Maybe they're all like that: boastful and defensive. In any case, her self-esteem is all tied up with the tower and her position as the guardian. Now she's failed. I'm pretty sure that she thinks the tower is ruined, and I don't think she'll be able to handle failure. I don't think she has the—what?—elasticity of spirit."

Derek made the gesture of doubt. "I think you underestimate that woman. Her technology is primitive—what you call primitive, anyway. But I don't think she's simple. I know Nia isn't. And the oracle is so damn complex, I don't know where I am with him. Most likely this lady—I've forgotten her name again."

"Inahooli."

"Most likely she'd do what I'd do in her place."

"What?" I started walking again.

Derek kept pace. "I'd lie. I'd pretend nothing had happened. When my people came, I'd say, 'Everything is fine.'"

I frowned. Derek glanced at me, then continued, "Every society has standards for proper conduct, and in every society people fail to meet those standards. Reality and human frailty get in the way. Well, you can't abandon the standards, and you can't have everyone in the society going around crying 'Mea culpa.' So you invent hypocrisy. It's present in every society I've ever studied. I'm sure they have it here on this planet."

"Maybe."

We turned away from the shore, walking toward the grove.

"Think of my people," Derek said. "To them two qualities are important. Mellowness and honesty. Well, what do you do when honesty will create an unpleasant situation?"

He paused. I said nothing. "First of all, you try to evade the problem. You eat a little peyote. You concentrate on the cosmic patterns. That's what's important, after all—all that energy, pouring down from the stars and rising up from the ground.

"The world is charged with the grandeur of God.
It will flame out, like shining from shook foil;
It gathers to a greatness, like the ooze of oil
Crushed . . .

"And so on. If you can't escape from the problem, if you are pulled back to the here and now, then you lie. Which is dishonest and hypocritical, but natural and human, and it keeps everything mellow."

We reached the camp. The oracle was up, rebuilding the fire. He glanced at us. "Nia has gone?"

"Yes," said Derek. "And that woman came. Inahooli. She's down by the water. I tied her up."

"Our luck is changing. Nia will find the bowhorn, and everything will come out the way it is supposed to. My spirit has promised me."

Derek made the gesture that meant he had heard what had been said, but was reserving judgment.

Late in the morning we went down to the canoe, all three of us. Inahooli was in the same position as before. Her head was turned, and her eyes closed against the glare of the sun.

I looked at her a moment. "This isn't going to work," I said in English. "Nia could be gone for days. We can't keep the woman like this."

She opened her eyes, frowning and squinting.

"It's uncomfortable. It's humiliating. And it's undemocratic. What right do we have to deprive her of freedom?"

"We have the right to protect ourselves," Derek said.

"Well, maybe. In any case, this isn't practical. How is she going to eat? Or go to the bathroom? We can't let her lie in her own excrement like a character in a novel about the old society."

The oracle bent over Inahooli. He loosened her gag.

"Demon," she said.

"No. I am a holy man. An oracle. I serve the Spirit of the Waterfall, who is large and powerful and able to handle any kind of evil."

141

An interesting word, that one. I translated it as "evil," an abstract noun. In his language it was an adjective coupled with a noun that meant "thing." The adjective meant "bad," as in a bad taste. It also meant "unlucky" or "peculiar."

"You are a demon," the woman said. "You travel with demons."

"They are not demons. They are people without hair."

"One of them is male. And you are a man."

The oracle made the gesture of agreement.

"Everyone knows that men are solitary by nature and have bad tempers and are unwilling to share anything with other men. But you travel with that one." She nodded toward Derek. "You must be a demon or a monster."

"You are thinking badly," the oracle said.

Again the same word, the one that meant "bad" or "evil" or "strange." This time the form was adverbial.

The oracle straightened up. "You have been alone too long. It isn't natural for a woman to sit by herself on an island."

"I am the guardian. And that one—the woman—has done harm to my tower."

"How?" asked the Voice of the Waterfall.

"She came to the island. She sat in the shadow of the tower."

"No I didn't. It was noon. There wasn't any shade. Right below the tower, maybe, but not where I was."

"You were on the island. Bad people—people who are unlucky—cannot go to a holy place. Not until they have taken part in a ceremony of purification. But there is no way to purify a demon."

"You said if I was a demon, the tower would harm me. I wasn't harmed. How can I be a demon?"

The woman closed her eyes for a moment, frowning. Then she looked at me. "I explained this before. You are a demon. I can see that now. You have to be a demon. Who else would travel with men? And with a woman like Nia? The magic in the tower should have destroyed you. Or—at the very least— given you a terrible pain. But you are fine. Therefore, it must be the tower that has come to harm. And I am the guardian! How will I ever explain?"

Derek said, "This kind of thinking goes around in a circle. If Lixia is a demon, the tower will hurt her. The tower does not hurt her, and this means she is a demon."

I made the gesture of disagreement. "You haven't understood the argument."

"Help me sit up," the woman said. "I can't talk like this."

The oracle took hold of her shoulders. He pulled her into a sitting position. She grunted and twisted, moving the upper portion of her body from side to side. "My arms are numb. I can't feel anything. And how can I talk without using my hands?"

The oracle looked at me.

"Free her. But only her hands."

"I need a knife," he said.

Derek gave him one.

The oracle cut.

"Are they free?" the woman said. "I can't move them."

"They are free."

She leaned forward. Her arms fell apart, and her hands knocked against the sides of the canoe. "I feel nothing! I cannot make them work!"

"Your arms are sleeping," Derek said. He pulled her arms forward, till her hands were resting on her thighs. Then he began to rub one of the arms.

"Aiya! It hurts! It tingles!"

Derek kept rubbing. "Lixia?"

"Yes?"

"Explain the argument. The one I didn't understand. And you—" He looked at Inahooli. "Remember, your feet are tied. Don't try anything humorous."

Inahooli frowned. "This is no time for a joke. And anyway, I am not good at joking. Everyone tells me that."

"The problem is Nia," I said. "I am a demon because I travel with her. And with you and the oracle."

The woman raised her arm. She clenched her hand, then opened it and made the gesture of agreement. Then she began to rub her other arm. Derek stood up and stepped back.

"If I am a demon, then it follows that the tower is my enemy. If the magic of the tower does not harm me, then it follows that my magic must have harmed the tower. —An elegant line of reasoning," I added in English. "I don't see any flaw."

"This is stupid," the oracle said. "You talk and talk, and you don't settle anything. You are all thinking badly and more than that"—he raised one hand for emphasis—"you are fooling around with words. You are like children with bright stones. You toss the words. You line them in rows. Aiya! How pretty! But what does it mean?" He paced around the canoe, then turned and stared at us. "Listen to me, all of you! Among my people there is a woman who is called the go-between. When there is an argument, she goes to the women who are involved. She asks questions. Each woman tells her side of the argument. Then the go-between goes off by herself. She thinks over everything she has heard. She picks through the stories, and she throws away anything that seems malicious or foolish. When people argue, they begin to brood. The memory of the argument stays in their minds. It becomes like food that has been stored all winter: half-rotten and full of bugs. And it is hard to tell what is good from the garbage.

143

"But the go-between learns to turn ideas over. She knows how to find the soft spots and the little holes where bugs have burrowed in. She throws away all the bad ideas. Whatever is left is the real reason for the argument. Once she knows that, she can begin to settle the argument."

He paused for a moment. Inahooli opened her mouth. He held up his hand, flat with the palm forward. The gesture meant "stop" or "wait." It was identical with the human gesture.

"Sometimes the go-between can find no good reason for the argument. Then she looks further. Is there a malicious neighbor who has been telling lies or carrying stories? Have the women in the argument done anything that is unlucky or likely to cause anger either in the land of the spirits or in the rest of the village? The go-between keeps looking until she finds a good reason for the argument. Now—" He touched his chest, then straightened his arm, moving it out to the side. I didn't recognize the gesture. It had a formal look, like the gestures used by professional speakers. Maybe it was a gesture reserved for special occasions: feasts and religious ceremonies. "I have been thinking about the reason for this argument. Everything you people have said is stupid. And we have no neighbors here to carry stories and tell lies. Therefore, the cause of this argument is magical."

Inahooli frowned. "You are talking too much. I am getting confused. Everything was simple and clear before you people arrived."

The oracle looked at Derek. "I thought maybe this is happening because of the bracelet. But I gave it back, and I performed a ceremony of propitiation."

I grabbed Derek's arm and pulled on his shirtsleeve. He jerked away from me. Too late. The cuff was open, and the thing on his wrist was visible. It was the bracelet, of course. Sunlight hit it. The metal glittered.

"He watched you last night," I told the oracle. "He saw where you threw the bracelet. This morning he went swimming. Derek never gives up. That's why he has tenure."

"What?" the oracle asked.

"It's difficult to explain."

Derek took off the bracelet. "Okay. You win, Lixia." He tossed the bracelet to the oracle. "Get rid of it. Lixia can watch me to make sure I don't watch you."

"What is this about?" Inahooli asked.

The Voice of the Waterfall answered. "This one"—he waved to Derek—"took the bracelet, and he had no right to. It was a gift to a spirit or demon, whoever inhabits the lake of boiling mud that is to the east of here."

"It belongs to the Trickster." The woman stared at Derek. "You are very unlucky. He does not forget. And it is very hard to get away from him."

"You see?" said the oracle. "There is always a good reason for everything. This"—he held up the bracelet—"is the reason for our argument."

144

"Do you believe this?" Derek asked the woman.

She frowned. "No. The Trickster is angry with you. But I am the one who is having the bad luck. That doesn't seem right." She closed her eyes and pressed her lips together. We all waited. After a minute she opened her eyes. "The Groundbird Clan!"

"What?" said Derek.

"Their ceremony follows ours, and we always overshadow them. Our tower is always taller and better-looking. Our dancers and storytellers have more skill. I know they are envious, and the new shamaness was born in their clan—though now, of course, she belongs to the Clan of the First Magician. But a woman does not forget what she learned as a child in the tent of her mother. Yes!" She made the gesture of affirmation. "She has performed some kind of magic rite and made this happen." She looked at the oracle. "You were right about the malicious neighbors. I should have thought of this before. There is nothing wrong with the tower. She drove me crazy with magic and made me think the tower is ruined."

"What about the bracelet?" the oracle said.

"That will certainly cause bad luck, but not to me. No, this is due to the Groundbird Clan." She fell quiet, obviously brooding.

"You said, the groundbird stole fire from the sky."

She looked at me, then made the gesture of agreement.

"Did you see the moon last night? It is on fire. Could that have anything to do with what is happening here? Could it be an omen? A sign of magic?"

"No." She paused. "Yes. Maybe. I have never been good with omens. Someone else has to explain them. I never understand what they mean. I have to get back to the tower. If the shamaness is trying to drive me crazy, then I must try to be ordinary. I have to go back to my usual behavior. I have to do what I'm supposed to do." She reached down and pulled at the fabric that held her feet. "Help me! I can't stay here. Who knows what is happening to the tower?"

The oracle cut her free. She pushed herself up on her knees, then tried to get up on one foot. She couldn't. "My ankles don't work."

"To hell with it," said Derek. He grabbed the woman under the arms and pulled her up. "Hold on to me." He lifted her out of the canoe. "Can you stand?"

"No."

He kept one arm around her. "Lean on me. Try to walk."

She stumbled forward.

"Okay. Keep going."

They walked back and forth. I watched and tried to figure out what had happened. What had we been talking about? What had been resolved?

After a while she was able to walk on her own. She made the gesture that indicated completion and then the gesture that meant gratitude. "I will go

145

now. The tower must be guarded. And if you are willing to take my advice, get rid of the bracelet. Give it back to the Trickster, or else he will cause you a lot of trouble." She pushed one of the canoes out into the water, jumped in, and began to paddle. In a minute or two she was gone, out of sight among the reeds.

"I am going to hide the bracelet," the oracle said. "Lixia, you watch that man. He cannot be trusted." The oracle walked away.

I looked at Derek.

He grinned and shrugged. "I seem to be getting a bad reputation."

"Uh-huh. And you deserve it. I've always heard that you were first-rate in the field. Well, if this is a sample . . ."

He began to frown, drawing down his thick blond eyebrows.

"You interfered with a ceremony. You stole something that's magical or—at least—owned by a magical being. Are you out of your mind? How could you risk your relationship with the oracle? He's an excellent informant. Do you think people like that grow on trees?"

"He never would have known except for you. You decided it was time for a big revelation."

I thought for a moment. "That's true enough."

"I ought to be angry with you, Lixia. I've lost a valuable artifact, and I'm going to have to spend a lot of time convincing the oracle that I am not—most of the time—a thief. Well—" He made the gesture that meant "so be it." "I'll talk him around. And I don't believe in holding a grudge. So what do you say we forget this?"

I laughed. The man was superb. After everything he'd done, he was willing to forgive me. "Okay. Do you want to shake on it?" I held out my hand. We shook.

"I'm getting hungry," Derek said. "What do you say we check the fish traps?"

I made the gesture of agreement. We waded out. The traps were empty, though something had paid a visit to them. The bait was gone.

"Dammit," I said.

We waded back to shore, bringing the traps with us.

The oracle came down the beach. His hands were empty. He had gotten rid of the bracelet. "No fish?"

"Not a thing."

"Aiya!" He paused and scratched his nose. "We should have asked the crazy woman if she had anything to spare. Well, I have seen plants that are edible. We will gather them."

Derek shook his head, then made the gesture that meant "no." "You two go. It's time I began to think about hunting. I'll look for wood. Maybe I can make a new bow or a spear."

146

I went with the oracle. We dug roots and gathered berries. He told me stories about the various kinds of vegetation: how the bloodroot got its color and why the sunleaf turned always toward the sun and why no man would eat any part of the *bubaia* vine, though women relished it.

Late in the afternoon we went back to camp. Derek was there. He had a long piece of wood. "A spear," he said.

We roasted the bloodroots. They were pale orange when we put them in the fire. By the time we raked them out, they had turned dark red. They had a sweet flavor and a mealy texture. Imagine a potato with the taste of a ripe sweet pepper. Not bad, I thought. But they needed butter.

Derek stripped the bark off his piece of wood and scraped the wood with a knife, cutting away irregularities I couldn't even see. Then he sat and twisted the bark into cord.

"This man is skillful," the oracle said. "Even though he has no hair, he knows the things a man has to know."

Derek glanced up and grinned, then went back to twisting.

"Though I don't understand," the oracle said, "why he likes to show his teeth. He does it over and over."

"It is an expression of pleasure or happiness," I said.

"Oh," said the oracle.

Night came. The wind was off the lake. It carried bugs to us: a new variety, tiny and numerous.

I cursed and waved my hands.

"Ignore them," Derek said.

I moved closer to the fire. Smoke swirled around me, and the bugs left me alone. But now—of course—my eyes were watering. I looked at the oracle. "Don't they bother you?"

"Yes," he said. "But there is nothing to be done. A lake like this always has bugs. And these ones do not bite. That is the best we can hope for." He opened his mouth in a really wide yawn and I saw his canines. They were long and sharp. No wonder these people did not express happiness by grinning. Those teeth looked menacing. "Are we going to keep watch?"

"Derek?" I asked.

"Yes. I'm not certain we did the right thing by letting that woman go. She gives me a humorous feeling. I don't like her aura."

"We couldn't keep her tied up for days," I said. "Anyway, she has a real problem to deal with now. Her enemies in the Groundbird Clan." I grinned.

The oracle lay down. I watched Derek. He split the piece of wood at one end and wedged the knife in, the blade pointing out. Then he wound the cord around the split wood and the knife. "Crude but effective. I hope." He kept winding and knotting. I put more branches on the fire. Then I lay down.

147

I woke. Something was biting my hand. A mosquito. I slapped and got the little varmint. At the same moment I remembered that it could not possibly be a mosquito. I looked at the fire. It was a heap of coals, glowing dimly, not giving off much smoke at all. Off to the west above the lake the Great Moon shone. It was getting close to full. I squinted and thought I saw a line above the upper edge. It was curved like a handle, going up and over the terminator, then back down—from sunlight into shadow. Derek had better eyes than I did. To me it was just barely visible.

"Goddammit!" Another biter got me on the neck. I looked around for wood. There wasn't any. I couldn't rebuild the fire.

I lay down and put my arm over my face, trying to protect it. The bugs hummed around me. They didn't bite often, but the sound and the expectation kept me awake. I gave up finally. It was time for a walk. Maybe I would find a late-night store that sold bug repellent or one of those hats with a veil made of mosquito netting.

I started toward the reeds. The wind was still blowing. Leaves rustled, and the grove was full of moving shadows. Here and there a beam of moonlight penetrated the foliage, and I could make out a branch or a stem of monster grass. But for the most part I saw very little, except for the moon ahead of me and the lake aglitter with yellow light. A lovely evening, except for the bugs.

When I was a short distance from camp—thirty meters at the most— hands grabbed my neck. I tried to yell and couldn't. The hands pressed in, choking. I grabbed at them. I couldn't break the grip. "Unh," said the person in back of me. It was a deep, low, satisfied sound. The person turned, dragging me around, and slammed my body against something that was hard.

The person let go. A moment later I was on the ground, belly down with my face pressed against something that felt lumpy. A root? The base of a tree?

The person rolled me onto my back. I kept still. Maybe he or she would think I was already dead. He or she leaned close. I heard heavy breathing, then smelled the person's breath.

Mouthwash, I thought.

More heavy breathing. I had a sense the person was going to touch me. Someone shouted nearby.

The person straightened up. A moment later he or she was gone.

My throat hurt. So did my shoulder and my arm. I inhaled slowly and carefully. So far, so good. My lungs still seemed to work. I exhaled, then raised myself up on one elbow. I could move. My neck was not broken.

I turned my head and felt a twinge of pain. The camp. Where was it? I saw a dim red glow. The fire. I got up on my knees. As I did so a figure jumped in front of the glow, visible for a moment. Then it was gone.

What?

There was something next to me. I touched it. Monster grass. A big smooth stem. That must have been what I'd hit when my attacker swung me around. I'd been picked up and slammed against a tree, the way a human would knock a shoe against a post to get off dry mud.

Aiya! I climbed to my feet, bracing myself against the stem of the monster grass. For a moment I felt dizzy. I closed my eyes and tried to breathe evenly, but not deeply.

"Monster!" It was a scream. Inahooli. That lunatic.

I opened my eyes. Next to the fire two figures struggled. They were on the ground, rolling over and over. I couldn't make out who they were.

I began to walk. It was possible, though I still felt dizzy. The campfire— and the two figures—went in and out of focus.

A voice cried, "Help me!"

It was the oracle. He was in the fight. But where was Derek? I reached the edge of the camp and looked around. There he was. Three meters away. He lay on his back, half in moonlight and half in shadow. His hair was loose and had fallen forward. Long, pale, and tangled, it covered most of his face. I bent and brushed it to one side. His eyes were closed. There was blood around his nose and mouth.

"Help!" the oracle cried again.

I saw Derek's spear near him on the ground. The blade shone faintly in the moonlight. He must have dropped it when Inahooli got him. I picked it up and walked around the fire, moving carefully. There was something wrong with my sense of balance.

Inahooli was on top. It had to be her. She wore a new tunic, pale with a lot of embroidery. The oracle had nothing like that. She straddled him. Her hands were on his face. I thought I saw her thumbs go into his eyes. The oracle screamed. I raised the spear and drove it into her back.

She cried out. There was fury in the sound. No pain. She twisted, trying to see who had done this thing. I let go of the spear. The oracle pushed up. She tumbled off him. A moment later he was on his feet. She was on the ground, on her side, groaning, beginning to feel the pain.

"Are you all right?" the oracle asked.

"No. Find out how Derek is." I went down on my knees next to the woman. The knife blade had gone into her lower back under the ribs. What had it hit? I had no idea. There wasn't much blood. Should I try to pull the spear out? Or would that increase the bleeding? My eyes went out of focus. I lifted my head and breathed fresh air. Inahooli was moving, trying to find a comfortable position. "Be still," I said.

"Demon."

149

I took her wrist and tried to find a pulse. She pulled her arm away. "Leave me alone." She grimaced. "Aiya! The pain!" She closed her eyes and pressed her lips together.

I took hold of her wrist again. This time she didn't pull away. I found the pulse. But how was I going to measure it? Not in beats per minute. I didn't have a way to measure time. And I didn't know what was normal for her people. Fifty beats a minute? Seventy? Or a hundred? I would have to compare her pulse rate with that of another native. "Oracle?"

"Give us a minute," Derek said in English.

I looked around. He was standing, holding on to the oracle with one hand. With the other hand he rubbed his forehead. "Ouch!"

"A concussion?" I said.

"Maybe. I can remember what happened. I think I can. That argues against a concussion. Maybe you had better check the size of my pupils."

"Okay."

The oracle said, "Speak a language I can understand."

Derek made the gesture of assent. "I was checking the grove, going in a circle, making sure everything was okay.

"When I got back to camp, you were gone, Lixia. I called your name and got no answer. That worried me—a little, not enough. I thought Inahooli was a fool. I didn't think she'd be able to get past me. I went looking for you.

"I found Inahooli." He sounded puzzled, as if he could not understand how any of this could have happened to Derek Sea Warrior, Ph.D. "I didn't see her coming. She appeared out of nowhere and grabbed the spear from me. She just grabbed and pulled and it was gone. She used it as a club. Right across the face." He felt his nose. "I don't think it's broken."

"Is that where the blood came from?"

"What blood?" He wiped below his nose, then looked at his hand. "Oh. That blood. I think so. The thing I don't understand is—why didn't she stab me?"

"She was going to," the oracle said. "After you fell. But you yelled before she hit you. I woke up and saw what was happening. I got to her before she drove the spear in. I jumped on her back and bit her shoulder. That made her drop the spear."

Inahooli groaned. I was still holding her wrist. Her pulse seemed slower than before. "Oracle, come here. I want to find out how quickly your heart is beating."

"Why?"

I thought for a moment. How was I going to explain? "When one of my people is sick, her heart beats differently."

"Than what?"

150

"Than it does when she is well. And a wise person—a person skilled in healing—can listen to the heart or feel the way it beats and tell how sick the woman is."

"I know that," the oracle said. "Remember, my mother is a shamaness. She taught me a few things when I lived in her house. But I haven't been injured. Why do you want to know how my heart is doing?"

"To compare." I waved at Inahooli with my free hand. "I don't know what her heartbeat ought to be. I don't know what is right for your people."

The oracle glanced at Derek. "Can you stand by yourself?"

"I think so." Derek let go of him.

The oracle walked over to Inahooli. He crouched down and took her wrist from me. "We don't belong to the same people, Inahooli and I. But all hearts beat in the same fashion." He paused, tilting his head and frowning. "It is going a little too fast, but remember she has been fighting." He laid the wrist down. "We will pull out the spear and bind up the wound. Even though I am a man and she is crazy, I cannot walk away and leave her in this condition."

Inahooli opened her eyes. "You are all demons."

"Don't talk," the oracle said. He took hold of her tunic where the spear had cut it and pulled gently. The fabric tore. In a moment or two he had the tunic off. He gave it to me. "Tear it in pieces."

I did what he asked. It wasn't easy. I kept running into embroidery. Fortunately I had sharp incisors. I bit through the threads, then went back to tearing. When I was done the oracle said, "We need more cloth."

What did we have? My shirt and Derek's. I looked at my comrade. He was still upright, but he hadn't moved any closer to us. He seemed—in the dim light—to be swaying. He looked worse than I felt. I unfastened my shirt and pulled it off.

The oracle looked at me. "What is that across your chest?"

How does one explain a brassiere to an alien? I tugged at the shirt. There was a weak seam. It tore. "I'll tell you later," I said.

Derek walked over to us. He stumbled once.

"How are you?" I asked.

"Okay. Dizzy and confused. I didn't really expect her to come back. I was only being careful. Why'd she do it?"

I finished tearing, then I made the gesture of uncertainty.

The oracle had his hand on the spear. He began to pull. Inahooli gasped. "It will be over soon," he told her. He glanced at me. "Have the cloth ready." He pulled again. The spear came out. I saw the blade, covered with dark blood. He laid the weapon down, then leaned forward and peered at the wound. "It is bleeding, but slowly. It is a flow, not a rush. That is a good sign. Give me the cloth."

I handed him a piece of tunic. He made it into a pad and tied it in place over the wound, using the rest of the cloth, the beautifully embroidered pieces of native fabric and my denim shirt.

A bug got me on my bare shoulder. I slapped it.

"Wood," said Derek. "There's a tree—I guess you would call it a tree— down and dry not far from here. Come on."

We went into the dark grove. Derek found his piece of monster grass: a huge fallen stem. It lay in moonlight. There was a growth on it, something analogous to fungus. It looked like coral, delicate and intricate. Pale branches divided and redivided. Either they were translucent or they glowed with their own light. I couldn't tell which. But the thing had a dim radiance. I stared at it. Another bug bit me, this time on the arm. "Let's hurry," I said.

We gathered wood and carried it back to camp. Derek rebuilt the fire. When it was burning brightly, I checked his eyes. The pupils were of equal size. No concussion.

I went over to the oracle. "How is she?"

"Her heartbeat has slowed down. But I do not like the way she breathes. My mother's sister made a noise like that when she had the coughing sickness. She did not live."

I listened. The oracle was right. Inahooli sounded congested, as if she had a bad cold or pneumonia.

"She told me she was cold," the oracle said. "I put Nia's cloak over her. Aiya! It is good that Nia left it!"

Derek spoke in English, "If she doesn't make it, remember it was self-defense."

"I should have hit her over the head or kicked her. Distracted her and given the oracle a chance to get away. Do you have any idea what this is going to do to my karma?"

"I told you before," the oracle said. "Speak a language I can understand."

"This will bring bad luck," I said. "To do this—to harm another person— is to act like an animal, without reason or compassion. People—true people— don't harm each other."

"Do you really believe that?" Derek asked. "And if so, what about the man in the canyon? He's dead, and—from what I heard—you helped."

"I didn't intend to kill him, and I did not deliver the fatal blow. Nia did. I don't know what was going through her mind. In any case, that's her problem, not mine. I try not to impose my system of ethics on the people I study. Here—" I paused. "I drove the blade in. So it's my problem and my karma. And I'm not entirely sure what I was intending. Maybe I wanted to kill Inahooli. I never expected to become a Buddha, but I thought I'd do better than this."

"What is a Buddha?" the oracle asked.

"A person who understands what is going on. Or maybe a person who doesn't understand what is going on and doesn't care."

"That makes no sense."

Inahooli groaned and moved restlessly. Her eyes opened, but she didn't look at us. She was staring up at nothing.

Derek leaned forward. "Inahooli? Can you hear what I'm saying?"

She looked at me. "I thought when autumn came I would be an important woman."

"Why did you come back?"

She moved her head slightly. Her eyes met his. "Do you think I believed you? Those crazy stories? I knew that you were demons."

I said, "You mean you were pretending? The story about the shamaness was a lie?"

"A trick." She pulled her lips back, so her teeth were exposed. It was not a smile. "You are very stupid demons." She paused for a moment and breathed in and out. Her eyes narrowed. "The pain is terrible." She looked at the oracle. "Will I live through this?"

"I don't know."

She blinked. "Aiya! The luck that I've been having!"

"What do you expect when you creep up on people in the darkness and try to do them harm? What spirit will approve of behavior like that?"

"I was angry."

The oracle frowned. "That is no excuse. When I get angry, I throw rocks or jump up and down and scream or—if I am very angry—I make up a nasty song and sing it as loudly as I can. That is the right way to be angry. It is not right to throw people around. Only crazy men do that."

"I tried to yell and jump up and down. It did no good. There was too much anger." Inahooli frowned. "It was like the lake of boiling mud—in me, in my gut, churning and exploding."

Derek said in English, "Bicarbonate of soda."

"Be quiet," I said.

"I could not endure the anger. I had to do something big." She closed her eyes a moment, then opened them. "I am not going to talk anymore. It hurts. It is too much trouble." She closed her eyes again.

I shivered. Derek put more wood on the fire. Flames leaped up. "It's burning too quickly. I don't think it will last till morning." He looked at me. "You're cold, aren't you?"

I made the gesture of agreement. "And the bugs are getting to me. They must have decided I smell like food."

He unfastened his shirt and took it off. "Here."

"What are you going to do?"

153

"Stay in motion." He looked at the lake. "The moon is still up. I think I have time. You stay here, Lixia." He walked into the darkness.

I opened my mouth to call after him, then decided what the heck. I put the shirt on.

The oracle said, "Where is he going?"

I made the gesture that meant "who knows?"

"He certainly moves quickly when he decides he ought to do something."

"Yes."

Inahooli groaned and bit her lip. The oracle took hold of her wrist. "The beat is getting weaker. I think she will die."

She opened her eyes. Her pupils had expanded, and I could barely see her irises. There was a little orange in the corners, but the middle of each eye was dark. "No."

"Yes," said the oracle. "I do not lie."

She closed her eyes and concentrated on breathing. It was becoming more difficult for her. Strange! To watch a person struggle to do something as easy and as ordinary as drawing a breath.

I got up and put more wood on the fire. Then I came back and sat down. I listened. Each inhalation was a gasp. When she exhaled I heard a whistle. The air was coming out through some kind of obstruction. A liquid. Blood. I must have gotten a lung when I drove the spear into her.

The breathing went on for another hour or two. I got up once and put more wood on the fire, then stood leaning over the flames. Hot air rose around me. My goose bumps disappeared, and feeling returned to my hands. Odd! That I was so cold. It was, after all, the middle of summer. But the night was cool, and there was a wind blowing. The bugs were gone. The wind must have blown them away.

I went back to Inahooli. I sat down and listened. Her breath went in and out. The sound was harsh and desperate. Toward dawn it became erratic. There were pauses, as if she were drifting in and out of sleep—the breath stopping for a moment as she came awake. But she wasn't ever really awake. I rubbed my hands. They were numb with cold. The oracle sat quietly.

At dawn the breathing stopped. The oracle felt her wrist and then her neck. "No beat." He stood up. "Aiya! I am stiff." He stretched and yawned, then rubbed his arms. "My feet are numb." He hopped from one foot to the other.

I got up and stretched. My neck and shoulder hurt, and there were minor things wrong all over my body: aches, twinges, areas of stiffness.

I looked at Inahooli. I could make out her position, even under the cloak. She lay on her side, her knees drawn up and her arms folded against her chest. Her head was bent forward. Her chin was tucked in. I couldn't see her face.

I was a killer. The real thing this time, not merely an accomplice. I looked east. Red light shone between two stems of monster grass. The sun was coming up.

The oracle stopped hopping. "This is a good time for a song. One came to me while I watched her." He pointed at Inahooli, then sang, using the language of gifts. I was able to get most of the song. Later he explained the verses I had not understood.

> "Aiya! Hai-aiya!
> What a situation!
> Even you, Inahooli,
> don't deserve
> to end like this.
>
> "Where are your sisters?
> They ought to mourn you,
> rocking and moaning
> at the entrance to your house.
>
> "Where are your cousins?
> They ought to mourn you,
> bringing gifts
> to bury in your grave.
>
> "Aiya! Hai-aiya!
> What a situation!
> Even you, Inahooli,
> don't deserve
> to end like this."

He paused for a moment, frowning and scratching the back of his neck. "There is one more verse," he said. "I just heard it in my mind. Give me a moment to arrange the words." He bit his thumbnail, then sang:

> "This is a man's death,
> to die without presents.
> This is a man's death,
> to die on the plain."

The sun finished rising. Derek came up from the lake. He was carrying a pair of saddlebags.

"Where have you been?" I asked.

"On the island, the one you visited." He set down the bags and opened one. "I'll trade you. My shirt for this." He pulled out a tunic. It was cream-white with blue and red embroidery.

I undid the fasteners on Derek's shirt. "Do you have something for Inahooli? I'd like to get Nia's cloak back. It doesn't seem right for it to be on her."

He glanced at the body. "Dead?"

"Yes."

He opened the other bag and pulled out a cloak. It was rust-brown with a yellow border. The oracle pulled Nia's cloak off Inahooli. I had a brief glimpse of the body, naked except for the dark fur and the bandage made of denim. Then it was gone from sight.

Derek said, "There was food on the island. Dried meat and fruit. I filled a bag."

"This has to be wrong, Derek. We're stealing from the dead."

He went down on his knees and put his hands on his thighs. For a moment or two he remained in that position, his arms braced, his head a little bent, looking at the body under the rust-brown cloak. "Listen to me, Inahooli. We take these things because we need them. We are cold. We are hungry. Two of us have traveled farther than you can imagine, and we may never make it home. Believe me, we aren't doing this out of malice or anger or any bad emotion, but out of need." He paused. "I promise you we will use what we take with respect. We won't be ungrateful, and we certainly won't use this as an excuse to go on a journey of strength.

"This happened the way it happened according to the turning of the wheel. Accept it, Inahooli. Don't be angry with us." He stood up and walked back to me.

"Journey of strength?" I said.

"Power trip," he said in English. "I couldn't think of a better way to translate it." He went back to the language of gifts. "I'd like my shirt back."

I gave it to him. He handed me the tunic in return. I pulled it over my head. The fabric was soft and warm, like fine wool. It had a furry aroma, the smell of the aliens.

"I'll get the food," Derek said. "After we eat, we can bury her."

We dug a grave in the sand by the lake, using the oars as shovels. Derek and the oracle got Inahooli and carried her to the grave. Hard work. They gasped and grunted and almost dropped her once. I carried the cloak, which was easy. They laid her in the grave. I laid the cloak over her.

"Wait for me," the oracle said. He walked into the grove.

I rubbed my shoulder, then looked at Derek. He had washed his face, but he still looked pretty awful. His nose was red and swollen, and one eye was almost closed. There was a bruise on his forehead above the eye.

"Why did you make that speech to Inahooli? To reassure the oracle?"

He nodded. "And me. One must never take without explaining and never kill without making an apology."

"How civilized are you, anyway?"

He grinned. "Not very."

The oracle came back. He carried food: a strip of dried meat and a handful of fresh berries. He laid these in the grave next to Inahooli. Then he unfastened his necklace of gold and turquoise and laid it next to the food. "Maybe she will be less angry if we give her presents. Though I doubt it. She is the kind that holds on to anger. What a bad way to be!"

We piled sand over Inahooli, then found rocks and put them on top of the sand. When we were done the oracle said, "We ought to perform ceremonies of aversion and purification. But I am not a shamaness. I don't know the ceremonies the holy women learn. I don't even know the ceremonies that men learn to help them after they leave the village. All I know is what the waterfall has told me." He sang:

> "O holy one!
> O being of power!
> Why don't you help me?
> What should I do next?
>
> "O holy one!
> O being of power!
> Why don't you help me?
> Tell me what to do!"

He tilted his head and listened. The wind blew. Reeds rustled. Water lapped the shore. "All I can hear is, 'Take a swim.' Maybe we can wash off what has happened in the last few days."

Derek made the gesture of agreement. The two of them undressed and waded in. They washed in the deep water by the reeds, then swam. I was worried about the cut on my arm. I didn't want to get it wet. And I didn't think my shoulder was up to swimming. I took off my boots and rolled up my jeans and waded in the shallows, looking for shells and polished stones. The stones were uninteresting: black stuff like pumice, worn round or oval. The shells were lovely: tiny spirals, pale lavender or pink. I gathered a dozen, then waded to the beach. I laid the shells on the grave. A ridiculous gesture. What use was the gift? I did not believe in an afterlife, so it wasn't an attempt to buy off Inahooli's anger. And it wasn't enough to buy off my feeling of responsibility.

"Killer," I said out loud.

That mood was dangerous. I refused to give in to it. Why should I? Guilt was not part of my heritage. The senior members of my family had disapproved of it. One must recognize mistakes and acknowledge them and work to break the patterns of behavior that led to them. But guilt was unproductive.

"Life is a process," Theresa had said. She was one of my co-mothers, a medical technician who specialized in psychology. Half the year she worked on a deep-sea mining ship, the *Pacific Aurora*, out of Pearl Harbor. The other half of the year, she helped to raise the junior members of the family. "We make and remake ourselves, responding to changes both external and internal. But guilt is static, as are related ideas and emotions: sin, for example, regret, and maybe shame. Though I am not certain about the effect of shame. But the others anchor you in the past. They hold you, so you can't move freely in the present.

"Imagine guilt as an iron band fastened around something that is growing: the trunk of a tree, the neck of a child. Sooner or later, one of two things must happen. If the band does not break, the growing thing will be deformed.

"Commit yourself to change, Lixia, to living in the present, to making and remaking who you are. Do the best you can. Understand what you do. And do not feel guilty."

Good advice, I told the memory of Theresa. I picked up my boots and walked to our camp.

Inzara

T he oracle went off to gather roots and berries. Derek went for wood, and I sorted through Inahooli's belongings. Two tunics—three, if I counted the one I had on, a leather cloak, a pair of sandals, and a knife. All the tunics had embroidery: geometric patterns. The cloak had a fastener, similar to a fibula, made of bronze and covered with silver. The silver was wearing thin.

"Lixia!" Derek shouted.

I threw down the cloak and ran through the grove. He was at the eastern edge.

"There!" He pointed.

Out on the plain was a rider. He or she was astride a bowhorn. I could make out the animal's long curving horns. A second animal—another bowhorn—followed the first.

"Nia?" I asked.

"I think so."

The rider came closer. I recognized the wide shoulders and the way she rode: easily, comfortably, slouching a little in the saddle. "We have to call Eddie at once," I said.

Derek glanced at me. "Shall I do the talking? I'm a better politician than you are, and we have some explaining to do. The unfortunate death of a native religious leader."

"Okay."

She reached us and dismounted. "Well, I found it." She waved at the bowhorn. "And the gear. I'm hungry. Is there any food?"

"Yes," I said.

"I'll take care of the animals," Derek said. He held out his hand. Nia gave him the reins.

"Where did you get that tunic? And what happened to his face?" She pointed to Derek.

"Inahooli came back."

"Aiya!"

"She came after us at night. We had to kill her. I had to kill her."

"You?" Nia stared at me, her eyes wide open.

"Yes."

Nia was silent for a while. At last she said, "Any unexpected death is bad. A death like this—that happens in a fight—is worse than other kinds. The ghost of the dead person is certain to be angry. There is likely to be bad luck. When we get to a place where there is a shamaness, we will ask for ceremonies to placate Inahooli or drive her away. We'd better do something about the man in the canyon as well. Though it doesn't matter in the same way when a man dies suddenly." She frowned. "Did you bury Inahooli?"

"Yes."

"With gifts?"

"Yes. The oracle gave his necklace."

"Good. Maybe there will be no bad luck." Nia did not sound confident. "The woman was crazy and dangerous. She brought this on herself. The spirits will not blame us, and ghosts do not usually travel any great distance. Once we are gone from here, we ought to be safe." Nia made the gesture that meant "I wish, I hope."

We returned to camp. I got out food: dried meat and dried fruit. Nia ate. "Hu! I have been starving on the plain." She leaned back and sighed. "The food is from the woman?"

I made the gesture of agreement. "Derek explained to her."

She looked at the piece of fruit in her hand. After a moment she popped it in her mouth. "I thought about it while I looked for the bowhorn. I thought—at first—that I was responsible for what was happening. But that can't be." She finished chewing and swallowed, then she scratched her nose. "Most of the time, bad luck comes from something that is unexpected or peculiar. Well, I have done strange things and had my share of bad luck. But in this case it was

160

Inahooli who was behaving oddly. We came to her land. We were strangers. But she did not welcome us. Instead she tried to kill us. Now, everyone knows that women do not quarrel with strangers. That is male behavior."

"Women never quarrel with strangers?" I asked.

"Once in a while. Hakht did. She is a bad person." Nia said this firmly with conviction. "And Inahooli did. She was crazy. And I killed the old man who killed Enshi. But ordinary women, women with self-respect, never quarrel except with people they know. Kinfolk and close neighbors. That is the right way to have an argument." Nia ate more fruit. "There is no way to be certain who a stranger is or what will happen if you give her trouble."

It made sense. The people on this planet did not have war—nor, as far as I could tell, any kind of organized theft. When they saw a stranger—a strange woman, at least—they did not have to wonder: Is this person a thief? A killer? Someone who will do us harm? They could instead anticipate with pleasure the gifts and the stories the stranger would bring.

Aggression and exchange were, or seemed to be, entirely separate. How different from Earth. The old Earth, anyway, where it had been legitimate to say, "Property is theft."

Derek walked into camp, carrying our two packs.

"What happened?" Nia asked. "How did Inahooli die?"

He set the packs down and told her. It was a fine report, brief and vivid with a lot of gesturing. "My luck was bad yesterday," he said at the end. "But hers was a lot worse. If things had gone a little more slowly, if she'd had a bit more time, Inahooli would have killed all three of us. Maybe the Trickster had decided that I had suffered enough."

"Who is the Trickster?" Nia asked. "And why does he want to make Derek suffer?"

"Remember the bracelet he found?" I said.

"Yes."

"It belonged to a spirit called the Trickster. Inahooli told Derek the Trickster was certain to be angry and give him a lot of grief."

"Ah!" said Nia.

"I know that spirit," said Derek. "Among my people he is called Coyote."

"I'm not entirely sure of that, Derek. Coyote is a sneak, but he isn't a bad person. I got the impression from Inahooli that the Trickster is bad. Selfish and malevolent. He's like Loki."

"Once again, I don't know what you are talking about," Nia said.

"Don't worry about it. Lixia has a habit of wandering away from whatever people are talking about. She thinks too much, and her thinking goes off in every possible direction."

I gave him the finger.

161

"Is that a gesture your people use?" asked Nia.

"Yes. It is a gesture of disrespect."

"Ah! Let me see it again."

I repeated the gesture. Nia imitated me. "I thought you people had no gestures. It is good to know you are not utterly strange." She looked at Derek. "Is your story over?"

He made the gesture of affirmation.

"Hu! I wish this had not happened. It has." She made the gesture that meant "so be it." "We'll go on tomorrow. I want to get away from here, before her ghost manages to pull free of her body."

"All right," said Derek.

The oracle came back with berries. We ate dinner. Derek called the ship.

"What happened?" asked Eddie. "Where in hell have you been?"

"We encountered some of the local fauna. Four meters tall with claws. Our animals bolted, and we lost them. Our radios were on the animals." Derek looked up. I was watching him. So were Nia and the oracle. "Have you managed to learn the native language, Eddie?"

"No. Why?"

"I have two natives here, and I think they're wondering what I'm saying."

"You let them know about the radios?"

"Yes."

"We were going to try to keep the natives ignorant of our technology," Eddie said. He spoke slowly and clearly, his voice even. "It was part of our policy of noninterference."

"Eddie, it wasn't possible. We couldn't keep creeping off into the darkness. 'Pardon me, I'm going to take this box and go off and pee. I'll be back in half an hour. Oh, by the way, I talk to myself while urinating, so if you hear voices in the night, don't worry.'"

Eddie said, "This is getting to be more and more of a mess." He paused. "Do you have anything to report?"

"Yes," said Derek. "A native attacked us. She's dead."

"What?"

Derek told the story. After he finished Eddie said, "I want to see what your recorders got. Transmit information."

Derek pulled off his medallion and put it into the radio. He looked at me. "I keep forgetting about the medallions."

"Don't worry, Derek. You can talk your way out of almost anything." I took off my medallion and tossed it to him. "Send that up, too."

A couple of minutes later Eddie came back on. "We'll get back to you after we've looked at your information. I warn you, I'm not happy about this. I am going to ask Lysenko if there is any place near you where he can land."

Lysenko was the senior rocket plane pilot: a man with an unfortunate name. Biologists laughed at him.

"Are you going to pull us out?" asked Derek.

"I want that option. Ask Nia and the oracle if they know of any place. A dry lakebed is best. A lake with water might be possible, if it's deep enough."

"Okay."

"And try to stay out of trouble for a while."

Derek turned the radio off. He got up and stretched. I could see the tension in his body. "One trouble with Eddie—he was born to sit at a desk. He can organize, supervise, analyze, and criticize, but he doesn't know what it's like in the field."

"What did your box say?" Nia asked. "Why is Derek angry?"

I stood up. "You explain, Derek. I'm tired of talking about Inahooli." I walked to the edge of the plain. Before me was the plain, dark and featureless. Above me the sky was full of stars. I listened to night noises: rustles in the branches and a low buzzing in the pseudo-grass. I thought about my career. There was a chance it was ruined. Who would trust me in the field after this? Especially if Eddie and the others on the soc. sci. committee decided I had been really out of line. They could attach a reprimand to my record or insist that I undergo group criticism.

Now that was an unpleasant idea. I had seen a group in action once. I'd made friends with a man on the long trip out of the solar system, before we went to sleep. A master chef from China. He had the moody personality that one associates with artists, and an extraordinary face: pale and smooth, like a mask carved out of white jade. His hair was black, long and thick and lustrous. When he cooked, it was tucked up in a cap. But when he sat and talked with friends, it fell around his face and touched his shoulders. I was maybe a little in love with him. I was certainly in love with his Mu Shu Iguana.

He woke at the edge of this system and realized—finally—what he had done. Left his family, his home, his society, his planet. When he returned, everything would be changed.

He got depressed—which was hardly surprising. Most of us got depressed at one point or another. But De was a real expert at depression. He brooded the same way as he cooked: with skill and passion.

He started drinking, which led to trouble on the job.

Most of his colleagues were Chinese, and they insisted on group criticism. I went to lend moral support—to De, not to his critics. We met in a small room with celadon walls. De sat in front, facing twenty people. Most were kitchen workers, a few were people he knew outside work, and a few were comparative strangers. The meeting was open to everyone, and everyone could speak. The voice of the masses had to be heard.

One by one the kitchen workers spoke. De had missed a lot of work, forcing others to cover for him. He had refused advice and constructive criticism.
His attitude was negative. He had argued with decisions made democratically
by the kitchen workers. He had lied about his drinking.

Someone from his dormitory got up. De had come in at all hours and
made a lot of noise, waking other people. Once he had thrown up in the hall,
right outside the speaker's cabin.

Another person—a blonde with a Scandinavian accent—got up and spoke
about the evils of drink. A couple of other people got up and argued with her.
The problem wasn't alcohol, it was the lack of a decent recreational program.
It was the Western cult of individuality. It was the miserable performance of
the psychology team.

De sat and listened. His face was paler than usual. There were dark patches under his eyes. He looked exhausted and unhappy. At last, when everyone
was done, he stood up. He apologized to his colleagues, to the people on the
ship, and to the entire human race. He promised to mend his ways, to come
to work promptly, and to go into therapy. Finally, he thanked everyone in
the room for their concern and good advice. As far as I could tell, he was
being sincere. My family had been in the West too long. I would never really understand the Chinese.

The senior nutritionist stood up and praised De for his new constructive
and cooperative attitude. The meeting ended. I went to find a drink.

Never, I thought. I would never go through group criticism. I wasn't sure
what I'd do if the committee insisted on it. I couldn't quit nor could they fire me.
Not this far from Earth. Most likely, if it came to a crisis, they'd relieve me of my
duties and refer me to the committee in charge of nonmechanical maintenance.
I'd wash walls or replace cracked tiles until it was time to leave the system.

Once again I was thinking too far ahead. Stop it! I told myself and went
back to camp. Derek sat by the fire, his knees up, his arms around them.

"Well?"

He glanced at me and grinned. "The oracle offered to talk to Eddie and
explain it isn't wrong to kill in self-defense. He seems to think Eddie is some
kind of idiot. And Nia said there is a river that goes between the country of
the Amber People and her country, the land of the Iron People. At one point
the river spreads out into a long narrow lake. The lake is deep and there are
no islands. It might be a safe place to land."

"How far?"

"She isn't entirely certain. Nine or ten days, she thinks."

"Do we go there?" I asked.

He made the gesture of affirmation. "It will make Eddie happy, and it's on
the way to Nia's people."

Sunlight woke me, slanting into the grove. A gray line of smoke curled up through it, moving languidly. The oracle crouched by the fire. He was skinning a fish.

"You reset the traps," I said.

"Yes, and we have been lucky. This is a greenfish. It is delicious, especially when baked. Go and perform your morning ceremony."

I obeyed him, doing yoga by the lake. I was still very stiff. But as far as I could tell, no major damage had been done. Talk about lucky!

When I got back to camp, Nia was pulling on one of Inahooli's tunics. It was dull blue, embroidered in orange: a pattern of triangles. She put on her own belt and her knife with the bone handle and the sheath of dark leather. After that she tugged at the hem of the tunic and smoothed it across her chest. "Hu! This is better! There is something to be said for new clothes with bright colors and no bad aroma."

We ate and broke camp, following the trail around the lake, then back onto the plain. To the west and south were clouds. They were high up, fluffy and thin, arranged in flocks or clusters. In the north the sky was clear. I could make out Hani Akhar.

I thought about the *China Clipper*: corridors and little rooms and far too many people. There would be no sky and no wind and no birds, except in the aviary. Maybe I should make a run for it, toss away my radio and AV recorder, and vanish into the wilderness. That was one way to avoid group criticism— unless, of course, they caught me.

I looked around at the plain. It was—or seemed to be—almost empty. A few orange bugs fluttered above the pseudo-grass. A few birds soared in the sky. Way off in the distance I saw a herd of animals. They were black dots moving through the yellow and green vegetation. I had no idea what they were.

This land was too vast and too alien. I couldn't turn my back on my civilization and live utterly alone without hope or help from my people.

That night we camped on top of a low hill. There was nothing in sight except for pseudo-grass. We ate Inahooli's food. Eddie did not call.

"Should we call him?" I asked.

Derek made the gesture that meant "no." "We don't have to go hunting for aggravation. It will find us, more than we want or need."

I made the gesture of agreement.

In the middle of the night rain began to fall. Thunder grumbled, and there were flashes of lightning. We huddled under our cloaks and ponchos and got wet.

By morning the rain had stopped, but the air remained humid, and the vegetation on the plain was beaded with water. It bent over the narrow path.

165

Derek and I pushed through it, getting wet a second time. The natives, riding in back of us, looked as if they were more comfortable, but not by much.

"A person is coming," Nia said.

I looked ahead. The trail was a dark line winding through the vegetation. A bowhorn moved along it. A person rode the animal.

"A man," said Nia. "He travels alone."

"No," said Derek. "There is someone else—off on the plain." He pointed north.

I peered and saw a dot moving down a slope. "Why aren't they together?"

"I don't know," Nia said. "Maybe they are both men."

The trail went into a hollow, and I lost sight of the riders, though only for a few minutes. We came out onto a low rise. A bowhorn stood in the middle of the trail: a large animal, dun-colored with a white spot on its chest. Its horns were as black and shiny as obsidian.

Derek and I stopped. The two natives rode up on either side of us and reined their animals. I looked at the bowhorn's rider.

A male, almost certainly. He was wide and tall with dark, shaggy fur. His tunic was like the one I had on: cream-colored with geometric embroidery. On his arms were thick gold bracelets, and he wore a necklace of gold and amber.

He looked us over calmly, then spoke in the language of gifts. "I see that you have met my sister." His voice was deep and soft.

"Inahooli," Derek said.

The man made the gesture of assent. "I am Toohala Inzara of the Clan of the Ropemaker and the People of Amber." He waved to the north. "My brother Tzoon is off in that direction. I haven't seen my brother Ara for a couple of days. But he is out there somewhere, probably to the south. How is our sister?"

"As well as can be expected," Derek said. "She has been alone for a long time."

The man made the gesture of agreement. "She has always been edgy and hard to get along with. I was hoping her temperament would improve, now that she has—at long last—achieved something of importance. But it hasn't?"

"No," said Derek.

"Aiya! Such a difficult person! If you don't mind, I'll be going. I don't like being with so many people. And two of you—I have to say it—are very odd-looking. That makes me even more uneasy." He looked us over again. "It's too bad Ara didn't see you. He is the curious one." He turned his animal off the trail and rode around us.

Derek started walking, more quickly than before. The rest of us followed. After a while Derek said, "He's going to visit Inahooli. Is that possible?"

166

"No one among my people would do a thing like that," said Nia. "Though I went to find my brother years ago."

The oracle said, "I visit with my mother from time to time. But I am holy and a little crazy as well. An ordinary man would not go looking for his relatives."

"This man must not be ordinary," Derek said. "He will reach the lake tomorrow in the afternoon and find the grave. What will he do then?"

Nia made the gesture of uncertainty. "I do not know."

"He was huge," I said. "Are most of your men that big?"

"No," said Nia.

"Thank God," said Derek. "I was beginning to think of meeting three brothers the size of gorillas and trying to explain to them what happened to their sister."

"As big as what?" asked Nia.

"Gorillas. They are relatives of ours, but much bigger than we are." Derek was still walking quickly. "He'll be a couple of days behind us when he starts."

"What are you talking about?" I asked.

"Inzara. If he decides to come after us. Maybe three days, if we're lucky and he spends time at the lake. Nia? How fast can a bowhorn travel?"

"The Amber People follow the herds. They understand animals and they understand patience. He will know better than to push his bowhorn too hard. Most likely, he will keep to a pace that is twice ours."

"I used to hate problems like this. Bob has twice as many pieces of fruit as Alice, who is half again as tall as Krishna. How many days until Inzara catches up with us?"

"What is he talking about now?" asked the oracle.

"Nothing important." I thought for a while. "It'll take him two days, Derek. We ought to start worrying in the evening of the day after tomorrow. No, the day after that."

"Okay. We are going to move as quickly as we can. Maybe the river is closer than we think."

"Are you frightened?" I asked.

"Yes, of course," he said in English. "If we kill any more natives, we are going to end up on the ship—cleaning out sewer lines, most likely. Or maybe cleaning cages in the laboratories. Anyway, we'll be finished down here forever." He glanced at me. "I bend rules a lot, and I operate close to the edge. But I have no intention of getting myself in serious trouble."

"Why do you bend rules?"

He laughed. "To prove I can."

We traveled till sunset, then made camp. The clouds parted and the Great Moon shone down on us. It was a little past full. Derek peered up at it. "The eruption must have ended."

167

"Uh-huh." I got out my one remaining human shirt and looked it over. A little dirty and with one tear. I decided to put it on.

"It's too late," said Derek. "That man has already seen Inahooli's shirt."

"Nonetheless . . ." I changed into my shirt and folded Inahooli's, putting it away.

My radio rang. I turned it on.

"First the good news," said Eddie. "The committee has decided to approve—with regret—your action in relation to Inahooli. You had no choice. Maybe if you hadn't been half-unconscious, you could have figured out another way to stop her. But it was her fault that you were in no condition to think. Her karma was working itself out. There should not be any increase in your karmic burden, at least in the opinion of the committee." I could hear a certain aloofness in his voice. Eddie had nothing against the various Asian religions—in their place, which was not a committee in charge of establishing policy for a scientific team. "Nothing bad is going on your record."

I felt my body relax. I let my breath out in a sigh, then rubbed the back of my neck. "Okay. What is the bad news?"

"There are three pieces. Derek got a reprimand for that silliness about the bracelet."

I looked over at Derek. He shrugged.

"However, that is not going to slow down anyone with his list of publications. The second piece of bad news is—the committee has decided to recommend a shipwide discussion of our policy re the natives."

"Nonintervention?" I asked.

"Uh-huh." Eddie sounded grim. "They want to reopen the question. I really would like you up here, or at least I would like the option. And that brings me to the third piece of bad news. Lysenko has gone over all the information we have about your part of the continent. The nearest place he is willing to land a plane is to the west of you. It's a river that widens into a lake. He says it's not good, but it's possible."

"How far?" I asked.

"Our best estimate is eight days. I am going to try to stall the first meeting of the all-ship committee."

"That isn't the worst of it, Eddie."

"Oh, no? What is?"

"We met a native today. Inahooli's brother. He is going to visit his sister."

"Does he know you met her?"

"I had on a tunic that belonged to Inahooli. So did Nia. He recognized the clothes. That didn't bother him. The natives are always exchanging gifts. But when he finds the grave . . ."

"Oh, damn."

"And he has two brothers. They are traveling together or—at least—in the same direction. We may have three large angry natives after us."

Eddie was silent for a minute or two. "What do you plan to do?"

Derek said, "Run like hell and hope they don't follow."

"I guess that's the best idea. The committee is right about one thing. There have been too many incidents. I can't figure out why." Eddie sounded plaintive.

"You aren't thinking," Derek said. "Consider the people who've been having all the trouble. Me. Harrison. Gregory. All men. We all ran into the same problem: the social role of adult males. I don't know how Santha managed to avoid trouble. Do his people allow men into their village?"

"Now, that is an interesting story," Eddie said. "But it is pretty long, and diagrams help a lot. I'll tell you about Santha when you get back up here."

"Okay," said Derek.

"I'm not sure your explanation works. What about Lixia? Why has she had so much trouble?"

"Remember her traveling companions. Two men and a woman who has a widespread reputation for perversion."

There was a silence. "You're right, aren't you? This is my mistake. I should have pulled Lixia out after the fiasco in that first village and reassigned her, maybe to the other continent."

Derek made the gesture of uncertainty, then said, "I don't know. I am not crazy about second-guessing history. And I don't like words like 'should.'"

"Well, do the best you can. Lysenko will be waiting when you reach the lake."

Derek turned off the radio. "Do you notice how much Eddie uses the first person singular? The way he talks, he is the one who makes all the decisions and takes all the responsibility with no help from the rest of the committee.

"I, me, my, mine—
Each one a danger sign.

"That's what the witches used to tell us. Listen for those words, they said. If a person uses them too often or with too much emphasis, then he or she is sinking down into the well of self. And that is a dangerous situation. You may be face-to-face with a greedhead or a power freak."

I made the gesture of acknowledgment. I didn't want to discuss the social theories of the California aborigines—not in English in front of Nia and the oracle. It was rude. I looked at Nia. "Our friend, the one whose voice is in the box, is worried about the amount of trouble we've encountered."

"It is never easy to travel," the oracle said. "I know that. One of my sisters is a great traveler. She has been as far north as the men go and met the

169

Iron People in their summer range. She has been south as well and seen the ocean and gotten gifts from the people who live there: the Fishbone People and the People of Dark Green Dye. My mother has told me about her adventures. Hola! What a tale!" He bit one of his fingernails. "What does your friend expect?"

"A good question. I'm not entirely sure."

For the next three days we traveled as quickly as possible. Nothing much happened. The sky was mostly clear, and the land rolled gently. We saw animals in the distance: flocks of grazing bipeds and once a solitary animal that Nia said was a killer of the plain.

"A male. See how big he is and how he shambles?"

"Nia, that thing is a black spot to me. I thought it might be a person."

"What eyes you have! It is certainly a killer and a male. A female would be traveling with her children. The children would be hungry, and she would be dangerous. But a male is not much of a problem."

"You say that!" the oracle put in. "I know better."

"You were alone and had no fire."

"We'll make one tonight," said the oracle.

This was in the middle of the third day. By then we were all getting uneasy, looking behind us and around us.

We stopped early atop a rise that was higher than the other little hills. Derek peered east. "Nothing," he said. "I can't see them. But nonetheless, we are going to keep watch. And I don't think I want to risk a fire."

"We have to," Nia said. "There are worse things here than men. I do not want to lie in the darkness and wait for a killer of the plain."

"All right," Derek said.

We built the fire and huddled around it. Derek took the first watch. I sat and worried. Finally, when I couldn't stand the worry anymore, I called Eddie.

"Any sign of the three brothers?" he asked.

"No. And I don't want to think about them. How are things on the ship?"

"Not good. Meiling went over to the opposition."

"What?"

"She has filed a report against nonintervention. The natives are not fools, according to her. They have eyes to see and minds to think with. They know that she is something utterly different, something utterly outside their experience *and* the experience of their ancestors. Hairless people are not mentioned in the stories about creation.

"Knowledge—by itself—is an intervention. Our presence changes the way the natives see the world. According to her, there is no way to study these people without causing change."

"The Heisenberg Uncertainty Principle," I said.

"So I am told. I'm not an expert on the history of science. And I don't think it's possible to apply the laws of physics to the behavior of people. That is like Social Darwinism. A stupid and dangerous theory.

"Meiling says the policy of nonintervention does only one thing. It makes life hard for the workers in the field. They can't trade information with the natives, and they can't offer help. Simple medical care, for example."

"I did," I said. "When Nia got hurt."

"I know. But that was only one person, and you and Nia were alone. It wasn't as if you had set yourself up as the village doctor. Meiling wants to. She has medical training and worked in Tibet. We told her no. She is still angry."

I thought of Meiling: thin and intense, a person who had trouble with detachment. Nonaction was not for her. She had no interest in the ideas of Lao Zi or the Buddha. She came from the second great tradition in China, that of Mao Zi and Men Zi and Master Kong. The tradition of social responsibility.

"She has a point," Eddie said. "I know that nonintervention makes everything more difficult. And maybe it is a farce. Maybe there is no way we can avoid changing this planet. But the policy makes us go slowly. If we abandon it or even begin to modify it, then it's only a matter of time—and not much time—before the planet looks the way America did in the nineteenth century. The natives will be knee deep in explorers and prospectors and Marxist missionaries."

"Eddie, you worry even more than I do."

"I'm not going to say wait and see. I'm going to do everything I can to make sure my predictions don't come true."

"Good night, Eddie."

I meditated for a while, looking at the fire. Then I dozed, sitting in the half-lotus position. Finally Derek shook me.

"It's your turn. I haven't seen anyone."

I kept watch until the middle of the night. Nothing much happened. Meteors fell, and a night bug came out of the darkness. It glided above the fire on huge pale wings. A moment later it was gone.

I woke Nia. She got up, groaning softly.

"I saw a bug this wide." I held my hands forty centimeters apart. "Is that possible?"

She frowned. "Is that why you woke me?"

"No. It's your turn to keep watch. Could the bug have been that big?"

"Yes." Nia stretched and yawned. "Go to sleep, Li-sa. I don't feel like talking."

I did as I was told.

The morning was bright. Above us and to the east the sky was clear. The west was full of clouds. They were a kind of cirrus.

"New weather," Nia said.

171

We saddled the animals and went on. I rode, as did the oracle.

The clouds spread east, covering the sky. By midmorning the sun shone through a white haze. Derek kept looking back. "Maybe they've decided to forget the whole thing," he said at last. He didn't speak with much conviction.

At noon we came to a valley. We stopped on the bluff above it. The bluff was low. The valley was shallow and not especially wide. A river ran through the middle of it, brown and slow. Monster grass grew on the banks. A new variety. The leaves were distinctly blue. The slopes of the valley were covered with the usual yellow vegetation. Here and there I saw patches of red: a plant I did not recognize.

The trail descended into the valley. We followed it over the yellow slopes. I saw animals: a herd or flock of quadrupeds. They were tiny, no more than a meter high, and shy. As soon as we came near they bounded away in great leaps like so many gazelles. They were brown with white stripes down their backs, and they looked furry.

"What are they?" asked Derek.

"Silverbacks," Nia said. "In the winter they turn entirely white, and their fur is warm and thick. Some people keep them. The People of Fur and Tin, for example. But we—the Iron People—think they are more trouble than they are worth. They do not keep their horns, but drop them every fall and grow new ones in the spring. While the horns are coming in the animals are irritable and hard to manage. They rub their horns against anything they can find: tent poles and the wheels of wagons and even the tripods we use to hang up cooking pots."

The trail went along the river. Bipeds with long necks grazed on the leaves of the monster grass. They were almost the same color as the grass. In the shadows, among the blue leaves, they were hard to make out. Often I did not see one until it moved, reaching up a long thin arm to grab some food or twisting its neck and cocking its tiny head in order to stare at us. And I had no idea how many there were. Two? Three? A dozen?

"We don't have to worry about killers of the plain," Nia said. "There are too many animals around. They aren't smart—these creatures—but they wouldn't stay if they saw one of their kind being eaten."

We continued along the river all afternoon. Gradually it widened, growing increasingly shallow. There were sandbars and patches of reed. The trail ended. We came to a halt.

Nia stared at the river. "This is the ford." She shaded her eyes. "There is a man on the other side in the shadows. He is standing watching us."

Derek shaded his eyes. "You're right. Goddammit!"

Behind us a voice spoke. "That is my brother Tzoon."

I looked around. A man stood five meters away from us, next to a stem of monster grass. Inzara. I recognized the tunic.

"And that is Ara." He waved and a man stepped onto the trail we had just come down. He was as big as Inzara. His tunic was blue and covered with embroidery. He wore a belt made of linked copper and a knife in a blue leather sheath. His boots were blue leather. Around one wrist he wore a dozen or so bracelets of copper wire. He moved his hand slightly, gesturing to his brother. I heard the bracelets chime.

"What do you want?" asked Derek.

"You killed Inahooli," Inzara said. "We dug her up. There was a deep wound in her back."

Derek said nothing.

After a moment Nia said, "Yes. We did. What about it?"

"We want an explanation."

Ara said, "The ceremony to honor the Ropemaker is ruined. We are men. We don't care about these things as much as the women do. But it is no good thing to see the clan of our mother embarrassed."

"Inahooli will be known as the guardian who failed," Inzara said. "Her ghost will be furious. She was never easy to get along with. Now, who knows what she will do? There will have to be ceremonies of aversion and ceremonies of purification." Inzara paused.

Ara continued, "And ceremonies to drive away the anger of Inahooli and of our ancestor the Ropemaker. This is a bad situation. We want to know how it came about."

"All right," Nia said. "We will tell you. Does the other one—the one across the river—want to hear?"

"Yes." Inzara waved and shouted.

The third brother appeared a few minutes later, riding out of the grove into sunlight. He led two bowhorns with empty saddles. They forded the river, splashing through the shallows. When they reached our side, the man reined his animal. "Well?" His voice was as deep as Inzara's but much harsher.

"Tie up the animals," Inzara said.

Nia looked at me and the oracle. "Get down, both of you."

We dismounted. Nia took our reins and led our animals into the nearest grove. The third brother rode after her.

They came back together, but walking some distance apart. Both of them looked wary. Nia was a big woman. The man dwarfed her. He was as huge as his brothers. He wore a kilt of dark green fabric and a yellow belt. The buckle was silver. His boots were green leather. On his broad chest he wore a necklace. It was tangled in his shaggy hair and more than half-hidden. I made out beads of silver, long and narrow, alternating with round amber beads as yellow as butter.

Inzara waved at him. "This, as I told you before, is my brother Tzoon."

173

The man looked at us, then grunted. "Unh!"

"Who are you?" asked Ara. He had remained to the north of us on the trail. Inzara was a little to the south, close to the bank of the river. The third brother was to the east, at the edge of the grove. We were surrounded. Trapped.

Nia scratched her nose. "Will you answer a question for me? Then I will tell you who we are."

Inzara made the gesture of assent.

"Why do you travel together?"

"We are not ordinary men," said Inzara. "We were born together, all three of us in one birth."

"Aiya!" said the oracle.

Nia said, "Hu!"

"No one in our village had ever seen a thing like that. Two children at once, yes. That has happened, though not often. Usually the children are small and weak. They die. But three—that was unheard of. And we were all large and healthy. People said our mother must have met the Trickster on the plain. We had to be unlucky. No woman could nurse three children. One of us, at least, would have to die."

Ara continued the story: "Our mother said we were all fine babies. She couldn't decide which one of us should be carried out on the plain and left for scavengers to find. She wanted to keep us all. Our mother never liked any kind of waste."

The third brother—Tzoon—made the gesture of agreement.

Ara went on. "Our mother took gifts to the shamaness: a fine long rope and a piece of cloth covered with embroidery."

"And a pot made by the Iron People," Inzara said. "She was never one to keep things hidden in her tent. She knew the importance of giving."

Ara made the gesture of agreement. "She asked the shamaness to perform the ceremony of interpretation. This took three days. Our mother nursed us as best she could. On the second day of the ceremony, when the shamaness was in a deep trance, our aunt Iatzi lost her baby."

"It had always been sick," Inzara added.

Once again Ara made the gesture of agreement. "It was her first child. Now her tent was empty and she had plenty of milk. She offered to help our mother.

"Our mother said that proved we were not unlucky. In fact we were luckier than most, since what we needed came to us."

Inzara said, "When the shamaness woke, she told the villagers she had gone up into the sky and met the Ropemaker, the Mother of Mothers, and the Master of the Herds. They told her, 'These children belong to us, and we will provide for them as we see fit. If we intend them to live, they will live. If we decide it is time for them to die—together or each one separately, you will see the result. Do not interfere and do not presume to understand our intentions.' That was the end of her vision.

"What else is there to say? When we were children, we liked to be together. We almost never argued. There were people in the village who said we had only one spirit among the three of us. Maybe they were right. We don't know. There are differences among us. Tzoon is silent. Ara is curious. I am unusually even-tempered. But it is true we are as close as sisters, and each one of us knows what the others are thinking. We went through the change at the same time exactly."

"Even then," Ara said, "we didn't quarrel, though Tzoon became more silent than before."

I looked at the third brother. He frowned.

"In the Summer Land and when the herd is moving, we stay close together. We like to look around and see a brother off in the distance. And we like to meet now and then to share food and talk. Inzara and I talk. Tzoon listens."

The third brother said, "In the spring we stay apart."

Inzara made the gesture of agreement. "We do not know what would happen then. What if a woman came out of the village full of lust, and two of us saw her? Would we fight? That would be terrible!"

"We make sure our territories are widely separated, though all equally close to the village," Ara said. "This has become difficult in recent years. We are all big men, and the territories we have now are almost in the village."

Inzara said, "We let other men—men we could face down—creep in between us. We lose some women that way. But our mother always said, 'Nothing is gained by greed.'"

"Now," said Tzoon. "Tell us who you are."

Nia pointed at each one of us and gave our names. She gave her name last.

"You are the woman who loved a man," Inzara said.

Nia made the gesture of agreement.

"And now you travel with another man." He pointed at the oracle. "And with two people who have almost no hair."

"Yes."

"What sex are those people?"

"One is a woman. The other is a man."

"Aiya!" said Inzara.

Tzoon made the gesture that meant "no matter." "This is no concern of ours. If they want to risk bad luck—well, let them. They do not belong to our village."

Ara made the gesture of agreement. "Our concern is Inahooli. How did she die?"

175

Nia rubbed the back of her neck. "This is not easy to explain."

Tzoon frowned.

She glanced at him, then at his brothers. "First of all, we met with a *shuwa-bara*. A male with a family to protect. He frightened our bowhorns, and they ran away. We were stuck on the shore of the Lake of Bugs and Stones. This is important for you to know. We had no way to escape Inahooli after she went crazy."

"Ah," said Inzara.

"The first time she came, Li-sa and I were alone. She wanted to show off her tower, and Li-sa was curious. She is a peculiar person, always asking questions, like a little girl, poking at things and prying them open and asking and asking. Aiya!"

Ara frowned. "Anything can be taken too far. But there is nothing wrong with curiosity."

"Anyway," Nia said. "Li-sa went to see the tower. Then Inahooli decided she was a demon and pulled out a knife. She tried to kill Li-sa. But Li-sa got away."

"Why did she think that one was a demon?" Ara waved at me.

Nia paused, frowning. She bit her thumbnail. "Inahooli remembered who I am. And she thought a person without hair who travels with a pervert must be a demon."

"That makes sense," said Tzoon.

Inzara made the gesture of disagreement. "The tower is protected. The shamaness performed ceremonies in the spring after it was built. There is magic all through it, woven into every piece of rope and around every piece of wood."

"Does the magic protect it against everything?" I asked.

"No. Of course not. A high wind can blow it down, and hail can tear the banners. Animals can chew on it or perch on it and cause damage. But the tower ought to be safe from demons. If that one"—he pointed at me—"was able to get near the tower, she isn't a demon. Though she might be something else unlucky. A person in need of purification, for example."

"No," said Nia. "Inahooli was definite. Li-sa was a demon. Inahooli decided the tower was ruined. Li-sa had taken away all of its power. She came to our camp at night, planning to get back at us in some way. That one"—she pointed at Derek—"saw her coming. He fought with Inahooli and won. He tied her up, and we tried to talk with her. They—the others—tried to talk with her. I was on the plain, looking for our bowhorns."

"I will tell this part," the oracle said. "We talked and talked, trying to convince her that we had done nothing to her tower. I understand these things. I am an oracle and the holiest person among the Copper People of the Plain."

176

"Aiya!" said Inzara.

"Oracles don't travel," said Ara. "Why are you here?"

"My spirit told me to go with these people. They are important in some way or other."

Ara looked at me and at Derek. He made the gesture of doubt and then the gesture of agreement. Together, they meant "if you say so."

The oracle continued: "In the end Inahooli decided that the cause of all her trouble was your shamaness. She had put a spell on Inahooli and made her believe the tower was ruined."

Tzoon grunted. "I never liked the shamaness. I remember what she was like as a girl. Always talking. Always being clever."

Inzara frowned. "Why would the shamaness do a thing like that?"

"Inahooli said she used to belong to the Groundbird Clan, and they are rivals of your clan."

I added, "She told us—the big moon was involved."

Inzara looked at me, frowning. "The moon? How?"

"It was boiling over then."

"We know," said Ara. "We saw it, but that has nothing to do with the making or unmaking of towers. That means we are going to be short of food in the winter."

"The old women say," Tzoon added.

Inzara made the gesture of disagreement. "Inahooli was not telling the truth. The moon had nothing to do with what was happening, and our shamaness is the daughter of the old shamaness. A true daughter, born out of the old woman's body. She has always belonged to the Clan of the First Magician."

Ara said, "The mother of the old shamaness was born in the Clan of the Groundbird. She was adopted by the shamaness of that time, who had only sons. Some people said that she—the mother of the old shamaness—favored the Groundbird Clan more than she should have. But that was three generations ago."

"Well, then," the oracle said. "Inahooli was lying. We believed her and let her go. She came back at night and attacked us. In my opinion she was crazy. She fought without caring what happened. She almost won. But one of us managed to stab her before she killed all of us. That is what she was trying to do."

"That is the whole story," Nia said.

There was a silence. The three brothers were frowning.

"Well?" said Tzoon at last. "Are they telling the truth?"

Inzara made the gesture of affirmation. "It sounds like Inahooli. Deep inside her, she always believed things would go wrong for her. She looked

177

for bad luck. When that one arrived"—he waved at Nia—"she must have thought, this is it. The thing I have been waiting for. The thing that will make me fail."

"What are you talking about?" I asked.

"I'm thirsty," Inzara replied. "Let's drink from the river and then sit down. I will tell you about Inahooli."

"All right," said Nia.

The three brothers drank, kneeling one by one at the edge of the river. As one drank, the other two kept watch, glancing at us and the grove of monster grass and the far side of the river. Tzoon was the last to drink. He rose and wiped his mouth. "Unh!"

Inzara moved away from the bank. He sat down with his back against a stem of monster grass, stretched out his legs, and rubbed one thigh. "It was a hard ride from the lake. We had to rebury Inahooli and do it the right way, with singing and with gifts of parting. All that took time."

Ara sat down at the edge of the grove, not far from Inzara. He folded his legs into a half-lotus position. "We could not do the entire ceremony. A shamaness is necessary for that. But we performed the parts we could remember from when we were children in the village."

"Tell the story," the third brother said. He remained standing on the bank of the river. How tall was he, anyway? Over two meters. In the sunlight his fur was dark brown instead of black. There were reddish highlights in the fur. His eyes were partially closed. The pupils had contracted to lines. The irises were pale yellow.

Inzara pointed at the ground, and the four of us sat down. We were facing Inzara and Ara. Tzoon was behind us. There was no way to watch him and his brothers at the same time. If anything went wrong, if the brothers became angry, he would be on us before we could rise and turn.

"Inahooli was the first born," Inzara said. "The oldest daughter. She should have been the most important child. But we came next, and we were magical."

"Ah," said Nia.

Inzara made the gesture of affirmation. "Everyone watched us. Everyone talked about us. We were the important ones."

Ara said, "I used to wonder why she looked unhappy. But I couldn't ask her. It was never easy talking to her. She was quieter than he is." Ara waved at Tzoon. "And she had a bad temper. Either she said nothing or she yelled and jumped up and down."

"I never noticed that she was unhappy," Inzara said. "But I have to say I never paid much attention to her. I was happy with my brothers and our mother and Iatzi."

Behind us Tzoon grunted. In agreement, I decided.

178

Inzara went on. "I met Inahooli again—for the first time since we left the village—the spring before last. I had a territory close to the village in between two men who were getting old. They no longer had the strength for confrontation, not with me or Ara or Tzoon. But we let them in, so we would be safe from one another.

"The first woman who came into my territory was Inahooli. She looked good. She was an impressive woman. And I was glad to see her. She was my sister, after all. We had shared the same tent and the same fire. I thought, this is good luck. I will be able to ask about our mother and about Iatzi.

"But the moment she saw who I was, she became furious. 'Can't I ever get away from you?' she yelled at me. I was surprised.

"We mated—"

"Why?" I asked.

"What do you mean?"

"Why did you mate, if she was angry with you?"

"Because that is what a man and woman do when they meet in the time of mating." He spoke slowly and clearly, as if he were talking to a child. "Unless, of course, they are mother and son."

An incest taboo, I thought. Why? Maybe to protect young boys from their mothers. Was that possible? Or maybe to allow the men one relationship that was not sexual.

"Go on," said Ara. "Tell the rest."

"After we mated, I asked her why she was angry. She said I was a child of the Trickster, born to cause trouble. She had waited and waited for the change. She had given us—all three of us—fine gifts and told us good-bye. At last, she told herself, she was out of the shadow and into the light. We were gone. She was free of us. But we wouldn't leave her alone. Every spring, Inahooli said, the women asked, 'Who has mated with Inzara and Ara and Tzoon? Are they all right? Did they make it through the winter? Are they as lucky as they have always been?'"

"Unh!"

I looked around at Tzoon. His eyes were almost entirely closed, and he looked as satisfied as a cat in a patch of sunlight. Nothing wrong with that, I told myself. Everyone enjoyed appreciation.

Inzara continued: "Her luck was always bad, she told me. Her children were ordinary. She had no special skill. No one respected her. She had no friends.

"I told her it wasn't my fault. Then she hit me. I thought, she will make me angry. I got out a mating gift. 'Get out of here,' I told her. 'If you still feel the lust, go east. Old Hoopatoo is there. He isn't much good at confronting, but he ought to be able to mate.'

179

"She gave me a gift, then rode away. I did not see her again until I dug into her grave." Inzara paused a moment. "The next spring I asked the women—the ones who came to me—how Inahooli was doing. She had gotten pregnant, they said. Her child had been born too early. It died. That was bad news. But there was good news. The clan had chosen her to be the guardian of the tower. She was a difficult woman, they told me, but impressive. Strong and forceful, and her family was respected by everyone. A good choice for the guardian, all the women said.

"I thought, Now she will have prestige. She will stop being envious." He looked at us. "I do not like being on bad terms with anyone—except other men, of course. And even then I don't want a serious quarrel. Everything will be fine, as far as I'm concerned, as long as they back down."

Ara made the gesture of agreement. Behind me Tzoon grunted.

Inzara went on. "No man ever sees the ceremonies in front of a clan tower—not unless he is very old and has gone through the second change and chosen to return to the village. But now and then, men go to look at a tower—usually after the ceremonies are over and the tower has been abandoned. Most of the time, the tower had been damaged in one way or another, and the holy masks are gone. They are always destroyed after the big dance. I thought, I want to see this tower—our sister's tower—when it is new. I talked to my brothers. They decided to come with me. We rode south ahead of the herd."

"We lost nothing," said Ara. "In the summer, in the north, it doesn't really matter what kind of territory a man has. Some areas are more comfortable than others. This summer, for example, I had a stretch of river full of fish and an outcropping of rock where berry vines grew. A good territory! I enjoyed it, especially the berries. They were as big as the end of my thumb and juicy. But it wasn't really difficult to ride away and leave everything to that fat fool Oopai. I knew he would sneak in the moment I was gone."

"No matter," said Tzoon. "When the herd reaches the Winter Land, we will be there. Then Oopai can remember his berries. We will be the ones who are close to the village."

Ara made the gesture of agreement.

"In any case," said Inzara. "We rode to the Lake of Bugs and Stones. We found our sister and we came after you."

Ara repeated the gesture of agreement. For a moment or two there was silence. What was next? What were they going to do? I glanced at the two brothers in front of me. Their faces—dark and furry—told me nothing. I twisted around and looked at Tzoon. He frowned and scratched his forehead—a wide, low expanse, covered with fur. The ridges above his eyes were prominent. His eyes were deep-set, his nose was flat, and his cheekbones were broad. An almost perfect Neanderthal. I had seen people like him in dioramas in museums. No. I was wrong. His jaw wasn't as heavy as the jaws of those museum people; and his forehead—though it was low—did not recede. From the look of it, he had a lot of forebrain. Whatever that might mean in his species.

He grunted and made the gesture that meant "so be it." After that he walked past us, away from the river.

Ara got up and stretched. A moment later Inzara stood.

We got up, all four of us.

"What now?" asked Derek.

"We got the explanation we wanted," Inzara said. "We don't mind being around each other, but you make us uneasy. We will go. East of here, we saw tracks. A flock of *shuwahara*. Tzoon is a fine archer, and Ara isn't bad. We will kill an animal—a young one, fat and tender—and roast it."

"Good," said Tzoon.

Ara said, "We will eat and then ride south and wait in the land of winter for the herd to arrive."

They got their animals and led them onto the trail, mounted and settled themselves in their saddles. Like Nia, they slouched, looking relaxed and comfortable. They gathered their reins, turned their animals, and rode away. At first they were close together. But after a short while Tzoon turned off the trail, riding into the grove. I lost sight of him. A minute or two later Ara turned his animal into the grove and—like his brother—was gone from view. Inzara rode on alone. The trail curved. He rode around the curve and was gone.

Derek exhaled. "Thank the Holy Unity or the wheel of fate or whatever is responsible. I hate to admit it, but that trio frightened me."

"Why?" asked the oracle. "They weren't crazy. Only crazy men fight when there is nothing to be won—no territory and no women."

Nia made the gesture of agreement. "They are big men. Those ones rarely go crazy. They know their own strength. They have the best of everything, and they know they are able to hold on to what they have. It is the young men in the hills who go crazy from frustration. Or the old men who have lost their territories."

"I forgot," a voice said.

I jumped. So did everyone else. We turned, all of us.

A bowhorn came out of the grove. The rider wore blue. Ara. The curious brother. He reined his animal and looked down at us.

"Yes?" said Derek. "What is it?"

"You two. The ones without hair. What are you?"

"People," I said. "We come from a long distance away. In our land all the people are more or less like us."

181

"With no hair?"

"Only on the head. And there are a few patches in other places."

"Where?"

"Under the arms and between our legs," I said.

"Aiya! You must get cold in the winter."

"We wear more clothes than you do," I said. "In the summer we take off almost everything, and we are probably more comfortable than you are."

Nia made the gesture of disagreement. "In the summer you have no protection against the bugs that sting or bite."

I thought for a moment. "We have ointments with aromas the bugs don't like. We smear them on us, and the bugs stay away."

"It sounds messy," Ara told me. "Fur would have been better. And handsomer, too. Whatever spirit made you wasn't thinking about what she was doing."

"That often happens," the oracle said. "The spirits are very powerful, but they aren't always smart."

Ara made the gesture of agreement. "You are right about that. Look at the Trickster. He thinks he is so clever. He runs around setting traps and telling lies. And what happens? He falls into his own traps half the time, and his lies get so complicated that he can't keep track of them. That isn't clever. It's stupid-smart." He paused. "What is the name of your people?"

"Humans," I said.

He repeated the word. "What does it mean?"

"People."

Ara frowned. "But what kind of people? What do you carry when you travel? What is your gift?"

Derek said, "At times we call ourselves *Homo sapiens*, which means the People of Wisdom."

"Aiya! That is a gift indeed! Do you have any with you? Tell me something wise."

Derek was silent for a moment. Then he looked pleased. He had come up with something. "If I tell you something wise, then you will have a gift from me. But I won't have anything from you. So I will have given you something for nothing, which is hardly wise."

"Ah," said Ara. He scratched his forehead. "You prove yourself wise by telling me nothing. Is that what you are trying to say?"

Derek made the gesture of agreement.

Ara made the gesture that meant "no." "Your answer is not wise. It is stupid-smart. You think the way the Trickster does. He worries about being cheated. He wastes his time looking for tricks and lies when there are none. 'Those branches by the trail hide a trap,' he says. 'A deep hole or a noose tied to a sapling. I'm no fool. I will go through the field.' And he leaves the safe way, trodden by people, and goes off to tangle himself in briers or to fall in a bog. If that is the best you can offer, I do not think your people are the People of Wisdom."

I looked at Derek. His face was red. He opened his mouth, then closed it. He wasn't going to argue with Ara. I could understand that. Ara was very large and not especially polite. Inzara was the one who liked to get along with people. Ara didn't seem to care.

"Most of the time," I said, "we call ourselves after the land we live in. Derek is an Angelino, because his people live near a place called Los Angeles. I am Hawaiian. I come from an island called Hawaii."

That wasn't exactly true. I was from the island of Kauai. But I didn't know the word for a collection of islands. Herd? Flock? Heap? Arrangement? Gathering? Lacking the word, I could not say I was from the Hawaiian Islands.

Ara frowned again. "You have a lot of names for yourselves. Can't you decide what you are?"

"No," I said.

"Ah. Well, if I meet any more hairless people, I will ask them for a name. Maybe they will come up with a better answer than you have." He turned his animal and rode off along the trail.

"I liked my answer," Derek said. "I guess these people don't appreciate wit." He used the English word for "wit." Was there a native word? I didn't know.

Nia got the bowhorns. We mounted double, Nia behind the oracle, Derek behind me. In that way we crossed the river. At the deepest point the water came to the bellies of our animals. I had to pull my feet up in order to keep them dry. Derek didn't bother. As usual he was barefooted. The water felt good, he said.

On the far side Nia and Derek dismounted. We found the trail. It went south and west along the river. We followed it.

Part Two

Tanajin

That evening we made camp in a grove by the river. We ate the last of our food.

Nia said, "Tomorrow I will hunt."

Derek made the gesture of assent and then the gesture of inclusion. The two together meant "I will hunt, too."

I thought of calling the ship. But I was tired and depressed and didn't feel up to a conversation with Eddie.

Rain fell during the night. I woke and heard the soft patter on foliage above me. It couldn't have been much of a rain. It didn't get through the leaves. I listened for a while, then went back to sleep.

By morning the rain had stopped. But the sky stayed overcast. Nia and Derek took off hunting. The oracle and I continued along the trail. To the right of us were groves of monster grass. To the left was the river. It ran over yellow stones and through beds of dull purple reeds. Birds clung to the reeds and made gurgling noises.

I thought about breakfast. My stomach gurgled, sounding like the birds. "Tell me a story."

"What kind?" asked the oracle.

"An important story. A story about something that matters."

"I will tell you about the moon."

"Which one?"

"The big one. It was not always up in the sky. It used to be down here on the ground. The Mother of Mothers kept it. It was her cooking pot. The pot was able to fill itself. It needed no help from anyone."

I thought of asking him to tell a different story.

"People could eat and eat. When the pot was empty, the people would sit down and wait. In a little while the pot was full again, all the way to the brim. It held porridge in the morning. At night it held a tasty meat stew. The Mother of Mothers fed everyone who was hungry. Everyone who was in need of food was able to come to her."

Too late. He was getting into the story. It would be rude to ask him to stop. My stomach made another gurgling noise.

"But the people became lazy and greedy. They thought if a village had that pot, no one in the village would ever have to work. So the fourteen kinds of people I know about all sent emissaries to the Mother. Each one said, 'Give me your pot, for then my people will be happy forever.'

"The Mother said no. The emissaries became angry. They went off together and consulted.

"'We will steal the pot, all of us together. When we have it, we'll draw straws. Whoever gets the longest straw can take the pot home and keep it for a year. At the end of the year she must give the pot to whoever got the second longest straw. In this way we'll share. Every village will have a good year, one out of fourteen.'

"They stole the pot. It wasn't hard. The Mother of Mothers was not suspicious. Then they drew straws and the trouble began. The women with long straws were happy. The women with short straws were furious. They began to quarrel and shout. They even hit one another.

"The noise attracted the Spirit of the Sky, who was far above them. He flew down and grabbed the pot and carried it away—though I don't know how he did it, since he has wings instead of arms. Maybe he grabbed the pot with his feet. There are women who say his feet are claws like the feet of a hunting bird.

"Then the Mother of Mothers said, 'You see what being greedy gets you. I am going to put my cooking pot in a safe place, and I am going to punish all of you, so that—in the future—women will think twice before they bother the spirits.'

"She put her cooking pot in the night sky. It became the moon. And she put the emissaries up there as well. 'Your punishment will be that your mission will never be completed. You will wander through the sky forever, unable to

188

get my cooking pot and unable to go home. The people of the world will learn from this to be less greedy and to treat the spirits with more consideration.'

"Those women became the little lights that travel across the sky night after night. We call them the Wanderers or the Thieves or the Women Without Respect."

The little moons, I thought. The captured planetoids. A very nice explanation, except we had counted only twelve little moons.

"You said there were fourteen emissaries," I said finally. "But I have seen only twelve lights."

"That is true," said the oracle.

"What happened to the other two?"

"That is another story, and I don't think a man should tell it to a woman."

"Oh."

"It is not decent." He used the negative form of the word that meant "well done," "well made," "in balance," or "appropriate."

"Oh," I said.

We rode on in silence. At last the oracle said, "I forgot one thing about the story of the cooking pot. If you look up into the sky, you will see the pot grow more and more empty night after night. And then—night after night—you will see the pot refill."

"Who eats from it?" I asked.

"People aren't certain. Maybe it is the great spirits, and maybe it is the people who die. They must go somewhere and when they get there, they have to eat."

I made the gesture of uncertainty and then the gesture of agreement. That meant I agreed, but not with any enthusiasm.

"Now I am hungry," the oracle said. "I should have told another story."

"Do you want to? I'm willing to listen."

"Not now. Maybe Nia will come back soon."

She didn't. After a while rain began to fall: a fine drizzle. We took shelter in a grove of monster grass. The rain grew heavier. Drops of water came down through the foliage above us.

The oracle said, "On a day like this, I remember the house of my mother."

"You do?"

He made the gesture of affirmation. "I remember it was always dry, even when rain came out of the sky like a river—like the waterfall my spirit inhabits. Aiya! It was comfortable! The flap was up over the smoke hole, and the fire burned low. Raindrops hissed in. The smoke coiled around itself under the ceiling—like lizards in the late spring when they mate." He paused for a moment. "When it was done coiling, the smoke would slide out around the lifted edges of the flap—the way the male lizards do when they are finished with their womenfolk and eager to get away but also tired."

189

What a speech! Amazing how well people were able to speak in a culture without books or holovision. We—who valued the written word and the projected image—talked in grunts and avoided metaphors as much as possible.

I looked at the oracle. His shoulders were hunched against the rain. His tunic clung to his body. The fabric was so thin that it offered almost no protection. Poor fellow.

Something clicked in my mind. Why didn't these people wear trousers? They rode astride. On Earth, through most of our history, trousers had been connected with the riding of horses. Cultures that traveled on horseback wore trousers. Other cultures did not.

The rule did not work for China. Everyone wore trousers there and had for centuries, but few people rode horses.

I had an idea that Chinese trousers had come from Central Asia. If that were so, I had my connection with horses.

There was another exception to the rule: the Indians of the North American plain. They had not worn trousers. But they did not have horses long, before they were overwhelmed by white "civilization." Maybe they would have developed trousers in time. And they did wear leggings.

I looked at the oracle again. His fur was a protection, of course, but surely not for his sexual organs. I realized I was up against the time-honored question. What does one wear under a kilt? Or a tunic, as the case might be. I searched my vocabulary, trying to find the right words.

The oracle said, "The rain has stopped." He touched his animal on the shoulder, and it moved out onto the trail. My animal followed. Maybe I'd better have Derek ask the question.

The rest of the morning I pondered on loincloths and shorts and bicycle pants and the problem of male fertility. If they mated only once a year, they could not afford a high rate of infertility. Maybe that was the reason they didn't wear trousers. But surely the men were uncomfortable.

Derek and Nia returned early in the afternoon. They brought food: a blue biped. It was a little one: a cub or chick or fawn.

We stopped and made camp. The rain began again. Derek and I went looking for dry wood. I asked him my questions about clothing.

He laughed. "I guess I should have told you. I asked the oracle about that long ago. Some men wear nothing. Others wear something that sounds like a jock strap. And there are people in the south who wear shorts instead of kilts. He doesn't know what they wear underneath."

"A jock strap ought to have some effect on fertility."

"I haven't seen the garment in question," Derek said. "I don't know how tightly it fits, and we don't know much about the physiology of these people.

190

For all we know those things the oracle has aren't testicles. Maybe he keeps his spermatozoa in his ears."

I made the gesture that meant "no." "It'd interfere with hearing. But—" I made the gesture of agreement. "We need to do more research."

He grinned.

I added, "I think I'll leave this particular problem to you."

"Okay. There's probably an article in it. 'Variations in Underwear among an Alien Humanoid Species.' The title isn't quite right. It isn't pompous enough. But it's a beginning."

"Do you always start with the title?"

"The title is very important, Lixia my love. And we had better get our wood before the rain gets any heavier."

By the time we got back to the camp, Nia had finished cleaning the biped. It looked less alien without its feathers, though I couldn't decide what it reminded me of. A rabbit? A monkey? We roasted it. It had a mild flavor, like chicken.

After dinner Derek called the ship. One of the computers answered. It had a female voice and a soft Caribbean accent. Eddie was busy, it told us. It would put our call through to Antonio. There were chiming noises, a whole series of them, then a beep.

Derek asked, "Where is Eddie?"

"At a meeting," Tony said. "Drafting a manifesto."

"Oh, yeah?" said Derek. "On what?"

"Need you ask? Nonintervention."

"Let's keep this brief," I said. "The natives are here, and they aren't comfortable when we speak a language they don't understand."

"Okay," said Tony. "Give me your report."

Derek told him about the three brothers.

Tony was silent for a while. At last he said, "You were lucky. We were lucky. If those men had gotten angry, we'd be up here arguing about how to pick up the pieces. And Eddie would be saying we shouldn't intervene."

"Yes," said Derek. "Do you have any information on the rendezvous?"

"Uh-huh. Keep going. The river you're following is a tributary of a much bigger river. When you reach it—the big river, I mean—turn downstream. The lake is south of you about eighty kilometers. The plane will land there, though Lysenko is still not happy. He keeps asking for a salt flat. We have told him beggars can't be choosers. He says there are no beggars in a socialist society."

"What?" I said.

"We think he was joking. Humor does not always cross cultural boundaries."

Derek said, "I'm going to turn the radio off."

191

"Good night," said Tony.

Derek hit the switch. He yawned. "So much for that. Maybe tomorrow it'll stop raining."

It didn't. We traveled through drizzle and mist. My body ached: mostly my shoulder and arm, but also much older injuries—a couple of root canals and the ankle I had broken at the Finland Station on my way to join the interstellar expedition. My first time in an L-5, my first experience with low g, and I decided to try the local form of dancing.

The valley grew narrow. I began to see outcroppings of rock. It was yellow and eroded. Limestone, almost certainly. We had passed out of the area of volcanic activity.

Most of the rock was high above us. The lower slopes of the valley were covered with vegetation. Not monster grass any longer. These were real trees. The bark was rough and gray. The leaves were round and green.

"It is going to be an early autumn," said Nia. "They have changed color already."

"Is that the color they will stay?" I asked.

She made the gesture of affirmation. "Some trees turn yellow after they turn green, but this kind changes no further. The leaves will be green when they fall."

"Aiya," I said.

Late in the afternoon we came to a place where the valley was very narrow, and the trail went under a cliff. There was an overhang. No. A shallow cave.

We dismounted and led our animals up a little slope to the cave. There were ashes on the floor and pieces of burnt wood.

"I thought so. We'll stay here tonight." Nia looked at Derek. "You get wood."

Derek made the gesture of assent. He left. We unsaddled the bowhorns and led them down to the river to drink, then tethered them where they could graze. One of the animals was limping a little. Nia crouched and examined a hoof.

The oracle called, "Lixia! Come here!"

I went into the cave. At the entrance it was maybe fifteen meters wide and ten meters tall, but it narrowed rapidly, and the ceiling dropped until I had to bend my head. The oracle stood where the cave ended or seemed to end. As I approached him I felt a cold wind: air coming toward me. "This is a holy place." He stepped to the side and pointed. I saw the opening: a meter high and half a meter wide. The wind came out of it. The oracle said, "The hair on my back is rising, and I have a queasy feeling in my gut. This is definitely a place that belongs to the spirits."

"Can we stay here?" I asked.

"I think so. I felt nothing in the front of the cave."

I looked at the hole. Once we had a fire going, I could make a torch. "Is it forbidden to go in?"

"I don't know. The spirits in this land are not the ones I know."

We returned to the front of the cave. Nia was there, dripping water. "Aiya! What a day!" She brushed off her arms and shoulders. "That hoof looks all right. The animal is tired and doesn't want to travel in weather like this. Who does? Either she is faking or there is an old injury that I can't see."

Derek came out of the woods, his arms full of branches. He ran up the slope, slipping a couple of times in the mud, reached the cave, and said, "This was dry when I got it. Now—I don't know."

"I will find out," said Nia.

She built a fire. I told Derek about the holy place.

"After dinner," he said. "We'll go and take a look."

Nia looked up. "Can't you learn? Remember what happened the last time you got curious about something holy. That crazy woman almost killed us."

"Don't you wonder about things?" asked Derek.

"No." Nia rocked back on her heels. "I have learned more about strange places than I ever wanted to know."

"What about strange people?"

She frowned. "I like Li-sa. I am glad that I met her. I was tired of living in the forest and I never really liked the Copper People."

"What do you mean?" asked the oracle.

"I don't mean your people. I have nothing against them. But I did not like the Copper People of the Forest."

"Them!" said the oracle. "They are peculiar."

Nia made the gesture of agreement. "It was good that Li-sa came and I had to leave. I might have stayed there my whole life. That would have been terrible!"

The oracle made the gesture of agreement.

"What about me?" asked Derek.

"I have not decided if I like you," said Nia.

"No?" Derek looked hurt.

The oracle said, "I will go into the back of the cave. I am used to holy places, and my spirit will protect me." He rummaged in one of the saddlebags and found a piece of meat. Cold roast biped. He bit into it.

"I won't," said Nia. "I have no spirit to protect me, and holy places have always made me uneasy. But it's good that you are going. You can make sure that Deragu does nothing that he shouldn't."

The oracle chewed, unable to talk. But one hand made the gesture that meant "why do you think I am doing this?"

We finished the biped, got branches, and lit them. Derek led the way to the back of the cave. Shadows moved around us. Our torches flared and

193

streamed in the wind coming out of the hole. Derek crouched. "A tight fit. I think I can make it." He turned sideways and squeezed in. His torch was the last thing to vanish.

The oracle and I waited. I was pretty calm, I thought, but the oracle fidgeted. A nervous fellow. I bit a fingernail.

"It opens out," said Derek. His voice echoed. "A lot."

The oracle crouched. "I can see his torch. I am going." He squeezed out of sight. A minute or two later he said, "Aiya!"

I glanced at the entrance to the cave. The fire burned brightly. Nia sat by it, hunched over, a dark shape. Beyond her was rain, a shining curtain.

I went in on my knees, remembering that I'd gone caving in college and had discovered that I was slightly claustrophobic. The claustrophobia was made worse by dark.

There was no darkness here. The torch blazed in front of me. Smoke blew in my face, making me want to cough or sneeze. The passage got narrower. My head brushed the ceiling, and my shoulders rubbed against rough wet stone.

"Hurry," called Derek. "You've got to see—"

The passage widened. I felt space above me and stood, lifting my torch. Nothing was visible except the floor—it was covered with a film of water and shone dimly—and two points of light in the distance, the torches my comrades carried.

"Here," said Derek.

I went toward the sound of his voice.

He stood by a wall, his torch held high. The wall was yellow limestone, covered with water. There were paintings on it. Animals. They were red and orange, dull blue, gray, and brown. I recognized the creature that had attacked us by the lake and the blue bipeds. Dinner.

People moved among the animals. They were stick figures, done without any detail, though the animals were carefully detailed. The people carried spears and bows.

"Hunting magic," said Derek. He walked along the wall.

I saw more animals: birds. They looked as if they ought to be large. The legs were heavy, the bodies round and solid. They had thick necks and large heads. The mouths were full of teeth.

"Do you notice what is missing?" asked Derek. "Bowhorns and silverbacks. The animals we think of as mammalian." He spoke the language of gifts, but the last word was English.

I made the gesture of agreement. We kept walking. There were more big birds and pseudo-dinosaurs. The figures were nothing like the other art I had seen on the planet. That had been intricate and often abstract: an art made of patterns, a decorative art. These figures were simple and realistic. They

194

looked alive—except for the people, who looked as if they had been drawn by children.

Derek pointed at the painting of a lizard. It had a long tail and spines along its back. Its feet were webbed. It was huge, at least in comparison with the hunters who surrounded it. The lizard and the hunters were painted in black. There were streaks of red on the lizard. Wounds, I was almost certain. Painted spears stuck out of the animal.

Derek looked at the oracle. "What is it?"

"I don't know. I have never seen an animal like that. Maybe it is a monster."

"Why are there no bowhorns?"

"I don't know." The oracle paused. "This place is very old. I can feel the spirits who live here, but I don't know who they are. They are old and hungry. I can feel that. Aiya! Their hunger! It is like a wind in the middle of winter!"

Derek turned and stared at the oracle. "What are they hungry for?"

"I don't know. There are many things the spirits like. Good food. Good weaving. Embroidery. The work of metal smiths. Some like flowers and branches of leaves. Others like blood."

"Hu!" said Derek. He went back to looking at the wall.

There were more paintings, one on top of another: lizards and birds and pseudo-dinosaurs. I didn't recognize most of the species. Most had spears in them.

"We'll have to ask the biologists about this," said Derek. "Look. This bird has arms."

The arms were tiny and ended in claws. The animal was definitely a bird. It had a beak. Its body was covered with feathers, rendered in soft strokes of red-brown paint. It had a tail made of plumes, nothing like the long and narrow tail of a lizard or a dinosaur.

"Weird," I said.

The oracle had moved away from us toward the center of the cave. "Come here."

He stood by a circle of stones about twenty meters across. The stones were painted red, and there were skulls among them. Some had beaks and others had muzzles full of irregular teeth. All were painted red. All pointed in toward the center of the circle.

At the center was an area of darkness. The stone floor was discolored.

"Now I know," the oracle said. "These spirits are the kind who like blood. Take this." He handed me his torch and stepped into the circle.

"Be careful," said Derek.

The oracle went to the area of darkness. He went down on one knee, then twisted and looked at us. I saw the glint of his eyes. "Come here. I am going to need light."

195

"Is it safe?" asked Derek.

"To come in the circle? I don't know. But you can hardly be worried, Deraku. You are fearless when it comes to the spirits. You are willing to steal what belongs to them."

"Maybe I have learned something." Derek glanced at the darkness around us. "And maybe this place is different. Maybe these spirits are more frightening than the Trickster."

"I think you will be all right," the oracle said. "I will speak for you."

We stepped over the red stones and walked to him. He had his knife out, and he was testing the blade with his thumb. "This is too dull." He put the knife back in its sheath, then held out his hand. "Give me your knife, Deraku."

Derek pulled out his knife.

"What are you going to do?" I asked.

"Keep quiet," said the oracle. "And hold the torches so the light falls on me." He took Derek's knife and tested the blade. "Good." He laid it on the ground, then put his right arm on his knee, the hand palm upward. The skin of the palm was hairless and black. I could see calluses at the bases of his fingers. The calluses were dark gray. The oracle felt along his arm. Then he picked up the knife. He was left-handed like most of the people I had met on the planet.

He made a little noise, a groan, and turned his arm slightly. Then he cut into it below the elbow. He drew the blade down toward his wrist. The motion was slow and careful. I imagined a surgeon would move like that. I knew a good tech did when putting an IV in. He reached the wrist and lifted the blade. There was blood along the edge.

"Aiya!" He wiped the blade on the fur of his leg and gave the knife back to Derek.

Derek put the knife away. I looked back at the oracle. He was still in the same position. His arm rested on his knee. He watched the cut. Blood welled up through his fur. It trickled into the palm of his hand and dripped on the floor.

"Have you done this often?" asked Derek.

The oracle glanced up. "No. My spirit likes beer and metalwork. It has no interest in blood. I do not think I would like to speak for spirits like these."

Derek made the gesture of agreement. The oracle pressed his arm, forcing blood out. I thought of the ancient ceremonies of North America: sun dancers on the middle-western plain and the priests of Mexico who drew thorns through their tongues. It was not the way of my ancestors. I did not understand it.

By this time there was a little pool of blood on the floor of the cave. It shone in the torchlight.

"Enough," said the oracle. "They may still be hungry, but I have only so much blood. They will understand, I think." He stood up.

Derek put down his torch. He pulled off his shirt and wrapped it around the oracle's arm, tying it in place. "Okay," he said and picked up the torch. "Let's get out of here."

The oracle stumbled a couple of times, crossing the cave.

"Will you be able to make it on your own?" asked Derek.

"Out through the opening? Yes."

We left our torches in the cave and crawled out: Derek first, then the oracle. I was last. I felt my way over the wet stone. Ahead of me in the darkness the oracle sighed and groaned. The cut must have been deeper than I had realized.

The tunnel ended. I stood up and saw the campfire, burning brightly in front of the curtain of rain. Nia stood and glanced toward us.

"Are you all right?" she asked.

Derek said, "The Voice of the Waterfall is injured."

"Aiya! That crazy man!"

The oracle groaned and swayed.

Derek grabbed him. "Lixia, get your medical kit." He lowered the furry man to the cave floor near the fire.

"Aiya!" said the oracle. "I do not feel entirely well."

Derek untied the shirt. The fabric—blue cotton—was spotted with blood, which looked black in the firelight.

"It's going to be hard to get these stains out." Derek put the shirt down. He looked at the wound. "It isn't bad. A good bleeder. Not deep."

"You say that," the oracle told him. "I do not like blood. I never did."

Derek opened the kit. He cleaned the wound, then adjusted the nozzle on the bandage can. "I ought to shave the arm," he said in English. "But I can't figure out how to do it without getting hair in the wound. I'm making the bandage as narrow as possible." He sprayed.

The oracle made a soft moaning sound.

"Will he be all right?" asked Nia.

"Yes," said Derek. "I don't know how to say it. There are people who feel pain more than other people."

"I know that," said Nia.

"I think he is one."

"It is my pain," said the oracle. "How can you know what it is like?"

"That's true," said Derek. He rocked back on his heels. "I'm done."

The oracle moved his arm. "Is your medicine good? Will it keep my arm from rotting?"

"Yes."

197

The oracle made the gesture that meant approval or satisfaction.
Derek closed the medical kit.

"I can't remain sitting," the oracle said and lay down.

Nia got her cloak and spread it over the oracle.

"Good, good," he said.

She put more wood on the fire. A gust of wind blew in, bringing drops of rain. They splattered over me. The fire leaped. I shivered.

"What was back there?" Nia asked.

I said, "A cave. There were animals in colors on the walls."

Nia frowned. "In colors?"

"Like the animals that people embroider on pieces of fabric."

"Not people," said Nia. "Men. They are the ones who do embroidery."

"Ah. The animals are"—I tried to think of the right word. How did one say "paint" in the language of gifts?—"are done in colors like the ones used for dying. The colors are put on stone, not fabric."

Nia frowned. "I think you are trying to say there are *atmi* back there?"

"*Atmi*?"

"Like this." She drew a figure in the dirt. It was a stick figure: a quadruped with two long curving horns. A bowhorn. *Atmi* meant drawing.

I made the gesture of agreement.

"I have seen these things before. In the hills to the south of here. I do not know who the people were who did such things. We do not draw on stone. We don't cut into stone either—only wood and metal. But those folks did. I have seen a cliff covered with engraving."

Derek leaned forward. "What kind of animals did those people draw? Did you recognize them?"

Nia made the gesture that meant "no." "Some I knew. Others were strange. Maybe they were spirit animals. Or maybe those folks came from another place. Like the place you are from, where all the people are hairless. Surely there must be strange animals in your country. Are they hairless like you?"

"No," I said. "Most of them have hair or scales or feathers."

"Aiya," said Nia. "I think I will go to sleep." She lay down close to the fire.

Derek and I stayed up. Nia's breathing changed, becoming slow and even. The oracle groaned, then snorted. Nia made a purring noise. A snore.

"Interesting," said Derek. He spoke in English. "The fauna must have changed, and in a dramatic way, and she has no idea a change of that magnitude is possible. She understands distance, but not time." He paused for a moment. "I can't think of a contemporary human society without a sense of history. My people know what California was like before the Big Quake. They think that they have escaped from history and gotten back to the eternal verities. But they know history used to happen in southern

198

California and that it still happens in most of the rest of the world. I'm not sure I'm being clear. I'm getting tired and I've never been good at thinking about abstractions."

"I thought you were good at everything, Derek."

He looked surprised, then pleased. He laughed. "No. I have my limitations, though I don't like to think about them. We'd better get to sleep."

I woke to sunlight glowing on the cave wall and rolled over. There it was: the planet's primary, just above the bluff on the far side of the river. There was no cloud near it, and it was so bright that I had to look away.

A day like this demanded a solar salute!

The oracle said, "They have gone fishing."

I looked around. He sat by the ashes of the fire.

"Derek and Nia?"

He made the gesture of agreement.

"How are you?"

"My arm hurts. I slept badly."

"Oh." I stood up and did a side bend. It felt good. I did another, bending toward the other side. Then I touched my toes.

"Spirits came to me."

I straightened up.

"They looked like the animals on the wall of the cave."

"Oh."

"They spoke to me. Their voices were like the voices of people, but I did not understand the language they spoke." He paused for a moment. "They were loud. I think they were angry. But I don't know if they were threatening me or trying to warn me about something. They might have been angry, because I did not understand. It was a bad dream."

Most likely he was right. "I have to go outside."

"Okay," said the oracle.

Derek and Nia were nowhere in sight. Instead I saw birds. They fluttered in the reeds and bushes. They flew from tree to tree. A tall, thin bird stalked along the far shore, looking for something to eat in the shallows.

I did my yoga. By the time I finished, the sun was high enough to light most of the valley. I walked back to the cave. Derek and the oracle sat by the fire. The oracle was eating. Derek licked his fingers, looking satisfied.

"Where's Nia?"

"Saddling the animals. Want something to eat?"

I made the gesture of agreement. He pulled something from the fire.

Leaves, burnt black. He unwrapped them with a couple of quick motions. "Ouch!" Inside was a piece of fish, steaming and fragrant. "No bones that I can find," he said in the language of gifts. "Dig it up."

199

It was delicious and there were no bones. "Did the oracle tell you about his dream?"

"Yes. It might mean nothing. He's been through a lot and he's in pain. I wish I could give him aspirin. Sometimes a dream means nothing important. Sometimes a cigar is only a cigar. However . . ." He paused. "He is an oracle and this is a holy place."

"Derek, you are a superstitious savage."

"Call me names, my love, and I will remind you that I have tenure and you do not."

"Screw you," I said.

He made the gesture of doubtful agreement.

I laughed.

"Nia is coming," he said. "Let's get the fire out."

We traveled south and west along the river. The sky remained clear. The day grew gradually hot. The oracle rode ahead of me. I watched him shift in the saddle and move his arm, trying to find a comfortable position.

We stopped in the middle of morning. Derek made a sling out of his bloodstained shirt. The oracle put it on and sighed. "Aiya! That is better."

The valley grew wider. The river spread out into marshes. At times I was unable to see the water, only the reeds, tall and purple, moving slightly in the very slight wind.

The birds grew quiet, as they did on Earth in the afternoon, and I drifted into a series of reveries: Earth, Hawaii, my family. They were all gone except for Charlie, a half sibling who'd gotten himself frozen. He was curious about the future, he told me in his last message. He'd be there to welcome me home.

The oracle sagged. I urged my bowhorn forward and grabbed him as he started to fall. "Derek!"

The oracle straightened. "I am only tired."

Derek reached us. He and I got the oracle onto the ground.

"We have gone far enough," said Nia. She glanced around. "This is not a good place to stop. But it isn't bad either."

We were in an open area. A meadow. Most of the vegetation was low and late-summer yellow. There was one really conspicuous exception: a plant that grew as tall as two meters. It dotted the meadow. I saw at least a dozen specimens. The lower half of the plant was a cluster of large, ragged, dusty-looking leaves. A stalk grew up from the leaves, ending in a cluster of flowers. The flowers were orange, an extraordinarily vivid color. It seemed to glow.

A weird-looking plant. Not really attractive.

"Are you dreaming?" asked Derek. "Get down here."

I dismounted.

The oracle sat on the ground. His shoulders sagged, and his head was down. "Nia, you take care of the animals. Lixia, get wood. I'll take care of the oracle."

I didn't much care for the way he ordered everyone around. On the other hand, I didn't have a better plan. I walked across the meadow. Bugs whirred and hummed around me. The sun was hot on my head and shoulders. The air had a sweet aroma: the orange flowers.

Bugs with orange wings fluttered around them, landed, and took off. I couldn't always tell what was a bug and what was a blossom. That was eerie, to see a flower fold up and suddenly take off, sailing on the still air to another plant.

I reached the far side of the meadow. Trees grew there. I gathered branches, moving slowly, made sleepy by the heat.

When I returned, the oracle was lying down in the shade of a flower. Derek sat next to him, cross-legged, holding the radio.

"Damn it, Eddie," he said. "I have a sick person on my hands. I need to talk to someone of the med team."

"We have agreed," the radio said. "No further intervention of any kind until we have discussed our policy."

I dropped my branches, then dropped to my knees. "This is ridiculous, Eddie."

There was silence except for static. "I have to admit, I think we have handled this badly. Though I am not sure how one works out a policy for something that has never happened before. We thought we had one. I thought we had one. But what I mean by nonintervention is not what you mean by it. And everyone seems to have a different idea of when—if ever—it is legitimate to bend the rules.

"For the time being, though, we are going to have no intervention at all.

"Do you have any idea when you're going to reach the lake?"

"That depends on how sick the oracle is," said Derek.

The radio made crackling noise. Finally Eddie said, "Call me when you have a better idea of his condition. I really don't think we can help. But it isn't my decision. I'll tell the committee for day-to-day administration what is going on."

"Thanks," said Derek. He turned the radio off.

"Do you really think we're going to need advice? We've dealt with injuries to two natives already."

"In the case of Inahooli, not very successfully," Derek said.

I made the gesture of unhappy agreement.

"No. I don't think it's necessary to have the med team in on this. It's a pretty minor injury. But this is a way to check up on what is going on upstairs. I get uneasy when I'm in the field too long. I once came back from a trip to the moon and found the worst asshole in the department had gotten an office I wanted. It was on a corner. Four big windows and one heck of a view. If I'd been in Berkeley, I would've stopped him. No question about that! But I was out of touch. There were things I should have known and didn't."

He sounded still angry, though he had lost the office over one hundred years ago.

"What do you think will happen?" I asked.

"I think we'll get to talk to the med team. Remember the people who are currently on the committee for day-to-day administration. Two biologists and three members of the crew."

"That isn't a majority," I said.

"The Chinese usually vote as a block, and I think they'll be in favor of intervention—in general and in this situation. Remember the theory of Jiang, the plumber. It's our revolutionary duty to rescue these unfortunate people from stagnation."

I considered for a moment, then made the gesture of uncertainty.

"I ought to take the oracle's temperature," Derek said. He glanced at my pile of branches. "And you ought to get more wood."

I got back a second time and found the oracle asleep.

"No sign of infection," Derek said. "His temperature is almost the same as Nia's. Most likely the heat got to him—and traveling—and maybe some kind of reaction to last night. Dealing with spirits takes a lot of energy. Shamans and witches often feel sick for several days afterward."

"So we don't need any help from the ship."

"No. But I'm not going to tell them that. If you're looking for Nia, she has borrowed my bow and gone hunting along the river."

The sun went down behind the valley wall, and Nia came back with a lizard. A big one, a meter and a half long. She gutted the animal and skinned it. We roasted it. The flesh was dark and tasted—more than anything else—like fish.

The next morning was clear. I did my yoga, ending with the solar salute. The oracle watched me. "What kind of ceremony is that?" he asked.

"I am welcoming the sun and giving it praise."

"Ah. I have not been able to decide what you believe in."

It was too early in the morning to discuss religion. "How are you doing?"

"I slept well. I had no dreams. My arm feels better. I think it is good that we left the cave. I think I might have gotten sicker, if we had stayed. The spirits there are very hungry, and I am not certain that my gift was big enough for them. But they are not the kind of spirits who travel. They have not followed me."

We ate some more of the lizard, cold this time, saddled the bowhorns, and went on.

The valley kept widening. A little after noon I glanced around and saw the bluffs were gone. I twisted in the saddle and looked back. There they were: a yellow wall, lit by the sun, extending north and south as far as I could see. We had come out the valley of our little tributary. We were in the valley of the Great River, traveling through a level forest. A number of the trees had fallen, and a lot more leaned at perilous angles. There were patches of color on the trunks: pale blue, pale green, and yellow. The patches were organisms, I decided. Most likely they fed on dead tissue. This was the bottomland. The flood plain. A lot of trees must die in the years when the river rose.

Late in the afternoon we came to a large pond or an inlet of the river. I couldn't tell which. Scum floated on it, a bright azure blue, and there were orange flowers that reminded me of lotuses. Our trail went close to the water. At the most we were ten meters away, traveling between the forest and the shore.

Ahead of us an animal waded in the shallows. It was a biped, a kind I had not seen before, very tall and very slender. Its color was tan or pale gray. It had the usual long neck and tiny head. It bent and pulled up flowers, stuffing the orange petals and blue stalks into its mouth.

The scene had an eerie beauty: the dark water, the gaudy flowers, the biped moving carefully and delicately—like a dancer, its long tail high so it didn't touch the surface of the water.

"There," said Derek and pointed. The water farther out was moving slightly. Flowers rose and fell. I saw ripples, then a head. It was a lizard, but much bigger than any lizard I had ever seen before.

"Aiya," said the oracle.

The head went under. I got a glimpse of a long back with a row of spines along it, then a tail, then nothing except a ripple that moved toward shore. Was the biped blind? I wanted to shout.

It gathered another handful of flowers and stuffed them into its mouth.

"Now," said Derek.

The lizard struck, the huge, dark body erupting from the water. The biped screamed and fell. Birds flew out of the trees and bushes along the shore.

I reined my bowhorn. The bodies rolled in the water. I saw a dark back, a long dark tail, the white underside of the biped.

The birds flew above me, crying out warning. There was another scream. God! What a sound!

My bowhorn shivered. I tightened my grip on the reins.

Nia was beside me. I hadn't seen her coming. She took hold of my animal's bridle. "Be calm," she said. "Be calm." Her free hand rubbed the furry brown neck.

I looked back at the water. The thrashing had ended. I could still see the white belly of the biped, floating just below the surface of the water. For a moment it was motionless. Then it jerked—and jerked again. It was moving toward shore. No. It was being moved. The lizard was pulling it. I saw the spiny back. The blunt head lifted. The jaws were clenched around a slender arm.

"Aiya," said the oracle. "That is an animal I have never seen before."

"Nor I," said Nia. "Though I've heard there are big lizards in the river."

"No excrement," said Derek. "Let's get moving. I want to get past that thing while it's still busy."

Nia let go of my animal's bridle. I slapped the reins. The bowhorn moved forward.

Our trail went around the inlet, leading us toward the lizard, which was entirely out of the water now. It dragged its prey up on the bank, then looked around. God, it was ugly! The dark skin was folded and sagging. The spines that went along the back were bent and torn. Some were missing entirely. These animals must fight. There were splotches on the heavy body: a lot of them, pale gray. A parasite, I decided, a kind of skin disease.

The lizard stared at us, then took a new grip on the biped, pulling it all the way out of the water. It let go and raised its head, looking at us again.

We were twenty meters from it with no choice except to go past it. We kept moving, none of us speaking. My bowhorn was flicking its ears. Ahead of me the other bowhorn seemed just as nervous. The short tail twitched back and forth, ready to give a warning sign. Nia stayed next to me, one hand on my animal's bridle.

The lizard bent its head and nosed the biped, turning it so it was belly up. Then it bit in.

It paid no attention to us after that. A couple of times I twisted in the saddle and looked back. The first time the lizard's head was low. The second time the head was lifted. Bits of flesh hung from the jaws and a long piece of gut was looped over the snout.

I shivered. My bowhorn snorted. The trail led back into the forest. I turned a final time. The inlet was gone from view.

"How big was that thing?" I asked.

Nia said, "The body was the same size as Derek."

"Two meters plus the tail," said Derek in English.

"Hu!" I said.

The oracle made the gesture of agreement.

A little before sundown we reached the bank of the river. The forest ended suddenly. Before us was a wide expanse of water. How far across? A kilometer? It was dotted with low islands. Some were bare: mud banks or sandbars.

Others were covered with vegetation. The water ran smoothly, gleaming in the light of the almost-gone sun.

"This is a sight I have not seen for many winters," Nia told us. "I crossed it in the winter to the north of here. It was frozen. That is the best time to cross."

"I have never seen it before," the oracle said. "It's certainly big."

We rested for a while. The sun went down. Birds flew over us, heading home.

"I'm tired," the oracle said. "Let's make camp."

Nia said, "Not here."

"Why not?" I asked.

She pointed north. A line of smoke drifted up into the sky. "We will spend the night with those people—if they are women. If it is a man, it's better to know that now, before we sleep."

We turned toward the smoke, traveling along the edge of the river. I made out a house. No. A tent, shaped like a hemisphere. The door faced the river. In front of the door was a fire, bright in the twilight.

Nia stopped and shouted, "People come!"

There was no answer.

"Is anyone home?"

A figure came out of the tent. He or she paused by the fire, looking toward us and frowning, trying to see into the darkness. "I can hear you, but I can't make out what you look like." The figure made the gesture that meant "come here."

I dismounted. So did the oracle. He staggered and Derek put an arm around him. Nia took the reins of the animals. The rest of us moved forward into the firelight.

"Atcha!" said the person. "You are something to look at!"

"We are travelers," said Derek. "Our friend is sick. We need a place to stay for the night."

The person was silent. I looked at him or her. I had reached the point where I could usually guess the gender of a native. This person baffled me. The voice was deep. The body was broad and solid. That indicated a male. But the fur was the fur of a woman: sleek and soft with a dull sheen like velvet.

The person wore a yellow tunic. There was embroidery on the sleeves and hem. The buckle on his belt—her belt?—was silver. He or she wore bracelets of gold or bronze.

A man, almost certainly. They loved finery. And yet I had never seen a man with fur like that.

"You can stay here," the person said.

Derek made the gesture of gratitude.

"I have to tell you, I am not willing to share my tent. It is small. I have gotten used to living alone. But I have plenty of blankets and enough food

205

for everyone. I want to know about you. I have never seen people as naked as you are."

Derek helped the oracle sit down, then straightened up. For once he was properly dressed in jeans and a shirt. The jeans were dirty. The shirt was torn. His boots were badly scuffed.

The person said, "I thought at first you were people who'd lost their fur. There are two bad diseases in the marshes to the south of here. One makes a person shake until she dies. The other makes hair fall out in patches. That one does not usually kill. But it certainly embarrasses!" He or she frowned. "Now I see you do not have the bodies of people. You are too thin. Your arms and legs are too long. The way you move does not look right to me. What are you?"

The oracle lifted his head. "I have traveled with them for many days. They are strange to look at, but they are not demons. Nor are they monsters like the ones the holy children drove out of the world long ago."

"That is a story I don't know," said the person. "Or at least it doesn't sound familiar. Where are you from?"

"My people live to the east of here. They are the Copper People of the Plain. I am their oracle. I travel with these folk"—he waved at Derek and me—"because my spirit told me to.

"The other person with us, the woman who stands in the darkness, was raised among the Iron People."

"Atcha." The person looked at Nia. "Many of your people come here. I ferry them across the river. What is your name?"

Nia said nothing.

"You are ashamed," said the person in yellow. "I can understand that. You are traveling with some very peculiar people. I will tell you something. I don't care. Everyone must come to me, even those who'd rather hide and keep what they do a secret. I have seen men who travel together. I have seen women who like to travel alone. I take them from one side of the river to the other. I keep my mouth shut. I do not criticize."

"My name is Nia. I am not ashamed of these people."

The person looked at us again. "I must say, they are strange. I am Tanajin. I grew up south of here. My people—the people who raised me—live in the marshes where the Great River goes into the plain of salt water. Their gift is leather, which is made from the skin of the *umazi*, which are lizards bigger than any found in the river."

"Aiya!" said the oracle.

"I am Lixia," I said. "This one is Derek. My people are the Hawaiians. His are the Angelinos."

"He is a man." Tanajin stared at Derek. "I had not realized. Are you a woman?"

206

I made the gesture of affirmation.

"You are welcome. Tether your animals in back of my tent. They'll be safe there. The lizards do not hunt out of the water, and the killers of the forest do not like to leave the shadows of the trees."

Nia made the gesture of acknowledgment. She led the animals away. Derek followed.

There was a large flat stone next to the fire. Tanajin pushed it into the flames, then took a stick and raked coals around the stone. A cooking surface. He or she made the gesture that meant "just a minute" and went in the tent.

"Is that a man or a woman?" I asked the oracle.

"A woman. Can't you tell?"

"No. And the name does not have an ending I recognize."

"I have gotten used to you," he said. "I keep forgetting that you are entirely out of the ordinary. It takes other people to remind me of that."

She came back out, carrying something that she put on the cooking stone. I leaned forward.

"It's bread." She lifted the top piece off the stack. It was flat and round like a pancake or a tortilla.

"Not a kind I know," said the oracle.

"I make it from the roots of the *talina* plant. It grows in marshes. The people in the south use it. And I add flour which travelers give me when I take them across the river."

"You have a boat?" I asked.

"A raft. These people of the plain insist on taking their animals everywhere. I cannot carry a bowhorn in a canoe—even a big one, like the ones the men use in the marshes. They have no other home—no tents like the men carry here on the plain and pitch when they make camp. When it rains the men in the marshes prop up a pair of spears. They stretch a cloak of *umazi* skin over the spears, and that is their shelter."

"It sounds uncomfortable," the oracle said.

"It isn't bad. I lived that way when I came up the river. But when I decided to settle here, I got a tent. A woman likes a home that does not rock."

She got up and went back in the tent. This time she brought out a bowl and a pan. The pan was shallow with a long handle. It looked to be made out of iron. She put it on the stone next to the stack of bread. The bowl went on the ground. It was full of a whitish liquid.

"I found eggs by the river this morning. Some fool of a lizard made her nest at the wrong time of year. If the young had hatched, they would have died."

"Why?" I asked.

"Look at the leaves! They are changing color." She tapped the side of the bowl. "By the time these little ones were ready to hatch, their mother would

207

have been gone. There would have been no one to guard them. No one to care for them."

The lizards were maternal. Funny, they didn't look maternal.

"Where does the mother go?"

"South along the river. All the big ones do. They keep going till they reach a place where the water does not freeze. A lot of them end up in the marshes. The *umazi* eat them and get fat and slow, and then it is possible to hunt the *umazi*."

"Aiya!" said the oracle.

"What about the little ones? Do they go south?"

Tanajin made the gesture that meant "no." "They dig holes in the mud at the edge of the river. They curl up and go to sleep and wake in the spring. You ask a lot of questions."

I made the gesture of agreement. "Do you mind?"

"If I don't want to answer you, I won't." She emptied the bowl into the pan. The liquid began to sizzle.

Derek and Nia came out of the darkness, our bags over their shoulders. Derek dropped the ones he carried. "I think I'll take another look at your arm."

"Good," said the oracle. "It hurts, and I am not entirely sure that your magic will work here by the river. The spirits here cannot be the same ones as in your country or my country. Tanajin does not know about the holy children."

"Neither do I," I said.

"Later," said Derek. He got out the medical kit.

The liquid in the pan was bubbling. Tanajin pulled a spoon out of her belt. She lifted the edges of whatever it was. Scrambled eggs? An omelette? The liquid on top flowed underneath. Using her free hand, she made the gesture of satisfaction.

"How did you get here?" I asked. "Why did you leave your home?"

"That is a long story. I don't like to tell it." She glanced at Nia. "Do you like to explain how you got so far from the village of your people?"

"No," said Nia.

Tanajin stood. "I need to get one other thing. Keep an eye on the eggs."

After she was gone Nia said, "I don't know what I am supposed to be looking for. What are the eggs supposed to be doing?"

I moved closer to the fire. Now I could see the pan clearly. The handle was inlaid with a gray metal: an animal pattern, two creatures with long bodies that wound around each other like ribbons in a braid. They grasped each other with clawed feet. Their heads confronted next to the pan, mouths open and almost touching, tongues curling out between rows of sharp teeth. What were they? The *umazi*? Tanajin had left the spoon. I used it to lift the edges of the omelette. Almost done.

"It looks as if the wound has been bleeding a little," said Derek. "But it isn't anything serious. There is no sign of any kind of rot."

"Good," said the oracle. "I do not want to die."

"Not many do," said Nia.

The oracle flexed his arm. Derek had put a new bandage on. "It still hurts. I hope I do not meet any more spirits like those in the cave. I don't like to give blood."

The eggs looked done. I lifted the pan from the fire, then put it down and waved my hand in the air. "Ouch!"

"I should have told you," Tanajin said. "The handle gets hot. Give me the spoon."

She knelt and divided the omelette in four, then took a piece of bread and laid a quarter of the omelette on it, folding the bread over. An egg sandwich. She handed it to me. "The jug on the ground is full of beer. I made it. It isn't as good as the beer the travelers bring. There are disadvantages to living alone."

I took the jug and moved away from the fire. The bread I held was warm and soft. It felt greasy. I took a bite. It was greasy—and tasty. The eggs had a strong flavor. Like what? Fish maybe. The beer was sour. I liked it.

My comrades got their sandwiches. We ate and drank. Tanajin watched us.

When we were done, Nia said, "There is a lake to the south of here."

Tanajin made the gesture of agreement.

"We need to get there."

Tanajin frowned. "There is no easy way. The trail goes across the river. It leads from the country of the Amber People to the country of your people, Nia. Before I came, travelers had to camp at the edge of the river and cut down trees. They made rafts to carry them across the river and then had to leave the rafts behind them to rot. A waste of good timber!

"And they did not know what to do, once they were on the water. They drifted downriver. They got caught on snags. Lizards came after them. I heard about this.

"I thought—here is something I can do which is useful. Here is a gift that people will appreciate.

"There is no trail that goes along the river. The way is hard. There are marshes and bogs. It will take you many days."

Derek said, "We have to get there soon."

"It cannot be done."

Derek leaned forward. "This is important. We are meeting with people. We have promised to be there."

Tanajin drank beer. She handed the jug to me, then wrapped her arms around her knees and stared at the fire. "I could take you downriver on my raft. But I'd lose it. The current is too strong. I could not get the raft back upriver.

209

And there is a place where the water goes down rapidly. You could get through in a boat. But I am not certain that a raft could make it." She paused. "Let me think. Maybe in the morning I will know what to do." She stood up. "I told you I had blankets. They are piled outside my door. Rest well."

Tanajin went in the tent. I took a blanket, too exhausted to examine it, though I noticed—lying underneath—that it was heavy and warm.

"Lixia?" It was Derek.

"Uh?"

"I called the ship."

I lifted my head. He was sitting by the fire. The ruddy light outlined a cheekbone and made an eye gleam.

"Yes?" I said.

"We aren't going to get our conversation with a doctor."

"What? You had it figured out. You were certain."

"Uh-huh." He smiled. I saw the corner of his mouth curl up. "Ivanova decided it would hurt their position if they voted for any kind of intervention before the big meeting. And the Chinese abstained. Every one."

"Why?"

"Don't ask me. I haven't the first idea."

"Do you really care so much?"

"Lixia, you will never get anywhere until you understand the importance of politics."

"Huh," I said and lay back down.

"One other thing," he said.

"Yes?"

"Gregory has been pulled out. He wasn't learning enough, sitting alone in his cabin, and the cabin stank, and the food was boring. We are the only people left on this continent."

"Eddie still wants us to leave?"

"He wants the option. If his side wins, he intends to quarantine the planet."

"Shit."

Derek smiled. "Yvonne is going up to join his faction in the big fight. Santha and Meiling are staying where they are, for the time being."

"Huh," I said again.

I woke at sunrise, stood and stretched, then walked down the bank till I found a cluster of bushes, peed, and washed my hands in the river. There was a flock of birds on the nearest island, roosting in the trees. They were large and white. They kept moving, flapping from one tree to another or leaving the island entirely, flying out over the river. One went over me. It was high enough up to be in sunlight. How splendid it was! How brilliantly white!

210

I went back to camp. Derek was gone—off to check the animals, most likely. The oracle lay wrapped in his blanket. Nia was going through one of the saddlebags, and Tanajin sat by the fire. A metal tripod stood over it. A pot hung suspended, flames licking around it. I looked in. Gray mush.

Tanajin said, "I have thought some more about your need."

I made the gesture that meant "go on."

"There is no quick way through the marshes. I told you that before. There is no safe way, either. The big lizards like to sun themselves on the banks of the river, and they hunt in the shallows. They are hungry this time of year. They know they must eat well, before they start the trip south.

"There are other animals that are dangerous. The killers of the forest. The little *mathadi*. They are no bigger than my hand. But their bite is poisonous. You must go on the river."

"How?" I asked.

"There is a man who lives near here. Like me, he comes from the south. He used to be a great hunter of the *umazi*. He knows the river—all of it. After we eat, I will build up the fire and signal him. If he is in the area, he will come. Maybe he will take you to the lake."

I made the gesture of gratitude. She gave the mush another stir. "You will have to leave the animals here. They will not fit in the boat."

I made the gesture that meant "no matter." "Would you like them? We owe you a gift in return for your help."

Tanajin frowned. "I do not travel on land. Not any long distance. I can walk to anyplace I want to visit."

Nia came over. She looked angry. "What are you saying, Li-sa? How can you offer the animals to this woman?"

I looked up, surprised. "She has found a way to get us to the lake."

"You will meet your friends and go off with them. That is your plan, isn't it?"

"I'm not certain. Maybe."

"If you do, what about me? What about the oracle? What will happen to us? We will be left alone in the middle of the plain." She squatted down and stared at me. "I do not want to go to the Amber People. I do not think the Iron People will make me welcome. We need those animals! We are going to have to travel a long distance before we find anyone who will give us through-the-winter hospitality."

"What have you done?" asked Tanajin.

"We've had bad luck," said Nia. She sounded curt.

"Worse than most, from the sound of it," said Tanajin. She took a bowl and filled it with mush. "I have heard of people who make one village mad at them. But two! That is something!"

211

"I wasn't thinking," I said to Nia. "You're right. You'll need the bowhorns. We'll have to find another gift for Tanajin." I paused. "You don't have to come with us the rest of the way to the lake. You could stay here."

"Is that what you want?" asked Nia.

"No. I want you to come. It won't be easy to leave you or the oracle. I don't want to do it now."

Nia made the gesture of assent. "I will go with you the rest of the way. Until you meet your friends."

I looked at Tanajin. "Will you take care of the animals till Nia and the oracle return?"

She handed me the bowl of mush, then made the gesture of assent.

I made the gesture of gratitude and tried the mush. It had a gritty texture. The flavor was nutty and sweet. Not bad.

"There is beer to drink," said Tanajin. "We'll eat, and then I'll build up the fire."

Nia woke the oracle. Derek returned. I explained our plan between mouthfuls of mush.

He made the gesture of agreement, then looked at Tanajin. "How safe is the river? I need to take a bath."

"The current is strong here. The lizards do not really like fast water. They are not likely to hunt in this area. You can go into the river, but stay close to shore and keep your eyes open. Those animals do not always do what is expected."

"Okay," said Derek.

Tanajin frowned.

"All right," said Derek in the language of gifts.

"I'll go with you," I said and stood.

"You need a something," said Tanajin.

"What?" asked Derek.

"Let me show you." Tanajin rose and went in the tent. She came out with an object about the size of a baseball. "This."

I took the object. It was yellow and felt oily. "We have nothing like this," I said.

"No wonder you look dirty and stink."

Derek said, "We have nothing like this with us. We have it at home. And we use it."

"Well, use it now," said Tanajin.

We went upriver till we were out of sight of the tent, stripped, and waded in. The water was lukewarm, about the same temperature as Tanajin's native beer. Even close to shore I could feel the current. I dunked down till the water covered me, then stood and rubbed myself with the yellow ball. It foamed. Wonderful!

212

Derek held out his hand. "Me, too."

"Just a minute." I covered myself with lather and rubbed lather in my hair. He stood watching, waist-deep in water, his hands on his hips. "Impatience on a monument," I said.

"What?"

"It's a quote, but I don't have it right."

"Shakespeare. *Twelfth Night.* 'She sat like Patience on a monument, smiling at grief.' I don't remember the act or scene, but it's Viola speaking to the duke. About herself, of course, though the duke does not know it. Give me the soap."

I handed it over. He lathered. I rinsed. Was there anything equal to getting clean? Especially after traveling so long. I got the soap back and covered myself with lather again.

Derek said, "I think we could use this stuff to wash our clothes. I have reached the point where I don't want to stand upwind of myself."

A log floated by. There was a lizard on it. A little one, no more than a meter long. It turned its head and looked at us, then inflated the sack in its throat. *Ca-roak!*

"The same to you," I said.

We waded back to shore, washed our clothes, and spread them on the sand to dry. The air was almost motionless. The day was getting hot. We sat down side by side. I glanced at Derek. His hair was blond again. His skin had returned to its usual color: brown and reddish brown. He looked attractive.

"The old saints were right," he said. "The ones who didn't take baths. Being dirty does interfere with sex. I'm not sure what the exact connection is, and it doesn't work for everyone, of course. But it certainly works for me." He made the gesture of inquiry.

I replied with the gesture of agreement and the gesture of assent.

We made love on the sand, then waded back into the river and washed ourselves off. We sat down again. He leaned over and kissed my ear. "Aristotle was not right. 'All animals are sad after sex.' I tend to feel mellow and sentimental after getting laid." He grinned. "And complacent, as if I've pulled off something out of the ordinary. A better-than-average card trick or a really clever essay."

"I didn't know you did card tricks."

"Not at the moment. I left my cards upstairs."

I looked downriver. A thick column of smoke rose into the sky. The signal fire.

"But I can prove that I'm clever," Derek said.

"Oh, yeah?"

"There was someone in the tent when we arrived last night. Hiding. I think it was a man."

213

"How do you know?"

"Footprints. Big ones. Entering and leaving. The ones close to the tent were scuffed. But I found others farther away. Good clear ones. One set was fresh. The ones leaving. My bet is he left after we went to sleep." Derek paused. "Not by the front. That would have wakened me. He cut apart two skins in the back."

I thought for a moment. "Do you think it's the man she's signaling?"

"Most likely. She didn't want us to know she was friendly with a man. Even though I am a man and so is the oracle. These people are careful."

I checked the clothes. They were still damp. "I just realized this morning—there's a chance our journey is almost over. We won't see Nia or the oracle after another day or two."

He made the gesture of agreement.

"I didn't mind leaving that village in New Jersey. Those people were loathsome. I barely got out alive. But every other time I've finished a study, it's been painful. At least a little. To go in and out of the lives of other people."

"I'm usually ready to go," said Derek. "I start thinking of my house in Berkeley. My books. The indoor plumbing. The kitchen with everything I need for cooking. And all the lovely women that are to be found around a university." He paused. "Later, when I'm back, I miss the people I was studying." He grinned. "In the comfort of my house."

I checked the clothes again. We talked about the people we had studied and the people we had known as friends and colleagues on Earth. A wandering conversation, full of pauses. We made love a second time and washed again in the lukewarm river. The day kept getting hotter. Clouds appeared in the west.

Around noon Nia came looking for us. "The man has arrived. He must live close to here. He's willing to take us to the lake. But he wants to go now. He says there will be a storm in the afternoon. He wants to be a good distance down the river by then."

We put on our underwear and shook the sand off the rest of our clothes, rolled them and carried them to camp.

There was a canoe drawn up on the shore. A dugout. Good-sized. Surprising that a single man would need a boat that big. The prow was high. The top was an animal head, elaborately carved. The eyes were inlaid with shell. The mouth was open and had real teeth: triangular and white. They were all the same size. Unspecialized. Most likely the teeth of a fish or reptile or a very large bird. The owner of the canoe was nowhere in sight.

"He's in the tent," said the oracle. "Talking to Tanajin. They are a strange pair."

"We'd better put on shirts," said Derek. "The day is bright. We'll get burned out on the water."

214

"Okay."

We packed the jeans and the rest of our belongings.

Nia said, "I talked with Tanajin this morning and told her I am a smith. She has tools here, left by a traveler. She says there is a hole in the bottom of her best cooking pot, and Ulzai—the man—has a knife that no longer holds an edge. And there is other work to be done."

"I am not much use at a forge," said the oracle. "But I know stories, and my dreams are useful."

Reciprocity. A gift must always be returned. What could we possibly give to Nia and the oracle in return for their help?

Tanajin came out, carrying a sack made of leather and a large metal jug. "Food," she said.

The man came after her. He wasn't tall, but he was broad and heavy. His fur was shaggy. It made him look even bigger than he was. He limped heavily. There was a patch of white fur on his leg. Was that evidence of scar tissue? He turned his head, looking us over. Two lines of white fur went down the side of his face. The inner line touched the corner of his mouth and the lip was twisted out. I could see the red mucous membrane.

His eyes were red. His pupils were contracted and so narrow I could not see them. The eyes were blank. Eerie!

"You are certainly different," he said. His voice was deep and harsh. "Tanajin says you have not been sick."

Derek made the gesture of affirmation.

"I am Ulzai."

He wore a kilt made of brown cloth. His belt was leather with a buckle of yellow metal. Brass, most likely. A long knife hung at his side. The sheath was leather and brass or bronze. The hilt was tarnished silver. His feet were bare. He wore no jewelry at all. He was the plainest-looking man I had seen on the planet. Plain in both senses. Unadorned and ugly.

"Get everything you own in the canoe. Does any one of you know how to paddle?"

"I do," I said.

"I will be in the stern. You sit in the prow. These others will go in between." He stared at Derek and Nia and the oracle. "The boat is going to be heavily laden. It may be that I am a fool to carry so many people. But I know what I am doing out on the water, and I have always been lucky there. Listen to me! Stay quiet! If you move around, the boat may turn over."

"Okay," said Derek.

"What?" asked Ulzai.

"That word means 'yes,'" said the oracle.

215

We loaded the canoe and pushed it into the water. Nia and the oracle got in clumsily.

"Be careful!" said Ulzai.

Derek did a little better.

Ulzai and I turned the boat, then climbed in. "You—at least—can get in a canoe," the furry man said. "Tell me your name."

"Lixia."

"Li-zha," he repeated.

Tanajin said, "Farewell."

I found my paddle. It was almost the same as the paddles I had used in northern Minnesota.

"Get to work," said Ulzai.

I dipped the paddle in the water. My first stroke was shallow.

"Is that the best you can do?"

"Give me time," I said. "I have not done this for many years, and I will not remember how to do it if you make me uneasy."

He made a barking noise. "All right."

The canoe moved out into the river. I glanced back once and saw Tanajin standing on the shore: a dark figure, motionless. Her tent was behind her. Smoke rose from her fire. It was still thick and dark.

"Don't look back," said Ulzai.

I turned my head and concentrated on paddling.

Ulzai

fter a while Ulzai said, "You are beginning to falter. Give the paddle to the man without hair. I'll watch him and tell him what he's doing wrong. You watch the river for logs."

Derek took the paddle. I rubbed my injured shoulder and looked around.

We were in the main channel: a broad expanse of water, empty except for an occasional bit of floating debris—a branch, a leaf, a mat of vegetation, a tree.

On my left was the eastern shore, covered with forest. The valley wall rose in the distance. It had not changed: a row of bluffs, made of soft rock and deeply eroded, pale yellow in the sunlight.

On my right were islands and sandbars and patches of marsh. Most of the islands were covered with trees. I couldn't make out the shoreline. There was no neat line between solid ground and water, no way to tell a large island from the riverbank.

Beyond the marsh and forest rose another line of cliffs, marking the western side of the valley. A lot of water must have run through here at some time in the past. Was this evidence for glaciation? A question for the planetologists. I wondered if they'd ever get down here, ever get to see this valley.

217

Midway through the afternoon Nia opened the food sack and handed out pieces of bread. We drank sour beer.

"There's our storm," Derek said.

I looked west. Clouds billowed above the cliffs: cumulonimbus, tall and grayish white. Other clouds—high and thin—extended to the middle of the sky. The sun shone through them, its brilliance barely dimmed.

Ulzai said, "You take the paddle back, o hairless woman. We are going to need whatever skill you have."

I followed orders. A wind began to blow, and the river grew choppy. Ulzai said, "Turn in."

"Where?" I asked.

"The island ahead. The big one."

We paddled toward it. Driftwood was piled on the upriver side: gray branches and roots, trunks worn smooth by water. We skirted the driftwood and came to shore on a little sandy beach. I climbed out. There was a low rumble of thunder in the west.

"Get the boat up on land," said Ulzai.

We unloaded the boat and pulled it out of the water, then carried it to the edge of the forest.

By this time the sky was dark. Ulzai made the gesture that meant "come along." We gathered our supplies and followed him into the forest. A path wound among the trees. Above us foliage rustled in the wind. The air smelled of damp earth and the approaching rain.

We reached a clearing. There was a pool in the middle, three meters across, clear and shallow. I could see leaves on the bottom. Last year's, maybe. They were dull yellow and gray. A dark blue mossy plant grew at the edges of the pool, and orange bugs skittered over the surface.

At the edge of the clearing was an awning, large and made of leather, stretched between four trees. All the debris of the forest floor had been cleared out from under it, and a pile of driftwood lay in the middle of the bare ground.

"That is my home," Ulzai said.

"Spartan," said Derek in English.

There was a crack of thunder. I jumped. Raindrops splattered down through the forest canopy.

Ulzai made a gesture.

We crowded under the awning, and the rain began in earnest. It drummed on the awning, dripped off the edges of the leather and fell into the clearing like—what? A gray curtain. A mountain torrent. I huddled, my arms around my knees. Wind blew water in on me. Lightning flashed. There was more thunder.

"This won't last," said Derek.

218

"I hope not," I said.

Again lightning. Again thunder. There was no pause between them. The lightning was close. I shivered, not from fear. The air was cold, and I was getting wet. Nia was closer to the edge of the awning than I was. Already her tunic clung to her body. Her fur was matted down, and she had a look of grim endurance.

"There has been a lot of rain this summer," the oracle said. "I wonder who is responsible."

Ulzai said, "One thing I have learned since I came up the river. The weather here is never reliable. To me it looks as if there are a lot of different spirits who take a hand in making the weather. They don't get along. They refuse to work together, and that explains why there are so many kinds of weather here and why the weather is always changing."

I looked at Nia. She was frowning. "You grew up on the plain, Nia. Is he right about the weather?"

"I do not know what causes the weather here, but in the country of my people—" She paused.

Hail fell with the rain. The hailstones bounced and rolled. A few ended under the awning. They were the size of gumballs.

"Everything comes from the Mother of Mothers," Nia said. "All the spirits are her children, and she has mated with a lot of them. This kind of behavior would be absolutely wrong, if people did it. If a man encounters his mother in the time for mating, they ride away from each other as fast as possible. But spirits are different. And who else did she have to mate with, the Great One? Every spirit came out of her body." Nia wiped the fur on her forehead, getting rid of some of the water.

"She mated with the Spirit of the Sky. They had four children in one birth. All were daughters. Each was a different color. When they grew up, they moved away from their mother and became the four directions. The pale yellow daughter settled in the east. The dark orange daughter settled in the west. The black daughter became the north. The last daughter was blue-green like her father. She became the south."

"This is a story I've never heard," Ulzai said.

The oracle made the gesture of agreement.

The hail piled up, turning the ground white. Nia went on.

"The Spirit of the Sky visited each daughter in turn, and each of the women gave birth to a son. They were the four winds. They grew up to be fierce and quarrelsome. They all laid claim to the land between the four directions. None would back down. They fought for the land, never ceasing, and life became impossible for everyone. Even the demons began to complain. They lived underground, but they liked to come out from time to time and

219

cause trouble. How could they do it now? They had no idea what they'd find. A flood to put out their fires. A deep snow in the middle of summer. Hail like this or a heavy rain.

"At last the Mother of Mothers took a hand. She called the four cousins. They came and stood around her. That must have been a sight! Each one was a different color, and each one was as tall as a thundercloud. The wind from the east was yellow like his mother. The wind from the west was orange-red like fire. The wind from the south was the color of the sky, and the wind from the north was iron-black.

"They towered over their grandmother and glared at one another.

"'You naughty boys,' she said. 'Why can't you stop fighting?'

"The north wind answered her. His voice was deep and rumbling. The breath that came from his mouth was cold. 'We are all big men. Not one of us is willing to back down. How can we let another man have the land in the middle? Each one of us wants the women. Each one of us wants the animals.'

"'Look around!' said the Mother of Mothers. 'You have destroyed everything that you have laid claim to. Your floods have washed away the villages. Your sudden frosts have killed the vegetation. The animals have fled. The demons are talking about leaving. What is left that is worth fighting over?'

"The four cousins looked around. Their grandmother was telling the truth. The plain was brown and black. Nothing lived there. No people. No animals. No vegetation.

"'And let me tell you something else,' said the old woman, the Great One. 'While you have been fighting here, other spirits have been visiting your mothers. Now you have sisters that are almost grown.'

"'Is that so? Then I will go home,' said the wind from the south. His breath was hot and dry. It smelled like the plain in the middle of summer. Aiya! What an aroma! How sweet and pleasant!

"'No,' said the Mother of Mothers. 'I will not let you mate with your sisters.'

"'Why not?' asked the wind from the east.

"'There has been too much of that kind of thing. If it continues, soon the children who are born will look like monsters or demons.'

"'But what are we going to do?' asked the wind from the west. 'You don't expect us to live without sex.'

"'No,' said the Mother of Mothers. 'In the time of mating, each of you will leave your home territory and go to another direction—north to south and west to east—until you meet your cousins or other women or even female demons. Mate with them! But remember this! I speak for the land in the middle. It does not belong to any of you. When you cross it, travel carefully. Treat everything with respect. Make no trouble. Cause no harm.'

"The four cousins frowned and glared.

220

"'What if we do not agree to this?' asked the northern wind.

"'Then I will deal with you, and don't think I can't.' All at once the old woman increased in size. She rose until her head almost touched the sky. The sun shone over her left shoulder.

"The four cousins looked up. Their mouths hung open. They shaded their eyes. They saw their father, the Spirit of the Sky. He floated above the old woman. The sun was the buckle on his belt. His wings spread from horizon to horizon. He looked down at them. His face was blue-green. His eyes glared angrily.

"They were afraid. 'All right,' they said. 'We will do as you suggest.'

"'Good,' said the Spirit of the Sky.

"That is the end of the story," said Nia. "The four winds stopped fighting. The weather became less violent. The people who had left came back to the land in the middle. So did the animals.

"But in the spring, at the time of mating, the four cousins travel across the land looking for women, and that is why the weather is bad in the spring."

She paused. I looked at the clearing. The hail had stopped. Rain still fell heavily.

"It is not spring now," said Ulzai. "Your story does not explain this weather."

"The cousins are restless and unruly," said Nia. "They prowl around the edges of the land in the middle. They try to be careful, but sometimes they meet one another. Then they shout and gesture. Lightning flashes. There is thunder and hail. But they do not fight the way they used to. Instead they back down and move apart. No real damage is done."

Ulzai made the barking sound. "I have seen black clouds that rose up to the sky. They leaped on the plain like dancers dressed in black tunics. I have seen two and three and four—all at the same time, one in each direction, dancing at the horizon. I think those clouds are able to do harm. And what about the hail that beats the vegetation flat? The winds that tear up trees? The storms of ice? Even the heat of summer can do damage. I have been out in the open and felt the heat like a blow to the head and a blow to the stomach. Those men have not kept their promise. They are still fighting, and this land is still a bad place for people."

Nia looked angry.

"Why are you here?" asked the oracle.

"The rain is getting lighter," Ulzai said. "And I am getting edgy. You may be used to being with other people. I am not." He stood and moved out from under the awning. "Stay here! I'll come back." He walked into the forest. His limp seemed worse than before. The weather, most likely.

"He has been in some kind of trouble," said the oracle. "And so has the woman. Why else would they have left their home?"

221

"People leave for no other reason?" Derek asked.

"Don't act as if you are stupid," Nia said. "You know there are travelers who carry gifts from one village to another. And men who like to wander. And women like Inahooli, who leave home for religious reasons. But the oracle is right. Those two people have done something wrong. I can tell. The rain is stopping."

She got up and went out into the clearing, stopped and looked at the sky. "It will clear. Hu! I am wet." She ran her hand down her arm, trying to squeeze the water out of her fur.

Most of the time the natives reminded me of bears, but there was something catlike about Nia at the moment. She grimaced and rubbed her other arm. "Aiya!" She pulled off her tunic and wrung it out, standing naked in the clearing. "I'm not going to stay in this place. It's too wet. Let the man find me, if he thinks it is important." She walked off, carrying her tunic.

Ulzai had headed inland. Nia went back toward the shore.

"Off in all directions, like the four spirits," Derek said.

The oracle opened the bag that Tanajin had given us. "I am going nowhere." He took out a piece of yellow fruit about the size of a z-gee ball. I was pretty certain it was a fruit. He bit in. Juice squirted. The oracle wiped his chin and licked his fingers, chewing all the while.

Derek got out his radio. "Nia is right. There ought to be a wind by the river and sunlight, if the clouds clear. I think I'll have a talk with Eddie. And when I'm done with that, I'll think about fishing."

He left. The oracle kept eating. A ray of sunlight touched the pool. It gleamed.

"It will get hot again," said the oracle.

I made the gesture of agreement. The air was humid. Clouds of tiny bugs appeared. In the sunlight over the pond they shone like motes of dust. In the forest shadow they were invisible. But I felt them hitting my face. I snorted and waved.

The oracle said, "Go. I can see you are getting angry. If the man comes back and wants to know where everyone is, I will tell him."

"Okay." I walked toward the river, moving slowly and looking around. The trees were tall, their trunks straight and narrow, their bark gray. The foliage, high above me, was blue. Here and there a few leaves shone, touched by sunlight, like pieces of blue glass in a window.

There must have been more than one path. The one I followed led me to a place I did not remember. A few dead trees stood among stands of a plant without leaves. Knobby green stalks moved stiffly in the wind.

I could go back and try to find the path I should have taken, but how would I recognize it? I looked down. My shadow pointed along the path. I was heading east. We had landed on the eastern shore of the island. Better to go forward.

The path grew mucky. The plants grew tall: a meter and a half, two meters. Water gleamed amid the vegetation. I was in a mire. It was time to give up. I turned.

There was a lizard on the path ten meters away. Not a really big one. I estimated it to be two meters long, tail and all. The animal lifted its head, turned it, and regarded me with a bright black eye.

Oh, hell.

The mouth opened. I saw ragged teeth. A tongue came out, thick and black. I kept still.

The animal's skin was brown with only a few wrinkles, and the spines along the back were in good condition. This fellow was comparatively young. He hadn't suffered from time and violence. Was he dangerous?

The mouth opened wider. The tongue extended farther. What was it doing? Tasting the air? Tasting my aroma? Finding out if I were edible?

I didn't want to go toward the animal. I didn't want to turn my back on it, either. There was marsh on either side of me. I began to sweat.

The long body whipped around. A moment later the animal was gone— off the path and out of sight among the reeds.

I let out my breath. Ulzai came into view, limping down the muddy trail, a spear in one hand. "I told you people to stay put. I got back, and no one was there except the little man. I went to find you. What did I discover? Your trail going off in the wrong direction! Are you crazy? Or merely a fool?"

"A fool," I said.

He barked. "It is good that you know what you are. Many people do not. This path leads into a marsh. There are lizards."

"I know. I saw one just before you came. On the path where you are standing."

He looked down at the mud in front of him. "I see. It wasn't big. An animal that size will not attack a full-grown person. You were in no danger. Come on."

By the time we reached the river, the western half of the sky was clear. The sun shone brilliantly. Nia had spread her tunic on the canoe. She lay on the sand on her back, one arm over her eyes. Derek sat close by. "I've been watching the river. There are big fish out there. I think I'll make a fishing pole."

"A what?" asked Ulzai.

The word that Derek had used meant—in common usage—a tent pole or the pole of a standard.

"What do you think I said?" asked Derek.

"That you wanted to make a tent for fishes. Or else—" Ulzai frowned. "That you wanted to set up a standard with a fish on top. Is that the animal of your lineage?"

"My animal lives in salt water," Derek said. "It looks like a fish, but it isn't one. The name for it is 'whale.'"

Ulzai grunted.

"What I meant to say is—I want to go fishing. I use a pole."

Nia said, "He does. I have seen him."

Ulzai looked interested. "In the marshes the women use nets to catch fish. The men use spears. And when I came up the river, I met people who use baskets and walls made of woven branches. The walls guide the fish into a trap. The baskets are the trap. But I have never heard of anyone using a tent pole."

Derek got up. "I need a branch. It has to be long and straight and flexible. Can you find me anything like that?"

Ulzai made the gesture of affirmation.

"Take care of the radio, will you?" Derek said.

"Yes. What did Eddie say?"

"The plane is coming down the day after tomorrow. Eddie expects us to be at the lake in three days. He's been able to stall the big discussion till then. He wants us to participate—not in the flesh, of course. We'll be in quarantine. But we can address the multitudes via holovision. He assumes that we are going to back him. We are going to have to make a choice, Lixia. Which side are we on?"

I made the gesture of uncertainty.

"You talk too much," Ulzai said. "And too many of the words you use are strange. Come on."

"Ulzai certainly likes to tell people what to do," said Nia. She yawned. "Aiya! It is comfortable in the sun. I think I will sleep."

I looked at the river. Nia began to snore. The clouds kept moving east until most of the sky was clear.

The two men came back. Derek had his branch and a coil of fishing line.

"How is the oracle?" I asked.

"Tired. His arm hurts. He's eaten all the fruit."

"Hu!"

"Uh-huh." Derek tied the line to the pole, then tied on a hook. He bit off the extra piece of poly and spat it out, then bent and picked it up. "We can't leave souvenirs of a higher culture." He stuck the poly into a pocket of his shirt and reached into the other pocket, pulling out a grub. It was fat and yellow. He slid the hook into the animal. It wriggled. I looked away.

Ulzai, I noticed, watched everything with interest. Nia continued to snore.

Derek reached into his pocket again and pulled out a lead weight, which he pressed into place on the line. "Fortunately, this is a metal-rich planet. If I lose the weight, it isn't likely to influence the course of history.

But I'd better not lose the line. The Unity knows what would happen if these savages discovered polypropylene."

Ulzai frowned. "I can understand only half of what you are saying."

"They always talk like this," said Nia. She sat up. Her fur was dry. It shone copper-red-brown. "It makes me angry. I have told them. They keep on the same way as before."

"I'm going down the beach," said Derek. "There's an eddy that looks interesting close to shore. In reach of this damn rig, I think. I wish I'd brought a folding rod with me, and a good spinning reel. I could have figured out a way to smuggle them down." He looked at Ulzai. "I may have to wade in the water. Is that going to be dangerous?"

"No. The lizards do not come to this side of the island. Not often, anyway. They like slow water. The river bottom goes down steeply here and the current is swift. Be careful. If you catch anything with your tent pole, bury the guts on land. Never put anything bloody in the water. The lizards will taste the blood and come."

"Okay," said Derek.

"What about my lizard?" I asked. "The one I saw? It was on this side of the island."

"It was on land," said Ulzai. "When it goes back into the water, it will find a place where the bottom is shallow and the current barely moves. I know these animals. They do not have the courage of the *umazi*."

Derek left us, going along the shore. He stopped and looked at the river, his head tilted, considering something not visible to me—the eddy, and waded into the water, swinging the long pole out. The line dropped in. He lifted the pole a little, then stood motionless. The rest of us watched him. Nothing happened.

"He knows how to keep still," Ulzai said at last. "All good hunters do."

Nia made the gesture of agreement, got up, and put on her tunic, the one that had belonged to Inahooli. It was wrinkled and there were stains on it. We were all looking pretty ratty.

"Atcha," said Ulzai.

The pole was bending. Derek had changed his grip. He was holding on tightly now. The pole bent more. He waded out a little farther.

"Be careful," called Ulzai.

The fish was going down.

No! It came out of the water in front of Derek: a long, dark body that twisted in midair and fell back into the river. *Splat!* The pole bent again.

"A good-sized fish," said Ulzai. "But it isn't worth catching. That kind is full of bones. And the flavor." He made the gesture that meant "it could be worse."

Derek lifted the pole. The fish must be rising. Yes! It jumped again, flashing in the sunlight, and fell. Derek lowered the pole. The fish ran toward the center of the river. The line gleamed, visible for a moment. I saw the tension in it. Derek turned, bringing the fish around in a circle, guiding it back toward shore.

"This is interesting," said Ulzai. "But I don't think it's a good way to catch fish. It takes a lot of time. That much is obvious. And the fish might get away—even now, after all the effort he has put into catching it."

I said, "Um."

The fish was in the shallows. Derek grinned. A moment later he said, "Goddammit."

The line was invisible at the moment. So was the fish. But I could see a zigzag pattern of ripples on the surface of the water, made by the line as it entered the water. The pattern led away from the shore. The fish had turned again.

Derek let it run till it reached the end of the line, then he started to bring it in a second time. He was sweating. His face gleamed, and there were dark patches on his shirt.

"I have seen that on certain animals," Ulzai said. "Water comes out of their skin in hot weather or when they have made some kind of big effort."

"Yes," I said.

"You certainly are unusual people. What does it mean? That he is working?"

"Yes."

"When a man uses a spear, he knows at once whether or not he has the fish. He may have to wait a long time before he has a chance to strike, but he doesn't have to work as hard as this man is working."

I was listening to a natural ice fisherman. What could I say to a person like that? He would never understand the pleasure that Derek took in fighting the fish. Though it didn't look like pleasure at the moment.

The fish surfaced. The dark back shone. I caught a glimpse of a ragged dorsal fin. It dove and resurfaced again.

"Come on, baby," said Derek. He lifted the pole and took a step backward. "That's it. I promise you, I'll be grateful. I'll give you praise. You won't be sorry you came to me."

The fish thrashed. Derek took another step toward shore. "That's it," he said again.

The fish floated just below the surface of the water. I could see it: a long, narrow shape like a cigar or a torpedo. It was almost motionless.

Derek changed his grip, going hand over hand along the pole, until he reached the tip. The butt dropped in the sand in back of him. He took hold of the line. The fish struggled weakly. Derek pulled it in and grabbed it, his fingers going behind the gill cover. He lifted. The animal twisted. It was half a meter long with a tan belly and a dark brown back. The fins were spiny and the mouth was full of teeth. Derek pulled out the hook. He was grinning.

"Another chapter for the book I'm planning to write. *Fighting Game Fish of the Galaxy.* I think I'll lie about the weight of the line."

"Ulzai says that kind isn't very tasty. And it has a lot of bones."

"Damn." He lifted the fish higher. "I promised that I would give it praise."

"You could throw it back," I said.

"It's exhausted. I've just done a lot of damage to its gills. If I let it go, it'll die. I'll have increased my karmic burden, and I won't have dinner." He shook his head. "As long as it isn't poisonous, I'm going to eat it."

"It is not poisonous," Ulzai said.

"Good. Take care of the fishing pole, will you, Lixia? I have to kill this fellow."

"Okay."

He walked up the beach. I went to retrieve the pole. By the time I had it, the fish was dead.

We went back to the clearing. Derek roasted the fish. It had more bones than a northern pike and even less flavor. Derek ate most of it. The rest of us made do with bread and dried meat.

When we were done, Derek said, "I told the fish I would praise it. That's a promise that has to be kept. It was handsome. It fought well. It kept me from hunger. I'll remember how it looked, leaping out of the water. And in time"—he grinned—"I'll forget what it tasted like."

Ulzai made the gesture of agreement.

"That was good praise," said the oracle. "And more than I expected of you. Most of the time you seem lacking in respect."

"I am an intricate person," said Derek. He used an adjective that was usually applied to metalwork or embroidery. As far as I could figure out, it had two connotations. It meant either an impressive technical achievement or something that was ornate and overdone.

Nia woke me the next day at dawn. By sunrise we were back on the water.

Derek and Ulzai paddled. I watched the river. We glided past islands and sandbars and a lot of floating debris. Clouds appeared sometime after noon. Cumuli. They loomed through the summer haze.

"Another storm," said Ulzai. "I know a place on the eastern shore. A stream runs into the river. There is a cave."

"Aiya!" said the oracle.

"Are there any spirits in the cave?" asked Nia.

"I have never seen any. I have camped there many times."

"Okay," said Derek.

The river wound toward the eastern side of the valley, and the main channel ran almost directly under the eastern bluffs. The riverbank was steep here, overgrown with green and yellow bushes. Above the foliage was a high wall of stone.

Ulzai pointed. I saw a notch in the cliff. A stream emerged from the bushes that grew below the notch: a thin sheen of water that ran over yellow rocks, then vanished into the river.

We landed south of the stream, unloaded the canoe, and pulled it up on the bank.

Birds wheeled above us, crying.

"What a lot of work," I said.

Derek made the gesture of assent. "One of the many reasons I am not entirely in love with pre-industrial technology. Though there are plenty of people on Earth who could make a better canoe using traditional methods. Maybe the problem here is a lack of the proper materials. Maybe we should introduce the birch tree."

"Aluminum," I said. "Plants scare me more than factories."

"You are doing it again," said the oracle. "Using words we don't know."

I made the gesture that meant "I'm sorry."

Ulzai said, "Come on."

We picked up our bags and followed him up the bank. The stream ran next to us in a ravine full of bushes. I couldn't see the water. I heard it: a faint gurgle. The birds kept crying. I looked up. A flock was chasing a single bird that was obviously of a different species. The bird that fled was the size of a gull. The members of the flock were—comparatively speaking—tiny.

The big bird fled toward the cliff. The little birds followed, swooping and screaming.

I tripped.

"Watch where you are going," said Derek in back of me. "Or you'll end up in that ravine."

We reached the cliff. Vines grew on it and overhung the entrance to the cave, so I didn't see it until Ulzai pushed through a patch of greenery and vanished. We followed him into a shallow space, five meters deep at most. I glanced around. There were no dark holes, no signs of an inner cave. I set down the bags I carried.

"We'll get wood," said Ulzai. "Before the rain."

Nia was right. He did like to give orders. A pity he was on this planet where the men had no chance to organize anything. He would have been a natural for disaster relief.

We went out. The sun had vanished behind a wall of clouds. The valley was dark and the sky was darkening rapidly as the clouds spread.

I gathered an armload of wood and returned to the cave. Ulzai was back already. He had a fire going, just inside the entrance. Smoke drifted up through the leaves of the vines. They were fluttering. The wind was rising.

"This will be worse than yesterday," said Ulzai. "Look at the sky in the west. It is a color between black and green." He laid another branch on the fire, then looked up, frowning. "The worst weather is in the spring. Nia is right about that. This time of year it is not likely that we'll see the black dancers. The clouds that hop and spin."

Tornadoes. I had seen one the first year I lived in Minnesota. I still had nightmares about the damn thing. They scared me more than tidal waves or volcanoes. Maybe because they were unpredictable.

Derek and the oracle came in. They dropped their wood next to mine in the back of the cave. The oracle said, "It looks terrible out there." He rubbed his neck. "Aiya! I am tired."

"How is your arm?" I asked.

"That isn't the problem. Now it is my belly. It was grumbling all night. I could not sleep, and I still feel queasy."

"The fruit," said Derek. "I wondered if it would get to you."

Nia returned. "The rain has begun. Big drops. When they hit the rock, they make a mark as wide as my hand."

She added her wood to the pile and sat down. "It has been a long time since I've been on the plain. And usually this time of year I'd be north of here with the herd and the village. I think—I am not certain—the storms are worse along the river."

"I don't think so," said Ulzai. "But I am not certain, either. I haven't spent a lot of time on the plain." He paused. "There is a question I have been wanting to ask."

"Yes?" said Derek.

"I do not want to ask you." Ulzai looked at Nia. "Tanajin told me that you are a smith."

Nia hesitated, then made the gesture of affirmation.

"She said that you belong to the Iron People."

"Yes." She paused. "I used to."

"Are you the woman we heard about?"

Nia said nothing.

"She was a smith, and she belonged to the Iron People. I don't remember her name. I am not certain that Tanajin ever told me. But she did tell me the story."

"What story?" asked Nia.

"The woman who loved a man. The Iron People tell it. So do the Amber People and the People of Fur and Tin. She is a famous woman! Are you the one?"

"Do you mean to cause trouble?" Nia asked.

"No. Why do you think I agreed to help you? Tanajin is the ferry woman. I am not." He paused for a moment. "Do you think it is easy for me to spend

229

three days with other people? There are so many of you! And those two are peculiar." He glanced at me and Derek.

Nia made a barking noise. "There is a woman to the east of here. She thought she knew me. She tried to kill us."

"When Tanajin first heard your story, she said to me, 'We are not alone. We are not the first people to have done this thing.'" Ulzai frowned. "I do not entirely agree with her. In the story they tell about you, you chose to treat a man like a sister or a female cousin. It was not an accident. You deliberately set out to do something offensive."

By this time the cave was dark, except for the light cast by the fire. It flickered on the walls. The eyes of the people around me gleamed: red, orange, yellow, and—most startling—blue. Thunder rumbled outside. Rain fell.

Nia said, "I will not argue with a story that has been told over and over. Let people believe what they want to believe."

"It was different with us," said Ulzai. He looked around. "I brought a jar of beer."

Derek found it and handed it over. Ulzai drank. "I have never told the story to anyone. I do not want to be famous on the plain."

Nia barked again. Ulzai gave the jar to her. She drank.

He hunched forward, staring at her, ignoring the rest of us. "It is not true that men like to be silent. We learn to be silent. Who is there to talk to in the marshes? The spirits. The lizards. The dead folk who wander at night. It is possible to see them. They are dim lights over the pools. They never speak. Neither do the spirits. Or if they do—" He glanced at the oracle. "I cannot hear them. I am not holy."

"I am," the oracle said.

"Tanajin told me." He looked at the fire. After a moment he rubbed the side of his face, running his hand along the lines of white fur. "I have kept the story in me for winter after winter. It is like a stone in my belly. It is like a bad taste in my mouth. It aches like an old wound in the time of rains. I do not understand it. I do not see what else we could have done."

Nia sighed. "Tell it then. I warn you. It will not help. Words are less use than you think."

"Maybe," said Ulzai.

The oracle said, "Can I have some beer?"

"What about your stomach?" asked Derek.

"Beer is good for the digestion."

Nia gave him the jar.

Ulzai scratched his head. "It's a long story."

"We have time," said Derek. "That storm isn't going to end soon."

"You two." He glared at Derek and me. "Keep quiet about what you hear. And you as well, o holy man."

We made the gesture of agreement, all three of us.

"First of all, I have to tell you about the People of Leather. I used to belong to them. So did Tanajin. They live in the marshes where the Great River goes into the plain of salt water. Their houses are not like any I have seen in other places. The marshland is flat and when the river rises, the land is flooded. All of it. The people build their houses on top of frames made of wood. I do not know how to describe these frames. They look something like the frames that people use to dry fabric or fish. But they are much bigger and solider. On top of each frame is a platform. On top of the platform is a house. The walls are made of reeds and branches woven together. The roof is made of bundles of reeds. The bundles are thick. Not even the heaviest rain can get through." He paused for a moment, his eyes half-closed, remembering. "There are no trees in the marsh, only reeds—though they can grow taller than a man. The houses rise above the reeds. They are taller than everything. A man can look up and see them, even at a distance. At night he can see the cooking fires on the platforms."

Derek leaned forward. "If there are no trees, where do you get wood for the houses?"

"The river brings it. When the river gets to the marshes, it spreads out. The water moves slowly then. The river drops whatever it has been carrying. There are sandbars at the entrance to the marshes and a great raft of wood. The raft fills most of the river, and it is so long that a man can paddle for days, going upstream, and never see the end of all that wood. There are more trees than anyone can count tangled together. Most are worn by the water. They have lost their bark. They are as gray as sand. They are as white as bone. But they are not rotten. They can be used."

"Aiya!" said the oracle.

Ulzai frowned at the fire. "Now I have forgotten what I was going to say."

"You were talking about your people," I said.

He made the gesture of agreement. "The women live in the houses, high above the reeds. The men live in boats. That is what every boy gets when it is time for him to leave the house of his mother: a boat with a carved prow and a set of spears, a knife for skinning and a cloak of lizard skin. Those four gifts are always the same.

"The boy gets them. He says farewell to his mother and to his other relatives. He paddles away. He does not return until he has killed a lizard. A big one. An *umazi*."

"What do you mean when you say, he returns?" asked Nia.

"I know the people here on the plain would not approve of our behavior. Our gift is leather. The men hunt the *umazi* and cut off their skins.

"But the skin is good for nothing, unless it is tanned, and the women do the tanning. They are the ones who have the big vats made of wood and iron.

231

They are the ones who have the urine. Where could a man possibly get enough urine to fill a tanning vat? And where would he keep the vat? Not in his canoe and not on the islands, which are often covered with water.

"When a man kills an *umazi*, he brings the skin to his mother or to a sister if his mother is dead."

"I have never heard of such a thing," said the oracle.

"It is done decently. The man waits till the big moon is full. Then—at night—he goes to the house of his mother. He ties up his boat. He climbs onto the platform. She is inside. The windows are covered. The door is fastened. She makes no noise at all.

"He lays down his gift. The raw *umazi* skin. He gathers up the gifts she has left for him outside the door. He goes. Nothing is said. They do not see each other.

"This must be done. Otherwise we have no leather, and we are the People of Leather."

"Hu!" said Nia.

"This is what you did?" asked the oracle.

Ulzai made the gesture of affirmation. "Until my mother died. My sisters were dead already. I had no female cousins. That is how it began."

"How what began?" asked Derek.

"I am a good hunter. No man killed more *umazi* than I did. My mother had more skins than she could handle. She gave away half of what I brought her.

"Sometimes at night I'd bring my boat in to the home channel. I'd drift below the houses in the darkness. I'd hear the women singing. They would praise my skill and her generosity. You have to understand, it was good to listen."

"You should not have been there," said Nia.

"I like praise," said Ulzai. "She died. I had no close relatives in the village. There was no one to bring my skins to. They were useless to me. All my skill as a hunter was useless."

"Aiya!" said Derek.

"Get more wood," said Ulzai.

Derek obeyed. Ulzai put two branches on the fire and watched until they caught. I listened. The rain was still falling.

He lifted his head. "Sometimes, when a thing like this happens, the man—the hunter—gives up hunting. He goes deep into the marsh and lives by fishing. He becomes ragged. He forgets how to speak. I have seen men like that at the time of mating. They try to force their way back into the area close to the village. I have faced two or three. They do not shout insults like ordinary men. They growl and make grunting noises. They draw their lips back and show their teeth. One raised his spear, as if he planned to use it against me.

232

In the end he did not. He made a strange noise—something like a groan—and ran away." Ulzai added branches to the fire.

"Other men look for another woman. Maybe there is a distant cousin who has no brothers. Maybe there is an old woman who has outlived all her relatives.

"But it is not easy to come to an agreement. The two people cannot speak. They cannot look at one another. The woman does not know who visits her, leaving the lizard skins. She has no idea of the right gifts to give him. A mother would know. So would a sister.

"Often the woman is afraid. The people in the village gossip when a woman who has no relations sets up a tanning vat. They ask questions. They have ideas. It is never good to attract the interest of your neighbors."

"That is true," said Nia.

"I was not willing to give up hunting. I didn't want to become a crazy man. I came into the village on dark nights. I stopped my boat under houses. I listened to the women talking. No one heard me. No one saw me. I am good at what I do.

"I learned that something had happened to the brothers of Tanajin. They had stopped coming to her house. She had nothing to tan. I decided to visit her." Ulzai got up and lifted the vines at the entrance to the cave. Water dripped off the leaves. I looked out and saw rain.

"I am getting tired of telling this story. It goes on and on. Maybe silence is better."

"Stop if you want," said Nia.

I kept my mouth shut, though I wanted to hear the rest of the story. Derek frowned.

"I will finish," Ulzai said. He sat down. "I left a skin. The next time the moon was full, I came again. She had put gifts outside her door. Food and a jar of beer and a knife. The hilt was black wood inlaid with silver. It wasn't the right size for my hand."

I made the gesture that indicated sympathy or regret.

"After that I came at every full moon. I brought her many skins. They were large and in good condition. She gave many away. But I did not hear the women sing in praise of her. And I did not always like the gifts she gave me.

"She gave me sandals made of lizard skin. They were too small. She gave me fabric for a kilt. It was dark green, covered with red and yellow embroidery. Most men would have liked it. But I like things that are plain."

"Why?" asked the oracle.

"It's the way I am." He paused. "There is nothing handsome about me. There never has been. I got this when I was a child." He touched the white fur on his face. "I fell off the platform of my mother's house. A lizard got me.

There are usually a few under the houses in the village. They are never big. The *umazi* do not live on garbage. But at the time the lizard seemed big enough to me. I shouted when it bit me. My mother dove in with a knife. She killed the lizard—and I was left with this." He touched his face a second time. "And this." He touched the white fur on his leg.

Nia said, "That must have been an experience."

Ulzai made the gesture of agreement. "Give me the beer."

I handed him the jar. He drank. "I decided to talk with Tanajin. But not in the village. I was afraid the old women would find out. I heard them talking on top of their platforms. They were like mothers hunting for vermin in the hair of their children. They hunted for bad ideas. They wanted to know something bad about Tanajin. I did not know why.

"I waited until the time of mating. I hid in the reeds near her house. When she left to go into the marshes, I went after her.

"I found her, but I wasn't the first one. There was a man with her. I confronted him. He became angry. We fought. I beat him, though it wasn't easy. He ran off into the marshes, and I spoke to Tanajin. I showed her the size of my feet and hands. I told her what kind of cloth I liked. I told her I always used the kind of spear that has a barbed head."

"Did you mate with her?" asked Derek.

Ulzai made the gesture of affirmation. "But nothing came of the mating. She had no child. That was the first mistake I made."

"What?" asked Derek. "The mating?"

Ulzai frowned. "No. Following her. Talking with her. Before that, she had been nothing. A shadow in the shadows of the house. Now she became something. A person. I knew what she looked like. I knew the sound of her voice. At times, when I was in the marsh or sitting on the platform in front of her house, I thought of her. I opened my mouth. I thought of speaking. Then I bit my tongue." He stood up again. "The rain is stopping. I am going out." He pushed through the vines.

"Interesting," said Derek in English. "How hard it is to maintain the barriers between people."

"You think so?" I said.

"Maybe I mean the opposite. Ulzai is right. It's time for a walk."

He left. I looked at Nia. Her dark face was expressionless.

"The world is full of strange people," said the oracle. "And stories which I never expected to hear. Maybe that is why my spirit told me to travel. I am going to drink more beer."

I decided to go out.

Ulzai was right about the rain. It had stopped. In the west, beyond the river, the clouds were beginning to break apart. I glanced around. Derek and

Ulzai were out of sight. I walked along the cliff until I found a place where I could climb. Up I went until I was high enough to see across the valley.

Winding channels. Islands. Marsh. The forest on the far side of the river. Rays of sunlight slanted between the clouds. Where they touched the forest, it was bright green or yellow.

The wind was cool and smelled of wet vegetation. I sat down and leaned against a rock. A flock of birds wheeled over the river. There must have been two or three hundred of them. They were too far away to be visible as anything except dots. I wondered what they were doing. Getting ready to fly south? I had seen birds do that on Earth. They flocked together and flew around, practicing migrating. Then one day—in October or November—one noticed that they were gone.

Well, hell, it couldn't be easy—flying south. I could understand why they had to practice. The birds in front of me flew off. I sat a while longer, then went back down the cliff.

Derek came up from the river. He carried a fishing rod and a string of fish. They were small, at least in comparison to the fish he'd caught the day before, with round, fat bodies and bright yellow bellies.

"I hope they're edible," he said.

We returned to the cave, and Derek held up the string. "How are these?"

"Delicious," said Nia. "But they are not easy to clean. I will do it. You might ruin them."

"Be my visitor," said Derek.

Nia frowned. "What does that mean?"

"Go ahead."

She cleaned the fish, and we roasted them. Ulzai came back. When he lifted the vines, sunlight came in. The sky in back of him was clear and bright.

"Are you going to finish your story?" asked Derek.

"Yes." He let the vines drop. We were back in shadow. "But first I will eat. Did you catch these?"

Derek made the gesture of affirmation.

"Your pole is good for something."

Derek made the gesture of gratitude.

Ulzai ate and drank the rest of the beer. He belched. "There isn't much left to the story. I brought more skins to Tanajin. The gifts she gave me were better than before. I hunted for her all summer. She gave away many skins. But the women did not praise her generosity. Or if they did, it was grudgingly. I heard them. They said, 'What right did she have to be prosperous, a woman with no relatives?'

"Winter came. It was warmer than usual. Few lizards came down the river from the north. The *umazi* were hungry. The hunger made them irritable,

235

and they were more willing to fight. Men died, and other men gave up. They hunted fish instead of the *umazi*. I kept on. I brought my skins into the village when the moon was full. I never failed." He lifted his head. I could see his pride.

"Tanajin was generous. I have said that before. She continued to give away skins. At night, when the moon was dark, I came into the village to listen."

Nia frowned. "I still say that was wrong."

"Have you done nothing worse, o woman of the Iron People?"

"I have done much that is worse." Nia's voice was even.

"I heard the women of the village. They sat in front of their houses and spoke together. They did not praise Tanajin. They said, 'Who is helping her, this woman without brothers? Who brings her fine skins when the rest of us get nothing?'

"They said, 'Even Ulzai was not able to kill this many *umazi*. And he was the best of the hunters. Tanajin has gotten help that is out of the ordinary. Maybe a spirit takes the luck from our sons and our brothers.'

"I wanted to shout up at them, 'You fools, I am the one who is helping Tanajin. Ulzai the hunter! I am no spirit!' But I could say nothing."

Nia made the gesture of agreement. "That is what happens when you listen in secret. You hear things you don't want to hear. You have to bite your tongue."

Ulzai looked angry. "Don't criticize me."

For a moment or two Nia was motionless. Then she made the gesture of agreement, followed by the gesture of apology.

Ulzai made the gesture of acknowledgment. "I left and came again. I heard more malicious gossip. They said it was dangerous to go near the house of Tanajin at night. A giant *umazi* lay in the dark water under the platform. A white bird sat on the rooftop."

"Aiya," said the oracle.

"I heard a boy speaking. He wasn't very old. I could tell that from the sound of his voice. He said he looked down from the house of his mother on a night when the moon was full. There was a man in the home channel, standing in a boat and poling it toward the house of Tanajin. The boat was full of the skins of lizards. The man looked up, the boy said. His eyes shone like sparks of fire. He opened his mouth. The mouth was empty. The man had no tongue. It was Ulzai, the boy said. It was me, and I was dead. Tanajin had worked magic and pulled me from the place where I lay in the cold water of the marsh. Now I worked for her.

"He was lying," said Ulzai. "I wanted to call him a liar. 'I am Ulzai,' I wanted to yell. 'I am alive and I use a paddle, not a pole.'"

"Hu!" said Derek.

236

"I do not know why any of this happened. Why did they praise my mother? Why did they say bad things about Tanajin? Do you know?" he asked Nia.

"No."

"I was angry. I decided I would kill no more *umazi*. I went into the distant marshes and lived on fish. The weather grew cold. Rain fell. I got the shivering sickness. I'd had it before. Most men get it after they have lived in the marsh for a while." He paused. "This time it was bad. First I became too sick to fish. Then I became too sick to eat. I lay in my boat under my cloak of well-tanned *umazi* skin. Rain fell. I shivered and dreamed.

"The great lizards came, swimming out of the marshes. They formed a circle around me. They spoke. 'Why have you given up on us? Is there anything more splendid than an *umazi*? Look at our sharp teeth! Look at our claws! We are huge and frightening. Will you ever find a prey more worthwhile?'

"I tried to answer. My teeth chattered, and I could not speak.

"'You have become a coward, Ulzai. You use your spear on little fish. You fear the voices of women. You lie here and wait to die of the shivering sickness.

"'We are your death. Not this miserable illness. We will get you one day, but only if you hunt us. Get up now! Paddle to the village. Go to Tanajin. She will help you. And when you are well, come after us.'

"They swam away, and I got up. I could hardly sit. The world moved in a circle around me, and I wanted to lie down, but I could not. The *umazi* had told me what to do.

"I paddled to the village. I came during the day, though I did not realize it. The world seemed dark to me. I reached the house of Tanajin. I tied my boat, but I could not climb up.

"She came down. I told her the lizards had said I must come to her. They were my death. I could not die of anything else. They had told me so.

"She helped me climb the ladder. She helped me into the house and made a bed for me—there, within the walls of her house. She cared for me until I was over the sickness.

"That is the end of the story. We could not stay in the village. They knew now—the old women—who had helped Tanajin. Ulzai the hunter! There was no magic. No bad spirit." He spread his hands. "Only Ulzai. Ulzai who would not die. Who came into the village.

"Now they were angry because of that. I should have died in the marshes. Tanajin should have left me in the boat."

He reached for the jar that had held the beer.

"It's empty," Derek said.

Ulzai made the gesture of regret. "Tanajin packed up. We loaded my boat. We left together."

"Why?" asked Nia.

"Tanajin needed help. She didn't know anything about living outside the village. And I was angry. I no longer cared about the opinions of other people. I had tried everything I could to win the praise of those women. I was even willing to die alone in the marshes until the *umazi* talked to me.

"I decided—from now on I would help those people who helped me. And I would listen to no one." He paused.

"Tanajin made a poem."

> "I am leaving
> these marshes.
> I am going far away."

> "I will never
> hear you again,
> O women of the village."

> "Making noises
> like the birds
> in the high reeds."

He made the gesture that meant "so be it" or "it is finished."

The rest of us were silent.

Ulzai stood up. "I am going out again. Maybe I'll return tonight. Maybe I won't." He left the cave.

Derek shifted position, bringing one knee up and resting his arm on it. His long hair was unfastened at the moment. It fell around his shoulders, and one lock was in his eyes. He brushed it back, then scratched his chin. "The first thing I'm going to do when we get back is get rid of some of this fur."

"But you have so little!" said Nia.

One of my fingernails was ragged. I gave it a bite. "I don't understand the story."

"You don't have to understand everything," said Derek.

"Why did the women of the village dislike Tanajin?"

"There are women like that," said Nia. "They don't fit in. Maybe they like to quarrel or maybe they hold themselves aloof from other people.

"I had a friend when I was young. Angai. She was the daughter of the shamaness, and she had a sharp tongue. Most people didn't like her. They talked about her, though not usually when I was around."

"What happened to her?" I asked. "Did she end up like Tanajin?"

Nia made the gesture that meant "no." "Her mother died. She became the shamaness. I have told you about her. I am sure of that."

"I don't remember. Were you a person like Tanajin?"

"No," said Nia. "I was ordinary. People didn't talk about me." She frowned. "I don't think they did. Not until they found out about me and Enshi. Then everything changed."

She looked uncomfortable. I changed the subject. We talked about the weather and then about the river. Ulzai did not return. The fire burnt down, becoming a heap of coals. One thin wisp of smoke still rose from it, curling into the leaves. I lay down, listening to the others. Their voices grew softer and more distant, until finally their words lost meaning.

Derek woke me in the morning. "Come on. Ulzai says it's going to be a long day."

I rolled over and groaned. The air felt damp. My arms ached. I went outside to pee.

A fog filled the valley. The river was invisible. The bushes, even the ones right in front of me, were dim and colorless. Not a day for the solar salute. I did some stretching exercises, then went back in the cave. No one had bothered to rebuild the fire. The cave was dark and warm. It smelled of furry bodies. A comforting aroma.

We packed up.

"How can we travel?" asked Nia. "I've been outside. The air is like the belly fur on a bowhorn. We are not going to be able to see anything."

"I know the river," said Ulzai. "We can travel half a day before we reach anything that is unusual or dangerous. And the fog will be gone by then. The air will be clear by the time we reach the place where the water goes down."

"Are you certain?" asked the oracle.

"Yes," said Ulzai. "Come on. And be careful."

We started down through the fog, Ulzai first. The rock we climbed over was slippery. I could see hardly anything: the dim figure of Ulzai, a few shadowy bushes. I brushed against one. The leaves were edged with drops of moisture. Somewhere close by, the stream made gurgling noises.

"Ai!" someone shouted.

I turned, seeing Nia and Derek. The oracle was gone.

"What happened?"

Nia made the gesture of uncertainty.

"The damn fool went into the ravine," said Derek.

"Help," said the oracle. His voice sounded distant, though he had to be close.

Derek peered into the ravine. "I can't see him. Oracle! Call again!"

"Help," said the oracle.

"Straight below." Derek set down the bags he carried, pulled off his boots and socks, and climbed into the ravine.

"What is going on?" asked Ulzai behind me.

"The oracle has fallen into the ravine."

"A clumsy man!"

I made the gesture of agreement.

"I have him," said Derek. "Can you stand?"

"I don't know," said the oracle.

"Try it."

There was a moment of silence.

"Aiya! My ankle hurts!"

Ulzai snorted. I walked to the edge of the ravine and looked in. There were shapes below me: rocks and branches, just barely visible through the fog.

"Come on," said Derek. "I'll help you climb."

The branches moved. Two figures appeared: one pale and human, the other dark and solid and alien. I knelt and reached down a hand. The oracle grabbed hold. I pulled. Derek lifted. We got him out.

"How could such a thing happen?" asked the oracle.

"Don't ask us," said Derek. He knelt by the oracle, who was sitting down, and felt the little man's ankle. The oracle moaned.

"I can't feel anything wrong, and you don't seem to be in a lot of pain."

"There you go again," said the oracle. "You are measuring the pain another person feels. How can you do that? What kind of magic do you have?"

"You aren't screaming when I do this," said Derek. He pressed.

The oracle gasped. "I will scream, if that is what you want. Let me breathe deeply first."

"We are wasting time," said Ulzai. "If the ankle is broken, the man will find out. The pain will get worse and the ankle will get bigger. If he's all right, he will find that out, too. Come on!"

Derek helped the oracle up. The little man groaned, but he was able to stand on the injured foot. He hobbled down the slope, leaning on Derek. Nia and I carried the bags.

The fog was lifting a little. I could see the edge of the river. Gray water lapped gently against a beach of gray sand. The center of the river was impenetrable whiteness.

We pushed the boat into the water. The oracle climbed in, settling down and groaning. The rest of us followed: Derek at the prow and Nia in back of him. I ended between the oracle and Ulzai. It wasn't an especially comfortable place to be. I was very much aware of Ulzai in back of me: huge and hairy and formidable. Something sharp and hard was pressing against my thigh. I shifted and looked. It was the blade of a spear, long and barbed, made of iron. It lay on the bottom of the boat, along with another spear and Derek's fishing pole. I had come close to sitting on the tip.

The boat moved away from shore.

I shifted back, trying to get away from the spear blade.

"Don't do that," said Ulzai. "I need room to paddle."

I shifted forward.

"Good."

We traveled through the fog all morning. The air was still, and there was no sound except the splash of the paddles. The silence had an effect on us. We barely spoke, and we moved carefully, trying to make as little noise as possible. The oracle was an exception. He moaned from time to time and shifted position. It seemed to me he was favoring his injured arm.

The fog grew thin. Islands emerged from the whiteness. The current picked up, and the surface of the river changed. There were ripples and eddies.

"We are getting to the place where the river goes down," said Ulzai. "The fog has lasted longer than I expected. I am trying to decide whether or not I want to go on. The boat is overloaded. There might be problems, and I don't want to come on them suddenly."

The oracle moved again, trying to find a comfortable position. His injured arm was resting on the side of the canoe. He lifted it. I saw blood drip into the water.

I leaned forward, grabbing the arm. He twisted. The boat rocked.

"Be still," I said.

The bandage had torn open. The edge of the foam was red with blood. Blood soaked the fur. A dark line of blood ran down the inside of the canoe. I leaned out. The boat rocked again.

"What are you doing?" asked Ulzai.

A second trail of blood ran down the outside of the canoe into the water.

"Blood," I said. "Didn't you say it was dangerous to let blood get into the water?"

"Yes."

"The oracle is bleeding."

"Move back," said Ulzai. "Take my paddle."

I obeyed. He stood and stepped over me. I tucked myself into the stern. Ulzai picked up a spear. He straightened up, glancing around.

"Nothing yet. But you, o holy man, keep your arm in the boat. I want no more blood in the water."

The oracle held his arm against his chest. His shoulders were hunched. I had a sense that he was frightened. Well, so was I.

Ulzai spoke again. "They do not like this part of the river. The water moves too quickly. They do not come here except in the time for migration, and that has not begun."

Derek said, "Good."

"If there are any around—if a few of them have decided to go south early, ahead of the rush—they're likely to be close to shore. Or else behind us.

241

Upriver. We'll keep going. Pay attention to the current. It is strong and getting stronger. Stay with it. There are rocks to the west. Watch out for them
and look to the east from time to time. If you see anything dark in the water
there, give a shout. It will be a lizard."

"Okay," I said.

He was right. The current was strong. I felt the water tug and pull every
time my paddle went in. The boat accelerated. Ulzai stood in front of me,
having no trouble keeping his balance. His arm was lifted. The spear was
poised. He glanced around, paying special attention to the water behind us.
That must be the area of real danger.

"Rocks," said Nia. "Ahead of us."

"Go to the east," said Ulzai. "You are too far out."

I shifted my paddle and drove the blade in, trying to turn the boat.
What I needed—really needed—was the kind of boat I had used on Earth.
Oh, for aluminum!

The canoe began to turn. I felt relief.

Ulzai exhaled. I glanced up. He was staring over my head. I glanced back.
There was something in the water. A dark head. Huge. It had to be twice the
size of the animal in the lagoon.

"*Umazi*," said the oracle.

"Don't look back," said Ulzai. "Keep paddling. And watch for trouble
ahead of us. I'll take care of this."

I paddled. After a moment he said, "It is no *umazi*. The shape of the head
is wrong. And it isn't big enough."

"Aiya!" said the oracle.

The current felt rougher. There was foam on the water ahead of us. Off to
the west a dark shape loomed out of the fog. A rock, not an island. We had
reached the rapids, and we were still too far out.

"The lizard will stop now," said Ulzai. "They hate fast water."

So did I, which gave me one thing in common with the lizard. Not enough
to form the basis for a friendship.

Ulzai said, "It must be hungry. Or crazy. It should have stopped."

"It hasn't?" I asked.

"It's getting close."

"Ratshit," I said in English.

Ulzai threw the spear.

Something roared, and I glanced around. The animal was behind us. My
God, almost in the boat! The enormous body twisted. I saw a pale belly and
a dark spiny back. Ulzai's spear stuck out of the back like yet another spine,
long and narrow. The animal opened its mouth. Teeth and more teeth. The
animal roared again.

I must have stopped paddling, though I wasn't aware of having done it. The boat rocked—turning, caught in an eddy, going sideways to the current.

"Fool!" Ulzai cried. "I told you—"

The boat went over. I went into the cold and rushing water. A moment later the river went over a drop.

I tumbled. My mouth filled with water. The river sucked me down. I didn't fight. Fighting would kill me. The rule was—go with the undertow. In the end it would surface. The rule was for swimming in the ocean.

God, it was hard not to struggle! My lungs hurt, and something was happening to my brain. A sense of pressure. A darkening.

The river went over another drop. I spun around. Aiya! Damn!

The current slowed. I was able to swim. Up. Up. I broke through the surface, spat out the river, and inhaled.

Ah!

I floated. The river carried me. I breathed in and out. My arms hurt and my shoulder and my lungs.

But I was alive. I lifted my head and saw fog. The water around me was gray. It rippled slightly. Ahead of me trees loomed: shadows, barely visible. An island. I was too exhausted to swim any farther. I let the current take me toward the trees.

There was driftwood on the upriver side. A great tangle. Branches and roots extended into the water, reaching out. I was going to pass them. I swam a few strokes, four or five—I couldn't have managed any more, grabbed hold of a root, and hung on. The current pulled at me. I breathed. In. Out. *So. Hum.* Gradually my heartbeat slowed. My lungs no longer hurt so badly.

The pain in my arms was getting worse. I was going to lose my grip on the root. I closed my eyes and prayed to Guan Yin, the goddess of mercy, the bodhisattva of compassion. Get me out of this alive.

She, standing on her lotus blossom, smiled and gestured reassuringly.

I pulled myself hand over hand into the tangle of wood and wedged myself there. The branches held me half out of the water. Aiya! I relaxed. My arms fell, and my hands went into the river. I rested for maybe an hour.

The fog burned off. In front of me the river shone blue-green-brown. A bird, a large one, paddled on the water. It dove and surfaced, then dove and surfaced again. I couldn't see if it caught anything.

At last I pulled myself entirely out of the water. I began to climb through the tangle of roots and branches, heading toward the shore of the island.

Lixia

B y the time I reached the shore I was exhausted again. I sat down on a beach of pale gray sand. In front of me was the driftwood: a white and gray wall that hid the river. In back of me I looked around: trees and bushes.

After a while I thought, what about the others?

I had seen Derek doing laps in the big pool on the ship. He was good in the water, almost as good as I was, and I had grown up by the ocean. He might not know as much as I did about rough water, but he'd survived a lot of really nasty situations.

As for the natives—I had no idea if any of them could swim. The river might have gotten them. A terrible idea. I shivered, though the sun was hot and my clothes were almost dry.

I decided to take an inventory. What did I have? A denim shirt. Jeans. Underwear. My boots were gone. One sock remained. I searched my pockets and found a lighter that didn't work. Maybe water had gotten into it. I'd try it later. A folding knife. A round gray stone with a fossil in it. Some lint.

That was it, except for the AV recorder on its chain around my neck. I touched it. It felt warm. There was a transmitter in there, a small one that broadcast a tracking signal. It didn't reach far, but the people on the ship already knew approximately where I was. If they decided to search for me, they'd find me. All I had to do was stay alive and hope that they came looking.

In order to find me quickly, they'd have to use machines: power boats or airplanes. I tried to imagine Eddie agreeing to a search like that. It was hardly likely. But he wasn't the only person on the ship.

I took off my one remaining sock, folded it, and put it in a pocket, then stood and brushed the sand off my clothes. Time to go exploring.

I went around the perimeter of the island, keeping as close to the shore as possible. I found no trails: a good sign. It meant there were no large animals on the island. It also meant I had to push through vegetation. I climbed over logs and under the branches of trees. Vines grew everywhere, forming lianas that were almost tropical. Bugs hummed around me. They did not bite.

A couple of times I came to foliage that was too dense to penetrate. I took to the river, wading through shallow water. Tiny fish darted ahead of me.

When I was halfway around the island, I cut my foot. I wasn't sure on what: a sharp stone or the shell of a river animal. The cut wasn't deep, but it did bleed. I kept out of the water after that.

By the time I got back to my starting point, it was late afternoon. Shadows extended across the beach, reaching the tangle of driftwood.

I sat down. What had I learned?

The island was below the rapids. I had gotten a glimpse of them while climbing through the bushes at the north end.

To the west were other islands. The water was quiet there, and the river shore was distant. I wasn't even sure that I was seeing it. That dim line might be a marsh or still more islands, their edges merging in the late summer haze.

To the east was the main channel of the river. The water looked deep. The current was swift. It had cut into the island, forming a steep bank, almost vertical. Trees grew along the top. Their roots extended into air, reaching for dirt that had vanished, and many leaned out over the water. A few had fallen in. The river rushed past them, tugging at yellow leaves.

The channel was not especially wide. I could swim to the mainland. But not today. I was tired, and the cut on my foot had not stopped bleeding. I didn't want to meet another lizard. A good night's sleep and I'd be able to get across the river. Maybe I'd find people. Nia. Derek. The oracle. Ulzai.

O Bodhisattva, Compassionate One, save those people.

I went to the edge of the river, scooped up water, and drank. It tasted funny, but it wasn't likely to kill me, and I had already swallowed plenty of it. I drank some more, then went to the edge of the wood and sat down, leaning against a tree.

245

Bugs woke me. They hummed in my ears and crawled on my face. A couple bit me. I brushed them away. It did no good. They came back and bit me again. I got up and walked along the beach. The sky was ablaze with stars. I could see the Milky Way clearly: a wide, glowing ribbon of light. A meteor fell to the east of me. A lovely night!

Except for the bugs. They followed me. They were much worse than they'd ever been before. Why? Had I finally found a species that liked the odor of humans? Or had I begun to smell like the natives? I'd been eating their food for more than sixty days.

I reached the edge of the river and looked out. I could wade in. The bugs would not be able to bite me if I were underwater. But lizards were there.

I turned and walked back the way I had come. There had to be something I could do. Cover myself with something. Figure out a way to build a fire.

I remembered a line from a teacher in college: "Always remember, in a society with a pre-industrial technology, everything takes far longer than you think it will. Everything involves a lot more work. And there are almost always a lot of bugs."

Another meteor fell: a big one to the south. It had a white head and a long reddish tail. I began to notice a funny sensation in the pit of my stomach. Or was it in my groin? An ache. No. More intense than that. A definite pain.

Menstrual cramps! I couldn't believe it. I had a capsule in my arm that was supposed to release hormones at a set rate for 180 days. I was safe for half a year. No menses. No cramps. No blood. Well, maybe a little spotting. They had warned us about that. The hormone level was set as low as possible.

What had gone wrong? Had the capsule been defective? Maybe it was stress. I'd been through a lot in the past few days. And stress could do a lot to the endocrine system.

I kept walking. The pain got worse, and the bugs kept following and biting.

I knew just what to do. Get a blanket and a container of tea spiked with whiskey. Crawl into bed in my cabin. Turn on the blanket and consume the tea. Listen to music. Go to sleep. Unfortunately—

At dawn the flow began. The cramps eased. The bugs became less active. I sat down. The sun came up, and the last of the bugs departed. I lay back and put an arm over my face.

I dreamt. There was a tower that looked like Inahooli's tower. It was in Hawaii in my front yard, surrounded by flowering plumeria trees.

I was sitting near the tower in the shadow of a tree, talking to someone, having an argument. At first I had no idea who the person was. Then I realized it was very small, about knee high to me. It kept changing as it talked, shrinking, then expanding, then shrinking again. Its shape changed as well as its size. At times it seemed to be a tiny human. At other times it was a tiny

246

furry person. Strangest of all, at times it seemed to be a bug, standing on six legs and waving a pair of forearms at me. At all times it was brown and shiny, the color of a cockroach. I couldn't tell what sex it was.

It had a high shrill voice.

"I am the Little Bug Spirit. I come to people when they begin to take themselves too seriously. They think they are big. I cut them down to size."

This angered me. I tried to speak, but I couldn't get my thoughts together.

The person went on, "I am the stone under your foot. I am the bug that bites you in the ass. I am the fart that comes when you are introduced to the important visiting professor. I am menstrual cramps and diarrhea."

I kept getting angrier.

"My tools are lies and tricks, misunderstandings and accidents. Everything stupid and undignified happens because of me. Hola! I am something!"

I reached to grab the person. It scurried away, and I was alone, feeling happy.

A voice said, "That does no good."

I looked up. The person was above me, sitting on a branch, surrounded by cream-white plumeria flowers. It waved its antennae. Its dark body glinted.

"The oracle will think this happened because of the spirits in the cave. Ulzai will think it happened because of the *umazi*. Nia will feel guilty and angry, as if she is responsible. And you will think the boat went over for no good reason.

"I tell you, I did it. Hola! I am something, even though I am small!" The person spread wings and flew away, making a whirring noise. It passed the tower and disappeared into the blue-green sky.

I woke. It was midmorning, and I lay in sunlight under a cloudless sky the color of the sky in my dream. I felt confused for a moment. Where was I? Not Hawaii. Nor Minnesota. I sat up and remembered. I was eighteen light-years from home. My skin itched. I looked at my arms. They were covered with lumps.

"Don't panic," I told myself after a moment in which I panicked. "Those are bug bites, and the mosquitoes in Minnesota have done a lot worse to you."

My voice sounded calm. That was a comfort. I stood up. My clothes stuck to me. Sweat, mostly. There was a dark stain in the crotch of my jeans. Sweat and blood.

The first thing to do was take a bath, then wash my clothes and do my yoga.

I walked down the beach till I was past the wall of driftwood. Then I dug a hole in the sand close to the water. It was slow work. I had no tools except my hands and a piece of driftwood.

When the hole was large enough, I dug a channel to the river. Water flowed in. I undressed and knelt in the sandy little pool and washed, using my one remaining sock as a washcloth.

Afterward, I put my clothing in to soak and did yoga, ending by meditating, looking out at the river with half-shut eyes. Light flashed off the green-brown water. O you jewel of the lotus.

I wrung out my clothes and spread them on the sand to dry, sat down and examined my tools. This time the lighter glowed. I tested it on my piece of driftwood. The wood caught fire. That solved two problems. The bugs and how to signal other people.

I put the lighter aside and examined the knife. The blade was ten centimeters long, made of rustproof steel. Sharp. I could use it to cut up food.

I had no intention of trying to cross the river until I'd stopped menstruating, which meant I was stuck on the island for at least four days. What was I going to eat?

I could fast, of course. I had done that before. But I might end up too weak to swim and looking for food was an occupation. I had once read a book by Leona Field, one of the leaders of the Second American Revolution. Leader was the wrong word. Leona was an anarchist; she didn't believe in leaders. She had spent a lot of her life waiting, in prison and out. Her advice was—plan the next step, be patient, keep busy. I decided to take her advice.

What was available? Fish in the river. The trees were full of birds, and I had seen a little animal about the size of a squirrel. It was furry and arboreal with a long tail that looked prehensile. The animal was common on the island.

I had no way of catching the birds or the furry animals. I might be able to make a fish trap. I had watched Nia.

There were plants. I was a little worried about them. Organisms that couldn't run often relied on poison as a protection.

I could collect some likely specimens and test them by eating small quantities.

There were bugs. Grubs were a source of protein. I didn't think they were likely to be poisonous.

What about animals other than fish? Were there things like clams or crayfish? There was a lot about this planet I didn't know.

Time for more exploring. I used the wet sock to wash off my legs, thinking—as I did so—that I was going to have to find something to use as a menstrual pad. This was awfully damn messy and maybe dangerous: I did not like the idea of leaving a trail of blood. I rinsed the sock and laid it out to dry, put on my underpants and shirt, and walked to the forest.

For the next couple of hours I lifted fallen branches and turned over stones, picked leaves and pulled up roots. It was hot among the trees. After a while I took off my shirt and turned it into a carry bag. Sweat ran down my back and between my breasts. Bugs hummed around me. Only a few bit. I didn't know why. Maybe there was only one species that thought I was edible, and that species came out at night. Maybe . . . To hell with it. I wasn't going to theorize.

I found a bush covered with round purple berries. Birds flew out of it as I approached. The ground was covered with purple-white droppings. That seemed to indicate edibility.

A dead branch turned out to be the home of many yellow grubs. I added them to my bag. They squirmed among the berries.

Another dead branch had no animal life that I could find, but the inner bark was soft and came off easily in long sheets. I ought to be able to fashion an absorbent pad. The bark went in with the grubs and berries.

I spent half an hour watching the arboreal animals. They whistled and chirped and threw things at me. Twigs, mostly. I stayed where I was and stared at them, hoping they'd throw something useful. One finally did. A half-eaten fruit. I picked it up.

Somewhere on the island was a tree that bore fruit that was oval and indigo-blue and edible. I put the fruit into my bag, added a few samples of plant life, and went back to the shore.

My clothes were almost dry. I washed again—myself and the underpants. Then I constructed a pad out of bark. The result was not lovely, and I had no way to attach it to my pants. One of the senior members of my family had told me over and over, "Never go *anywhere* without at least two safety pins."

Here I was, years and light-years from home on a planet in another star system, proving that Perdita had been right.

I put on my jeans and tucked the pad into them. With luck, it would stay in place.

I got out the indigo fruit—the grubs were still lively—and cut away the part that had been chewed by the arboreal animal. I ate the rest. It was mushy and sweet. Not bad, though I preferred fruit that was a little less ripe.

What next? I was getting hungry, but not hungry enough to eat the grubs. I ought to find a use for them. It would be wasteful to let them die. If they weren't going to be dinner, then they'd have to be bait.

I glanced at the sky. It was still full of light. I ought to have time to make a fish trap. I had seen a plant in the middle of the island that I might be able to use.

I carried my bag full of maggots into the shade, left it there, and went back into the forest.

There was a slight depression in the middle of the island. The ground was boggy, and the chief form of vegetation was something that looked like a reed. Each plant consisted of a single purple stalk a little over two meters tall. At the top of each stalk was a crest made of magenta fibers—like gossamer, they were so fine and light.

I cut a dozen of the stalks. As I sawed, the plants shook, and the magenta fibers broke free.

When I was half done, I noticed that all the plants were losing their fibers—even the ones I had not touched and hadn't gone near. Some of the fibers drifted down and lay in the mud. Most floated off, twisting and coiling in currents I could not feel. A few landed on me. They were quite ordinary—like thread. I brushed them off and finished cutting. By the time I was done the entire grove was bare.

No way of telling what my recorder had seen, dangling and swaying at the end of its chain. I described what had happened out loud. "My bet is—the fibers are flowers or maybe runners that travel through the air. The plants release them when they are injured. Somehow the plants are connected. An injury to one is an injury to all. If I'm wrong and the fibers are a method of protection—maybe this message will serve as a warning." I carried my stalks back to the beach.

Now. String. I decided to use my sock. It was made of a really remarkable yarn, a cotton-and-synthetic combination—not as absorbent as cotton, but far more durable. The sock had no holes, even after all the traveling I had done.

I made my trap, stopping now and then to close my eyes and visualize Nia at work, bending and fastening branches. She had deft fingers, the backs covered with brown fur. Dark bare palms. Muscular forearms. Her voice—deep and slow—explained what she was doing.

How I missed those people!

I added a stone for weight, as she had told me, then the grubs. They were getting less lively. I waded into the river. In that area—in front of my beach—it was shallow. There was an inlet protected by the tangle of driftwood. Where the driftwood stopped, the river bottom went down. The water changed from transparent to a dark opaque greenish brown. A drop-off. I set my trap there, next to the drop-off and close to the tangle of driftwood.

I waded back, looking down through the water. There were trails in the sand. I followed one. Where it ended, I dug. Aiya! Something hard! I pulled it out. A gray cone, full of pink tentacles. The tentacles waved in an agitated fashion.

I tossed the creature on the shore and went on hunting. I found half a dozen of the animals. Hermit squid, I called them. The shells ranged in size from five to ten centimeters. The animals looked edible to me. More edible than the grubs or the various plants I had gathered.

The sun was low by now. My beach was in shadow. I gathered driftwood and built a fire. The stars came out. I wrapped a hermit squid in leaves and baked it in the coals. It sizzled but did not scream, for which I was grateful. I was willing to kill animals and eat them. I accepted that addition to my karmic burden. But I didn't like my victims to be noisy.

I pulled the bundle of leaves out of the fire and unwrapped it. The shell was still gray. The tentacles had turned a lovely cherry-red. I opened my knife and dug the animal out of its shell. The body was cone-shaped and mottled red and orange. I sniffed. It smelled of nothing in particular. I cut it open. There was nothing repulsive inside. No gut full of black gunk. No sack of ink or venom. No bones and no spines.

"Here goes." I ate the thing. It was rubbery and had a peppery flavor. I liked it.

I thought of cooking another animal, but decided to wait and see if the first one killed me.

A hard decision. My stomach rumbled. I could eat some berries. No. One food at a time. If I got sick, I wanted to be able to tell what to avoid in the future.

Bugs appeared out of the darkness. I put more wood on the fire and shifted position. I was in the smoke now. The bugs left me alone.

After an hour or so I looked at the rest of the animals. Their tentacles waved feebly. They were dying. If they were like shellfish on Earth, they would go bad fast. And I was getting really hungry. I decided to take the risk. I wrapped them up and stuck them in the coals. They sizzled.

How could I ask the bodhisattva for compassion when I felt nothing for these little beings except an ineffectual guilt? And what in hell was wrong with me? Was I reverting? I was a modern person, a native of Hawaii. I knew nothing about the religious beliefs of the ancient Chinese, except what I had read in books or heard when I did a study of the Chinese community in Melbourne. So why was I praying to the bodhisattva? And why did I care what happened to these wretched little animals? I added more wood to the fire.

I ate the rest of the hermit squid, then told the recorder what I had done and went to sleep. I woke in the morning, feeling perfectly okay.

Another bright day. I paid a visit to a log in the wood and—as I did so—thought longingly of the bathrooms on the ship. Washed at the edge of the river. Ate berries. Got bark and made a new menstrual pad. I put the damn thing on and buried the previous one. Then I waded out to my fish trap. I pulled it up.

I had something. It was not a fish.

It sat hunched in the middle of the trap, legs folded up. There were—I counted—ten legs. Each was long and narrow, folded three times. The body was round and hard, striped and spotted brown and tan. There was a head at one end. The head consisted of mandibles and eyes. The mandibles clicked. The eyes glared up at me. I counted. The animal had six eyes, four large and

251

two small. All were faceted. What I had was a large spider in a hard shell. A spider with too many legs.

Click. Click.

I had wanted a tasty little fish.

"Okay," I said. "Are you edible? How do I cook you?"

Click.

It might be delicious, as good as the hermit squid. The folded legs moved slightly. The eyes glared. I was—of course—reading expression into the eyes, which looked like black beads and did not, in reality, express anything. The mandibles clicked. I opened the trap and shook.

The animal fell into the water and was gone. I carried the trap back to shore and set it down. Then I returned to the inlet. I waded around, looking for trails in the sand, and found three hermit squid. They were breakfast.

After I was done I went exploring in the wood. I found more grubs and a plant that looked familiar. It had frilly blue leaves and a fat root. I was pretty sure that Nia had gathered plants like this. The root was baked, as I remembered. It was starchy and tasteless but filling. I pulled up nine or ten.

The arboreal animals made noises above me. They threw more twigs. I waited, hoping for another piece of fruit. No such luck. I gave up finally and went back to the shore, rebaited my trap and gathered driftwood. I was starting to feel a little bored. I was going to be stuck on the island for another three or four days. I wasn't going to starve and I didn't need a shelter. What was I going to do?

I scratched myself absently. I could look for a natural bug repellent. I could practice my calligraphy in the sand. I could sleep a lot. I could negotiate with the spirits: Guan Yin and the Mother of Mothers or the odd little spirit who had appeared in my dream.

Ask them for what? To save me and my friends.

I could think about what I was going to do after I crossed the river. There was forest over there. Tanajin had mentioned an animal called the killer of the forest. It did not sound like anything I wanted to meet. What about the lizards? They were migratory. They did not like fast water. Maybe they went overland when they came to the rapids. I imagined them, huge and dark and dangerous, moving through the shadows of the forest.

How fast were they on land? Could I outrun them?

I could build a signal fire. If my friends were alive, they'd see it.

I decided to build the fire. Not today. The sun was well into the west. By the time I had enough wood gathered, it'd be night. That would be tomorrow's project.

I checked the trap again. It was empty. I looked for hermit squid. I found none. Dinner would have to be the roots. I washed them in the river and baked them in my fire.

The sun went down. I ate the roots. They tasted like nothing in particular. I described them—and the creature I had found in the trap—to my recorder. Then I went to sleep.

I woke with indigestion. The fire was a heap of coals. Stars filled the sky. And I had a really terrible case of gas.

Those damn roots! I must have been wrong. They weren't the kind that Nia had found. I rebuilt the fire and sat next to it, waiting for the pain to go away or worsen.

If I got out alive, I was going to name this place. If I had to, I would stand over the members of the cartography team as they input the information. Most likely I would call it Little Bug Island, though I also liked the Island of Petty Aggravations. That had a ring. I imagined people in the future looking at the name and saying, "There has to be a story here. What were the aggravations? And who was the person who was aggravated?"

The pain stopped finally. I went back to sleep.

The next morning was sunny with a bit of haze, cool at the moment. I waded out to my trap.

Ah! I had a fish. It was large and orange with a dark blue dorsal fin. There were long, narrow, pale blue tendrils around its mouth. They moved slowly, feeling the air or maybe tasting it.

"You're ugly," I said.

The fish opened its mouth and croaked.

"The same to me, eh?"

The fish croaked again.

I wasn't especially hungry, not after a night of indigestion. The fish would keep. I lowered the trap into the water and waded to shore.

I spent the morning gathering driftwood. By noon I was covered with sweat and a little queasy from the heat. The sky was full of high clouds, barely visible through the haze. The trees along my beach were motionless. There was going to be a storm, but not for a while. I lit the signal fire.

It caught slowly. I added dry leaves and pieces of bark. The flames licked around the twisted white branches. Smoke rose. The heat was intense. I moved back and looked around. The sky was empty except for the clouds and the haze.

No one else was signaling.

Be patient, I told myself. I added more wood.

I kept the fire going most of the afternoon. More clouds moved in. A wind began to blow. My trail of smoke went sideways rather than up. I went and got my fish and killed it, cleaned it, and baked it in the coals at the edge of the fire.

There were whitecaps on the river now. Thunder rumbled to the west of me. I ate the fish. It had a muddy flavor. I should have kept it alive for three

253

days in clean running water or else smoked it. That's what you did with carp. I licked my fingers. The first drops of rain came down, hissing in my fire. I moved into the shelter of the trees.

Lightning flashed. Thunder made loud noises. Rain fell in sheets that swept over the river, billowing in front of the wind. I huddled under a bush, and water dripped through the foliage above me, forming pools on the ground.

The storm moved east finally. The rain stopped. I crawled out from under my bush, took off my clothes, and wrung them out, then went to look at my fire. It was soaked. There was no way to relight it. Tomorrow maybe.

But everything was still wet then, and I spent the day foraging. The hermit squid had vanished. I found new grubs and the tree with indigo fruit. The tree had a straight trunk, and the fruit was high up. This was no problem. The branches were full of animals. I stood and waited. The animals became uneasy. They chirped and whistled.

"The same to you," I said.

They threw fruit. I gathered it. They made more angry noises.

"T.S."

I rebaited my trap and rebuilt my cooking fire, then made a new menstrual pad. The flow had almost stopped. I was going to be able to leave the island in another day or two.

Lunch was cold fish. Dessert was a piece of fruit. I spent the afternoon resting. Around sunset I checked the trap. Nothing. I lowered it and heard a noise. I looked up. Birds. They were so high that I couldn't make out any detail. They certainly were numerous. The flock extended from north to south as far as I could see in either direction. It was a band that wavered continuously, growing broad, then narrow, sometimes breaking, then re-forming. There were thousands of birds up there. Maybe millions. They called to one another as they flew. Their cry was high and shrill—clearly audible, in spite of distance. On and on it went. I had never seen this many birds.

The end came in sight. A few stragglers—subsidiary bunches—followed all the rest. A hundred here. Two hundred there. Flying south, crying, "Hey, wait for us."

Then the sky was empty. I waded back to shore.

A fall migration. The lizards went south by water. The birds went south by air. But so many! I remembered what I'd read about America before the coming of civilization. Herds of buffalo that covered the prairie. Flocks of birds that made the sky go dark at noon.

I scratched my head. It itched. I needed soap and a shower.

The next day was clear and bright. I rebuilt the signal fire. This time it caught. At noon I checked my trap. The grubs were gone. Something had eaten them and left. I went foraging again, along the edges of the island. I found a few dead fish. They had been dead for a while, and they did not look appealing. At the southern end of the island I found an animal. A biped. It lay on the beach, half in the water. Dead, but not for long. It was less than a meter. Its feathers were blue-green, the color of the sky, and it had a long red crest. The arms ended in delicate claws. The hind legs were designed for running. The open mouth was full of teeth. A lovely little predator. An eater of what? Large flying bugs? Or maybe little furry creatures.

I carried it back to my fire and cut it up. Most of it I buried, but I used a couple of pieces to rebait my trap.

After that I sat and watched the river, looking for lizards. I saw none. It ought to be safe to swim across.

Toward evening I saw a trail of smoke to the east of me. Downriver. I stood and grinned at the narrow line—like the stroke of a pencil. I had company. I'd wait another day. Keep my fire burning. If no one came to me, I'd head downriver.

I wondered briefly who had made the fire. Was it one of my comrades or someone else? A solitary hunter. A group of women on a journey. Traders from the Amber People.

There was no point in constructing theories. I had no real information. I did my yoga, then meditated, looking at the smoke.

Dinner was a piece of fruit. I slept badly, troubled by indigestion.

The morning was overcast. I could feel rain in the air. Damn! I looked east. There was no sign of the other fire. Maybe they had let it go out overnight. Maybe the smoke was invisible against the low gray sky.

I checked my trap—it was empty again—dug up the biped and used another piece for bait. Then I checked my menstrual pad. No sign of blood. I ought to be able to swim across the river. I took the pad off and buried it and then rebuilt my fire.

Midway through the morning, the rain began. It was fine and misty. My fire kept burning, but who was going to see it? The eastern shore of the river was dim. I cursed whoever was in charge of the weather. The four winds. Those unruly men! I prayed to Guan Yin, though I didn't remember that she had anything to do with meteorology, and I asked the Mother of Mothers to straighten out her grandsons.

"And do something about the Little Bug Spirit, if you can."

Maybe I was getting a little crazy. I didn't usually talk to spirits. My stomach grumbled. I decided the fruit was the problem. I needed meat or a vegetable. I drank a little water and checked my trap. The bait was still there.

At noon the boat came into view: a launch with a cabin and good-sized engine. It was moving slowly upriver through the rain.

255

I put on my jeans and gathered my belongings: the knife, the lighter, my half-unraveled sock. I ought to put the fire out. But how? It was pretty big. I'd let the others worry about it. I went down to the shore and waved and shouted.

The person at the stern waved in reply. The boat turned toward me. I waded into the water.

The person was dressed in olive-green. A member of the crew. In theory there were no uniforms on the ship. But the crewmembers tended to dress alike: olive-green denim pants and olive-green pullover sweaters, soft caps with brims, olive-green or black.

I waded farther out, right to the edge of the drop-off. The boat came in, moving increasingly slowly. Ivanova. I recognized her squat, broad body. I was being rescued by the chief pilot of the I.S.S. *Number One*.

Someone else came out of the cabin, taller than Ivanova and broader, dressed in jeans and a blue denim jacket. His shirt was red. His hair was long and black, worn loose. It flowed over his shoulders. Edward Antoine Whirlwind, Ph.D.

The boat stopped next to me. Eddie reached down and pulled me onboard. He hugged me. "Lixia! Are you all right?"

"Yeah." I held on to him. I was shaking, and I felt as if my knees were going to give way.

"Get her inside," said Ivanova. Her voice—as always—took me by surprise. It was a rich contralto, which ought to have belonged to an actress or a singer. "Tell Agopian to get out here. We need to do something about the fire."

A moment later I was in the cabin. There was a carpet under my bare feet. Eddie helped me into a chair. I leaned back and felt the fabric through my shirt: a rough texture, most likely handmade.

My arms rested on the arms of the chair. I curled my fingers under and felt metal tubing. How long had it been since I had sat like this—up, off the ground, in a chair with a back? I did not remember.

Eddie leaned over me, looking concerned. There were other people behind him. A crewwoman with a Central Asian face. A crewman who looked vaguely Middle Eastern. A tall blond man in a pair of light-blue coveralls.

The blond man grinned at me and made the gesture that meant "welcome." Derek.

Eddie spoke to the crew people, and they left.

Derek said, "Are you okay?"

"Yes. Eddie, you're looming."

"Sorry."

They sat down. I looked at Derek. "How are you? What happened? Do you know what happened to the others?"

256

He made the gesture that indicated lack of knowledge. "I ended by myself. You must have, too."

"Yes."

"I lost the boat as soon as it went over and caught hold of a tree that was hung up in the rapids." He grinned. "There I was—in the middle of white water, holding on to this damn tree trunk and wondering what to do next. I saw no one. I have no idea what happened to the others."

"What did you do?"

"It wasn't a good place for swimming. I was pretty sure of that. And I haven't had any experience with white-water swimming. I worked the tree free and floated out of the rapids."

I made the gesture that meant "good" or "clever."

"That's what I thought until I found out how hard it is to steer a tree. Especially this one. It was very badly designed—for navigation, anyway. It may have done just fine in its previous line of work." Derek glanced at Eddie. "I'll tell you the rest later."

Eddie leaned forward. "Are you certain that you're all right, Lixia?"

"Nothing hurts. I have no injuries. I'm tired, and I'm going to want to eat pretty soon, but not at this moment."

"Okay." He stood. "I have to talk to Ivanova. There are decisions to be made, and she'll make them on her own if I don't get out there quickly. Derek, you take care of Lixia."

"To hear is to obey."

"Cut the crap."

Eddie left the cabin. I looked around, seeing curved walls and oval windows. The carpet on the floor was a neutral color: gray or tan. All the furniture looked as if it folded or disassembled or turned into something else. The couches along the walls, for example. They obviously became beds. The little tables between them folded into the walls. Our chairs had hinges. I was in a home for nomads. It occurred to me that I was spending my entire life traveling.

"I have my orders," Derek said. "What do you need? Or want?"

"Nothing yet. Give me a minute."

He made the gesture of acquiescence.

I closed my eyes. Time passed. The sound of the engine changed. I opened my eyes and stood. The boat was moving away from my island. The beach—my beach—was empty. People had been there. I saw their footprints in the sand, and my fire was covered with yellow foam. The foam was melting in the rain, dripping off the branches and forming a pool of yellowish water. Blobs of foam floated in the pool.

Ugly!

We passed the tangle of driftwood, heading upstream toward the rapids. "Where are we going?"

Derek made the gesture that indicated lack of knowledge.

The short man—Agopian—came into the cabin. He closed the door. "Ivanova has asked me to look after you. She is having an argument with Eddie."

"About what?"

"Whether to look for your companions. Eddie says no, as you might expect. Ivanova says a cosmonaut does not refuse to look for people who might be alive and in trouble. In space we have only each other. What can I do for you?"

I made a decision. "Food."

"We don't have a proper kitchen. I can offer you a sandwich."

"Okay."

He crossed the cabin, aft to fore, and went through another door. A light went on, and I saw him crouching, looking into something: a cooling unit. "We have egg salad, caviar, onion and tomato, and something that claims to be chopped chicken liver on Russian black bread."

I made the gesture of inquiry. He looked puzzled. I said, "What do you mean 'claims'?"

"I am Armenian, and Armenians have long memories. I remember the taste of Russian black bread. We have given up a lot in order to go to the stars."

True enough. I made the gesture of agreement.

"What do you want?" asked Agopian.

"The egg salad. Unless it's on black bread."

"Rye. Not great, but adequate. Do you want mineral water or beer? We also have the local water, distilled and free of everything that might do harm."

"Mineral water."

He brought the food out. The sandwich was wrapped in paper. The water was in a glass bottle. "Please return to recycling" was stamped on the side. There was a chip in the bottom.

I opened the bottle. The water fizzed. I drank a little, then unwrapped the sandwich and took a bite. It was delicious. I forced myself to eat slowly, stopping after each bite to drink the water, which had—very faintly—the taste of a citrus fruit.

"Derek?" said Agopian.

"Nothing for me."

The crewman went back into the galley and came out with another bottle. This one was amber rather than clear. Most likely, it held beer. He sat down, opening the bottle. For a while after that, there was silence. I was eating. Derek looked tired, content to do nothing. Agopian drank his beer.

"Of course, there are benefits," he said at last.

"What?" asked Derek.

"To going to the stars. When I was a kid, I had two ambitions. To take part in a revolution and to walk on another planet in the light of another sun. I've achieved one ambition, and depending on how you define revolution, I may achieve the other. Meeting these people—the natives here—is going to change our history."

I finished the sandwich and licked my fingers, then made the gesture of agreement.

"What does that mean?" asked Agopian.

Derek said, "Yes. Okay. I agree with you."

"Your English is excellent," I said.

He nodded. "I was in Detroit for two years—more like three—studying at the School for Labor History."

"You're a historian? And you're on the crew?"

"I have a degree in—what would be the right translation? Computer science? Computer theory? *Not* computer engineering. I know how to work with the machines and I know a lot about the way they interact with humans. I don't really know what goes on inside them.

"I also have a degree in history and a certificate that says I am competent to astrogate."

"He's a political officer," said Derek.

"There is no such position on the I.S.S. *One.* I am a member of the astrogation team."

Derek made the gesture of polite lack of conviction.

"I can imagine what that means," Agopian said. He glanced at me. "I was a political officer. Three years onboard the *Alexandra Kollontai.* It's a freighter that goes between Transfer Station One and the L-5 colonies. I'd better use the past tense. It was a freighter. It must have been recycled by now." He paused for a moment. He was thinking about the passage of time, something we all did on the expedition. "But I am not a political officer any longer."

"He gives classes on Marxist theory," said Derek. "And on the history of class struggle."

"On my own time," said Agopian. "No one is required to attend."

"A lot of the crewmembers go."

"Why shouldn't they? It's no crime to study the ideas of Karl Marx. Not in this century and on this ship."

I tried to think of a way to change the subject. Nothing came immediately to mind. The boat began to rock. Agopian stood up and looked out a window. "We're going around the north end of your island, Lixia. Across the current and maybe a little too close to the rapids. I like ships that go through

space. These little things that travel on water make me nervous. But Ivanova
is good."

Eddie came in, ducking through the cabin doorway. It was too low for him
and almost too narrow. "We're going to look for Nia and the oracle."

"Good," said Derek.

Eddie shrugged. "I'm getting used to losing arguments. I feel like the old
chiefs and medicine men who told the Europeans, 'You're making a mistake.
You can't treat the Earth like this.' They were right. It only took two hundred
years for everyone to see it."

"He's angry," said Derek.

"Of course I am." He went to the kitchen and got a bottle of mineral water.
"We're going to cross the river and go down the west side—slowly. We won't
reach camp till evening." He opened the bottle and sat down, stretching out
his legs. The mineral water was gone in two gulps. He set the bottle down.

I wanted no part of his anger or of whatever game Derek was playing with
Agopian. My head itched. "I need a shower."

"We have a portable shower," Agopian said. "But we can't set it up onboard
the ship."

"Boat," said Derek.

I said, "Do you have a bathroom? And a sponge?"

"Across from the kitchen. You ought to find everything you need."

I made the gesture of gratitude, got up, and went to the bathroom.

The toilet filled half of it. A cabinet was set into the opposite wall. I slid
it open and—as promised—found everything I needed: soap in a bottle, a
toothbrush, a comb, a pile of neatly folded coveralls, a sponge. The sponge
was genuine and had once been alive, most likely on the ship.

The soap was peppermint. The label said it could be used on body, hair,
teeth, and clothing, but should not be swallowed or otherwise eaten.

I stripped and washed all over—not easy to do in the tiny space. By the
time I finished, there was water everywhere. I brushed my teeth and combed
my wet hair, dried myself and the room, then smiled at my reflection. Not
bad, though I looked a little thin and a little too pale. I needed makeup and a
pair of earrings.

Ah, yes! And clothing. I put on coveralls, size small, blue, the color of
peace and unity. It wasn't my favorite color, but the only other option was
olive drab.

That was it, except for lifting the basin back into the wall above the toilet, turning off the fan and going out to the main cabin. The three men
glanced at me. Curious, to feel again the tension between men and women.
"What do I do with my old clothes?"

"Do you want them back?" asked Agopian.

"Never."

"There's a recycling box in the kitchen. Put them there."

I did and said, "I'm going out on deck. It's too—" I hesitated.

"Close in here," said Derek.

I made the gesture of agreement and opened the door.

It was still raining. An overhang protected the deck. Ivanova sat in a tall chair, which enabled her to see over the cabin roof. Her hands rested on the steering wheel. They were broad and blunt-fingered, strong-looking, even at rest. A wiping blade went across the window in front of her. *Snick.* Pause. *Snick.*

Ivanova glanced at me, nodded, then glanced at the crewwoman. "This is Li Lixia of the sociology team. Lixia, this is Tatiana Valikhanova."

"Of the auxiliary transportation maintenance team," the woman said.

We shook. I looked around. The boat had turned and was moving south. The western shore was on my right, low and gray, a mixture of forest and marsh. To my left were islands: clumps of trees, rising out of the water.

"Watch for smoke," said Ivanova. "That is how we spotted you and Derek."

"In this?" I asked.

"The weather is unfortunate."

I made the gesture of acknowledgment.

The boat continued downriver. After a while Tatiana spoke in Russian. Ivanova turned the wheel. The boat turned toward a long island covered with bushes. There were white spots on the bushes, which became a flock of birds. They flew up as we approached. Tatiana scanned the island with binoculars. "Nothing," she said in English. The boat turned again, out into the channel. The rain was getting heavier. Raindrops pocked the surface of the water, and the shore was barely visible.

"This is really bad," I said.

"We'll try again in two or three days," Ivanova said. "We will be traveling this way. The nearest village is north of here on a tributary of this river."

I stared at her. "You're going to visit a village?"

"Yes."

"You must have had the meeting."

"On the problem of intervention? Yes."

"What happened?"

Ivanova laughed. "What do you expect? You and Derek had vanished. We could not reach you by radio. People wanted to look for you. Eddie said no. It was too risky. The precedent was too dangerous. We had to adhere to his ridiculous—what do you call it?"

I frowned, looking toward the shore. It was a gray line now. "Do you mean the policy of nonintervention?"

261

"No. It is a term invented by writers. American writers, I think. Prime something."

I grinned. "The Prime Directive."

"Agopian told me about it. He is full of information about America and science fiction."

"So you decided to look for us. Believe me, I am grateful. But why the village? Why are you going there?"

"Eddie said no. I said—the crew said—this is crazy. We can't leave people in trouble. We can't let other humans die. Eddie kept pounding at the danger of the precedent. I don't understand him. I am from the Chukotka National District. Do you know where that is?"

"No."

"Siberia, as far east and north as anyone can go and still be on the continent of Asia. Most of my ancestors were ethnic Russians. But no one in Siberia is entirely one thing. I have ancestors who were Chukchi and Inuit. I know what happened to the Small Peoples, the original natives, for good and for bad. We learned it in school.

"That's over. We can't undo it, and we can't stop history. We can only act more carefully, more thoughtfully, with more respect and less greed." She paused. "We can only act like socialists."

I thought for a moment. "I don't understand what this has to do with being here."

"It was a deadlock," said Tatiana. "No one wanted to leave you on the planet. But there are a lot of people on the ship from Asia and Africa and Latin America. They remember the stories they learned in school. Comrade Ivanova is from Siberia. I am from Kazakhstan. From the Kazakh A.S.S.R. I know what happened to our good pastureland when the Russians—the Soviet Russians—came."

"What?" I asked.

"Plowed up. Gone. We had to pasture our herds in the dry land—the desert—or the mountains." The woman lifted her binoculars. "Comrade, could you bring us closer to the shore?"

"Yes." Ivanova turned the wheel. The boat turned toward the rainy marsh: gray reeds, bent under the weight of water. They moved gently in the wind. "As Tatiana says, it was a deadlock. We sat and glared at one another. Until the Chinese said it was not our problem."

I looked at Ivanova, surprised.

"They said the planet does not belong to us. And it is not our history that we are afraid of changing. They said—Mr. Fang said—consult the natives. Ask them if they want to have us here." Ivanova paused. "That is why we are going to the village."

"One village is going to decide this issue for the entire planet?"

"No. Of course not. We are going to the nearest village to explain who we are and why we have come into their territory. To ask if we can stay. If they say no, we will apologize and leave. If they say yes . . ."

Tatiana said, "There is something on the shore."

The boat slowed. I made out the thing. It lay on a mud bank, entirely out of the water. A long object, narrow and dark. A lizard?

Tatiana said, "A canoe."

"What?" I held out my hand. She gave me the binoculars. She was right. "We tipped over next to the eastern shore. How could it possibly have gotten here?"

"The current certainly would not have brought it," Ivanova said.

The boat slowed, edging toward the bank. Ivanova spoke in Russian. Tatiana went into the cabin. The boat stopped. Eddie came out on deck, Agopian following.

"How deep?" asked Eddie.

Ivanova glanced at the instruments in front of her. "A little over a meter."

Eddie went over the side and waded to shore.

"Comrade?" asked Agopian.

"Stay here. Unless you want to go."

"Of course I do. It's clearly an artifact—made by aliens. I'd like to touch it. I'm already wet."

She laughed. He followed Eddie. I raised the binoculars again. Eddie was at the canoe. I could estimate the size now. It was too small. Eddie touched the wood. Agopian came up, his shoulders hunched against the rain, his pants soaked to the waist. They spoke. If they'd been natives, I would have understood them. But the gestures they made had no clear meaning. Agopian pointed. Eddie shook his head. They looked around them. Agopian pulled out a camera. He took pictures of the canoe. Eddie walked back toward us.

"It isn't our canoe," I said to Ivanova.

"No?"

"Too small. And there's something else. The shape of the prow."

Eddie climbed back onboard. "It's old. The wood is rotten. There are plants growing inside it." He glanced back at Agopian. The short man was still taking pictures. "There aren't any footprints on the shore. I'd say it washed up, maybe in the spring. This river must flood. I don't think it was new then. It looks as if it's been in the water for years."

"There isn't much chance of finding them, is there?" I said.

"No."

"They should have been on the eastern side of the river," said Ivanova. "Near the main channel, like you and Derek." She paused, then shouted. "Comrade!"

I jumped.

Eddie grinned. "You see what it's been like on the ship. She has one hell of a bellow."

"I have almost never yelled at you," said Ivanova.

Agopian waded back out. Eddie helped him onboard.

"It isn't much to look at," he said. "But it *is* an artifact." I heard an odd tone in his voice. "They aren't a figment of our imagination."

"Who?" asked Eddie.

"The aliens. The natives. Other people. Sentient life." He laughed. "And I'm here." He looked down at his pants. "I'm going to have to change my clothes."

Eddie nodded. The boat began to move, edging out toward deeper water. The men went into the cabin.

I stayed next to Ivanova. The boat picked up speed. The rain grew heavier. The islands and the shore became dim shadows. Water ran down the windshield and beat on the unprotected deck in back of us. The wind carried it under the overhang. It touched me. I shivered.

"Go inside, comrade. I don't know what diseases it is possible to catch on this planet, but whatever they are, you are asking to catch them. You are exhausted. You haven't eaten properly for days. And now you are getting wet and cold. Give the binoculars to Tatiana. I don't believe she will be able to see anything. But one does not give up when lives are at stake."

I went in. Derek was lounging in a chair, his legs out, his shoulders against the back. Not the way he usually sat. He looked exhausted. The others sat around him, drinking tea and talking softly. Lights glowed pale yellow.

Tatiana glanced up. "She wants me?"

"Yes." I handed over the binoculars. She left. I sat down on a couch, feeling disoriented. Maybe it was the light. So pale and steady. So foreign. Nothing like firelight. I rubbed my neck. The others glanced at me, then continued their conversation. It had something to do with a concert on the ship. A composer who was using elements of native music taken from our reports. Eddie thought the work was superficial. Agopian thought it was interesting. Derek asked a question now and then.

I lay down and closed my eyes. Someone put a blanket over me.

Derek said, "We're almost to the camp."

I sat up. The lights were off. The cabin was empty, except for the two of us.

"It stopped raining," he said. "Come out."

I stood, stretching, and followed him onto the deck. Tatiana was at the wheel. The other three leaned against the stern railing. Eddie's long hair fluttered in the wind. Behind them was the river valley, dark with forest. Above them the sky was iron-gray. In the west—on my right—it was clearing. Rays of sunlight came through the clouds and touched the river. No. The lake. It stretched around us, wide and silver-gray. Birds soared over the choppy water. I looked to my left. I could just barely make out the eastern shore. "It's bigger than I expected."

"You probably were thinking of something on Earth," said Eddie. "I noticed in your reports—you kept trying to make this world a second Earth. Not only you. All the field-workers. Everything was compared to something at home. Most of the comparisons are going to turn out to be false and wrong. This place is *alien*. We don't belong here."

"That has not been determined," said Ivanova.

The boat turned in toward the western shore. It was close, and the bluffs were easy to see. They were tall and eroded, topped with forest and cut by deep ravines.

"It really is a lovely planet," said Agopian. "Earth must have looked like this, before the capitalists got hold of it."

"Huh," said Eddie.

There were domes on the shore: tan and soft blue, creamy off-white, celadon-green. In front of them was a dock, extending into the lake. It floated, long and jointed, moving up and down section by section as the waves washed in.

People came out of the buildings. They ran toward the dock. So many!

"Eddie," said Derek.

"Yes."

"I don't think we have the energy for any kind of celebration."

"Leave it to me." The boat stopped. Eddie climbed onto the dock and ran toward the people.

The engine stopped. I heard water and the wind. Birds cried. Human voices spoke. I did not understand them. Eddie gestured. The people turned and walked back to the camp.

We climbed out, and Agopian tied the boat. Eddie returned, one person with him: a tall and slender woman. Her skin was dark brown. Her hair was shoulder-length and wavy. Her coveralls were terra-cotta red.

"This is Liberation Minh. She's a member of the medical team."

"A pleasure." She shook our hands. "We're going to need to do a preliminary examination. It won't take long. We will take you apart once we have you on the ship. But now—all we need is a few samples. A few tests." She turned and led the way. Derek and I followed.

"We have found parasites in your colleagues. A few worms or wormlike creatures. A number of microbes. None doing really well, but trying. If they were larger, we'd speak of courage and enterprise." Her accent was African. That surprised me. I would have bet she came from the Americas. That name and that coloring. Maybe her parents had been American.

"Also, we have found malnutrition. Our microbes—the ones that were supposed to help you metabolize the native flora and fauna—did not work as well as we had hoped."

We reached the end of the dock. Vehicles had gone over the muddy ground, mashing down the vegetation and leaving deep ruts. I saw one machine: a hillclimber with huge wheels. It was parked next to a dome.

Liberation Mihn said, "That is it, except for a little metal poisoning. The crust of this planet is rich."

Oh, good, I thought. Our microbes were failing, other microbes had moved in, and we were being poisoned by who knew what? Zinc. Copper. Manganese. Lead.

We followed her into a blue-gray dome. Inside was a pale gray carpet. Hexagonal windows looked out on the evening lake. There were rooms full of medical equipment. I entered one, and a tech came in, tall, with a hawk face. "Please undress, unless you are uncomfortable with nudity or men."

"No." I put on a gown. He attached machines to me. They made the usual machine noises. He made the kind of human noises that were usual during a medical examination.

"No trouble there. Or there. You seem to be in the—what is the term?—pink of health. I don't know if that refers to the color of healthy Europeans. If so, it is another example of racism. How hard it is to get such things out of a language!"

There were more noises, machine and human. Finally he said, "I can see no trouble at all. Except your weight. It's down a bit, and it is never a good idea to be too thin. Try to eat a little more until your weight is back up to where it should be."

"Okay."

"And the problem with menstruation. That is most interesting! I will refer it to the proper committee, along with your test results. The bathroom is next door. Please read the instructions on the monitor and follow them exactly. Thank you for your patience." He gave me a dazzling white smile. "And welcome back. God is great!"

He left. I found the bathroom, followed the instructions, dressed, and went down the hall. By this time it was night. When I looked out the windows, I saw only my own reflection and the gleam of the corridor lights. I came to a room with chairs. Derek and Eddie sat there. Both looked tired.

"How are you?" I asked Derek.

"Some scratches and bruises. One ugly bite. But otherwise okay."

"One ugly bite?"

"I'll tell you about it later."

I glanced at Eddie. "What next?"

266

"You are assigned to dome number five. I'll take you there. Dome three—the big one—has the commons and the dining room."

"Not tonight. I just want to go to sleep."

"Yes," said Derek.

"Okay." Eddie stood.

We went out. The sky had cleared. Stars gleamed overhead. To the east I saw a planet. It was yellow and so bright that it cast a reflection: a yellow line that barely wavered. The water must be quiet. The air was still. We moved past buildings and machinery. Metal gleamed dimly in the light that came out windows.

Eddie stopped and pushed open a door. We followed him into a corridor made of glazed yellow panels. Lamps shaped like flowers were fastened to the walls. Their stems were ceramic. Their petals were frosted glass. A light blue carpet covered the floor. I felt its texture through my slippers. Soft. Our feet made no noise as we followed Eddie.

"Here." He opened another door. A light came on. I saw a bedroom: blue walls and a pale tan carpet. There was a hexagonal window over the bed. The window was at an angle, set in a wall that curved.

"This is yours, Lixia."

I made the gesture of gratitude.

"Derek will be next door. The bathroom is down the hall. I can get you food, if you're hungry."

"No." The bed had a cover: a floral pattern done in white, dark blue, and tan. It looked comforting. Was that the right word? Comfortable. Like home.

"Good night," said Eddie.

They left me. I dimmed the light, undressed, and lay down. The bed was soft. The cover felt cool and smooth. I thought of getting under it, but could not manage the effort. I closed my eyes.

I woke to darkness. Above me was the window. Stars burned outside. There was someone in the room. I wasn't sure how I could tell, but I was certain. Where was the light? I didn't remember turning it off. I reached out carefully, feeling along the wall. Surely there ought to be a switch.

"Relax," said Derek. "It's only me." His voice came from the floor.

"What in hell?"

"The bed was too soft, and I was lonely. I wanted something familiar."

"Oh."

"They smell funny, Lixia. I think it's the difference in diet. And the lack of fur."

"Could be."

"And there's something about the air in these buildings. It doesn't feel right. It barely moves."

267

"If you want to sleep on the floor, it's okay with me."

"Thank you."

"What happened to you, Derek? After you got to the sandbar."

He laughed. "Nothing much. The nearest land was a marsh. I swam over there. I thought maybe I'd be able to find a trail. I got bit."

"Is that what you were talking about?"

"More or less. It was a kind of lizard. Not even as long as my forearm. But brightly colored and fearless. I thought those colors had to mean something, and there had to be a reason why the animal was fearless. Either it scared other animals or it tasted like shit.

"I figured I didn't want to take the chance. I had to get the wound open and bleeding. I didn't have a knife on me. I'd lost it. I didn't want to take the time to find something sharp." He paused. "I chewed the wound open."

"What?"

"I was lucky it was in a place I could reach. If that animal had bit me on the ass, I'd probably be dead. I got it bleeding freely, and I sucked out everything I could. But I still got goddamn sick. The animal was poisonous."

"Where was it?"

"The wound? On my arm, right above the bracelet. I wondered if maybe the brightness attracted the animal—or angered it."

"The bracelet?"

"The one that belonged to the Trickster. I tracked the oracle and found where he threw it into the lake."

"You took it back a second time."

"Uh-huh."

"Do you still have it?"

"Not anymore. I don't like being pushed around by anyone, even a spirit. But too many bad things have happened. I threw it in the river. I apologized to the Trickster. I told him I'd find a way to make up for everything." He paused. "After I got over being sick, I decided to stay where I was. My arm hurt. I wasn't sure that I'd be able to swim any distance at all. And I didn't want to go back in the marsh. I figured, I'd wait for a rescue or until I was feeling a bit better. I gathered wood and built a fire. I'm tired, Lixia."

I said, "Good night."

His breathing changed almost at once, becoming deep and even and slow. He had gone to sleep.

I followed his example.

I dreamed that I was back on the ship in a corridor. The walls were made of ceramic tile, glazed oxblood-red. Derek was in the corridor. He was dancing. The gold bracelet was on his wrist. It shone brightly. Derek sang in the language of gifts:

> "I am the Trickster,
> O, you foolish woman.
> What I want, I take.
> What I take, I keep."

Eddie

S unlight came through the window. I groaned and sat up. Derek was
gone. He'd left a pillow on the floor. The covering was brown and
gray: a pattern of swallows in flight.

I found my clothes and went looking for the bathroom, which had
been used. There was steam on the mirror and two damp towels. They'd been
hung up, not especially neatly. I straightened them, turned on the shower, and
climbed in. Ah! The simple pleasures of civilization! Hot spray beat on my
head and back. The soap smelled of lemon. There was a loofah hanging on a
hook in the stall. I got it wet and scrubbed.

The water went off. I pressed the button that turned it on.

A voice said, "If you wish to obtain more water, wait a minute, then press
the 'On' button. But remember, you have already used your daily allotment."

"There's a whole lake out there. A river as big as the Mississippi. And the
water is clean."

The shower did not answer. I pressed the button again, though I felt guilty
about it—as I was supposed to. The water came on, and I washed my hair.

When I was done I got dressed and wandered through the dome. I found
evidence of occupation in almost every room: rumpled beds and pieces of

clothing. A necklace lay on a table. It was antique silver and coral. Sunlight touched it. It gleamed.

Another room held a book, which I turned on. The title appeared on the screen: À la Recherche du Temps Perdu par Marcel Proust. My French was close to nonexistent. I turned the book off and put it back where I had found it and then went out of the dome.

The day was bright and windy. The lake glittered. Clouds moved across the sky. Eddie waited for me. He wore a flower-print shirt, dark-green and red. His hair was in braids. His jeans were tucked into high boots made of real leather. He had sunglasses on. The lenses were green-gold and highly reflective. I could not see his eyes.

"Good morning, Lixia. I thought I'd make sure you found the dining room."

"Thanks."

We walked toward the biggest dome.

"How'd you sleep?"

"Okay. Where do I get new clothes?"

"Dome one. It's all standard issue. I'm sorry about that. No one thought to bring anything from your cabin."

"You didn't expect to find me."

He laughed. "Maybe so. We've gone to a hell of a lot of trouble—and set a dangerous precedent—and you may be right. We may not have believed that you and Derek were alive."

"Lucky for us that you came down anyway."

Eddie did not answer. I glanced at him. He was frowning. I knew what he was thinking. It wasn't lucky for the people on the planet.

The dining room was almost empty. A crewmember sat reading, a glass of tea on the table in front of him. A woman gathered dishes, stacking them neatly. She was large, with red-brown coloring. Her clothing—a pair of jeans and a white blouse—told me nothing about her occupation.

Eddie led the way to the serving table. A little man was putting bagels on a plate. His hair was long and blond, covered by a hair net, and his clothing was kitchen-white.

"You're late," he said. "The eggs are gone."

"What's left?" Eddie asked.

"Noodles and sausage. We have three kinds of sausage." He tapped a heating unit. "These are made from chicken and are relatively spicy. The ones in the next unit are made from iguana. They're mild. The ones at the end are soybean. I don't recommend them, unless you're really worried about your karma. No animal was killed to make them, and that's the best I can say." He paused and glanced down the table. "That's it, except for the bagels, which turned out pretty well today."

I helped myself to chicken sausage, a bagel, and a pot of coffee. Eddie got noodles and tea.

We sat down at a table next to a wall made up of hexagonal windows. Outside was the lake. I squinted. Two objects floated there, a good distance out. They were hard to see amid the glitter of the waves. I shaded my eyes. They were long and dark, low in the water.

"The rocket planes," said Eddie.

I poured coffee and drank. "Ivanova told me a little of what happened at the meeting. But I can't say that I understood it."

"I wish to hell you and Derek had made it back in time. I wish you hadn't vanished. I was trying to argue a principle while Ivanova recited the Code of Space. One does not abandon a comrade in trouble. It had a definite impact." He paused and twirled noodles onto a fork. "Did you know—in the century after the conquest of Mexico, ninety percent of the native population died? The population of Peru fell by ninety-five percent. Three million people vanished off the Caribbean Islands." He ate the noodles, chewing them carefully. "They died in the mines and on the plantations. They were sent to Europe as slaves. Disease got them. War and execution. Starvation. There is a quote I have memorized by a Spanish writer of the time.

"'Who of those born in future generations will believe this? I myself who saw it can hardly believe that such was possible.'"

I ate as he talked. The sausage was not really spicy. The bagel was excellent.

"Eddie, that was hundreds of years ago. You don't seriously think that something like that is going to happen again?"

He paused, then sighed. "I don't know. But I've been listening to the conversations on the ship." He ate another forkful of noodles, then reached for a bottle of Sichuan hot oil, which was on the table along with other condiments. He sprinkled the oil all over his plate. "Everyone wants to get down to the surface of the planet. No. That isn't entirely true. There are astronomers who don't care, and some planetologists who want to look at the other planets in the system. But they're the exceptions. The biologists are going crazy."

"What do you expect? These people came eighteen point two light-years to study the life on this planet."

"I know." He ate more noodles. "That's better. I'm telling you what I've been hearing. Most of the people on the ship are talking about the research they plan to do, once they get down here."

I drank more coffee. Eddie was not a linear thinker, going from A to B to C. Sometimes, when I listened to him, I was reminded of weaving, of how the pattern emerged bit by bit as the shuttle went back and forth. If I waited long enough, I would understand his argument.

272

He said, "That isn't what bothers me, though I wonder what all these people will do if the natives say, 'No. We don't want you. Go home.'

"What bothers me is the speculation. It's especially bad among members of the crew.

"There's a lot of discussion about the feasibility of interstellar trade. What is so valuable—and so unique—that it'd be worth moving from star to star? And what would keep its value for one hundred twenty years? Most people figure life and art."

"Eddie, this has been talked about for centuries."

"There are people on the ship who are building economic models. The economists, of course. We should never have brought them along. They are running everything they can think of through the models. Is it worthwhile to ship iridium? Or platinum? Or copper? What if we assume improvements in our technology? Ships that move a lot faster or use a lot less energy?

"What about people? Think of the knowledge and skill that's contained in almost any human brain. Why send art to Earth? Send the artist.

"And when we send samples of the life here—or anywhere—back to Earth, we ought to send the people who understand that life. The farmers and hunters and animal trainers. The old women who know which herbs are medicinal.

"How else can we possibly know what we have when we grow an organism? How else can we take care of it? And use it?"

I poured myself more coffee. "The ship is full of people who like to play with ideas. And as you have pointed out before, the crew doesn't have enough to do at present. Neither do the social scientists. I think you're taking this way too seriously."

"Maybe." He finished eating. "There are problems with all the models. For example, how can we send people on a trip that will last one hundred twenty years? Not humans. Natives, who may not understand the nature of the journey.

"No one has an answer to that question, though some of the crew are hypothesizing natives who like to travel and who don't care if they ever come home."

"Um."

He made the gesture of agreement.

"Eddie! You're learning."

He repeated the gesture and then went on.

"Let's suppose that it is economic to ship iridium or platinum. Who's going to mine it? And refine it? We're going to have to assume a good-sized colony. Maybe the natives will help us. Maybe we'll teach them our technology.

"There are people who say it's crazy to think of moving raw materials— even raw materials that have been at least partially processed, such as ingots of metal. They say, why not build the factories here and produce a finished product? For example, why not build ships? We could fill them with good-ies—with life and art—and send them back to Earth. Or else we could go on from here and find other planets in other systems.

"As you might imagine, this plan would require a really large colony. Or a lot of help from the natives. We'd have to bring them into the industrial age." He pushed his plate to the side. "And this brings us to Comrade Lu Jiang. Do you remember her?"

I made the gesture of indecision, then added, "I'm not certain."

"She's the woman who thinks the natives are trapped in their present his-torical stage. They can't gather in cities because the men are solitary. The women need men during the mating season and maybe at other times. In most of the societies we've studied, the men are important economically. At least to some extent." He paused, frowning, obviously trying to get his ideas in order.

"They're not likely to develop the kind of trade and manufacture that leads to industrial capitalism. Without industrial capitalism, there can be no revo-lution. These people will always be tribal. Unless we help them, they can never develop a socialist society.

"It is our duty to help them, according to Comrade Jiang."

"I am getting a headache," I said.

"I've had one for days." He stood up. "Come on."

We took our dishes to the recycling table and stacked them, then went out to the lake. The beach was gravel. Little birds ran over it, stopping now and then to peck. What—if anything—were they finding? Small animals? Bits of debris?

"You see why I think it was dangerous to come down, even to find you?"

"I guess so."

"I told the meeting, if we did this now—if we hunted for you—we'd do it again. There'd be another good reason and another.

"I said we had to draw a line. We had to make an unbreakable rule."

I was angry with Eddie, of course. Anyone would have been. He'd been willing to let us die for a theory—in order to defend a bunch of people he didn't know against a danger that might be imaginary. It was too damn abstract for me. I thought of myself on the island and Derek on his sandbar. We could have died. Easily.

"The meeting didn't listen to you."

"No. They were hungry, and they heard Ivanova make her speech on the Code of Space."

"Why'd you come on this expedition if you didn't want to meet aliens?"

"I was hoping they'd be so damn different that we couldn't harm each other. I thought—if there were people here and they were vulnerable, there had to be someone on the ship with a good memory. Someone who'd be ready to defend them." He looked out at the shining lake. "Eddie the Galactic Hero. The man who tried to save his people—four hundred years after the fact and more than eighteen light-years from home." He glanced at me. His glasses had been transparent in the dining room. Now they were like polished metal again.

I kept silent.

"I've gotten myself angry. I think I'll take a walk."

"Okay."

He started down the beach. I went looking for dome number one.

It was empty: no other shoppers and no volunteer fashion consultants, nothing except a computer on a table next to the door. I punched in a request for clothing, and it answered with a map. Aisle two, shelves one through nine. "Please remember to input your selections," it added in luminous yellow letters. "Without this information we cannot charge your account."

I got my clothing and went back to my room. My bed was made. There was a note on the pillow from Derek.

"Always remember: Neatness is next to revolutionary zeal."

I crumpled the note and tossed it into the recycling bin, then put on a pair of jeans, a bright pink shirt, high boots, a belt of lizard skin. I needed jewelry. The computer had none, which was hardly surprising. If I wanted jewelry on the ship, I didn't punch the supply department. I punched arts and artifacts or I went to the personal exchange.

The rest of the clothing went into a cabinet. I decided to take a walk—not south, the way Eddie had gone. North along the shore.

The beach was narrow in that direction. Bushes grew almost to the water. There were outcroppings of rock.

After a while I looked back. I could see the dock and the rocket planes, but not the domes. Vegetation hid them. I found a hunk of limestone and sat down on it. Birds darted along the shore. They were like the ones I'd seen earlier: little and brown. Runners, not fliers. One stopped and stretched its wings. There were claws at the tips and joints.

"Li-sa?" a voice said.

I turned.

Nia stood there. Her tunic was ripped. Her fur was matted. She looked miserable.

I jumped off the rock and grabbed her, hugging tightly. She stiffened, then returned my embrace.

"You're alive!"

"Both of us."

275

I let go and stepped back. "Who?"

"I," said the oracle.

His kilt was in worse shape than Nia's tunic. It was a gray rag that barely covered his pubic area.

"Ulzai?"

Nia made the gesture that indicated lack of knowledge. "We caught onto the boat after it went over. It floated upside down and carried us through the rapids. Aiya! What an experience!"

"I can't swim," the oracle said. "But my spirit took care of me, as always. And of Nia, too."

Nia made the gesture of gratitude. The oracle replied with the gesture of acknowledgment.

I made the gesture that asked for more information.

Nia said, "The boat went downriver. We held on. All day. All night. At last it drifted into shallow water. We were able to stand."

"Just barely," the oracle said. "My legs were like string. Aiya!"

Nia glanced at him, frowning a little. "We pulled the boat to shore and rested, then I looked around. We were on an island. It was large and covered with bushes. There was no water—except the water in the river, which tasted muddy to me. And not much food.

"We decided to go farther down the river. I found branches that would serve as paddles. I am going to sit."

I made the gesture of agreement. The two natives settled themselves on the ground. I followed suit.

"It was not an easy journey," the oracle said. "The branches were not good paddles."

"Maybe we should have stayed where we were," Nia said. "But I thought your friends were going to be at the lake. We could tell them what happened. Maybe they would know how to find you." She paused and scratched her nose. "We spent three days traveling on the river. The first day we stayed close to the shore. Then—in the late afternoon—we saw a lizard. A big one, lying on the bank. It took no interest in us, but we became frightened. We paddled out into the middle of the river.

"We found an island with trees and made camp. I was pretty sure that the lizards could not climb.

"The next day we went on. In the afternoon we came to the lake. We made camp on the eastern shore. There was something in the water a long way out. It was low and dark. We thought it was an island.

"At night lights shone on it, and there were more lights on the shore. I thought, those are Li-sa's people. We are going to have to cross the lake.

"The next morning something unexpected happened." Nia paused.

276

"Something fell out of the sky," the oracle said. "There was a lot of noise. We ran and hid. When the noise stopped we came back. There were two islands in the lake."

"I've heard of stones falling out of the sky," Nia said. "But stones do not float. I thought to myself, this is new. And it is big."

Nia looked at me. Her gaze was steady. "I did not like it, Li-sa. I began to feel uneasy. I thought, there is something going on that I do not understand, and it is something big."

The oracle said, "After that, we were careful."

Nia made the gesture of agreement. "We were at the place where the river entered the lake. We waited till nightfall and paddled across. It wasn't easy. We were going across the current. But we made it. We hid the boat. Then we traveled through the forest below the river bluff. There was no trail. We had to go up and down over the rocks. We had to push through the vegetation. Aiya!

"We came to the village. The one that belongs to your people. We hid." She paused for a moment. "This is the hard part of the story."

"We decided not to go in," the oracle said. "Not at once. We wanted to be sure that the village really did belong to your people. We stayed in the forest and watched. We saw." The oracle paused. "There were boats on the lake that moved by themselves. They went back and forth between the islands and the shore. There were other things. Wagons. People rode in them. The wagons moved the way the boats did, with no one doing any work. And the wagons made noises. They roared like killers of the forest. They honked like *osubai*. We could tell they were made of metal. We knew they were not alive. But how were they moving? And why were they making so much noise?"

"We should have gone into the camp," Nia said. "We knew these were your kinfolk. They wore clothing like yours, and they had no fur. It was my responsibility to tell them what had happened to you and Deragu." She straightened her shoulders and looked directly at me. "I could not do it, Li-sa. Even though you might be in trouble. Even though these people might have been able to help you. I was afraid."

"How long did you watch?" I asked.

"A day," said the oracle. "And part of another. Then you came with Deraku, riding in one of the boats that moved even though the people on it did nothing. We saw you get off. We saw your relatives greet you."

"That was a relief," Nia said.

"This morning we saw you go off on your own. We followed." He made the gesture that meant "it is over" or "the story is done."

"I probably would have done the same thing," I said. "Hidden and watched. I know my people are strange. But there is nothing in the camp to worry about. Are you willing to come with me?"

277

"Yes," said the oracle. "I have heard nothing new from my spirit. And this is what I came for. To meet your people who have no hair."

Nia made the gesture of doubtful agreement.

We turned back toward camp.

"I am worried about Ulzai," I said.

"He will be all right," the oracle said. "The *umazi* promised him that they would kill him, and he has told us that there are no *umazi* here in the north. Therefore, he is safe."

Good reasoning, if one believed in messages from spirits.

"Why did the camp frighten you?" I asked. "You weren't frightened by my box with voices."

"Your radio," Nia said, pronouncing the word carefully and almost correctly. "That thing is small. I told you, I am not afraid of new things if they are small. And if there are not too many of them." She paused for a moment. "And you are a friend of mine. I do not know these people."

We reached the dock. There was a boat tied up, maybe the one we had come on. A couple of people were standing next to it. They looked at me and the natives, then froze—motionless, watching.

We turned up into the camp.

"Are you hungry?" I asked.

"Yes," said the oracle.

"I'll get you some food." I turned toward the big dome. They followed, keeping close to me.

There was a hillclimber parked by the entrance to the dome. It wasn't the same one I had seen before. I would have recognized the big dent in the side. How had they managed to do that in only a few days? A man was lifting a box marked "fragile" out of the back. He stopped, the box in midair, and stared, his mouth open.

"Brian!" I said. "How are you?"

"Those are aliens," he said.

"It'd be more accurate to say that we're the aliens. These people are native." He smiled at Nia.

"This person is showing teeth the way that Deragu always does."

"It means that he's friendly."

"This is a man?" asked Nia.

I made the gesture of affirmation.

"What are the signs? He is no bigger than you are, and I can't tell if his fur is different from yours. You both have so little."

"The texture of the fur doesn't matter. But the location does. Only men have fur on the lower part of the face. But not all men do. His voice is deeper than mine, and his shoulders are wider. Those are signs."

278

Nia frowned. "I cannot hear much difference in your voices, and you both look slender to me." She made the gesture that meant "so be it." "Tell the man, it is my wish to be friendly."

"Okay. If Nia could smile, she would," I said in English. "But among her people, smiling is not an act of friendship. And—as far as I have been able to tell—they don't have a comparable expression."

"Shit," said Brian. "Does that mean I've done something wrong?"

"No. She's been with me and Derek, who—as you may remember—smiles a lot."

"Yeah. I remember. The famous Sea Warrior shit-eating grin. Tell her I'm glad to meet her. Tell her this is a great day."

"I will."

We entered the dome. The entrance area had a carpet: light brown with a tight weave. The oracle stopped and rubbed his bare foot across it. "Is this a gift that your people offer? Or does it come from another village?"

Most likely the carpet came from Earth. I said, "It comes from another village a long way from here."

"The people on the plain—my folk and Nia's—make carpets that are softer and that have patterns done in many fine colors. This is nothing much to look at."

Nia said, "I know you are crazy, but you ought to remember something about good manners. It is not right to criticize the things that other people have."

"I would have kept quiet, if this had been made by Lixia's people."

We went on down the hall. The dining room was empty. I led my companions into the kitchen, which was empty, too. Sunlight came in through high windows and everything gleamed, even the wooden cutting table, which had just been washed. The kitchen people must have left a few minutes before.

I looked around. "There must be food here somewhere."

Derek pushed through the doors. "They said—I was hoping. Nia, can I embrace you?"

Nia looked surprised, then made the gesture of assent.

He gave her a quick hug.

"But not me," the oracle said. "I am a man, even if I am crazy. I do not like to be touched."

"Okay." Derek looked at me. "Everyone is running around out there shouting, 'The natives are coming, the natives are coming.' I told Agopian to find the kitchen team."

"Good. What about Eddie?"

"We're looking for him."

"What are you saying?" asked Nia.

Agopian came in with the little blond man. He was dressed in denim now, and his long hair was down. He wore it clipped at the nape of his neck. From there it flowed most of the way to his waist.

"Glory be to heaven," he said.

I said, "They're hungry."

He nodded. "Sandwiches. And we have a pretty good lentil soup."

I glanced at Derek. "Do you think it's safe for them to eat our food?"

"An interesting question, and one I don't want to answer on my own. I'd better go find a biologist."

"I'd like to know what you are saying," Nia said.

"We are trying to decide if you can eat our food."

"Why not?"

The blond man said, "Could you people get out of my kitchen? We have strict regulations re sanitation."

"Does that remark indicate prejudice?" I asked.

"It certainly does. I have a strong prejudice against dirt and against many microorganisms. Now, please, out."

We went back into the dining room. Derek left with Agopian, and I sat down at the table. Nia and the oracle followed my example. They looked nervous. I couldn't remember seeing a chair in any native house.

"Your people are noisy," Nia said.

I made the gesture of agreement.

The oracle looked out the window. "They run around a lot."

"Only when strangers arrive or when something happens that is unusual."

"Hu!"

The blond man came in, carrying a pitcher and two glasses. "This is local water. It's been analyzed and then distilled. It ought to be safe for everyone."

He set the glasses down and filled them. "Here you are." He handed one to Nia and the other to the oracle.

They frowned. Nia set her glass down. She touched it lightly. "What is this? It looks like ice, but it is not cold."

"It is called 'glass.' It won't melt, and you can't eat it. It breaks easily. If it breaks, the edges are sharp."

There was ice floating in the glass. A cube. She prodded it. "Is this more guh—more of the same thing?"

I made the gesture of disagreement. "That is ice."

"Why is it shaped like a box? Why does it have a hole in the middle?"

"And why is it in our water?" the oracle asked.

"My people like their water to be cold, that's why we put ice in it. The ice is like a box because . . ." I hesitated. "We make it. We cast it like metal in a mold, and the mold is square on all sides."

280

"Aiya!" She lifted the glass and tilted it. Water ran over her chin and dripped on her ragged tunic. "This cup is not well made!"

"That may be," I said.

The oracle tried. Like Nia, he spilled a fair amount of water. They were nervous, both of them. Why, I could not imagine. Here they sat, surrounded by hairless magicians, trying to make conversation while their stomachs made hungry noises.

They finished drinking the water. The oracle pulled an ice cube out of his glass. He held it on his palm, looking at it. Then he poked it with a finger. "It is ice." He popped it into his mouth. I heard a crunch.

"You can do that with the ice," I said. "But not with the glass."

The oracle made the gesture that indicated understanding. Derek returned, a woman with him as tall as he was and as black as coal. She wore a bright yellow coverall and a pair of truly amazing earrings. Two huge disks made of hammered metal. When she got closer, I saw her eyes. The irises were silver, the same color as the earrings. There were no pupils.

Contact lenses, of course. It wasn't an Earth fashion. She was from one of the L-5 colonies or from Luna or Mars.

She had a bag in one hand. After a moment I realized the bag was moving. Something inside it was alive. She looked at Nia and the oracle. "Well, they certainly are alien. There can be no doubt of that."

Derek said, "According to Marina, they *ought* to be able to eat our food."

"The trouble isn't that we are poisonous to one another," the woman said. "The trouble is the members of one system cannot metabolize the food that comes from the other system. If these people eat our food for any length of time, they are going to end up with some really terrible deficiency diseases. But one or two meals should not hurt them.

"However," she paused. "Having said all that, I do not recommend that we give them our food. Instead—" She reached into the bag and pulled out a fish. It twisted in her hand. "Ask your friends if this is edible."

I did. Nia made the gesture of affirmation. Marina gave the fish to the blond man. "Broil it. Add nothing. No butter. No salt."

"All right," the man said. He went into the kitchen.

Marina sat down. "There are always allergies, and unpredictable reactions of one kind or another. We don't want to kill the first aliens we have ever met."

"No," I said.

"What is going on?" asked Nia.

"The little man is going to cook the fish," I said. "The woman who just came in says it is possible that our food might harm you."

"Aiya!" said the oracle. "This is a strange experience."

Nia made the gesture of agreement.

The black woman introduced herself. Her name was Marina in Sight of Olympus, and she was from Mars. She was a biologist. Her specialty was taxonomy. She had spent years classifying the fossil life of her home planet.

"It got to be depressing. All those wonderful little creatures! As strange as anything we had on Earth during the Precambrian. And all of them were gone. Everything was gone. The planet was dead except for us. You can see why I jumped at the chance to join the expedition."

Nia looked irritated. "It is hard to be around people who do not understand the language of gifts."

I made the gesture of agreement. The blond man came back with two plates of broiled fish.

"It was hard," he said. "I couldn't even add a garnish."

Nia and the oracle ate quickly and neatly with their hands. The rest of us tried not to stare at them.

When they were done, Nia said, "I am going into the forest. If I can find the right kind of wood, I'll make a trap. I have been afraid to go down by the lake, since your people seemed to be everywhere on it. But now I am less afraid. And if I cannot eat your food, I will have to find food for myself."

I made the gesture of agreement.

"So many new things! How do I get out of this house?"

I led her to the door.

"I will be back at nightfall." She turned and walked through the camp toward the forest. People watched her. I returned to the dining room.

The oracle said, "I would like to sleep."

"Okay," said Derek.

They left. The blond man made a stack of plates and glasses. "They are going to have to learn to pick up after themselves."

"They aren't likely to be using the dining room much," I said.

"Maybe not." He went into the kitchen.

I looked at Marina who said, "I have to go feed an ugly-nasty."

"What?"

"I am collecting specimens, and I haven't started giving them Latin names. This has been an amazing day. See you later."

She left. I sat a while longer, alone, thinking, they are alive. Then I went outside.

The wind blew south and east, carrying the clouds away. By midafternoon the sky was clear. I located the biology dome. It was pale yellow and full of cages. Most of the cages were occupied. Birds whistled. Bipeds made piping noises. The ugly-nasty grunted and snuffled.

"What is it?" I asked.

"I figure it's a prince, under some kind of a curse," Marina said. "Look at those warts! Look at those bristles!"

The creature paced, claws clicking. It was designed for digging and had a long narrow snout. Not like an anteater. This creature had a lot of teeth.

"I can see what's ugly about it."

"But what is nasty? It throws up when it gets nervous. I think it's a defense mechanism. It surely put me off."

"What is it?"

"That is an interesting question." Marina seated herself on a corner of a table. Next to her was a cage full of little lizards, striped yellow and bright pink. The lizards scurried up the sides of the cage and hung from the top. "There, there, honeys. I didn't mean to frighten you."

The lizards stopped moving. They hung upside-down, frozen. I had the sense they thought they were invisible.

"Remember that cave you found just before you reached the river valley?"

I looked at her surprised. "Yes."

She grinned. "I've seen the reports. There were paintings on the walls. People and bipeds and some mighty big lizards, but no—I'm not certain what to call them—pseudo-mammals. Or mammaloids. No furry critters.

"We think there is a chance that the two continents here have been separated for a long time and have developed really different ecologies.

"There are birds on the big continent. They could have flown there. And a lot of animals that remind us of mammals. But no bipeds.

"This continent is full of birds and bipeds and animals that remind us of lizards. But there are not a lot of animals with fur. Most are small or, if not small, they are domesticated."

"They came with the people," I said. "And the people came from the big continent."

"Right. That's what we think. But we are working from almost no data.

"We think the paintings that you saw were done after the first people arrived, but before they'd had much of an effect on the local fauna. Maybe the first people came before the domestication of animals. Or maybe they had boats too small to carry much of anything. As I said, we have almost no data.

"Which brings me to the ugly-nasty." She waved at it.

It snuffled, then yawned, showing rows of pointed teeth. A black tongue curled. What did it eat?

"Raw meat and leaves," Marina said. "It is an omnivore."

"Can you read minds?"

"I can make obvious deductions." She waved again. "It's too big to have hidden on a boat—or raft—or whatever the people used to get here. And I can't think of any reason why anyone'd want to bring a thing like that on an ocean voyage. And it isn't all that similar to the mammaloids I've seen."

283

I made the gesture of inquiry.

"You'd better speak English."

"It isn't?"

"No. For one thing, it doesn't have tits. I can find no evidence that it lactates. The animals on the big continent do. For another thing, it has vestigial scales. They're hidden in among the warts and bristles."

"Really?" I took another look at the animal. It was hard to figure out what it looked like. A sloth? Not really. A spiny anteater? No. How about a hairy lizard? Maybe. Or how about a cross between a badger and a toad?

Nothing fit. It was its own kind of creature.

"Do you think it lays eggs?"

"Maybe. I won't know till I cut it open."

I decided not to think about that. "Where do you think it comes from?"

"I have no idea. Maybe it evolved here. Maybe it came from one of the islands. Maybe it's from the big continent. It might have changed after it got here, found an empty ecological niche, and grown to fill it.

"It has been pure hell on the ship. We've had too many questions and too little information. We've been sitting up there and weaving crazy theories, like a bunch of spiders who've been given a hallucinogen." Marina stood up. "Well, that's over. I'm going out to check my traps." She grinned. "It's just amazing. I have no idea what I'm going to find."

I stayed behind and watched the animals. They all had the faintly miserable look of creatures in cages. Maybe I was reading in. I wouldn't like to be where they were. Maybe they didn't mind.

The ugly-nasty looked at me, then paced some more. Was it getting nervous? I decided to leave.

There were two boats at the dock now, and people were unloading boxes. I went to help.

We finished about the time the sun went down. The river bluffs cast long shadows over the camp. The lake still gleamed, reflecting the blue-green sky. The people I'd been helping thanked me. I went back to my dome and found Derek in the hall outside my room. He was dressed in a pair of white denim pants. The pants were soaked. He had nothing else on. "I've just introduced the oracle to hot and cold running water. I'd better get back there. He might drown. Go to the supply dome. Get medium shorts and a shirt. There is no way he can wear that rag any longer."

"Okay." I turned and went back the way I had come.

By the time I returned, the oracle was out of the bathroom. He wandered in the hall, wearing a floral-print towel. One of our dome mates—an Asian woman—watched him. She looked bemused.

"Where is Derek?" I asked.

"In the water room. Have you brought me something to wear?"

"Yes. Come on in here." I led the way to my room. The woman shook her head and went about her business.

I helped him put on the shorts. They were Earth blue with a lot of pockets. The shirt was cotton and short-sleeved: a pullover, yellow with the name of the expedition in bright red Chinese characters. He needed help with that, too.

When the struggle was over, I stepped back and looked. His fly was closed. His fur was only a little disheveled.

Derek came in.

"How do I look?" asked the oracle. "Am I impressive? Is this the way a man is supposed to dress among your people?"

"Yes," said Derek.

"Look behind you," I said.

He turned and faced a mirror. "Aiya! It is big! Even my mother the shamaness did not have a whatever as big as this one." He peered at his reflection, frowning, then baring his teeth. He picked a fleck of something out from between his upper incisors. "I hope Nia comes back soon. I am hungry. It's hard work taking a bath the way you people do it."

"You can say that again," Derek said.

"No," said the oracle. "Once is enough. I want to go out now. Your houses are too little. I feel as if the walls are pressing in on me." He pressed his hands together in illustration.

"You take him," Derek said. "I want to change my clothes and take a nap."

"Okay."

The camp lights had come on. They shone over doors and from the tops of metal poles. A hillclimber bumped past over the rutted ground. Someone called to me. I smiled and waved, not recognizing the voice.

We ended on the dock. There were lights on it: little yellow ones that illuminated our feet and the surface of the dock. I wasn't entirely certain what it was made of. Cermet? Fiberglass? Something gray and rough. It rocked under our weight. The segments rose and fell every time a wave came in.

Bugs crawled around the lights. They were all the same kind: narrow green bodies and huge transparent wings. The wings glittered.

"I am almost ready to eat those," the oracle said.

I looked down the beach. A person came out of the darkness carrying a string of fish. "Nia?" I called.

"Li-sa! I need a knife."

I felt in my pocket. "I have one."

"I have found a place to camp. A cave." She turned and waved toward the bluff, which was visible only as an area of darkness between the camp lights and the stars. "There is water and dry wood."

285

"You are welcome to stay with us," I said.

She made the gesture that meant "thanks, but no thanks."

"Then can I go with you?"

"Why?"

I hesitated. How to explain? The day had been too busy. I had gotten too much information. I needed peace and quiet. An environment that was familiar.

"Come along," said the oracle. "We do not need to know why."

We walked through the camp, keeping to the shadows, and climbed the bluff. There must have been a path. I couldn't see it. I followed the sound that Nia made, brushing past branches, clambering over rocks. In back of me the oracle gasped for breath. I was gasping, too.

Nia said, "This is the place."

I stopped.

"Stay where you are, Li-sa. I know your eyes are almost useless in the dark."

I obeyed.

"Aiya!" said the oracle. "What a climb! I don't like the way these clothes fit. They are too tight."

A flame appeared. I made out Nia, crouching and blowing. The flame grew brighter. She rocked back on her heels and reached for a handful of twigs. Carefully, one by one, she placed them in the fire. It burned in the middle of a clearing. On one side was the river bluff, rising perpendicular and almost bare of vegetation. I made out the cave. It was extremely shallow—an overhang, really.

The rest of the clearing was edged with scrubby little trees. Vines grew up the trunks and over the branches. Entire trees were mantled or shrouded. The leaves of the vines were purple-red.

Nia said, "Give me your knife."

I unfolded it and handed it over. She cleaned the fish and wrapped them in leaves, laying them in the coals at the edge of the fire.

"There is water nearby. I forgot to ask for something to put it in."

"I'm not thirsty," I said and sat down.

"What will happen now, Li-sa? Will your people leave and take you with them?"

"Not yet." I put my arms around my knees. I looked at the fire and thought, she must have managed to keep her fire-making kit after the canoe went over. Or had she managed to find stones that worked as well as her flint and steel? "They want to exchange gifts. They say there is a village north and west of here, on a little river that goes into the big river. They plan to go there and ask the people if they can stay in this country, at least for a while."

Nia was silent. I glanced at her.

"Do you think they'll say no?"

"I do not know what they will do."

The oracle said, "It seems to me you told us your people live on the western side of the river."

"Yes."

I glanced at her again. The broad, low forehead was wrinkled, and her brow ridges seemed more prominent than usual. Her eyes were hidden in shadow.

"Does the village belong to the Iron People, Nia?" I asked.

"I think so. It ought to. This is their country."

"What will happen if they find you here?"

"I told you before. They will treat me the way all strangers are treated."

"There is no possibility that you will be . . . ." I hesitated, then used a word than meant to be damaged by accident. There didn't seem to be a word that meant to be harmed or injured by intent, unless I went to the words that described the quarrels of men.

She looked surprised. "No. They are not crazy. They are not the People Whose Gift Is Folly."

"What?"

"You know that story?" said the oracle "I have always liked it."

I looked at him. "What is it about?"

Nia picked up a stick and used it to pull the fish out of the fire. She spat on her fingers, then unwrapped the leaves. "Hu! Is that hot!"

"Is the fish done?" asked the oracle.

Nia made the gesture of affirmation.

"Good." The oracle moved closer to the fire.

They ate.

When they were finished and licking their fingers, I said, "Tell me the story."

Nia made the gesture of inquiry.

"The People Whose Gift Is Folly."

"Yes," said the oracle. "Tell it."

"In the far north live a people," Nia said.

"No," said the oracle. "They live in the west."

Nia looked angry.

"I will let you tell it the way you want," the oracle said. "Even though you are wrong."

Nia made the gesture that meant "so be it."

"In the far north live a people. They do everything backward and inside out. The men stay at home. They care for the children. The women herd and hunt."

"That is right," the oracle said.

"The people are stupid and clumsy. They tether their animals inside their tents. They live outside under the sky. The rain beats down on them. The snow piles up around them. The wind moans and bellows in their ears."

The oracle made the gesture of agreement, followed by the gesture of satisfaction.

"When they try to cook a meal, they build the fire in the pot, and when it is burning well, they pile their meat around the pot, against the hot metal. Everything is done stupidly. There are many stories about the ways they get mating wrong. They do not seem to be able to remember what goes where."

The oracle leaned forward. "There is a story about a man. The time for mating came, and he went out of the village. He found a pot lying on the plain. Someone—some other fool—had left it there. It was well made and handsome. It shone in the light of the sun.

"'How lovely you are,' he said to the pot. 'I will look no further.'

"He mated with the pot, and then he returned to his village.

"Later he became angry when the pot did not come into the village and bring him children to raise. He went out and found it, lying where he had left it. 'Where are my sons, you stupid thing? Where are my lovely strong daughters?'

"He kicked the pot and turned it over. Inside it was red with rust.

"The man fell on his knees. 'O pot! O pot! You have miscarried! Did I do it? Did my anger kill my children?'"

The oracle stopped.

"Is that the end of the story?" I asked.

"I don't know any more."

"I have never heard that one," Nia said.

"Until now," the oracle said.

Nia made the gesture of agreement. "The story I know is about the woman who became confused at the time of mating. Instead of waiting for a man to come out of the village and into the territory she guarded, this woman found an *osupa*. She mated with it. I don't know why the animal agreed. Maybe animals are stupid too in that country.

"Time passed. The woman had a child. The child was covered with feathers and had a tail.

"'What a fine child,' the woman said. 'He is not usual at all.'

"The child grew up. He would not learn the crafts of men. Instead he wanted to hunt on the plain. He ran more quickly than any ordinary person. He caught little animals with his claws and teeth.

"'My child is special,' the woman said. 'No one has ever seen a child like this.' She bragged to the other women when she met them. They became angry, because they had ordinary children, who did what was expected of them.

"'We all want unusual children,' they said.

"The next time for mating came, and they all mated with animals."

288

"I don't know this story," the oracle said. "I think it is disgusting."

Nia looked worried.

"If you don't like it, move out of hearing," I said. "I want to hear the end."

The oracle stood up, then he sat down again. "The story is disgusting, but I am curious."

"I was not thinking," Nia said. "I have spent too much time with strange people. This is not a story for a man."

"Nia, you can't stop now."

"Yes, I can."

I looked at the oracle. "Go."

He frowned. "Do I have to?"

I made the gesture of affirmation.

He got up with obvious reluctance and moved to the edge of the clearing, sat down with his back to us and stared out at the dark.

I looked to Nia.

"There isn't much more. The women all had peculiar children. Some were like groundbirds. Others were like bowhorns. One woman mated with a killer of the plain. I don't know how she managed it. Her daughter was made entirely of teeth and claws.

"None of these children wanted to go into the village. They stayed on the plain and hunted one another. They did not learn the skills of people.

"At first the women were happy. 'All our children are unusual. We have done something that has never been done before.'

"Then they noticed they had no one to help them. And the men in the village noticed the same thing. They went out, both men and women, and pleaded with the children. 'Come off the plain. Learn the skills of people. We need smiths and weavers. We need herders and women who know how to do fine embroidery.'

"But the children did not listen. Instead they ran away. They became animals entirely.

"The People Whose Gift Is Folly had to turn to each other. They mated the proper way. The women had ordinary children. The men raised them. They were like their parents. Stupid, yes. Clumsy and foolish. But people." She made the gesture that meant "it is done."

"Come back," I said to the oracle.

He returned. We sat quietly. Nia looked depressed, and the oracle looked sulky. I was feeling bothered.

What did the stories mean? Both were about the loss of children. Was that a problem here? Did they worry about miscarriages and damaged children as we did on Earth?

It did not seem likely. This planet was clean. These people had not filled their environment with toxins.

289

There was another explanation. The stories were about a people who did everything backward. Maybe the message was sociological, not biological. If you want healthy children, be ordinary.

A good message. Relevant and true. Look at me. Look at everyone on the ship. We were not ordinary. Most of us had no children. Those who did had parted with them 120 years ago.

My neck hurt. I rubbed it. "I'm going back down to the village. We need blankets, if we are going to stay the night, and something to keep water in. I have to tell Derek where I am."

Nia made the gesture of agreement, then pointed. "The path begins there."

I stood and stretched, made the gesture of acknowledgment and went in the direction she had indicated.

I lost the path in the darkness and had to scramble down over rocks. Branches caught my clothes. Thorns scratched me. I fell a couple of times. Finally I reached level ground; and the lights of the camp shone in front of me.

The main hall of my dome was empty. Voices came through a closed door: a pair of women talking. Farther down someone played a Chinese flute. The performance was live. I could tell by the mistakes.

I flicked on the light in my room and opened the closet under my bed. As I had hoped, it held a blanket.

"Where have you been?" asked Derek. He came in, closing the door after him. He had changed to blue jeans and a light blue cotton shirt. His beard was gone. The skin on his face was parti-colored: reddish brown above and white below. An odd sight. His blond hair was very short.

"You found a barber?"

He made the gesture that meant "it doesn't matter" or "let's talk about something else." "I have been all over camp looking for you."

"I was up on the bluff. I need your blanket."

"Why?"

"Nia and the oracle have made a camp of their own. They don't have anything to sleep on."

"Why don't they come down?"

"I didn't ask. Maybe they feel the way I do. There are too many people here. Everything is too complicated."

"You don't know the half of it. I'll get my blanket." He left, returning in a couple of minutes. "What else do you need?"

"No pillows. It's going to be hard enough getting the blankets up the bluff. And the natives don't use pillows. I'm trying to decide if I want to stay with Nia."

He tossed his blanket toward me. It unfolded in midair and fell in a heap.

290

"Damn you."

"I'll be back."

I picked the blanket up and refolded it. Derek returned with another blanket, which he added to the pile. "Janos won't need this."

"You think not?"

"The dome is way too warm. I'll go to the edge of camp with you. I don't entirely like being inside."

I remembered stories about Derek. He had a house in Berkeley full of artifacts and books. A lot of books. Most of them were made of paper. Some were new and came from specialty presses. Others were old and fragile.

He worked in the house. Guests stayed in it. If one of the guests was a lover of his, he stayed inside with her. But when he was alone, he slept in a lean-to in the backyard. The roof was a piece of canvas stretched over living bamboo. The floor was grass. He didn't use a sleeping bag or any kind of mattress. In hot weather he slept on the grass. In cold weather—in the rain and fog of the northern California winter—he used a ragged blanket.

That was the story. I didn't know if I believed it.

We left the dome and walked up into the darkness under the bluff. I carried the blankets.

"Okay." He stopped. "This is far enough." He looked back at the lights of camp. "Did you turn in your recorder?"

"Yes. Goddamn!"

"What?"

"Nia and the oracle were telling stories this evening. I forgot that I didn't have a recorder on."

"That shouldn't be a problem for you. I know your reputation. If something interests you, you'll remember it."

"Huh," I said. "I always like a backup."

"That also is part of your reputation." He touched my arm. "I have something to tell you."

"What?"

"I had a talk with Eddie this evening. He came in after you wandered off with the oracle."

"Yes?"

"He wants us to go upriver with Ivanova and him. He wants us to translate for them."

"Eddie is going? A man?"

"That was part of the compromise. We are supposed to send representatives of each of the three factions. For intervention. Against intervention. And the compromise position."

"Why?"

"To explain our problem to the natives. To give our problem to the natives and ask them for the solution. Since it's their planet." I thought I could hear sarcasm in Derek's voice.

"That might make sense, though I'm not saying it does. But why are they sending a man?"

"Eddie is the chief advocate of nonintervention. And we are supposed to be honest with the natives. We have to explain to them—to show them—what we are like."

"It's crazy."

"Uh-huh. And it isn't what I want to talk about." Derek paused. "He wants us to lie."

"What?"

"He wants us to change what Ivanova says when she speaks to the natives. He wants us to make certain that the natives do not like her argument."

"No! We'd be certain to be caught. The meeting will be recorded, and someone will check our translation. Maybe not right away, but soon."

"I told him that. He said we could do it without being obvious. We could slant the words. Twist them just a little. Change the intonation."

"I can't believe this of Eddie. I've worked with him for years."

"Do you think I'm lying?"

I looked at him, but saw almost nothing. "No," I said at last. "What did you say to him?"

"I said the risk was too great, and all we'd gain would be a little time. Ivanova and her people aren't going to pack up and go home. They want to be on this planet. They'll go to the next village over and ask permission to land. We'd have to lie again.

"And what is he going to do, I asked him, when the rest of the sociology team comes down? Ask all of them to lie? How long before someone says no and goes to the all-ship council?"

"This isn't an ethical question for you," I said.

"I'm willing to lie. But only for my own reasons and only if I'm pretty certain I will not get caught. I won't lie for Eddie." He paused. When he spoke again, his voice had changed. The mocking tone was gone. "I am not certain that intervention is a bad idea. Eddie does not come from a culture with a pre-industrial technology. When he goes into the field, he takes a modern first-aid kit and a radio. If he gets into trouble, he can yell for help. He has never been through the kind of experience we've gone through, here on this planet. And he has never been through what I went through, when I was growing up."

"You told him no," I said.

"I told him maybe. As carefully as possible, in case there was a recorder on. But he thinks he has a chance to pull me in."

"Why'd you do that?"

"I never make a decision in haste, my love. And I never limit my options until I have to."

"I don't understand you."

He laughed.

I waited.

"Eddie admits that his plan will do nothing except buy time. Interesting, isn't it, how metaphors of buying and selling have stayed in the language? We buy time. We sell out our honor. He says he doesn't really know what he is going to do with the time. But he will not let these people go the way of his people in the Americas. He's willing to risk everything in the hope of stopping that."

"Huh," I said.

"Go on up to Nia and the oracle. I think I'll go and find a bottle of wine. It's been a long time since I've been drunk."

I climbed the bluff, getting lost again. I have no idea how long I blundered around, tangling myself in bushes, tripping over roots, and sliding down slopes of dirt and stone, then climbing up again, cursing.

In the end I found the camp. I walked into firelight. The oracle looked up. "Your hair is full of leaves. And there is dirt on your face."

"I'm not surprised." I dropped the blankets. "There you are. Goddamn! I forgot something to hold water!"

Nia made the gesture that meant "no matter." The oracle took a blanket and rubbed it with one hand. "I like the texture, though it isn't as soft as the wool that comes from a silverback." He wrapped the blanket around himself.

I got a blanket of my own and lay down in the cave. For a while I looked at the firelight, flickering on the stone wall and ceiling.

I woke to sunlight. The oracle sat in the clearing by the fire, adding branches. His clothing—the blue shorts and the yellow cotton shirt—were already a little dirty.

"Where is Nia?"

"She went down to look at her fish traps."

I got up and pulled my knife out of my pocket. "She'll need this. I'm going down to the village to eat."

"You have the luck! I wish I had a place to eat. I am getting tired of fish."

"Maybe I can work something out."

This time the trip was easy. The path down was clear. Who had made it? I wondered. Did people come here?

I went to my dome and showered, putting on new clothes: burgundy-red coveralls, a white belt, white socks, and Japanese sandals. I fastened my hair at the nape of my neck and frowned at my reflection. I definitely needed a haircut. But what style? Maybe I should wait till I got to the ship. Meiling always knew what was in fashion. I went to the dining hall.

Eddie and Derek sat together. They were in the shade today, and Eddie was not wearing glasses. I got coffee and a muffin and went over.

"It's a good thing you showed up," Derek said. "Eddie has decided that we need to hold a meeting."

I sat down and poured out coffee. What an aroma! How had I lived without it?

Eddie said, "I've been telling Derek, you ought to start work on your reports. You're in a new environment now. You're getting a different kind of information. It's going to start interfering."

"Gresham's Law of Memory," Derek said.

"What?"

"New information drives out old. Bad information drives out good."

I buttered the muffin, which was banana walnut bran. "I don't think that formulation is right."

"It is frivolous and unuseful," Eddie said. "Which seems to be Derek's mood this morning." He glanced at the notebook in front of him. It was open, and there was print on the screen. "Will you start work on the report, Lixia?"

"Yes."

"Today?"

"Yes."

Eddie pressed a button in the notebook. A line of print vanished. "The medical team says they want to watch you for another day."

"Not us personally," Derek said. "They are watching our cultures. If nothing strange and terrible has appeared by tomorrow evening, we can go back to work."

Eddie looked impatient, but he let Derek finish talking. Then he leaned forward. "Ivanova and I want you to accompany us when we go upriver."

I made the gesture that meant "I know."

"Will you go?"

"Yes."

He pressed the button again. Another line of print vanished. "Derek has suggested that we ask Nia and the oracle to come along."

"I don't know if that's a good idea. She's from that village. They sent her into exile. They won't harm her if she goes back, but they might not welcome her especially warmly."

"Ask her," Derek said.

"Why do you want her to go?"

"She and the oracle know more about humans than anyone else on this planet. They might have something useful to say about the problem at hand.

And I don't want to leave the two of them alone in the middle of nowhere. We can't give them food, and I don't know how people are going to feel about giving them tools or weapons. God knows what will happen if these savages get fishing hooks or knives with stainless steel blades. And—" He grinned. "I'm afraid to leave them here unprotected. The med people want to examine them. So do the biologists and the psychologists and . . ."

"What do you think?" Eddie asked.

I finished the muffin, washing it down with coffee. "We might as well ask her. Derek is right. She is something of an expert on humanity. We can't leave her alone on the plain. And I'd hate to come back and find that she'd left because of the medical people. She might. She isn't entirely easy with us, and a medical examination can be pretty dehumanizing, even if you know what is going on."

Eddie nodded. More print disappeared out of the notebook. I glanced over. The screen was empty except for two characters. I squinted. The number four and a question mark. "Is that it?"

He looked at me somberly, his eyes unprotected. He wore a blue shirt this morning: plain chambray, open at the neck to show a bone-and-shell necklace. His hair was clipped at the back of his neck. The clip was beaded: a geometric design. Dakota work, like the necklace. Most of his ancestors were Anishinabe, but a few had come from the Seven Council Fires. A few more were French or English.

"There's one more thing." He paused.

"I told her," said Derek.

"What do you think, Lixia?"

"I think it's a lousy idea."

Eddie sighed. Number four vanished. He turned the notebook off and closed it, folding the screen over the keyboard. The notebook was still too big to go into an ordinary pocket. The problem was human fingers. They had not been miniaturized. The keyboard had to be at least twenty centimeters wide in order for most people to use it.

"I was afraid of that," Eddie said. "I'll talk to you later. Please start on the report." He walked away from us, carrying the notebook in one hand.

"That is going to be an unpleasant conversation," I said.

Derek made the gesture of agreement.

"If you had told him no, I could have avoided it."

"Uh-huh."

"If you had told him no, he'd be angry with you. Now, he is going to be angry with me."

"Maybe."

"Did you plan this?"

"I don't plan nearly as much as you think I do."

"Huh." I took my dishes to the recycling table, then went to the supply dome and got a notebook with a 256K memory.

I spent the morning in my room. First I wrote down the stories that I'd heard the night before: the People Whose Gift Is Folly.

After that I did an outline of my report.

I stopped at noon and went and got a sandwich. I was missing a gorgeous day. Huge clouds blew across the sky. The lake glittered. There were people on the dock, unloading more boxes. I took the sandwich back to my room and ate it as I wrote.

I noticed, finally, that my back hurt. No more sunlight came in my window, and the sky was more green than blue. A late afternoon color. I saved my work and shut off the notebook, then stood and stretched.

It was too early for dinner. In any case I wasn't hungry. I decided to take a walk.

I went south along the lake. The beach was flat and comparatively wide. Easy to walk on. Here and there streams came down off the bluff. They were small and almost dry. I stepped over them.

The beach narrowed. Vegetation loomed on my right, and I could smell the damp, close aroma of a forest. I looked back. The camp was out of sight.

"Ha-runh," said something.

I looked ahead. A creature had emerged from the vegetation. It stood on the beach, about ten meters away, regarding me with a tiny dark eye. It didn't seem worried. Why should it be? It was as big as a rhinoceros.

I kept still, frightened but also interested.

It was a quadruped. Nothing like a bowhorn. Its skin was brown and hairless. Its legs were thick. It had a long tail, which it held in a graceful curve. The tip waved slowly back and forth. What did that mean? Was it a sign of good humor?

Odd flat horns stuck off the animal's head. There were two pairs. They reminded me of the cantilevered roofs of certain modern buildings. Or of shelf fungus. They were covered with a fine short down or fur.

Brown velvet fungus. Brown velvet cantilevered roofs.

The animal watched me for another moment or two. Then it picked its way delicately to the lake, the huge feet making hardly any noise, and waded into the water. It had a flexible, almost-prehensile upper lip, which it lifted as it drank, exposing its teeth. They were long and flat and shovel-like.

A herbivore, almost certainly. I suspected it was a browser.

It lifted its head and looked at me again, then went back to drinking.

Time to leave. I backed down the beach. The animal kept on drinking, though its tail began to twitch. A rapid, nervous motion. My hunch was it indicated irritation.

I stopped moving.

The animal waded back to shore.

Where could I run to? Would I be safer in the water or the forest?

The animal paused a moment and stared at me, then turned and trotted south along the beach. I watched it go, the wide backside swaying, the tail moving to and fro. From this angle the animal looked silly. I did not think it would have looked silly if it had been coming toward me.

I walked back to camp, glancing over my shoulder from time to time to make sure nothing was coming up behind me. The beach remained empty.

Marina was in her dome, feeding leaves to a biped. "It doesn't like anything I give it. I'm going to have to let it go. Unless I decide to dissect it."

"I've got to tell you what I saw."

She glanced at me. Today she wore golden contacts. They matched her earrings, which were intricate and dangly and chimed every time she moved. "Do I need a recorder?"

"Yes."

She found one and turned it on. "Okay."

I described the animal.

"That big?"

"I'm not especially good at judging sizes. But it had legs like an elephant. How big does that make it?"

"Not small. Could it have been a domestic animal?"

"I don't know. But I haven't seen anything like it in any village."

"If it isn't." She tugged her lower lip. "More problems. More questions. I wish I knew which god to thank." She turned off the recorder. "I'll go down there tomorrow and look at the prints. If I'm lucky, I'll find some droppings. That will tell us what the critter eats."

"Nia might know what it is."

Marina nodded. "I really ought to spend some time with her. How about tomorrow? You introduce us. She can come with me and look for piles of shit."

"Sounds great."

I left her there, still trying to feed the biped, which was a lovely specimen. The feathers on the back were pale soft gray. The belly was cream-white. The forearms ended in pink claws, and the clawed feet were the same delicate color. The animal moved restlessly back and forth in its cage. The clawed hands picked up Marina's food, then dropped it. The clawed feet kicked the leaves away.

I went to the big dome. This time I followed a sign, which led me to the commons—a large room full of low tables and comfortable chairs. It was almost empty. I saw Brian, sitting with a pair of Chinese. He lifted a hand in greeting. I waved and went over to the bar.

297

The bartender was a stocky man with Mayan features. Most of the time his eyes were ordinary dark brown. Now and then, when the light hit them at just the right angle, the irises turned green—a shimmering metallic color, stunning and disturbing.

"Li Lixia." He held out his hand. "Gustavo Isidis Planitia. I'm on the medical team."

We shook. He asked me to name my toxin. I said chablis.

He filled a glass. "Are you still in quarantine?"

"What do you mean?"

"Eddie put out the word to leave you alone. We are supposed to give you plenty of time to recover from whatever."

I tasted the wine. It was young and harsh. There had been no practical way to keep the winery going on the long trip out and no good reason to. The people were sleeping. The computers did not drink. All our wine had been made in the last year or so. It all tasted like this or worse.

"Eddie is probably right," I said. "We are having some trouble readjusting."

"I think it's a plot," Gustavo said. "We know Eddie's position. I think he is trying to control information—from you to us and from us to you."

I looked at him. His eyes were green at the moment, shining like the plumage of some kind of tropical bird.

"That sounds like paranoia," I said.

"That's a technical term, and it's out of date. What you mean is—you think I'm harboring an unfounded suspicion. What you said is—you think I am crazy."

"Okay. I withdraw paranoia. But I think you are wrong. Thank you for the wine."

"My pleasure. And I'm glad to have met you."

I sat down by myself. There was a bowl of bar mix on the table: nuts and dried fruit and other things I could not identify. Pretty tasty. I ate a handful and sipped at my wine.

It might be true. Eddie might be trying to isolate us. On the other hand I wasn't in the mood for political game-playing. Maybe he knew that and was simply protecting me.

Brian stopped on the way out and introduced me to his companions. They were young and earnest-looking, from the planetology team. They bowed and shook hands and said it was a pleasure.

"We're going to have to talk," said Brian.

"Okay."

"We look forward," said one of the Chinese.

"Eagerly," said the other.

They left. I drank more wine and looked at the window above me. It was hexagonal, set in the curving ceiling. Above it was a cloud, moving in the wind and darkening as the last sunlight faded off it.

"Can I join you?" asked Eddie.

I made the gesture of assent.

He lowered himself into a chair. "Derek has talked to Nia and the oracle. He is willing to go. She says she has to think."

I made the gesture of acknowledgment.

He took a long swallow from the bottle he carried—it was mineral water—and set the bottle on the table, then took a big handful of the bar mix. He glanced at me. "Is there coconut in this?"

"No."

"I don't like coconut." He ate the mix, washing it down with more mineral water. "You really think my idea is lousy."

"It won't work. We'll get in trouble. And it's immoral. The people here have the right to make their own decision, using good information."

He frowned. "I think Ivanova has an advantage. I'm trying to do something about it."

"How so?" I ate some more of the bar mix.

"These people know about strangers and trade. When Ivanova talks about cultural exchange, they are going to understand her. But they know nothing about modern technology. And they have no idea what happens when an industrial society meets a society that is barely agricultural."

"I wouldn't say 'barely.' It seems to me they have a pretty highly developed agriculture. And animal husbandry. What they don't have is a state apparatus— which can be a sign of a primitive society or of a very highly developed one."

"You are playing games, Lixia. These people are tribal, pre-urban, and pre-industrial. They don't have the kind of society that the anarchists imagine. They have what my people had till the end of the nineteenth century." He paused for a moment and looked at me, his expression thoughtful. "You aren't going to help me, are you?"

"No."

"Will you report me?"

"To the all-ship committee? No. I'm not sure what the charge would be. Corrupting a translator? Conduct unbefitting a scholar?"

"God, what a mess." He stood and walked out of the room.

I couldn't tell from the tone of his voice whether he was angry or merely depressed. Angry, most likely. At the moment I did not care. I would in the morning when I was sober. But now . . . I finished drinking my wine and ate another handful of the bar mix, then I stood. My coordination was off. I swayed slightly.

"Are you all right?" asked Gustavo.

"Yes." I decided to skip dinner. I wasn't hungry, and I didn't like to be the only drunk in a room. Curious, that one glass of wine should hit so hard. I went to my room and to bed.

299

Waking, I looked up and saw nothing outside my window. A dim grayness. There were fine beads of water on the glass. I could feel moisture in the air, even inside.

I got up and showered, putting on coveralls, a jacket, heavy socks and shoes.

Outside it was cool, maybe even cold. The bluff was invisible. I could barely see the trees at the edge of camp. The domes around me had lost most of their color and most of their solidity. They seemed to float in the fog: shadows or bubbles.

I walked to the lake. I could see the first few meters of water. It barely moved, making no noise as it touched the pebble beach. Why was fog so appealing? Was it the mystery? The sense of possibility? There was an old story that argued for the existence of many alternate worlds in close proximity. Sometimes the worlds touched and—for a time—blurred together. That made fog. It was the blending of different realities. Sometimes, when the worlds separated and the fog cleared, people found themselves in unexpected places. They had crossed over. They were in an alternate reality.

I decided I wasn't interested in an alternate reality. Not at the moment. Though I liked the idea that life was blurred and shadowed by possibility. Nothing was fixed. Nothing was certain. There were no sharp edges, no immutable courses.

I walked up to the big dome and had breakfast with Marina and a trio of biologists. They asked me questions about the natives. I answered as best I could.

"Chia met a native," Marina said and pointed at a tiny brown woman.

"You did?"

"Yes. North of the camp. I was looking for—" She hesitated. "We haven't got a name for them. They look like centipedes. They are twenty centimeters long, and they live under rocks in the water." She paused. "Most of them are blue."

"About the native," Marina said.

"He was pulling traps out of the water. We looked at one another for a while. Then he went back to his work, and I went back to mine. I had not realized they were so big."

"That was Nia," I said. "She is female, and she is no taller than I am."

"You are tall, Lixia, compared to people in my country. And the native was very—" She hesitated again. "Very wide and solid."

"The fur makes a difference. She doesn't look as big when she's wet."

"Ah," said the little woman. "Like a cat." She added, "I have met tigers in the jungle. They like to swim. They look big even when they climb out of a river."

I made the gesture that meant "I don't know from personal experience, but most likely you are right."

Marina said, "I miss cats. I keep saying we ought to grow a few."

"No mice," said one of the other biologists. "Except in the labs, and they aren't a problem."

"They will be," said Marina. "Someone will lose a few. They'll get in the gardens. We'll have a plague, just like in the Bible. Mice and hemorrhoids."

"What?" said the third biologist. He was huge and almost certainly Polynesian.

"The Philistines stole the Ark of the Covenant, whatever that might be, and the Lord Almighty afflicted them with mice and hemorrhoids. I'm not lying. It's in the Bible."

"If that happens, we'll grow some cats," the man said. He sounded calm and practical.

The tiny woman frowned. "I do not understand how cats will be any use in dealing with hemorrhoids."

"I have to work," I said and left.

By noon the sky above my window was hazy blue-green. My report was a mess. I had a lot of information, but no structure. No ideological frame.

Oh, to be a Marxist! Especially a vulgar Marxist. They always had an explanation. Usually it came from the nineteenth century. Engels on *The Origin of the Family, Private Property and the State.* Surely Fred could explain this planet to me. Maybe I ought to find a library computer and call up ancient documents on social theory. I tossed my notebook on the bed.

The door opened. Derek leaned in and said, "You have a visitor."

Nia entered, dressed in light gray shorts and a burgundy shirt. The shirt had big white letters on it. They said, "Best Wishes from the Iroquois Confederation."

A donation. Everyone had wanted to contribute to the expedition. The ship was full of objects with names on them given by clubs and co-ops, cities, unions, tribes, and kibbutzim. The lamp in my cabin came from the Association of Airship Workers. The union emblem was on the shade: two hands clasped in front of a dirigible.

Derek said, "I looked for something without writing. But it is impossible to find a short-sleeved cotton shirt without a motto."

Nia said, "Speak a language that I can understand."

"He has said nothing important," I told her.

"Good. I have decided to go with you."

"Why?"

She made the gesture that meant "why not?"

"Is that a good answer?"

She came in and sat on the floor, folding herself neatly into a cross-legged position. "No. I want to find out what has happened to my children and cousins. I have told you that before. And I have to go in that direction.

301

I promised to do work for Tanajin." She paused for a moment. "Someone has to tell her what happened to the boat. Someone has to tell her that Ulzai has vanished. These clothes are tight. How can your people be comfortable?"

"Not easily," I said.

"I'll get new clothes at the village. And food. And tools. They will give me that even though they know me and can be almost certain that I am not the Dark One."

Did I have a recorder? I glanced around.

"Here," said Derek.

He tossed. I caught. It was an audio recorder the size of a box of matches. I turned it on. "Who is the Dark One?"

"A spirit. She comes to villages as a stranger—usually a woman, sometimes a man. Often she is ragged and hungry. She may be ill. She may look peculiar.

"Hua—the woman who taught me smithing—said her true shape is an old woman with black fur, bent and twisted. She has an odd aroma. She asks for help, though not in a pleasant way. Most of the time she is surly.

"If the village is generous, she continues on her way. If the village is stingy or rude, then . . ." Nia made the gesture that meant "you know" or "what do you expect?"

"Bad things happen," Derek said.

Nia made the gesture of agreement.

"What kind of bad things?" I asked.

"People get sick. Animals die. There is not enough food." She paused and looked at me. It must have been obvious that I wanted to know more. "The shamaness finds out which spirit is angry. Then the village must perform a ceremony. It is called 'Welcoming the Stranger.' They gather everything they like best: good food, knives with sharp edges, clothing that is covered with embroidery, gifts that come from the most distant places. They build a fire. The people sing.

> "Notice
> how we welcome you.
> Notice
> the fine provisions.

"The food goes in. The knives. The clothing. Everything is burnt. If the people are fortunate, the Dark One will be satisfied. But it takes a lot. It is better to give her what she needs when she comes as an old woman."

"What would happen if the Dark One came to the village of the People Whose Gift Is Folly?"

"I have never heard a story about that, and I don't expect to."

"Why not?"

"Stories about the Dark One are told in the summer and fall. That is when most people travel. That is when strangers are met.

"Stories about the People Whose Gift Is Folly are told in winter when the snow is deep and travel is impossible. That is when people like to hear about stupid behavior that has happened a long distance away."

"The snow is deep," said Derek in English. "The wind is howling. Let's sit by the fire and laugh at foreigners."

I turned off the recorder.

Nia stood. "If you are going to talk in that language, I am going to leave."

"Do you want to eat?" asked Derek. He spoke the language of gifts.

I made the gesture of affirmation.

Nia said, "I'm making a bow. I've found some wood that isn't bad. Deragu has given me a string."

"You did?"

"Don't tell anyone."

We left together, going out into the hazy sunlight. Nia made the gesture of farewell and headed inland toward the bluff. Derek and I went to the dining room.

We ate with Agopian and a thin black man, Cyril Johnson. He was the hydrology team, and his equipment hadn't arrived. He made a speech about bloody incompetence on the ship and throughout human history.

We listened politely. I ate something that tried to be a Greek salad. The cheese was goat cheese, and there were too few olives. Most of the olive trees had died on the trip out. It would be years before the new trees were old enough to bear.

"We've scheduled a general meeting tonight," said Agopian. "These people have the right to know what is going on."

"You're right," said Derek. "They do. Unfortunately, we haven't any idea."

"You know more about the natives than anyone else."

"Are they going to let us stay?" asked Cyril.

"I don't know," I said.

He frowned, pressing narrow lips together. Another example of bloody incompetence.

I finished my coffee and took my tray to the recycling table. Agopian followed me. We went outside. The sky was clear. The air was hot and damp. I took off my jacket.

"I'm going with you," Agopian said.

"Upriver?"

He nodded.

"I'm sure there's a good reason why Ivanova is taking an astrogator." I looked at the dock. Both boats were tied up. People were working on them, doing maintenance or repair.

"I am a historian as well."

"Of labor history, I think you said."

"Every society has work and workers."

I glanced at him. He wasn't wearing the crew uniform today. Instead he looked almost American: faded jeans and a cotton shirt with narrow vertical blue and white stripes. Huaraches on his feet. His belt had a large metal buckle. There was a rocket plane on it and some writing in the Cyrillic alphabet.

"In North America we'd called that a railroad shirt."

He grinned. "I got it in Detroit, in the gift store at the Museum of Working-class Culture."

We walked toward the lake.

"The belt is from the gift shop on Transfer Station Number One. I got it when I joined the *Kollontai*. I am—I used to be—a great collector of souvenirs."

"Not anymore?"

"Not really. Though I wouldn't mind taking something back from here. If we go back."

"If?"

"It is a long journey; and we have no idea what Earth will be like when we get there. Here—maybe—we have a future. There we'll be curious leftovers from the distant past, like the mammoths they have reconstructed."

"I thought they were going to be the new beast of burden in Siberia."

"They are stupider than elephants; and their tempers are not reliable. It is not easy to domesticate a new species. Or, in this case, a very old species."

We stopped at the edge of the water. There were the usual little brown birds running over the pebbles, hunting and pecking.

"How in hell did you end up with an astrogation certificate?"

He laughed. "You are wondering if Derek is right, and I am a—what is that word?—a vegetable."

"I think you mean a plant."

He nodded. "Or a vole."

"All at once your English is deteriorating."

"I have trouble with the language of paranoia. It does not come naturally to me."

"Oh."

"I got the certificate because I was a failure as a political officer."

"You were?"

He nodded again. "You have to realize—from the time I was a boy, I had two dreams. Two passions. Space and political theory."

304

An odd combination, I thought. But there was no accounting for tastes or passions.

"I knew from early on that I wanted to be a political officer in the Soviet fleet. I made it, and I found I was no good." He pushed at a stone with the toe of his boot. It flipped over, revealing a bright yellow bug. The bug scurried away.

"The *Kollontai* was a freighter. I think I told you that. The crew were the kind of people you find in warehouses and on ships. Have you ever met any?"

I made the gesture of affirmation.

"There is something about the people who move freight around. All over the world and even in space, they are the same. How should I describe them? Robust? Down to earth? Though that sounds strange when I am talking about space travelers.

"They are certainly blue collar. The kind of people who made all three of our revolutions. I had no idea how to get along with them."

He paused a moment, looking at the lake. "I am an intellectual. I think it would be fair to say that. I study ideas. That is what interests me. Political theory. The theory of history. The philosophy of science. The relationship between people and machines.

"I don't really care for a lot of ordinary human activities. I play no games. I have no hobbies. I don't like sports. I almost never watch holovision. I have never married. I have no children. I drink wine and beer, usually in moderation. I never drink brandy or vodka."

"What do you do for entertainment?"

"I read science fiction, and I think."

"It sounds like a heck of a lot of fun."

"You see? Can you imagine me surrounded by blue-collar workers?"

I grinned. "No. Not really."

He nodded. "It was terrible. I organized classes on Marxist theory. No one came. I tried to celebrate important events in the history of class struggle. Either they ignored me or they used the event as an excuse to get drunk. I spent time in the recreational areas, trying to get to know the crew.

"I couldn't talk to them. It seemed to me as if we were speaking different languages. I had no idea of what was going on inside them.

"Things floated to the surface. I knew they liked sex and alcohol, z-gee and soccer. I knew the names of all their favorite shows, and I had seen most of them at least once. *War and Peace. Crossing the Urals. Deep-Ocean Adventure. The Potato Cosmonauts.*

"But I did not understand the pattern of their thinking. The intellectual framework. The underlying ideology. They made no sense to me.

305

"I should have quit and gone back to Earth. I could have gotten a job teaching. I would have fit in at a college or a polytechnic.

"But I stayed, even after I stopped trying to be a political officer." He glanced at me, smiling. "I gave up. I went through the motions."

Agopian reminded me of someone; and I had been trying to figure out who. Now it came to me. Eddie. They both lived in their heads. They were both moved to passion by theory.

What did I love? I wondered. Sunlight. Food. Certain human bodies. A landscape like the one in front of me, big enough to put human activity in perspective, and alive.

"It got boring," Agopian said. "I had to do something. I decided to learn a new skill. I took up astrogation."

"That's how you got your certificate."

He nodded. "And it is how I finally got to know some of the people on the ship. We had two astrogators. I asked them questions when I got into trouble with the learning program.

"One of them read science fiction. She told me the cook had a remarkable personal collection. He was from Siberia. A huge man. He talked in grunts, and I hadn't been sure he was entirely human. After he realized that I read science fiction, he began to use entire sentences.

"He loaned me his books. We talked about them and about Siberia. One of his brothers is—or was—a mammoth trainer. That's how I know about the mammoths."

He pushed another stone over. There was nothing under it except wet pebbles. "That is the end of the story. I got my certificate, and I never really learned to get along with those people. It got better, but there was always something about the way they think—" He shook his head. "Or the way I think. They, after all, are in the majority."

Did I really believe this clever little man had been a failure? "You don't have the same trouble here?"

"No. For one thing, I am no longer a political officer. An astrogator doesn't have to worry about agitation and propaganda. All I have to do is get the numbers right.

"For another thing, it takes a special kind of person to go to the stars. We are not better than the rest of humanity, but we are different. I understand most of the people here."

"Who else is going upriver?" I asked.

"Tatiana. Ivanova. Eddie. You and Derek. The natives. Mr. Fang."

"Is he here?"

"Yes. He is the representative for the majority position. He's here to observe and to make sure that the natives understand this is their decision."

306

I thought for a moment. "It sounds crowded."

"We are going to have to take both boats. It leaves the camp in a bad position. I think Ivanova is planning to send one of the planes up for more supplies, including another boat."

"We're certainly moving in."

"Only provisionally," Agopian said.

We talked about the meeting scheduled for that evening, then separated. I went back to my room and changed into lighter clothing, turned on the air system and opened my notebook.

It was an unpleasant afternoon. The air coming in was hot and muggy. My work went badly. In the end I gave up. I had no gift for analysis, only for observation. The reality I saw was too complex and fluid and ambiguous to fit neatly into any theory.

Derek stopped by. "Marina wants to meet Nia. I'm taking her up the bluff."

I made the gesture of acknowledgment. He left, and I went walking. I felt trapped, frustrated, discouraged. I needed to work, but not with ideas. I stopped in the kitchen. It was full of people making dinner. "Can I help?"

"By all means," said the little blond man. "Take those canisters to the incinerator and empty them. Be careful. Don't spill anything. We are trying not to contaminate the environment." He shook his head. "I hate to destroy that stuff. It'd make a wonderful compost heap."

"You mean we aren't recycling?"

"Only dishes."

I felt something akin to horror.

"We are trying to make the camp entirely self-contained. Nothing from Earth goes into the biosystem. Especially nothing organic. Either we destroy it, or we pack it and take it back up there." He pointed at the ceiling. "It was decided *not* to pack the coffee grounds and the orange peelings. It's a real pity. I hate to see waste."

I made the gesture of agreement, then said, "We haven't really met."

"My name is Peace-with-Justice."

I waited.

"My people don't believe in family names. We don't belong to a bloodline or a kinship group. We belong to ourselves and to all of humanity."

"Oh," I said and picked up a canister.

It was good hard work. The canisters were heavy and the incinerator port was badly placed. I had to lift each canister to shoulder height in order to empty it.

When I was done, I cleaned the canisters and washed the floor of the incinerator room. The canisters went into a sterilizer. The incinerator went on with much blinking of warning lights.

My shoulders ached, which felt good. My report seemed less of a problem.

I ate dinner with the kitchen crew: tofu and vegetables on top of a pile of sticky brown rice. On one side I added soy sauce with ginger and garlic. On the other side I added fermented plum juice. Delicious!

When I was finished, Peace-with-Justice said, "We'll clean up. You'd better get ready for the meeting. Thank you, Lixia."

I went back to my dome, washed, and changed into clean clothes, then went to the lounge. A gusty wind was blowing, and there were clouds across most of the sky. Rain, I was almost certain.

I thought of a poem suddenly. It was Anishinabe.

> Sometimes I go around feeling sorry for myself,
> and all the while
> a great wind is carrying me across the sky.

The lounge was crowded. People were bringing chairs from the dining room. Derek and Eddie stood at the bar.

"How did it go?" I asked Derek.

"With Nia? All right. She identified the animal. It's rare and solitary. It lays eggs."

"Something that big?"

"The dinosaurs laid eggs. Marina is excited. She thinks we are looking at a biosystem in transition. Animals that are native to this continent are being replaced by animals from the islands or from the other continent."

"Or from Earth," said Eddie.

"No," said Derek. "The med team says our bugs do very badly in the native organisms. The bacteria starve to death. The viruses do nothing. They aren't able to use the native genetic material. They cannot reproduce." He grinned. "The native organisms are doing rather better in us, especially several species of microscopic parasitic worm. Liberation Minh is very excited by them. They have abilities we did not expect at all."

"You make it sound like good news," said Eddie.

"I find it interesting. And Liberation doesn't think the worms represent any real danger."

"Huh!"

Derek glanced at me. "The med team says that we can go upriver."

"Good."

Ivanova came in, accompanied by a dozen or so crewmembers. It was disturbing to watch them. They moved as a unit and sat down together in chairs that had been saved by other members of the crew.

"Time to start," Derek said. He lifted himself onto the bar.

I got up beside him, though less gracefully.

Derek raised a hand in the native gesture that asked for attention. The people grew quiet. "Okay. Who is moderating?"

"Someone neutral," Ivanova said.

A man called, "Is Mr. Fang here?"

I looked around. There he was, sitting in the third row back. He was thin and wiry, with upright posture and an alert expression. His gray-white hair was fastened in a bun. He wore his usual costume: a faded blue cotton shirt over faded blue cotton pants.

He whispered to the young woman next to him. She stood. "Mr. Fang does not feel able to moderate. His voice is not strong enough."

"Then you do it," the man said.

The young woman blushed. "I am Mr. Fang's apprentice. I know nothing about public speaking."

At that point I stopped listening. In all likelihood the Chinese had picked someone to moderate. But they wouldn't put the person forward. That would be undemocratic and immodest. Instead there would be a discussion. I looked around the room trying to estimate the size of the crowd. Over a hundred. About a third were crew. They must have brought in everyone from the rocket planes. I smiled at people I knew. Harrison Yee stood in the back, leaning against the wall, his arms folded. He raised a hand in greeting. Funny, I should have seen him before this.

The moderator was picked. A middle-aged Chinese woman. She had a strong firm voice and not much of an accent.

"It is getting late. These people have to get up early. I am going to suggest a very limited agenda. I think two questions are of special interest to everyone here.

"First, what happened to Lixia and Derek? Why did we lose contact with them?

"And second, what do they think is going to happen tomorrow? What are the natives going to do?"

The agenda was approved by a show of hands. Derek gave a report on our accident. He was brief and clear. I stood next to him, feeling uncomfortable. I wasn't especially fond of meetings, and I did not like being the center of attention. I was an observer. I wanted to be in the audience. When he finished, the moderator asked if I had anything to add.

"No."

"Do you want to answer the next question?"

"What are the natives going to do? I have no idea."

Derek added, "They are used to travelers; and they aren't afraid of strangers. But the strangers are only passing through. As far as we can tell, each culture is discrete. They don't mix. Maybe because they don't have a

309

tradition of war. They don't conquer their neighbors. They don't carry one another off into slavery. They don't rape. They don't steal wives."

"Is this a tangent?" asked the moderator.

"No. If we were travelers, they'd welcome us. But we are going to ask for permission to stay. I have no idea how they will respond."

Harrison Yee raised his hand. The moderator pointed at him. "This situation can't be completely new. This planet has diseases and volcanoes. There must have been villages that were so damaged by some natural disaster that they couldn't continue on their own."

"Yes," said Derek. "But we haven't heard about them."

Another person said, "Are you sure there has been no exchange of genetic material? Have you seen evidence of inbreeding?"

"No," I said. "And I think Derek is overstating the situation. We know that individuals move from one culture to another. There is probably enough of this kind of movement to prevent serious inbreeding. But as far as we can tell, there isn't the kind of mixing of entire populations that has been common on Earth."

"In that case," the person said, "there ought to be a lot more genetic diversity. I think you're wrong. I think these people are managing to interbreed."

"I'm only telling you what I've seen. And my conclusion, which is—we don't know how these people will react to a bunch of strangers who want to settle down in their midst."

"We are not talking about a permanent stay," a woman said. She had an East Indian accent. "Are we?"

"Please raise your hand before you speak," the moderator said. "We do not want this meeting to get out of control."

A black man raised his hand. The moderator pointed to him. He said, "I know it was decided to send a mixed group. Men and women. I think that's crazy. The natives have driven away how many men? Gregory. Derek. Harrison. We're just going to make them angry."

Ivanova said, "I agree with you absolutely."

Eddie said, "We are not planning to go into the village until we've explained the situation and asked for permission. If they say the men can't come in, we won't." He smiled briefly. "Which could be a problem for my position. If necessary, I will ask Lixia to give the argument for nonintervention, though I'd prefer to give it myself."

"They're likely to tell all of you to go away," the black man said. "What you are doing has nothing to do with honesty. This is lack of respect for the culture and beliefs of another people."

Ivanova nodded. "You are right. But remember—we have already achieved what we wanted in this region. Derek and Lixia have been rescued. If the

310

natives tell all of us to leave, not much is lost. We can send a team of women to another village."

"If honesty doesn't work, we can always try a lie," a woman said.

The moderator said, "Please."

People kept talking. Nothing new was said and no one went back to the question asked by the Indian woman, either to answer it or ask it again. *We are not talking about a permanent stay. Are we?*

The meeting ended. I jumped off the bar. Harrison came up and hugged me. "Where have you been?"

"On one of the planes. Eddie's been keeping me busy, sending reports to the ship."

I must have looked dubious or maybe hurt.

"He said you were having trouble adjusting to the camp. You needed time alone."

"Maybe."

People were leaving, taking chairs. Gustavo moved in behind the bar. His eyes shone green. He said, "I'm reopening. Can I get you anything?"

Harrison and I ordered wine.

Eddie said, "Be careful with that stuff. We want to start early tomorrow."

"When?" I asked.

"Sunrise."

"I'll be careful. Are you sure that you want me to give the argument for nonintervention? If you can't, I mean?"

"You know the argument. You know how to speak to the natives. You believe in democracy." He smiled. "Maybe more than I do. If the natives are going to make an informed decision, they need to know what I have to say. You'll see that they get the information."

"I guess I will."

He paused for a moment. "As Derek would say, we have to learn to deal with people as they are. If they can't be corrupted, then we have to find a way to use their honesty."

"You're talking in the first person plural, Eddie. That's always a dangerous sign."

"You're right." He made the gesture of farewell.

Harrison watched him leave, then said, "What was that about?"

"Eddie is having trouble dealing with the current situation."

Harrison nodded. "If he doesn't get himself together, I think we are going to have to find another coordinator for the team."

"No more politics! Tell me what's been happening on the ship. The gossip. Not the faction fighting."

He did. I finished my wine.

311

Gustavo said, "In my role as a bartender I should offer you another. But I'm also a psychotherapist, and you don't need any more alcohol."

"You are?"

"Of course. My area of competence is psychopharmacology." He took my glass, then wiped the ring of moisture off the bar. "You don't have to worry. I took a course in bartending. I can mix almost anything you might want to drink."

Harrison grinned. "And then tell you what kind of damage it will do."

Gustavo nodded. He took Harrison's glass. "Sunrise, Lixia. You might want to pack tonight."

He was right. Harrison and I left the lounge. The air outside was damp and cool, and the clouds above the river bluffs had spread. Now they covered a third of the sky.

"New weather," said Harrison. "I envy you. I have to go back to the plane."

"You do?"

He nodded. "Eddie wants me to handle communications between you people and the ship, which means I'll be trapped out there—" He waved at the lake. "I don't really mind. There is the most beautiful young man on the communications team. They thawed him out recently. His eyes are like the sky in summer, and his hair is like autumn wheat."

"Huh," I said.

Harrison glanced at me and grinned. "Now, Lixia, you know I have not been in love with anyone for a long, long time. Not since we went to sleep. I think it may be a side effect of hibernation. Are bears amorous when they first awake?"

"I haven't the vaguest idea. But some people are. Remember what Derek was like when we were coming into this system."

Harrison laughed. "Maybe people recover from hibernation at different rates. Maybe some bears are amorous when they first awake." He paused. "I'd better go find out when the last boat leaves. If I don't make it, I'm going to have to swim."

We said good-bye. I went to the supply dome and got a bag, went to my room and packed.

I did not sleep well. My dreams mixed the planet with the ship. I walked down a corridor made of cermet and ceramic. There were natives there, moving among the shipboard humans. I turned a corner and was in a garden. An enormous quadruped grazed on lettuce plants. It regarded me serenely with a tiny dark eye. The ugly-nasty scuttled over a floor of yellow tile. I heard the clicking of its nails.

I turned another corner. There was a native camp in the middle of a ceramic meeting room. Smoke rose from a fire. A native woman was crouched over a metal cooking pot. A native child was playing with a cat. It was a perfectly ordinary Earth cat, a domestic short hair, half-grown. Its fur was spotted black and white. The child's fur was brown.

Derek woke me. I stared at him, thinking about the cat. Marina was right. We ought to grow a few.

"Rise and shine," he said.

"I've been having damn strange dreams."

"You've been getting too much information. And you're trying to process it."

I got up and went to the bathroom.

We ate breakfast in the dining hall. It was empty except for the people who were going upriver and Peace-with-Justice. He recommended eggs Benedict.

"The egg gives you cholesterol. The ham does damage to your karma. And the sauce contains enough calories to—"

"Have we started killing the pigs?"

He nodded. I felt queasy. They were a special miniature breed, originally developed for lab work. They were bright, clean, well mannered, and extremely cute. I could eat the chickens. I could eat the iguanas. But I wasn't sure about the pigs.

"I'll tell you what," he said. "I'll fix you a serving with no ham. I can tell by your expression that you are willing to do damage to yourself in this life only. So—here you are." He gave me a plate. "Cholesterol and calories, but no bad karma."

"Thanks," I said.

I ate. The sun rose. The landscape outside the dome became visible.

"Time to go," said Ivanova.

I gulped my second cup of coffee. Peace-with-Justice said, "Good-bye." We went down to the boats.

Nia and the oracle were there, standing on the dock, looking uneasy. Nia had a bow and half a dozen arrows with pale gray feathers. The color reminded me of Marina's biped, the one that hadn't been eating.

"Five people on each boat," said Ivanova. "I have given thought on how to split us up. The natives should stay together. Lixia will go with them. And Agopian. And Tatiana.

"The rest of us will take the other boat."

Eddie frowned.

"You are putting all the politicians on one boat," Derek said. "Is that wise?"

"We will aggravate each other," Ivanova said. "But the other people will be safe."

"It's fine with me," I said.

"And with me," said Mr. Fang. His apprentice was with him. "Poor Yunqi may suffer. She has no interest in politics."

The young woman blushed and nodded.

"But it is good for the young to experience adversity."

I climbed onboard and stowed my bag, then went out on deck. Ivanova had already started her engine. Agopian was casting off for her. The two natives were on the dock, watching. They looked interested and nervous.

"Come on," I said. "Get on."

Ivanova's boat moved out from the dock and turned, going in a wide circle away from shore. Tatiana started the engine on our boat. Agopian cast off. I leaned on the railing and felt relaxed for the first time in days. I was moving again. There was nothing I liked better than travel.

We followed the first boat out into the lake, turning south, then east, then north. Ahead of us was the dark river valley.

Angai

A wind blew. The lake was flecked with foam. Ahead of us and to one side Ivanova's boat bounced over the waves. We were bouncing, too. Nia and the oracle grabbed on to the railing.

"This thing goes quickly," the oracle said.

"What makes it move?" asked Nia.

How to explain the internal combustion engine?

"There is a fire inside," I said finally.

She frowned. "That does not make sense. Fire can move, but it does not make other things move, unless they are alive."

The oracle made the gesture of agreement.

Nia looked at the water. "I have seen the plain on fire with everything running before it. Bowhorns and *osupai*. Every kind of bird and bug, the ones that fly and the ones that jump, all hurrying ahead of the fire. Even the killers were running and the little animals that tunnel underground.

"But they were alive. Fire changes. It does not carry."

"Maybe Derek can explain."

We reached the north end of the lake midway through the morning. The wind dropped as soon as we got among the little forested islands. The sky

315

remained partly cloudy. There were patches of sunlight on the river and on the green and blue-green trees.

The boats moved slowly. Tatiana said, "Keep an eye out for debris."

After a while I saw a lizard. It was in midchannel, swimming steadily, its head held out of the water. The spines along its back were visible, but nothing else, and it wasn't easy to estimate the animal's size. About ten meters long.

"Aiya!" said the oracle. "I am glad we are not in Ulzai's boat."

"Going south," said Agopian in English. "I wonder if it is true about the migration?"

By noon we had seen five lizards. All were big, and all were heading south. Only one was out of the water. That one dragged its enormous bulk over a mud bank, going south like all the rest.

The radio crackled and spoke Russian.

Tatiana said, "Ivanova has warned the camp. If those animals decide to leave the water, there may be trouble."

We ate lunch in the cabin: sandwiches and tea. The natives had the haunch of a biped.

"Sacrificed by Marina," Agopian said. "And cooked without anything. It ought to be safe."

"How does it taste?" I asked in the language of gifts.

The oracle made the gesture that meant "it could be worse."

"It needs salt," Nia said. "And other things. I will be glad to be in a village again."

I took food out to Tatiana. She remained at the wheel, guiding the boat with one hand while she ate a smoked-fish sandwich.

"We are almost to the tributary. If the satellite pictures are not telling a lie, we ought to be able to go up it."

I made the gesture of acknowledgment.

The others came out on deck.

"It's frustrating," Agopian said. "I'm sitting with people from another star system. My mind is full of questions; and all I can do is point and make faces."

"He has been making improper gestures," said the oracle. "And baring his teeth."

"We decided he is ignorant, like most of your people," said Nia.

About this time I noticed the bugs. They had bright yellow wings. I saw two of them fluttering over the water. Another pair rested on a log that floated past our boat.

Agopian pointed at an island. The trees were dotted with yellow. More bugs, resting on the foliage.

"It looks like autumn," said Tatiana. "At home when the poplars start turning."

We passed other islands where the foliage was partially yellow. Clouds of bugs drifted over the river like leaves in the wind. But there was no wind—at least none sufficient to explain this whirling and dancing.

Bugs landed on the roof of our boat, on the deck and railing.

"What are they doing?" I asked.

"Going south like the lizards," Nia said. She looked pleased. "We see them on the plain. They are lucky."

The bugs took off one after another, rejoining the migration. We were almost through it by now. A few stragglers danced in the air, and the surface of the river was dotted with bugs, like a river on Earth dotted with the leaves of poplars.

Ivanova's boat turned toward the western shore. We followed, entering a new channel.

"This is the tributary," Tatiana said.

The water changed color, becoming a deep clear brown. It moved quickly between steep banks covered with forest. Above the trees were limestone cliffs, close to us on both sides. We were going almost due west.

Midway through the afternoon we came to rapids. They were nothing to write home about: a series of gradual drops. No rocks were visible. There was only a little foam. But they closed the river. We weren't going any farther. Above us a trail of white smoke twisted out from the top of the valley wall.

The other boat turned toward shore. We followed, edging in against the bank. Agopian clambered forward and tied our prow to a tree that leaned over the river. I wrapped a second mooring line around a sapling near the stern. The engine stopped. I heard leaves rustle, the cries of birds. The muscles in my neck relaxed.

"Do you notice," I said, "the sound of machinery is always an irritant?"

He looked surprised. "If that is so, we're in trouble in space."

He was right. Every ship and station was full of the sound of machinery.

Nia said, "I have been thinking."

I made the gesture that meant "go on."

"It's a bad idea to show anyone too many strange things at once. You come into the village with me. If Angai is there, and she ought to be, we'll explain about your people. She can decide what to do. Maybe she will permit the men to come in."

"Okay," I said.

We climbed out of the boat.

Eddie came toward us along the bank. "I've talked to Ivanova and Mr. Fang. We think you ought to go up to the village, alone or with Nia." He smiled. "Ivanova is worried about Nia, since she has had a difficult relation-

317

ship with her people. But I want her to go. Mr. Fang thinks we ought to leave the decision to you and Nia."

I glanced at Nia. "The people on the other boat have come up with the same idea. They want the two of us to go."

"It is hard to understand your people, Li-sa. When I begin to think that you are ordinary, you do something that is utterly crazy. When I decide you are really crazy, you make a decision like this one, which is ordinary and right. I never know what to expect."

I made the gesture that meant "maybe so."

We pushed through the bushes at the river's edge. Beyond was a trail. Nia turned onto it. I followed her up the river bluff.

On top was the plain: almost flat here. An erratic wind swept over it, changing direction often. The vegetation changed color as leaves flipped over. Tan. Yellow. Gray-green. Silver-gray. The colors moved across the plain, through light and shadow, brightening and darkening.

Nia said,

> "Now, at last,
> there is room enough.
>
> "Hai-ya!
> There is room!
>
> "My inner person
> is able to straighten.
>
> "My inner person
> is able to expand."

Off to our left was a village made of tents and wagons. Smoke rose from many fires. Beyond the village—to the north and west—animals dotted the plain. Bowhorns. The edge of the herd. Or were these merely the domestic animals?

"Come on," said Nia. "I want this meeting over."

There were children playing at the edge of the village: about a dozen. Some wore kilts. Others were naked, except for various kinds of ornamentation: belts made of leather and brass, copper bracelets, necklaces of brightly colored beads.

The children were organized in two rows, which faced each other. Between the rows were two children with sticks. The children in rows tossed a ball back and forth. The children with sticks tried to knock it down.

That much I figured out before the children saw us. One shouted. A couple ran. The rest turned and stared.

Nia said, "This person looks strange, but she is more or less ordinary. There are more like her below on the river. They have come to visit. They have fine gifts and interesting stories."

"Hu," said one of the children. I could not tell the gender. He or she was tall and thin, with auburn fur and a yellow kilt. The kilt was embroidered with dark blue thread. The child wore a pair of silver bracelets, one on each wrist. He or she held a stick. "You are certain they are not demons?"

"I have traveled with this person all the way from the eastern forest. She has never done anything the least bit demonlike. She's a good companion."

"Hu!" the child repeated. "You'd better come with me. My foster mother is the shamaness."

"What is your name?" asked Nia.

"Hua," said the child.

"I am Nia."

The child had turned, ready to lead us. Now she turned back, regarding Nia with large, clear yellow eyes.

"How is your brother?" Nia asked.

"He is getting difficult. Angai says the change is coming."

Nia frowned. "Isn't he too young?"

"It will be early. But not that early. You have been gone a long time."

"That's true," said Nia.

The child led us into the village. The tents at the edge were small and widely scattered. I saw no people around them.

"What are they?" I asked.

Nia answered. "They belong to the men. The old ones, who have come into the village."

"I don't see anyone. Where are they?"

"Hunting. Or maybe sitting where they are not visible. Men set up their tents so the entrances face the plain. If they are home, they will be—" She made a circling gesture.

"What's wrong with this person?" asked Hua. "Doesn't she know anything?"

"Not much," said Nia.

Farther in, the tents were larger and closer together. They were made of leather, stretched over a series of poles. Each tent had six to eight peaks. In spite of their size, they were not especially tall—more like a mountain range than like a tepee.

The flaps were open, held up by poles so they formed awnings, which shaded the entrances. Women sat under the awnings, and children played in the streets.

319

The women called out in a language I did not understand. Hua answered in the same language. The women got up, leaving their work. They gathered their children and followed. Soon we were at the head of a procession.

"What's going on?" I asked.

"They are asking about you. Hua is telling them—come along and listen while Angai finds out what you are."

"Oh."

Nia added, "I do not like being followed."

I made the gesture of agreement.

The village was obviously new to this location. Plants grew between tents and under wagons. Flowers bloomed. Bugs jumped and hummed. A tethered bowhorn ate leaves off a bush in the middle of what seemed to be the main thoroughfare.

We passed the animal. It stopped eating and looked at us, then lifted its tail and defecated.

More evidence that the village was new. I had seen very little dung or garbage.

I looked at the wagons. They were everywhere, scattered among the tents. They had rectangular bodies made of wood and curved tops made of leather stretched on a frame of wood. The sides were elaborately carved. The tops were decorated with strips of brightly colored cloth that hung down in the front and back, making curtains of ribbon that fluttered in the wind: red, yellow, blue, green, orange. Each wagon had four wheels, bound with iron. The spokes were carved and painted.

We crossed an open area, full of more plants. Hua stopped in front of a tent. It was large, and there were poles around it: standards. One was a metal tree, full of gold and silver birds. Bells hung from the lower branches, moving in the wind and chiming.

"I know that," Nia said. "I made it." She looked at her hands. "I have been traveling too long. I need to have tools again."

The other standards were animals made of bronze or brass: a bowhorn, a killer of the plain, a biped.

"My name-mother made the others," Hua said. "They are very old."

Nia's teacher. I remembered now. "Did you know her?" I asked the girl.

Hua looked shocked. "No! Never! How can you ask a question like that? What do you mean by it?"

"This person comes from a long way off," said Nia. "When I first met her, she didn't know the language we are speaking. I sometimes think she doesn't know it yet. Don't worry too much about the things she says."

Hua made the gesture of acquiescence. But she looked worried.

A woman came out of the tent. She was tall and thin, dressed in a full-length orange robe. Her fur was dark brown, flecked with gray, though I didn't get the impression that she was old. She wore at least a dozen necklaces made of gold and silver and amber. Bracelets covered her arms from wrist to elbow. Like the necklaces, they were a mixture: gold, silver, copper, ivory. There were even a couple made of carved wood. She had a gold stud in the side of her low, flat, furry nose.

She looked us over, then spoke to Nia. "Can you never behave in an acceptable fashion? What are you doing back here? And where did you find a person like this one?"

"This is my foster mother," Hua said.

"Her name is Angai," Nia said. She gestured toward me. "This person is named Li-sa. I met her in the east, in the village of the Copper People of the Forest. I've been living there."

"This is no Copper Person," said Angai.

Nia made the gesture of agreement. "I don't know where she's from. A long distance away, she told me. But I met her in the village of the Copper People in the house of their shamaness Nahusai."

People murmured in back of me. A baby started to cry.

"There are more hairless people below the village in two boats. They want permission to come up."

Angai frowned. "What have you told them about us, Nia? Have you been lying? We always make visitors welcome! There is no reason for them to wait below." She paused. "Unless they are sick. Is that what has happened to their hair?"

"Four of them are men."

"Sit down," Angai said. "Here, under the tent flap. There is no reason why we should be uncomfortable while we talk."

We obeyed, even Hua. Angai glared at her. "I am not certain this is a matter for children."

"The whole village is here. Everyone is listening."

Angai made the gesture that meant "very well." "But keep quiet. Pay attention! Learn what makes a shamaness!"

Hua made the gesture of assent.

"Now." Angai looked at Nia. "Tell me what this is about."

"These people are different. It isn't simply the lack of hair. Look at her eyes." She pointed at me. "They are brown and white like the ground in early spring, when the snow has begun to melt. Who has ever seen eyes like these? Look at her hands. She has two extra fingers, and they are not deformed. All her people have two extra fingers. Friend of my childhood, draw in a breath! Does she smell like any person you have ever met before?"

Angai sniffed. "No."

Nia hunched forward. "She is not a person the way you are a person, Angai."

I opened my mouth to object, then closed it. Nia was far from stupid. She must have a reason for what she was doing.

"They have tools that are different from our tools. Their language sounds like an animal spitting and chittering.

"But—" Nia paused. "They do have tools, and they do have a language. They aren't animals. Nor are they spirits. I don't believe they are demons. They are utterly strange and unfamiliar people."

Angai made the gesture that meant "that may be."

"Among these people the men are not solitary. They live with the women."

"Aiya!" cried a woman. Others called, "Hu!"

Angai made the gesture that demanded silence. "Go on."

"That's why they are waiting. They know we have different customs. They do not want to anger the Iron People. They do not want to show disrespect or be dishonest."

"But they want to come into the village," Angai said.

Nia glanced at me.

"Yes," I said. "They—we—have a difficulty. An argument we cannot settle. We want your advice, the advice of your people."

"It's hardly surprising that they argue," a woman said. "Men and women together! What a perversion!"

Another woman added, "Except at the time of mating."

"Bowhorns mate in the autumn," Angai said. "And there are animals that bear two or three litters in a summer. Are you like that? Is this your time for mating?"

I hesitated.

Nia said, "I have watched these people carefully and listened to them. It's my belief that they're always ready to mate."

There was more hu-ing from the audience. Angai made the gesture for silence. We all waited. She frowned. "You are certain these are people, Nia?"

"You are the shamaness. Is this one a spirit? A demon? Or a ghost?"

Angai touched my arm. "She is solid. It is daylight. She cannot be a ghost."

"What about a demon?" asked one of the villagers. "They are solid. They can go out in the light of the sun."

Angai stared at me. "I have seen demons in my dreams. Their eyes burn like fire. Their hands and feet have long curving claws. Otherwise they look like people. I have never heard of a demon without hair." She paused. "You are certain they are not spirits, Nia?"

"Spirits have many disguises," Nia said. "Even a clever woman can fail to discover them. But I have traveled with these people for three cycles of the big moon. They have never changed their shape. They have never

322

changed their size. They eat. They sleep. They produce dung and urine. Their dung and urine is ordinary, though it does not smell exactly like ours. Even when they are angry, even when they seem to be in danger, they do nothing spiritlike."

Angai made a gesture I did not know. "They are not animals. They are not spirits. They are not ghosts or demons. Therefore they must be people. They have asked us for help. It is my opinion that we ought to help them. They have asked to come into our village, it is my opinion that we ought to give them permission."

A woman spoke loudly, but not in the language of gifts.

Angai lifted a hand. "They are not like us. We cannot judge them the way we judge ourselves."

Several women spoke in the tribal language. I turned to look at the crowd.

The sun was low by now. Rays of light—almost horizontal—shone between the tents. They lit the open area, the vegetation and the people: solid matrons, bent old crones, lithe girls, a lot of children. The adults shouted and gestured. Their jewelry flashed.

I knew most of the gestures. "Yes." "No." "You are wrong or crazy." "We are in agreement." "Agreement is utterly impossible."

I looked back at Angai. She watched and listened, expressionless.

"What is going on?" I asked Nia.

"Some of them agree with Angai. Others do not. They will all shout until they get tired."

I looked back at the crowd. The argument went on. Children—the older ones—wandered off, obviously bored. The younger children began to cry. Their mothers picked them up and hugged them and rocked them.

The other women continued the argument, but everything was less violent now. The voices had grown softer. The gestures were less broad.

Light faded out of the square. Only the peaks of the tents were lit and the tips of the metal standards. Gold, silver, and bronze gleamed in front of the sky, which was cloudless and deep blue-green.

At last there was silence except for the whimpering of babies and the high, clear voices of a group of children who had started to play a game.

"Hai! Hai! Ah-tsa-hai!"

The women looked at Angai, who spoke loudly and firmly.

The women replied with gestures of uncertain agreement.

Angai looked at me. "The day is almost finished. It is a bad idea to begin anything important in the dark. Therefore, I ask you to return to your boats. Come back in the morning with everyone. All your people. We will listen to your problem."

323

I made the gesture of gratitude and stood.

"You, Nia." Angai looked at my companion. "Go with the hairless person. People have known you too long. They will forget that you are a stranger now. They won't treat you with the courtesy due a traveler."

Nia made the gesture of assent.

Hua said, "I want to go with them."

Angai frowned.

Nia said, "No. I don't want people saying that you are like me."

"Nia is right," said Angai. She looked at her foster daughter. "Tomorrow you will see the hairless people. Tonight, stay here."

Hua made the gesture of reluctant acquiescence.

The crowd parted. Nia and I passed through it.

"Aiya!" said Nia. "What a day!"

We went down the bluff. The lights on the first boat had been turned on. Pale and steady, they lit the open deck at the rear of the boat. The oracle sat there, gnawing on the forearm of a biped. He looked up as we climbed onboard. "What happened? Did you get any food?"

"No," said Nia.

"You'd better soon. Everything is gone except for this and the food of Lixia's people."

"You saved nothing for me?"

"I thought you would eat in the village."

"Aiya!"

He handed her the bone.

She made the gesture of effusive gratitude.

I opened the cabin door. Agopian and Ivanova were inside playing chess. Agopian looked up. "You're back."

"Uh-huh. It went all right. We can go up tomorrow. All of us."

"Congratulations." Ivanova tipped over her king. "I concede. I can do nothing without my pawns."

Agopian grinned. "One of her pawns became a revolutionary socialist and convinced the others to form a soviet, which means—of course—that white has no ordinary soldiers left."

"And red wins," said Ivanova grimly.

"What are you talking about?"

"Brechtian chess." Agopian began to put the pieces away. "It was named in honor of the German playwright Bertolt Brecht, who said that ordinary chess was boring. The pieces ought to change according to where they were on the board and how long they'd been there. A madman named Robik actually invented the game early in the twenty-second century."

"It is a thoroughly irritating game," said Ivanova.

"Karl Marx hated losing at chess. It didn't bother Lenin—at least according to Gorki." Agopian folded the board, then folded it a second time. "Lenin was interested in *how* he lost. That kept him from getting angry over the fact that he'd lost. He said chess taught him a lot about strategy and tactics. But he had to give it up. It was interfering with his revolutionary activity."

"Where is everyone else?" I asked.

"On the other boat. Mr. Fang is fixing dinner. Iguana with red peppers and green onions. We wanted to finish our game."

"Though I don't know why," said Ivanova. She stood up and stretched.

"You thought you were going to win, comrade, when my commissar developed ugly revisionist tendencies."

"Commissar," I said.

Agopian smiled. "Robik wanted to get rid of the feudal elements in chess. He changed the knights into commissars."

"Don't tell me any more."

"I won't. Are you coming to dinner?"

"No."

"There is beer in the gallery and the makings for sandwiches." He went out on deck.

Ivanova followed, pausing at the door. "You have done good work, Lixia."

I made the gesture that indicated the modest acceptance of praise.

She left. I got a beer and drank it, then made a sandwich. I took it out on deck along with another beer.

Nia and the oracle were still there. "Did you get enough to eat?"

"I did," the oracle said. "But Nia is going to be hungry when she wakes."

Nia made the gesture that meant "no big deal."

I sat down facing the natives. "Nia, why was your daughter upset when I asked if she had known old Hua?"

"Ai!" said the oracle. "You asked that?"

"Yes. What is wrong with the question?"

"No one ever names a child after a living woman," Nia said. "If a woman meets her name-mother, she is meeting a ghost."

I said, "Hu!" and drank some beer, then asked, "Is that true of men as well?"

"No," said the oracle.

Nia added, "Boy children are named after men who have left the village. Usually it is the brother of their mother. My son is named after my brother Anasu. As far as I know, he is still alive." She paused. "I hope he is." She looked at the bone she held. It was gnawed clean. No shred of meat remained. "When my son leaves the village, he may well meet Anasu. That will not be especially frightening."

"Unless they try to claim the same territory," the oracle said.

325

"That is hardly likely." Nia tossed the bone down. It rattled on the deck. "I am going to get a blanket and sleep up there." She pointed toward the prow of the boat.

"All right," I said.

She got up stiffly, as if she had been working hard at some kind of physical labor. Well, someday I would find out what it was like to go home.

I finished the beer, went into the cabin, and unfolded a bed.

"I need a blanket," the oracle said.

I got one for him. He took it outside. I undressed and lay down. For a while I thought about the day—the tents and wagons, the people, especially the children. How must it feel to have a daughter? I reached for the button on the wall above me. I pressed it, and the lights went out.

Derek said, "You never came over to report last night. We were disappointed, Lixia."

I opened my eyes. The cabin was full of people: Derek, Agopian, Tatiana.

"Do all of you have to be here?" I asked.

"We have limited space at the moment," said Derek.

Agopian nodded. "Two boats and a planet."

"What happened in the village?" asked Tatiana.

"I told Agopian. The shamaness—her name is Angai—has agreed to help us with our problem. Excuse me." I went to the bathroom.

When I came back out, the cabin had been rearranged. The beds were couches again. The chairs and tables had been unfolded. Agopian and Derek were setting out plates.

Agopian glanced at me. "We are serving an American breakfast on this boat. The only decent food I ever had in America was served at breakfast. Though the hamburger has a certain *je ne sais quoi*. As does the Coney Island hot dog. Yunqi is serving a Chinese breakfast on the other boat. I hear she's a really bad cook."

"Are all Armenians oral-dependent?"

"That is a racist question." He finished setting the table. "We like to eat. A lot of us have died of starvation over the centuries."

"You might want to go outside," said Derek.

"Why?"

"Nia's son is there."

I went on deck. Nia and the oracle sat on either side of an iron pot full of stew. They were eating, pulling out hunks of meat with their fingers, and they wore new clothes. Nothing impressive. Nia had on a dark green tunic, plain except for a single line of yellow embroidery at the neck. The oracle wore a reddish-orange kilt with no embroidery at all.

"Where is Anasu?" I asked.

326

She pointed.

The boy sat on the railing. He was the same height as the oracle, but not as solid-looking, and very dark brown. His eyes were gray. I had never seen that color in a native before.

His kilt was blue-gray. He wore boots designed—I was almost certain—for riding, not walking. They were knee high, made of thin flexible gray leather, which bagged at the ankles. The heels were decorated with silver studs. His belt had a silver buckle, and he wore four narrow silver bracelets, two on each wrist.

Nia said, "He came down last night, after everyone was asleep. He woke me. I told him I was hungry. He went and got food."

The oracle, chewing, made the gesture of gratitude.

The boy said, "I was away yesterday—out on the plain, hunting. When I got back, Hua told me our mother had returned. Angai told me to leave her alone. I didn't listen. I will be a man—if not this winter, then the winter after. It is not the voices of women that keep a man alive on the plain. It is his own voice. The one he hears in his mind when his tongue is silent."

The oracle made the gesture of agreement.

"He brought us clothing, too," said Nia.

"I saw what my mother looked like. Shabby! And foreign! I don't really understand what's going on. Who are you, anyway? Why do you need help from our shamaness?"

I opened my mouth to explain. The boy held up his hand.

"But I know that Nia is in the middle, and it seems to me she ought to be dressed in decent clothing."

"How old are you?" I asked.

"Thirteen. Everyone says that I have grown up quickly. I don't know if that's a good thing. People expect me to leave the village soon. I suppose I don't mind."

"Don't mind," said Nia. "Your father got in trouble because he didn't want to leave the village."

"I've heard about that." The boy paused and turned his head, then jumped down off the railing.

Foliage moved. Eddie climbed onto the boat. "Good morning, Lixia." He glanced at the boy. "Nia's son?"

I made the gesture of affirmation.

"Introduce me."

I did.

The boy looked him up and down. "Is this a man?"

"Yes."

"He is a big man," the boy said.

327

Eddie wore jeans, a turquoise-blue shirt, and a vest covered with bead-work. The vest was Anishinabe: a bold pattern of brightly colored flowers. The beads were tiny, made of glass. They shimmered in the early morning light. His hair was in braids. The buckle on his belt was turquoise and gold. Of course he was a big man. I made the gesture of affirmation.

"Is he likely to confront anyone?" the boy asked.

"No."

The boy made the gesture that meant "good."

Nia stood. "Didn't you hear in the village? These people are not like any other people."

"I heard," said the boy.

Agopian leaned out the cabin door. "Breakfast is ready."

"This is another male," said Nia.

"You are really certain they are not going to confront each other?" asked the boy.

"Yes."

"Hu!"

The oracle looked up. "The little one won't back down or run away, even though it is obvious that he is no match for Eddie."

"We have to eat," I said in the language of gifts.

The oracle made the gesture that meant "go ahead."

Eddie and I went in. There was a plate of bagels already on the table, toasted and buttered. Derek was setting down a plate of scrambled eggs. Tatiana came out of the galley, carrying a pot of coffee.

"Ivanova is staying on the other boat," Eddie said. "I think she is trying to make points with the Chinese by eating their breakfast."

"Never put politics above digestion," Agopian said. He sat down and reached for a bagel.

We ate in silence, aware—I think—of the aliens outside. Their voices came through the open door, low and even, speaking the language of their tribe.

Tatiana cleared the table. Eddie washed. I dried. Ivanova arrived and spoke to Tatiana in Russian. I glanced out of the galley. It was obvious they were arguing—speaking softly and intently, both of them frowning. Agopian listened and said nothing.

We finished with the dishes.

Ivanova said, "There have been noises in the wood. Voices. I have seen a couple of children in the trees, looking at us, doing nothing. But I don't think it would be a good idea to leave the boats unattended."

"I have to stay," said Tatiana. "And Yunqi. The rest of you are needed in the village. I've come so far, and now I have to be a watchdog while history is made a few hundred meters away."

328

"Agopian could stay," I said.

Agopian said, "I will never forgive you for that remark."

Ivanova shook her head. "He is a historian. I want him along."

I went out on deck and looked up. The sky was empty except for one lit-tle group of clouds. They were shaped like scales and arranged in rows.

"Lizard-hide clouds," said Nia. She stood up, then bent and put a cover on the stew pot. The handle was a biped—a carnivore, bending over and feeding on another biped that lay dead, a relief on the curving lid.

The boy was gone.

I made the gesture of inquiry.

"I said we'd be in the village soon. He went ahead."

Ivanova came out. "We'd better get going."

I followed her onto the bank. The natives followed me. Mr. Fang was on the trail, leaning on a cane. The others joined us: Agopian, Eddie, Derek, who had changed his clothing. Now he was dressed entirely in white: close-fitting jeans and a loose thin shirt. The sleeves were blouselike. The shoulders were covered with embroidery, white on white.

"Where'd you get that?" I asked. "Not from supply."

"Barter."

His shoes were a highly reflective white cloth, trimmed with white leather. They shimmered and flashed, even in the forest shadow.

"Huh!" said Eddie.

We went up the bluff. Nia led the way into the village. It was empty. The wind lifted dust and blew it around us. The bells on the metal standards rang.

Agopian said, "Where is everybody?"

Derek made the gesture that meant he did not know.

We came to the open area: the village square. It was full of people: women and children dressed in fine clothing. Everywhere I looked, I saw bright col-ors, embroidery, jewelry.

A woman shouted. Everyone looked at us.

"Aiya!" said the oracle. "Do I have to go into that?"

"You can go back," Derek said.

"No. My spirit told me to stay with you."

The crowd parted. We walked through. The oracle kept his head down, looking at no one until we reached Angai.

She stood in front of her tent, under the awning. Her robe was covered with so much embroidery that I could not tell the color of the underlying fabric.

Her jewelry was less impressive: a nose stud made of gold and a necklace that looked as if it ought to belong to a girl. Each link was a small and deli-cate silver bird. Hardly the right thing for a middle-aged shamaness, dressed up for a major social occasion.

"Be seated." She pitched her voice so everyone could hear. "Tell me your problem. The village will listen. We'll do what we can."

There were rugs spread under the awning. Angai gestured, and we sat down.

The villagers moved in. The old women were closest. They sat on the ground. Behind them stood the matrons. I could not see the girls or the children. I heard the children though—high voices shouting, "Tsa! Tsa! Tsa!"

Angai said, "Begin."

I introduced myself, then the other humans.

"What sex are they?" asked Angai.

I told her.

"Four men," said Angai. "One of them looks old. Is that right?"

I made the gesture of affirmation.

"But the other three?"

"Are neither old nor young."

"Two of them." She glanced at Derek and Eddie. "Look like big men. The way they dress is big. So is the way they hold themselves."

"Yes."

"But they are able to sit next to each other—and to women—and to a pair of little men—and do nothing."

"Yes."

"Nia is right. You people are different." She looked at the oracle. "Li-sa did not give your name. Who are you and why do you travel with the hairless people? Why have you come into this village? Are you a pervert?"

"No. I am holy and crazy. My name is the Voice of the Waterfall. I belong to the Copper People of the Plain. I am an oracle. I travel with the hairless people because my spirit told me to. I came into your village, o shamaness, because these people came. I will not leave them until I hear from my spirit."

Angai frowned. "I have never heard of a spirit that used a man for speaking. But the old women say the farther off a village is, the more things are done wrong. The Copper People are a long way off." She glanced back at me. "What is your problem? Tell me! Maybe if I know what kinds of things worry you, I will understand you better." She glanced at Nia. "You!"

Nia made the gesture that indicated she was listening with respect.

"Pay careful attention! If this hairless woman says something that does not seem right to you, speak up. Tell me!"

"Yes."

"Okay," I said in English. "She is ready to hear about the problem."

"I will speak first," said Mr. Fang. "Please continue to translate, Lixia."

I made the gesture of agreement.

He looked puzzled. I nodded. He began.

330

"First of all, thank Angai for making us welcome. Explain to her that we come from a long distance away.

"After we reached this planet—this place—we developed a difference of opinion. We have not been able to settle the argument among ourselves. Therefore, we have decided to turn to people outside our expedition."

I translated.

Angai made the gesture of approval. "When two women cannot agree, they must turn to a third. To act differently is to act like men." She frowned, evidently remembering that Mr. Fang was a man. "Go on."

The old man hesitated. Dots of reflected sunlight danced over his brown skin and his faded blue cotton clothing. The light came from ornaments that hung from the edges of the awning: chains of bronze, which ended in little flat fishes and birds. They moved in the wind, chiming softly. The old man's hair was loose today, and it moved too, lifting as the wind blew under the awning: wispy, untidy, whitish gray. "This is difficult. How can ideas be removed from their context? How can we explain our dilemma to people whose history and technology are different from our own?"

"I am willing to try," said Eddie.

"No," said Mr. Fang. "Your turn will come later. Lixia, tell her that we come from a planet—a place—where there are many different kinds of society. These societies have different levels of technology and, therefore, different kinds of social organization and different ideologies."

"The old man says in our country there are many different peoples. They have different tools and different ideas."

"They could hardly have the same tools," said Angai. "Every village must have its own smith. Every smith must have her own tools. As for ideas, I know that people do not always agree."

Mr. Fang went on. "In the past there have been problems when people with different levels of technology have met." He paused. "I don't want to talk about war or exploitation. Those are Eddie's subjects.

"Tell the shamaness—when different societies encounter one another, they exchange information and this can cause changes in one society or the other. These changes are not always pleasant."

I made the gesture that meant "I will." "The old man says when different people get together, they teach each other new ways of doing things, and this can be disturbing."

The word I used for "disturbing" meant "to turn around or over," "to stir porridge by moving a spoon in a circle," "to empty a pot by turning it upside down."

Angai looked puzzled.

"Because of this," said Mr. Fang, "people have always disagreed about the benefits of travel and the exchange of information. According to Master Lao,

331

in a country that follows the Way, people will avoid technological improvements. They will spend their whole lives in one village even though the next village may be so close that they can hear the dogs barking and the crowing of the roosters."

I said, "There are people in our country who think it is a bad idea to learn new things. These people don't like to travel."

Angai made the gesture that meant "go on."

Mr. Fang said, "But Master Kong said the two great pleasures of life are acquiring knowledge and having friends come to visit from a long distance.

"The literature of China is full of traveling, of friends parting and meeting again. That is how our civilization was created and held together—by the poets on horseback and the soldiers on the frontier, the women sent to marry foreigners, the ordinary workers who took caravans over the mountains and boats through the gorges of the Yangtze." He glanced up and realized where he was. For a moment he looked startled.

I said, "There are other people who like to learn new things. These people like to travel."

"I come from Sichuan, from ancient Shu. Without travel and the exchange of information, we would not be Chinese. On the other hand we might still have our native culture and ecology. I am the heir to Kong and Lao, Du Fu and Wang Anshi. That is an obvious good. But we have lost our ancient traditions, whatever they may have been. And we have lost our tigers, our elephants, our pandas, and our leopards. That is a terrible loss."

"There is both gain and loss in all this travel," I said. "New stories are learned. Old stories are forgotten. New things come into the country. Old things go away."

"Even in the twentieth century, it was possible to find giant pandas in the forests of Sichuan. The snow leopard is—or was—remarkably elusive, but there were people who saw prints in the snow of the high mountains in the twentieth century. How does one balance that loss against the poetry of Du Fu, the philosophy of Master Kong, the benefits of socialism?"

"This is not easy to explain," I said to Angai. "He's talking about his country. You don't know the places or the people or the animals."

"Do the best you can," said Angai.

"All right." I thought for a moment. "He is making a pile of the things that have been gained through travel. He is comparing it to the things that have been lost. Which pile is bigger? he asks. He can't make up his mind."

"Aiya!" said the villagers.

Mr. Fang lifted his head, looking directly at Angai. "We cannot decide whether or not it's a good idea to visit you. Therefore we are asking you to decide."

I translated, then added, "Eddie and Ivanova are going to speak. Eddie is against this visit. Ivanova thinks it is a good idea."

"This is going to take a long time," Angai said. "My people need to care for their children. The old women need to get up and walk around. We will stop for a while. There is so much information! So much to think about! So many questions to ask!"

She made a gesture. The old women stood up, groaning. Some of them had to be helped to their feet. The crowd of villagers broke apart and we were alone.

Angai looked at Nia. "Have you heard anything that sounds wrong?"

"No. But there is a lot about these people that I don't know." Nia scratched her forehead. "Li-sa did not speak as much as the old man did." She looked at Derek. "What was not said?"

"She told you," Derek said. "The old man was speaking about his country."

"Is what he said important?" Nia asked.

"Judge for yourself." Derek gave a meticulously exact translation.

The natives frowned and began to ask questions. What is a panda? What is a Wang Anshi?

I got up and walked into the sunlight, stretched and touched my toes. The morning clouds had vanished. The air was getting hot.

I glanced at the group under the awning. Hua had joined them. She carried a jar made of silver. The body was round. The neck was long and narrow. She looked at me and lifted it. I went back, hunkered down, and drank a cool liquid that tasted bitter and made my mouth go numb.

"What is it?" I asked.

"It makes people happy," Hua said. "When the old women drink it, they forget that their bodies hurt and their strength is leaving them. They dance and sing like girls."

"Hu!" I took another swig, then handed the jar to Derek.

"You were in the tent," I said to Hua.

She made the gesture of affirmation. "If I had stayed out there," she waved at the open area, "the old women would have pushed in front of me. I would have seen nothing and not heard much, either. I am going to be the next shamaness. It is important for me to see and hear what my foster mother does."

Eddie took the jar. "What is this stuff?"

"A mind-altering substance," Derek said.

Eddie handed it to Ivanova, who handed it to Agopian. "Be careful, comrade," she said.

"I will," said Agopian. He drank, choked, coughed, and gave the jar to Mr. Fang.

I looked at Hua. "Why couldn't you be out here with us?"

"There is no room under the awning."

"Girls do not sit with women when they make important decisions," Angai said.

And maybe, I thought, it would not be a good idea for Hua and Nia and Angai to sit together in front of the entire village. The villagers might remember how close their shamaness had been to the woman they had exiled.

People were coming back now. They carried objects: poles, which they dug into the ground, and pieces of fabric, which they stretched over the poles. Light shone through the fabric, taking on the color of each piece: red, green, blue, yellow, and orange.

The people spread rugs and settled down. They handed around food: pieces of bread, bowls of meat, jars made of silver and bronze. Babies crawled through the colored shadows. Little children ran.

Hua ducked back into the tent. A moment later she reappeared—or rather, her hand did, furry and brown, holding a large flat piece of bread. Eddie took it. We passed it around.

Angai made a commanding gesture. The people in the square grew quiet. Angai looked at us. "Begin."

"Elizaveta and I flipped a coin," said Eddie. "I lost. I have to go first. Derek, will you translate?"

"Yes."

Eddie drew in a breath, then exhaled slowly. "First of all, repeat what Mr. Fang said: When different people meet, changes occur.

"Most likely these people—the Iron People—will change more than we will, since they have a less developed technology. They may not like the changes they experience. And they may not find it possible to go back to the way they were."

Derek thought for a moment. "All right." He looked at Angai. "Eddie says when people meet, they change one another."

Angai made the gesture of qualified agreement.

"If the people have different kinds of tools, then the people with large and powerful tools will change less than the people with small and weak tools.

"Eddie says our tools are large and powerful. Your tools are small and weak. Therefore you will change more than we do, and you may not like the changes."

Angai frowned. "This man is not being courteous. Our people are skillful. The tools we make are good."

The women around her made gestures of unqualified agreement.

"However, it is true that new ideas make people uncomfortable. Maybe we will not like the stories you tell or the ways that you behave."

Derek translated this into English.

Eddie frowned, then nodded. "Next, tell the shamaness that we have a long history of bad behavior toward people who are different. We have improved in the past two or three centuries, but we don't know that the change is permanent. We may revert—especially here in this country, which is so much like North America."

"Is this necessary?" asked Ivanova. "Do we have to bring up all the ancient crimes of feudalism and capitalism? We are not those people. And most of us have not had to endure anything like those economic systems."

Mr. Fang said, "Eddie is not a Marxist. He does not share our analysis of human nature or of human history. For him this is a real concern."

Derek said, "Eddie says in the past our people acted badly toward people in other villages. He is afraid it will happen again."

"What do you mean by acting badly?" Angai asked.

Derek translated.

Eddie said, "Tell her about war."

"In the past our men used to go around in groups. They fought with men from other villages. The men who won stole things from the men who lost."

"What kind of things?" asked Angai.

"Belongings, animals, land. Sometimes they took away people: men and women and children."

"How can you steal land? It cannot be carried away in a saddlebag or even in a wagon. And what purpose could there be in stealing people?"

An old woman said, "There are stories about demons who eat people."

Angai frowned. "Is that what your people did?"

"No," said Derek. "Let Eddie explain." He translated Angai's questions.

Eddie frowned. "This is really difficult. Wait a minute." He stared at the sky. "There are two ways to steal land.

"First, you drive off the people who are on the land and take it over yourself. That was done in North America.

"Second, you take over ownership of the land. You don't get rid of the original people. You keep them to work the land. You own them as well as the land. That was done in South America and Africa and—I guess—in Europe in the Middle Ages."

Derek translated.

Angai said, "Why would people agree to work for strangers? What bond holds them together? They are not kin. They cannot possibly have any obligations to people who are thieves."

Eddie answered, "If they did not work, they got no food. Often they were beaten or hurt in other ways."

Derek translated, having trouble with the word "beaten." He hesitated, then used the word that meant to hammer metal at the forge.

335

"This is impossible to understand," said Angai. "Why didn't the people leave?"

"There was no place to go," said Eddie. "The world was full of people who fought and stole. Everything was owned."

"Hu!" said Angai. She looked at Nia. "Does this sound right to you?"

"No. I have never heard any of this before. I know this man does not want you to welcome his people. Maybe he is lying."

Angai looked at me. "Is he lying?"

"No. But what he is describing happened a long time ago."

"How long ago?"

I did some figuring. "At least twelve generations have passed."

Angai leaned back and exhaled. "Are you certain these things really happened? A story can change when it is told and retold."

"We are certain."

"What happened? It is easier to change words than to change people. If the story is true, if it has not changed, then what happened to you? Why are you different now?"

I hesitated. Derek translated our conversation.

Eddie said, "I'm not certain that we are any different."

"Can I answer the question?" I asked.

Mr. Fang and Ivanova nodded.

"I think you are trying to undercut me," Eddie said.

"I'm trying to answer a question that Angai has asked. Derek will translate everything I say. If you want to comment, you'll be able to."

Eddie made the gesture of reluctant assent.

I looked at Angai. "Eddie does not believe that we have changed. But I do."

"How? And why?" asked Angai.

I thought for a while, aware of the people listening—of the small noises, coughs and whispers, a baby crying, older children playing on the far side of the square. I could hear their voices, high and clear, not all that different from the voices of children on Earth.

But when I looked, I saw dark fur and yellow eyes, slit pupils, flat broad faces that reminded me of no kind of human.

"Eddie has told you that these people—our ancestors—stole from one another. That is true. They also stole from the entire world. People will treat everything the way they treat one another."

A very old lady—bent over and gray—said, "Hu! Yes! I know!"

"They tore up the land, looking for various kinds of wealth: gold and silver and copper and other things. They cut down forests. They took water out of rivers so the rivers went dry. They put poison into other rivers so the water could not be used. They were even able to do harm to the sky. Burning rains began to fall, and the heat of the sun grew more intense."

336

"This is terrible," a woman said. "Weren't your shamanesses able to do anything? Couldn't they plead with the spirits? Couldn't they perform ceremonies of propitiation and aversion?"

"They tried. But nothing worked. It was not spirits that were doing these things. It was people."

"Hu!" the woman said.

"What happened?" asked Angai.

"You have to understand, most of our ancestors were not deliberately evil. They did not intend to ruin the world. But they didn't think about the results of what they were doing. They thought they could take without giving. They thought the world was like a fish in a shell. They could open it and eat it and throw the shell away."

I paused. Derek translated.

"Fish in a shell?" asked Mr. Fang.

Eddie said, "I'm surprised that Derek missed that one. Our ancestors thought the world was their oyster."

Mr. Fang still looked puzzled.

Angai said, "They must have realized that they were acting wrongly. It is always wrong to steal. It is always wrong to harm other people—except when two men fight in the spring."

"They lied to one another about what they were doing," I told her.

"In the beginning—in the early days—they said, 'We are making the world better. When we came to this place there was nothing except forest and wild animals and people who ran around naked. We have ended this. We have cut down the trees and planted gardens. We have made meadows where we can raise the kind of animals we like. We have taught the naked people how to wear clothing. All this is good! And look at the other things we've done! We have dug rivers and brought water to our gardens. We have turned dry canyons into lakes. Now there is more food. Now there can be more people. Now our villages can grow large and rich!'

"After a while they began to notice that the world did not seem to be a better place. Everything seemed smaller and dirtier. Everything was wearing out—the soil, the hills, the rivers and lakes. The people said, 'There is nothing new in this. There have always been places where the land is thin and useless. There have always been rivers where the water is not fit to drink. There is no problem.'

"Things kept getting worse. Now the people said, 'For everything that is gained, something must be lost. Look at what we have gained! Look at our villages full of big houses! Look at our houses full of many gifts! The forests that are gone have come back to us in gold. The rivers we cannot drink from have become jars full of *bara*.'

337

"Finally everything became so bad that no one could come up with any-thing comforting to say. Then the people said, 'Change is impossible. It's already too late. Anyway, we don't really mind the way things are.'" I paused. "Those are the four kinds of lie the people told. 'We are making things better.' 'There is no problem.' 'There are no real gifts.' 'It is too late to change.'"

"This is the worst thing I have ever heard," a woman said.

Angai said, "This can't be the end of the story."

"In the end the people looked around and saw how terrible the world had become. Lying was no longer possible. They saw where anger and greed had taken them—to the edge of destruction. They had to choose. If they wanted to live, they would have to give up anger and greed. If they wanted to remain angry and greedy, they would certainly die.

"Most people decided they wanted to live. They were like someone walk-ing in her sleep, troubled by terrible dreams. All at once she wakes and sees where she is standing—at the edge of a cliff. One more step will take her over. The rocks below look hard."

Derek translated.

Agopian said, "That's a wonderful speech, Lixia. I'm impressed. But you left out class warfare and a lot of very serious revolutionary struggle."

"And you have ignored the benefits of technology," said Ivanova. "Civilization is more than organized lying and stealing—though lying and steal-ing have certainly been important. Do you really think that we'd be better off if we were still digging for grubs with our fingers in the African savannah?"

"I can't get everything in," I said. "And like Eddie, I am not a Marxist."

Angai said, "Is that all? Or is there more to your explanation?"

"One other thing. Derek told you that groups of men used to go around and fight each other. That is how everything started—when one kind of peo-ple began to steal from another kind of people."

Angai made the gesture of acknowledgment.

"Our men don't go off on their own anymore. They stay with the women, and women do not like to confront and fight."

"That is true," Angai said. "Maybe you are right to keep your men in the villages—if they get together and make trouble once they are on their own."

The other women made gestures of agreement.

"How lucky we are," one said. "Our men would never think of getting together."

"They might, if they heard about these people," another said.

"I think you have just done us in," Derek said in English.

Angai made the gesture of disagreement. "These people are obviously dif-ferent from us. I think it's likely their men are different from our men." She looked at me. "Did your men ever live alone the way our men do?"

"No. Our men have always done things in groups."

Angai made the gesture that meant "you see." She glanced up. "The sun is in the western half of the sky, and we are reaching the hottest part of the day. We have heard from Eddie. Now we have to hear the other person. Ifana."

I translated.

Ivanova nodded. "You take care of this, Lixia." She straightened up. "I don't have much to add. What Eddie has described is not the nature of humanity, but the nature of capitalism—and the various economic and political systems that arose in response to capitalism, some of which, I know, called themselves proletarian. The question of what those societies actually were—"

Agopian spoke in Russian.

Ivanova nodded and said, "—is not relevant here. The dominant system was capitalism. It squatted like a dragon in the center of the twentieth century. Its tentacles reached everywhere."

A lovely metaphor, and Ivanova would not be able to disown it. We had too many recorders on.

"That era is over, at least for the majority of the population of Earth." She paused.

I said, "Ivanova says, our ancestors were not bad people. They had bad customs, and we have given those customs up."

"We have learned the hard way—through terrible suffering—that a society based on individual greed is very dangerous. In order to survive we have to think in large terms. We have to think about the species and the planet. If we do not, we'll die—or our children will die—or their children. We have no choice! We must cooperate!"

I said, "We have learned that we can't be greedy or selfish."

"Good!" said the gray old lady, the one who had spoken before.

"A proletarian society is based on cooperation. People do not exploit each other. Nor do they exploit their neighbors. When they meet with members of other societies, it is with respect for the rights of others and a concern for the benefit of all."

I said, "We work together now. We don't steal. When we meet people from other villages, we exchange gifts."

Ivanova looked at Angai. "We would like to spend time in your country in order to learn about your people and this planet. In return we will teach you about our people and Earth. I sincerely believe this exchange of information will do no harm. Instead, it will work for the benefit of everyone."

"She says that our people want to come and visit and exchange stories. She thinks this will be good for everyone."

"Is she telling the truth?" asked Angai.

"She believes what she has told you. So does Eddie."

"Does the old man have anything to say?"

339

I translated the question.

"Only this," said Mr. Fang. He looked at the shamaness. "This is your planet and your decision. It will remain your decision. If—in the future—you want us to leave, we will."

"He says this is your country. You can tell us to stay. You can tell us to go, now or anytime."

Angai frowned. "I know all that. Does he think I am stupid?" She climbed to her feet. "We will end now. I will go and think about everything these people have told us. I'll ask the advice of the spirits and the old women of the village. Tomorrow I will tell you what my decision is." She made the gesture that meant "it is over" and went into her tent.

The villagers began to disassemble their awnings.

I helped Mr. Fang get up.

"I do not really agree with the Daoists," he said. "But maybe we take too much upon ourselves. Making history is hard work, and it may be dangerous. I think I will have a cup of tea, look at the river, and contemplate inaction."

We walked through the village. He leaned on my arm. I realized how thin he was, and frail.

"On the other hand," said Mr. Fang, "there is the story of Yu the Engineer. He was traveling on government business and had to cross a river. A large yellow dragon bumped the boat.

"The boatmen were terrified. Yu remained calm. He said, 'I am doing my utmost in the interest of the people, discharging my duties in obedience to Heaven. Living, I am a guest. Dying, I go home. Why should I be disturbed? This dragon is no more than a lizard.'

"The dragon flattened its ears and dropped its tail and swam away. Yu continued on his journey. I have always liked that story."

We went down the river bluff. I helped him onto Ivanova's boat and settled him in a chair on the deck. The cabin was empty. Yunqi must have gone to see Tatiana. I made tea and brought it out. Lapsang Souchong. We sipped and watched birds fishing in the river.

Yunqi returned and prepared lunch. Cold noodles and pickled vegetables. We ate together on the deck. The pickles were delicious.

After a while Derek joined us and drank a beer, his feet up on the railing, his new shoes gleaming. "Much better! I don't like speeches. They aren't what life is about. If life is about anything."

I made the gesture of agreement.

"What will they do?" asked Yunqi. "Will we be allowed to stay?"

I said, "I don't know."

Yunqi frowned. "Our work is important."

"This is their country," said Mr. Fang.

I decided that I was hot and sticky and not especially willing to listen to speculation about the villagers. "I'm going for a swim."

Derek made the gesture that meant "that's a good idea."

I went to the other boat.

Agopian and Ivanova sat on the deck. They were talking softly and intently in Russian. They glanced at me, then went back to their conversation.

Eddie was in the cabin on a couch reading.

"Where is Tatiana?" I asked.

"In the village. She wanted to see the people. It might be her only chance. They may tell us to go." There was something in his voice. Hope? Satisfaction?

I got a towel and a bottle of soap from the bathroom. "What are the comrades talking about?"

"I have no idea. It never occurred to me that I'd need Russian. Their work in the social sciences is not that good, at least in the areas that interest me."

"It's probably nothing." I got a new pair of coveralls: bright yellow. "I'm going into the river. If I'm not back in an hour, get out the nets."

"Okay."

I washed in the shallow water close to shore, then swam out to midchannel. It was midafternoon now. The cliffs above me were still bright with sunlight, but the forest along the river was shadowy. I floated on my back, letting the current take me south and east.

Something whistled. I lifted my head. There was a biped on the shore. It was two meters tall, yellow with blue stripes and a lovely azure throat. A predator. I saw the clawed hands and the mouth full of pointed teeth. An *osupa* maybe? It watched me, fearless, then whistled again. Other animals came out of the shadows: a pack. The young were half the size of their parents and spotted rather than striped. Ten in all. On land they would have frightened me. But they didn't look like swimmers. I flipped over and slowly swam upriver to the boat. The current was stronger than I had realized. By the time I pulled myself onboard I was tired. I sat on the prow, breathing heavily.

The dominant predators seemed to be the animals called killers. They were four-footed and looked something like badgers or leopards, if the art of the natives was accurate. Were the predatory bipeds being pushed out? Or did they fill another ecological niche? Maybe the killers preyed mostly on bowhorns, while these animals preyed on their herbivorous cousins. More questions for Marina to answer. I got dressed and went aft.

Ivanova was gone. Agopian sat at the folding table, laying down cards. A native watched him, standing at the other end of the table, leaning forward on furry hands.

341

Agopian looked up. "He or she wants you, I think. It's really hard trying to relate to utterly strange beings who don't speak a language I understand."

"What is he doing?" asked the native. It was Nia's son.

"It's a . . ." I hesitated. I still didn't know the word for game. "A ceremony. Or else, it's the kind of thing that children do with a stick and a ball."

"Hu! He puts red on black and black on red. But I don't understand the rest. Are the colors important?"

I translated.

Agopian said, "Red for blood and fire. Black for night and death." He laid down a card. "Black for anarchy. Red for revolution."

I looked at Anasu. "He says, they are the colors of blood and fire, night and death, confusion and change."

"That is plenty! What a ceremony this person is performing! Is he? I don't know the word. Is he a male shamaness?"

I translated.

"I am a Marxist."

I made the gesture that meant "yes."

"Aiya!" The boy straightened up, taking his hands off the table. "Is there a place where we can go? I don't want to disturb a shaman." He paused. "A shaman person."

"He doesn't want to bother you," I said in English.

"Take him away," Agopian said. "I have to do some thinking." He glanced up. "I may want to tell you something later."

"About the conversation you were having with Ivanova?"

"Yes. I think I've gotten myself into something stupid, and now I have to get out." He looked at the array of cards, frowning. "That's life, as Lenin said. One step forward. Two steps back." He laid down another card. "I'd prefer it if you didn't mention my remarks to Ivanova."

"Okay."

The boy followed me forward to the prow. We sat down on the fiberglass deck. He wrapped his furry arms around his furry knees.

"One of your people is in the village, walking around and looking. She doesn't understand a word that people say to her. Or is she a male? I don't know."

"A woman. Her name is Tatiana."

He made the gesture of acknowledgment: a quick flip of one hand. "Hua is with her, making sure that she does not get into trouble."

A voice called out in the language of the village. It came from a tree that leaned over the river. I glanced up and saw leaves moving. "Is that a friend of yours?"

"Gerat. He always makes a lot of noise. You won't hear the others. They told me I would not dare go onto the boat."

"Is that why you came down?"

"Because of the dare? No. We wanted to see the boats, and everyone in the village is arguing." He hugged his knees. "Hu! What a situation! They don't want the children around, especially the boys. They don't want us to see that they are confused."

"Do you know what they're going to decide?"

"No. It depends on Angai and the spirits. Also on the old women. I think the old women will say that you have to leave. But I don't know about Angai." He tilted his head, considering. His strange pale gray eyes were half-closed. Finally he made the gesture of uncertainty. "Hua might have some idea. She understands Angai better than I do. And she knows more about the spirits." He opened his eyes. "I have something to ask you."

I made the gesture that meant "go ahead and ask."

"People say this boat moves on its own. I'd like to see that. Is it possible?"

I thought for a moment. It was a reasonable request. One must always help the young acquire knowledge. And I liked this kid. He was intelligent and charming. Odd that charm crossed species lines. Odd that his charm should have a sexual component. It did.

"Okay." I stood up. "I'll talk to the shaman person."

Anasu lifted a hand. "I don't want to interrupt a ceremony."

"He might be done by now."

I walked back to the stern. Agopian was still playing solitaire. "Can you run the boat?"

"Of course."

"Take it out."

"Why?"

"The boy. Anasu. He wants to see a boat in motion."

Agopian frowned.

"It isn't a lot to ask."

Agopian stood and gathered up the cards. "Okay."

The boy joined us, looking nervous. "Was the shaman person done?"

"I think so."

Agopian settled himself in the pilot's chair, flipped a switch, and spoke in Russian. "What is he saying?" asked the boy.

"I don't know. We have many languages, and I know only a few."

"Then you aren't all from the same village?"

"No."

The radio spoke in Russian. Agopian started the engine. Next to me, the boy clenched his hands. Agopian said, "Get the mooring lines, Lixia."

343

I did, scrambling through the underbrush. A voice spoke overhead. I did-
n't think it was the child who had spoken before. I climbed back on the boat,
and it moved away from shore. Eddie came out of the cabin.

"What's going on?"

I told him.

He frowned.

"Think of it this way," I said. "It may be his last chance."

"Like Tatiana in the village?" Eddie grinned. "Okay."

"Is the big man angry?" asked Anasu.

"No." I looked at the shore. A couple of the children were visible now.
One stood quietly on the bank, looking out at us. The other hung one-hand-
ed from a branch like a gibbon. His feet kicked. Or did I mean her feet?

"That is Gerat," said Anasu.

A moment later Gerat lost his grip. He fell into the water and splashed
around, shouting. The other child paid no attention.

"I told you," said Anasu. "He is always noisy."

We reached the middle of the river. Agopian brought the boat around so
it pointed upstream toward the rapids, then throttled down. The sound of the
engine went from a roar to a growl.

"Why does your boat make so much noise?" asked Anasu. "Is it hungry?"

"It won't eat us, if that is what you are wondering."

"Is it alive?"

Gerat climbed onto the bank. His fur was soaked and matted. He looked
miserable, even at a distance.

"No," I said. "It's a tool."

The boy ran three steps forward, jumped and caught the edge of the cabin
roof, swinging himself up.

"Hey!" said Eddie.

Anasu stood, his legs wide.

"Get down!" Eddie shouted.

The boy waved.

The other children made whooping noises. I could see five.

"I will be a big man!" Anasu called. "I'll be like my uncle. You little ones,
listen! Get ready to back down!"

"You say it!" a voice called in reply.

The boat was drifting downriver very slowly. Anasu tried a dance step: a
slide and hop.

"I am on the boat!
I am on the boat
that growls!

"I am on the boat!
I am on the boat
that ROARS!

"I am dancing!
Aiya! Dancing
on the broad
and shaking back."

"Big mouth!" cried one of the children. I thought it was Gerat.

Anasu spun around.

Agopian said, "Get him down, Lixia."

"The shaman person is getting angry," I said. "Get down."

Anasu shouted again, then rolled forward in a somersault that took him off the roof. He straightened in midair and landed on his feet.

"Gymnastics," said Agopian. "That's what these kids need. With the proper training, they'd beat the Chinese."

"They need to be left alone," said Eddie.

Agopian turned the wheel. The boat turned in a circle, heading back to shore.

Anasu was breathing heavily. Not from exertion. From excitement and maybe fear. "Is the shaman person seriously angry?"

"I don't think so."

"What about the big man? He did most of the shouting."

"No."

Anasu made the gesture of happiness.

The other children met the boat, calling to Anasu in their own language. He ignored them, standing with his shoulders back.

Interesting. The process of establishing dominance must begin early. That was true of humans in societies where hierarchies were important. In New Jersey, for example.

It was possible that the children already knew—before they went through the change—where they stood in relation to one another.

I climbed out of the boat and tied it up. Anasu followed, helping as best he could. When we were done, he made the gesture of gratitude. "Tell the shaman person, I am grateful to him. I hope he isn't angry. It is never a good idea to get in quarrels with holy people."

He turned and ran into the forest. The other children followed. I went back to the boat.

"He could have fallen off," said Eddie. "What if he came down near the prop?"

"I think it's called a screw," said Agopian. "Though I wouldn't swear to that."

345

I went in the cabin. Eddie's book lay on the floor. The fast-forward button shone red and on the screen was the three-lobed symbol used to mark the end of anything precious: literature, art, air, clean water, unpolluted soil. The symbol was painted on outside airlocks. It stood at the edge of the various ruined lands. It ended holodramas and shone over the exits in museums.

I turned the book off and tossed it on the couch, went to the galley and got a beer.

Tatiana came back.

"How did you like the village?" I asked.

"God is great." She laughed. "That's what I kept thinking. *Allah akbar.*"

"'O brave new world, that has such people in it,'" said Eddie.

Agopian said, "Miranda in *The Tempest*. Has anyone ever told you that Shakespeare is better in Russian?"

Eddie made the gesture that meant "no."

I said, "I've always heard that he was best in German."

"That line never reminds me of Shakespeare," Eddie said. "I know it from Aldous Huxley. His novel *Brave New World*."

"You've read it?" I asked.

"I've taught it—in my survey course on the collapse of Western civilization."

Ah, yes. How could I have forgotten?

We made sandwiches and ate them on the deck. Bugs danced above the surface of the river. The sky darkened.

Tatiana went to bed. The rest of us stayed on deck. I opened another beer.

"Be careful," said Eddie. "That stuff can be dangerous."

"I'm of Chinese descent, and the Chinese are famous for not having a drinking problem."

Derek chose that moment to climb over the railing. "For example," he said. "There is the famous Chinese poet Li Bo. The story is—he was out in a boat, drinking rice wine and enjoying the evening. He saw the reflection of the moon on the water and leaned over to embrace it. He fell in and drowned."

"Where have you been?" I asked.

"Up at the village."

Eddie frowned. "We were told—"

"I wasn't in the village. I was outside it, taking a walk, looking at the night sky, listening to the music."

"Music?" I asked.

He made the gesture of affirmation. "One instrument sounded like a flute. Another was like a xylophone, and there was a third that made a noise like a foghorn.

"I wanted to go in. But the old men were prowling at the edges of the village. The music must have gotten to them. They didn't go in, but they couldn't seem to pull themselves away. They kept pacing, stopping, peering at the fire—there was a big one in the middle of the village—then pacing again. I couldn't figure out a way to get past them. Damn! I hate to pass up any ceremony!"

I finished my beer and went into the cabin. Tatiana was already asleep. I unfolded one of the couches, undressed, and lay down. The window above me was open. I heard the rustle of foliage and the river lapping gently against our boat.

I woke early. The cabin was dark and cool. Someone was snoring. I got up and went to the bathroom, then out on the deck, carrying my clothes. Light shone out the windows of the other boat. A gust of wind brought me the scent of Chinese cooking and music: the piano version of "Pictures from an Exhibition."

I did my yoga, dressed, and climbed the river bluff.

The sun was visible from the top. It hung just above the horizon: a reddish-orange disk, too bright to look at directly. I followed a trail through the pseudo-grass. Leaves brushed against me, wet with dew. In a minute or two my pants were soaked.

A flower bloomed just off the trail: large and low to the ground. The petals were pale yellow, almost the same color as the plain. The center was dark. The entire plant was fleshy—like a succulent on Earth.

I knelt and touched the edge of the flower.

Damn! I waved my hand in the air. The flower curled into a ball. I looked at my finger. It felt as if a bee had gotten it.

A shadow fell over me. I glanced up and saw Nia.

"That is a stinging flower."

"I never would have known."

"Come into camp. There is a lotion that will make you feel better. My cousin is certain to have it."

I stood, my hand throbbing. We walked toward the village.

Nia said, "They eat bugs and other animals. Very small lizards. Sometimes an *aipit.*"

"A what?"

"It is an animal with four feet, covered with fur. The body is as long as the first joint of my thumb. The poison in the plant will kill something that small. But the plant does no real harm to people. It can't get through a good coat of fur, the kind we have. People get stung if they touch the plant the way you did—or if they are foolish enough to walk on the plain with bare feet." She paused for a moment. "A bowhorn can walk through a cluster of the plants and feel nothing, unless it is a fawn and tries to nibble. They do that once."

347

We reached the village. Nia stopped in front of a big tent. A woman sat at the entrance, large and handsome, dressed in a navy tunic. Her necklace was silver and amber. Her bracelets were gold.

"This person touched a stinging flower," Nia said.

The woman spoke in the language of the village. A child came out carrying a pot.

"Sit down," the woman said. "My name is Ti-antai. Nia said your people are like children, always touching and turning things over. You see what happens? Hold out your hand."

I followed orders. She looked at my finger, which was swollen by this time and bright red. "Aiya! How peculiar!"

"What?" I asked, feeling a little nervous.

"The color of your skin." She dug into the pot, bringing out a glob of something yellow, grabbed my hand firmly, and smeared the stuff on my finger. The pain diminished at once.

"What is the flower?" I asked. "A plant or an animal?"

"That's hard to say. When it is full-grown, it has roots like a plant. But it hunts like an animal and it has a mouth—the dark hole in the center. Did you see it?"

"Yes, but I didn't realize what it was."

"You weren't looking carefully," the woman said. "You must always look carefully before you touch."

I made the gesture of courteous acknowledgment for good advice.

Nia said, "The flowers have young that move around."

I thought for a moment. "How do the flowers reproduce?"

Ti-antai looked at Nia. "You are right about these people. They poke into things they know nothing about and they ask a lot of questions." She looked at me. "The flowers shrivel up at the time of the first frost. There is nothing left except a black pod. That stays the way it is all winter. In the spring it breaks open and the young come out. They are green and like worms with feet. They crawl away into the vegetation. I don't know what they do under the leaves. But in time they root themselves. They grow. They become flowers. That's all I know— except this. The lotion that cures the sting comes from the bodies of the young. I gather them in the spring and tie them onto a drying rack. They move for a day or two or three. Then they dry up. When they are entirely dry, I grind them up.

"Other things go into the lotion, but it is the bodies of the young that are important."

Weird, I thought. And I was the wrong person to be listening. Marina in Sight of Olympus ought to be here.

"Now, go away," the woman said. "You make me uneasy. Nia has always been friends with the strangest kinds of people."

348

I stood and made the gesture of gratitude.

Nia said, "I will go to the boats with you. I have a message from Angai."

We left the village, following the trail down the river bluff.

Nia said, "Angai has come to a decision."

"What is it?"

"She will tell us this afternoon. Come up to the village just before sunset. All of you. The women and the men." She moved her shoulders and rubbed the back of her neck. "Aiya! It was hard! All day we talked and argued. Angai and I and the oracle. The old women. The rest of the village. I got a headache.

"At night there was a feast. Angai sent the oracle away. He had to stay in a tent that had been abandoned by one of the old men. A man who went suddenly crazy and rode off onto the plain. I was allowed to stay.

"We always hold a feast after a big argument. It reminds us that we are one people. But the arguing didn't end. Anhar told a story."

"Who?"

"She is the best storyteller in the village. Most people like her. I don't. She was one of the people who spoke against me the last time I was here. She had many reasons why I could not stay among the Iron People."

We were halfway down the cliff, moving through shadowy forest. My finger had stopped hurting.

"The story isn't one of ours. It came from the Amber People. It tells about the Trickster."

"Do you remember it?" I asked.

Nia made the gesture that meant "yes." "He came to a village, disguised as an old woman. The villagers thought he was the Dark One. He played many malicious tricks. Do you want to hear about them? I think I can remember most."

"Not now. Later, when I have one of the little boxes that can remember what is said to it."

"Aiya!" said Nia.

I asked, "What happened next?"

"In the story? The villagers realized he could not be the Dark One. He was too nasty. Even she sets a limit on her behavior.

"They tricked him into climbing into a pot of water. They put on the lid and boiled him until he was dead. The story ends with a song. It goes like this." Nia sang:

"Hu! My flesh
was fed to lizards!

"Hu! My bones
were made into flutes!

349

"Hu! My music
is loud and nasty!

"Hu! My music
sounds like this!"

"The Trickster died?" I asked.

"Only for a while. He always comes back. Angai was furious."

"Why?" We had reached the riverbank. My boat was in front of us. It smelled of coffee and bacon.

Nia said, "Anhar was saying that you are troublemakers like the Trickster, imposing on the village. But the argument was over. The decision was made. It was time to be pleasant to one another. Anhar could not stop. There are people like that. They pick at the edges of a quarrel like a child picking at the edges of a healing wound.

"I don't know what Angai has decided, but I know she does not want to make Anhar happy." Nia waved at the boat. "That's all I have to tell you. Come up to the village at sunset."

"Okay," I said.

She left. I went onboard the boat. The folding table was up. Agopian, Eddie, and Ivanova sat around it.

"Elizaveta has been talking to the camp," Eddie said.

"Oh, yeah?" I sat down and poured myself a cup of coffee.

She nodded. "They have seen lizards in the lake. Big ones. Half a dozen so far—keeping to the shallow water close to shore."

I paused, my hand halfway to the milk. "Oh-oh."

"They are putting up new spotlights and making sure that everything that smells like food is burned."

"I thought they were doing that before."

"Only with material from the ship. Organic matter from the planet was being buried."

The remains of Marina's specimens.

Agopian ate a piece of bacon. "No one is going swimming."

"Here?"

"No. At the camp."

"What happened to your finger?" asked Eddie.

I told them about the flower.

Eddie shook his head. "We keep thinking this planet is like Earth. I think—if we stay—we're going to be surprised over and over, not always pleasantly."

350

"Maybe. I ran into Nia up on the bluff. She said we're supposed to go into the village late this afternoon. Angai has made a decision. Don't ask me what it is. Nia didn't even want to guess."

I ate breakfast, then went for a swim. Afterward I put on jeans and a red silk shirt.

We had silkworms on the ship, of course, and a garden full of mulberry trees. But the shirt had been made on Earth. There was a union label in the back of the collar. "Shanghai Textile Workers," it said. Next to the writing was a person—I couldn't tell the sex—riding on the back of a flying crane. Robes flew out behind the person, and he or she held a spindle. Behind the crane was a five-pointed star.

The person on the crane was almost certainly a Daoist immortal, and the five-pointed star was an emblem of the revolution. The shirt felt wonderful against my skin.

It was a bad day: still and hot. Everyone was restless. Eddie and Derek and I worked on reports. Tatiana and Agopian ran checks on equipment. Ivanova paced from boat to boat. Only Mr. Fang seemed calm. I went over to his boat after lunch. He sat on the deck. There was a chessboard in front of him. Next to the board was a pot of tea.

"If you are looking for Yunqi, she has gone for a swim, leaving herself in a really terrible position. I can see no way out for her." He waved at the pieces on the board.

"They're driving me crazy over there. I'm driving me crazy."

"Master Lao tells us that heaviness is the foundation of lightness, and stillness is the lord of action."

"What?"

"Lenin tells us that a revolutionary needs two things: patience and a sense of irony." He looked up and smiled. "Get yourself a cup, Lixia. I will set up the board again. We will drink tea and play chess and not worry about problems which are outside our control."

"Are you being wise?"

"Not especially."

"Good. I'm in no mood for wisdom."

I went and got a cup. We played chess. He beat me.

Yunqi came back, wearing a swimsuit. It was single-piece and solid blue. Her short black hair was dripping wet. Her eyes had the out-of-focus look of severe myopia.

"Why don't you wear contacts?" I asked.

"I like the way I look in glasses." She put them on: two plain clear lenses in plain round metal frames.

"Yunqi is like Comrade Agopian," said Mr. Fang. "A romantic. She likes glasses with the look of the early twentieth century. That was the age of heroes. Luxemburg. Lenin. Trotsky. Mao and Zhou."

"I thought you didn't like politics," I said.

She blushed. "I don't like endless talking—especially when people get angry. But I have always enjoyed stories of the Long March and Comrade Trotsky on the armored train."

"She likes war," said Mr. Fang. "As an idea. Do you want to play another game of chess?"

I said, "Okay."

I lost again. Mr. Fang said, "It's time to go."

The people from the other boat met us on the trail: Derek, Eddie, Ivanova, Agopian. We climbed the bluff together.

It was hot and windy on the plain. In the village awnings flapped.

Standards jingled. Campfires danced. A tiny quadruped bounded down the street in front of us. It was the size of a dik-dik, with little curved horns. Its fur was dark green. It wore a collar made of leather and brass.

"What is it?" asked Eddie.

I made the gesture of ignorance.

Derek said, "We don't know."

We reached the town square. Once again it was full of people—at least the edges. The center of the square was a heap of ashes.

Angai waited for us in front of her tent. She wore a robe of dark blue fabric with no embroidery. Her belt was made of links of gold, interwoven like chain mail. The buckle was huge: a gold biped, folded back on itself. The neck was twisted. The head touched the rump. The long tail curled around the entire body. The animal's eye was a dark red stone.

Nia and the oracle stood with her.

The crowd murmured around us. Angai held up a hand. There was silence, except for the chiming of metal and the rush of the wind.

"I've talked to various people," Angai said loudly. "The old women who have learned much in their lives. The old men who have traveled far and are certainly not foolish. I have talked with Nia and the Voice of the Waterfall, who know these hairless people. I have gone in my tent alone and consulted with the spirits, inhaling the smoke of dreams.

"After listening to everything and thinking, I have come to a decision.

"I bring it to you, o people of the village. You are the ones who must approve or disapprove.

"But remember, if you disapprove, you are going against me and the spirits and the elders of the village."

She paused and gestured toward us. Derek translated.

Ivanova said, "A smart woman. It won't be easy to vote her down."

Angai went on. "If you want to know what the old people said, ask them. I will tell you what the spirits told me. But I want Nia and the oracle to speak for themselves."

"Why?" asked a voice.

Angai made the gesture that demanded silence. "I asked Nia her opinion, because she traveled a long distance with two of the hairless people. She has seen the town that they have built next to the Long Lake. She has ridden on one of their boats."

"So has Anasu!" a child cried.

"Be quiet," said a woman.

Angai went on. "Only a fool—only a worthless woman—refuses to ask for information from those who know.

"As for the oracle, he also has traveled with these people, and he is holy. A spirit has given him advice."

She paused. Derek translated. Nia spoke.

"Angai asked me if these people are reliable. I said yes. So far as I know. But there are many of them, and they have differences of opinion. I have heard them argue.

"I think we can trust them. I think we can believe what they say. But I do not know for certain.

"She asked if they will do harm to the Iron People. They are not crazy. They will not harm us intentionally. But they are very different. If we make them welcome, they will change the way we see the world. They have done that to me.

"That is disturbing. Maybe it is harmful. I do not know."

Nia paused. Derek translated. She went on. "I don't think they will vanish. They are not a mirage. They are here and solid. If we send them off, they will go to other villages. Someone on the plain will make them welcome. I do not think there is a way to drive them out of the world. Maybe if everyone got together, it could be done. But that will not happen, and I don't know if it ought to happen. Change is not always bad. There was a time when nothing existed. Spirits appeared out of the nothing. They made the world and everything in it. Most of us think this was a change for the good.

"My advice to Angai is—make them welcome. But do it carefully. O my people! *Think* about what you are doing!"

The oracle stepped forward. "I don't have much to say. My spirit is old and powerful. It has given good advice to the people of my village for many generations. It told me to go with these hairless people and learn from them. What they know is important, my spirit said.

"I have done this, traveling a long distance with Lixia and Deraku. We have met many people and also several spirits. Some bad things have happened, but not because of those two."

I thought he was being kind. I had mishandled the meeting with Inahooli, and Derek had been irresponsible about the bracelet he had found in the old volcano.

Someone asked, "What kind of bad things?"

"We had trouble with the Trickster," the oracle said. "You know what he is like. A malevolent troublemaker! He likes to turn people against one another. He likes to make them forget all the old customs and the right way to behave.

"And we met a spirit north of here, not far from the river. It was in a cave." He paused. "It was one of those things that are found in dark places, usually underground. They have various names. The Old Ones. The Unseen. The Hungry.

"Most of the time, they aren't a problem. They sleep in their dark place. Sometimes they wake up and notice people. Then they are likely to cause trouble—out of hunger or a stupid anger." He paused. "I have forgotten what I was going to say."

"I asked you to give your opinion of the hairless people," Angai said. "But you went off about spirits."

He made the gesture of agreement. "I can't tell you what to do. You aren't my people, and you have your own spirits to give advice. But I like Lixia and Deraku, and I don't think these people without hair are dangerous."

He stopped. Derek translated.

Eddie said, "Wrong!"

The square was darkening. People brought out poles made of metal and stuck them in the ground. They placed torches in brackets on the poles. The torches streamed in the wind, flaring and dimming. Most were close to Angai. She and Nia and the oracle were pretty well lit. But the light kept changing in intensity. Shadows jumped and flickered. Faces, hands, eyes, and metal ornaments went in and out of darkness.

"Nia has spoken clearly," Angai said. "And the oracle is worth listening to, even if he is not always clear."

A voice said, "What is your opinion? You are the shamaness here. These other people are strangers."

"I will tell you." She waited a moment. The bells on the standards went *ching-ching* in the wind. A baby cried briefly.

"I think Nia is right. We ought to welcome these people, as we have always welcomed strangers, not out of fear of the Dark One, but out of the respect for the spirits and for decent behavior.

354

"I think Nia is right in a second way. This is a time for changes. We cannot ignore the changes. When the ground shakes and old trails go in new directions, only a fool pretends she can travel the same way as before. The wise woman says, 'This rock is new. That slope was not here last summer.'"

Angai straightened up to her full height. She looked around commandingly. "Listen to me! This is my decision! We will welcome the hairless people. But we will do it carefully. Like a wise traveler, we will go one step at a time."

She paused. Derek translated.

Eddie said, "Damn!"

Angai went on. "The hairless people can stay in the village they have built so long as they remember that this is not their country. They are visitors." She looked at us. "Do not move your village without asking permission, and do not ask more of your relatives to come and stay with you. I don't want our country to fill up with hairless people.

"Nia says among your people men and women cannot be separated. Therefore—it is my decision—you can live in your village according to your customs. But when you visit us or any other ordinary people, leave your men at home."

"Shit," said Derek.

"I will not have men in this village again. It is too disturbing. The old women become angry. The children get new ideas."

Angai stopped. Derek translated.

"This is good," said Ivanova. "But not as good as I had hoped." She paused for a moment. "It's a beginning."

"It stinks," said Derek. "How can I do fieldwork? I have to be able to go into the villages!"

"Talk to the men," I said.

"They'll try to kill me."

Angai went on. "Nia says you are going to want to travel all over and ask questions and look at things. Is she right? Is this true?"

"Yes," I said.

Angai frowned. "I am not certain what to do about that. I do not want to find hairless people in every part of our country, turning over rocks and poking sticks into holes. It is hard enough to have children." She paused. "Stay close to the village until I have had a chance to think more about this."

Derek translated.

Eddie said, "This isn't going to work."

"Yes, it will," said Mr. Fang. "They have the right to set these kinds of limits. We have the discipline to keep within the limits they have set."

"What about Nia?" asked a voice.

"I have not decided," Angai said.

"We have," said the voice. "Ten winters ago we told her to leave. She has not changed. She was a pervert then. She is a pervert now. Look at the people she travels with! Tell her to go with them. Tell her to live in their village—not here, among people who know how to behave."

The crowd parted. I saw the speaker now: a stocky woman of middle age. Her fur was medium brown and oddly dull. It soaked up light like clay.

"That is Anhar," Nia said.

"I will ask the spirits what to do about Nia," Angai said. "Not today. They don't like a lot of questions all at once."

"You have always liked Nia," Anhar said. "You have always protected her. You are trying to bring her back into the village."

Angai said, "You never know when to be quiet, Anhar. I am tired of your opinions! You have a little mind, full of nasty ideas. It is like a cheese eaten out by cheese bugs. It is like a dead animal eaten out by worms."

"Wow," said Derek.

Anhar turned. The crowd let her through. She walked away from Angai out of the torch-lit square. I lost sight of her in the darkness.

"What about the man?" another woman asked. "The Voice of the Waterfall?"

The oracle answered. "I am going to the village of the hairless people. My spirit told me to learn from them. I have not had any new dreams telling me to do anything else."

Angai said, "I am done speaking. You have heard my decision. Do you agree with me? Or is there going to be an argument?"

There was silence. I had a sense that the people around me were unhappy. But no one was willing to speak.

At last someone said, "What did the spirits tell you, Angai?"

"I dreamed I was on a trail I did not recognize. The country around me was unfamiliar. The ground under my feet was hot. Smoke rose from holes. I could not see where I was going."

"That does not sound like a good dream, Angai."

The shamaness frowned. "I am not finished! There was an old woman with me. She had a fat belly and drooping breasts. She carried a staff and it seemed to me that she was having trouble walking. Sometimes she walked next to me. Sometimes ahead. Sometimes in back. She never left me. She made noises from time to time: grunts and moans. Most of the time she was silent. Once she was in back of me, and I thought I heard her stumble. I stopped and looked back. She said, 'Keep going. Don't worry about me. As old as I am, I will keep up with you.' I went on. That was the end of the dream."

The woman who had asked the question said, "All right. I will go along with you, Angai. Even though I am made uneasy by these new people. And even though I think Anhar is right about Nia."

356

Angai made the gesture that meant "it is over." She turned and went into her tent.

I said, "You finish translating, Derek. I want to speak to Nia."

He made the gesture of agreement.

I walked over to Nia and the oracle. A couple of women removed the torches from their holders, taking them away.

Nia said, "I am not certain that Angai was being clever. She ought to have been more polite to Anhar. Now she's made an enemy of her."

"No," said the oracle. "She has changed nothing. They were enemies already. Now they can stop pretending. I have never had an enemy, but I know it's hard work being polite to someone you hate. It makes a woman tired. She loses strength. She cannot do things that are important."

"You've never had an enemy?" I asked.

"Most men do not. If a man gets angry, he confronts the person who has made him angry. Or else he leaves. The women are trapped in their villages. They spend winter after winter next to people they dislike. They do not speak their anger. They cannot get away. That makes enemies. I have seen it happen."

"Do you want to stay in the village?" I asked Nia.

She made the gesture of uncertainty.

"Do you have a place to stay tonight?"

"Here. With Angai." Nia paused. "That was Ti-antai. The woman who spoke last. The woman who cared for your hand this morning. She was a good friend of mine when we were young."

"Aiya!" I said.

The oracle said, "I will go with you. Angai made me stay at the edge of the village last night in an old tent that was full of holes. Even with the holes and the wind blowing through, it smelled of old age and craziness." He paused. "Not holy craziness. The other kind."

The square was empty except for my companions. The torches were all gone. There was no noise except the wind and Derek's voice, still translating.

"What was the dream about?" I asked. "Why did it satisfy your cousin?"

"You don't know much, do you?" Nia said.

"No. Who was the old woman?"

"The Mother of Mothers. If she tells us to go on through a strange country, then we will."

"It was a good dream," said the oracle. "I have had only a few that were that easy to understand. No one can possibly argue with it."

Derek said, "I'm done."

"Coming," I said.

We left the square, walking through the dark village.

357

Ivanova said, "This decision is not going to satisfy anyone. The research teams are going to want to be able to travel. And Eddie, of course, is horrified that we have not been ordered off the planet."

"That's right," Eddie said.

"I think the problem is vulgar Marxism," said Mr. Fang.

"Oh, yeah?" I said.

"We oversimplify the dialectical process and we become fascinated by the drama of revolution. We forget that human history is very complex and very slow. Every big change is preceded by a multitude of small changes. There are compromises. There are failures. We take a step forward and then are forced to go back a step or even two.

"Even revolutions are full of compromise and failure. Even in the midst of great transformations, we go back. After the triumph of the October Revolution came Kronstadt and the crushing of the Workers' Opposition."

"I don't understand where this is leading," Ivanova said.

"We expected this meeting to resolve everything. We expected a revolution, the simple kind that we see on the holovision.

"We are in the middle of a revolution. It has gone on for over five hundred years. I have no idea when it will end, if ever. But it is not a simple drama. It does not move forward all the time. And there are no neat divisions. No scenes and acts. At least none that we can see. Historians put in such things later.

"Today—I think—the revolution has moved into a new stage. It has certainly moved *onto* a new stage. There are new actors and new problems. But there is no resolution."

"True enough," said Eddie. "What we have is goddamned compromise. It isn't going to hold. Once we are down here—"

Ivanova said, "For once I agree with Eddie. We have to be able to travel. We have come so far." She paused. "Maybe we can find another people who will set fewer limitations."

"Not tonight," said Mr. Fang.

We reached the river. There were lights on one of the boats. Tatiana and Yunqi sat together on the deck. They helped Mr. Fang onboard. Ivanova and Eddie followed.

The oracle said, "I want to sleep. This has been a long day."

"You're right about that," I said.

We took him to the other boat and got him bedded down in the cabin.

Derek and Agopian and I went out on deck. The river air was cool and full of bugs. They swarmed around the deck lights once we turned them on. Agopian and I sat down. Derek went and got beers.

We drank, not speaking. We could hear voices from the other boat: Ivanova and Eddie, describing what had happened to Tatiana and Yunqi.

Agopian said, "I don't know how long that conversation will go on."

"Hours, most likely."

"Maybe." He set down his bottle. "There is something I have to tell you."

I looked at him. "Your secret. Your ethical complexity."

"Yes."

"Can't it wait?"

"I'm not sure I'll be able to get you alone. This is perfect now, if I have enough time."

Derek said, "I'm willing to listen."

Agopian looked at me.

I nodded.

"I'm going to try to tell this as quickly as possible. I don't know when that conversation will end, and Tatiana will come over. There is information that has been kept hidden and lies that have been told. I think it's time this situation was rectified."

Derek leaned forward. "What kind of information?"

"History. What's been happening on Earth during the past one hundred years."

"We have the messages from Earth," I said.

"They are lies."

"You know this for certain?" asked Derek.

"I wrote them—with help, of course. It was too big a job for any one person."

"Why?" I asked.

Derek asked, "When?"

"You know there was trouble coming into the system."

Derek made the gesture of agreement.

Agopian looked puzzled and went on. "There was a lot more junk than we had expected, and a lot of it was a long way out. A kind of super Oort cloud. And there were problems with the astrogation system. The computers decided it was an emergency. They woke the crew up early. We brought the ship in.

"We didn't have time to wake up any other people. But we did have time to check the messages that had been coming in from Earth. They were crazy."

"What do you mean?" I asked.

"I mean exactly that. The messages are crazy. Earth has changed a lot." He paused. "We thought history would stop because our lives had stopped, because we were sleeping a magic sleep like children in a fairy tale.

"Not true. History went on and took a turn . . ." He paused again. "Progress is not inevitable. That is an error the vulgar Marxists make. I've always liked that term. I imagine a man with a big thick beard, farting at the dinner table as he explains commodity fetishism or the labor theory of value. And of course he gets the theory wrong."

"What are you talking about?" I asked.

"Progress. There is no law that says humanity has to evolve ever higher social forms. Collapse is possible. Regression or stagnation. That's essentially what happened after the twentieth century. Not regression but stagnation. We thought it was a characteristic of post-capitalist societies: extreme stability, as opposed to the extreme instability of capitalism, the crazy rate of change during the nineteenth and twentieth centuries.

"I think now the stability came from the terrible mess created in the twentieth century, the lack of resources and precarious state of the environment. We spent two hundred years cleaning up—trying to return the planet to its former state, trying to undo what those creeps and epigones had done. We didn't have time for innovation."

"We built the L-5 colonies," I said.

"And the ship," said Derek.

"Those are new objects. I am talking about new ideas. Most of our ideology and technology comes—came—from the old society. Most of what we have done is based on what people already knew prior to the collapse."

"That isn't entirely true," I said.

Agopian said, "It is mostly true. We have been like the people of the early Middle Ages. We used the old knowledge in new ways. But we did not add to it."

Derek frowned. "I question that analogy."

"I don't want to argue about the Middle Ages."

Derek made the gesture that meant "forget what I said."

"In any case, the stability—or stagnation—was only temporary. That's what we learned when we woke up and listened to the messages from home. About the time we left, the various societies on Earth began to change rapidly."

He paused, frowning. "The changes were disturbing. We—I mean the crew—could barely handle the information we were getting, and we are—without a question—the most disciplined people on the ship. We had no idea what would happen if the rest of you woke up and heard. We imagined panic and a collapse of morale. Some people would want to run home, though home to what is a question. Others would fall apart. There would have been months of argument and a decline in the quality of work. It seemed to us that the expedition had to be protected. We took a vote—everyone who wasn't frozen. We decided to change the messages."

I opened my mouth.

He held up a hand. "Don't ask questions. I don't know how much time I have, and I want to tell you as much as possible."

"Okay."

360

"We started by changing history. That was comparatively easy. We drafted—I drafted—an alternative history, one we felt more comfortable with. After that it was a matter of searching and replacing. We told the computer system to look for certain kinds of events—and remove them and replace them with other kinds of events."

He smiled. "I have to say, I have a new respect for liars, especially those who lived before computers. I have no idea how you can manage to rewrite history without a computer."

"Why did you do it?" I asked. "What could possibly be so terrible about the messages from Earth?"

He sat next to one of the deck lights. I could see him clearly: a rectangular face, pale brown in color. His eyes were large and dark. His nose was high and narrow, with a slight curve. His mouth was ordinary. It was the eyes that dominated the face and the unruly curly hair, worn slightly longer than was fashionable among members of the crew.

"There are three things that matter to me: socialism, Marxism, and the Soviet Union. I don't think that what I feel is chauvinism. It's love for a place and pride in what the people there have done. How they fought again and again, generation after generation, to build a society that really embodied the principles of socialism. They succeeded, though just barely. The revolution was not destroyed by Stalinism or Fascism or nationalism or even by the many crimes and the amazing stupidity of the apparatchiks. The people managed finally to create a society that was decent and just."

"If it makes you feel better, we'll tell you that your feeling is not chauvinism," Derek said.

Agopian smiled. "My life has been built around socialism and Marxism and the Soviet Union. They are like coordinates. They give me a place in space and time. They give me a framework: moral, intellectual, historical, social, and personal.

"When I think of losing them—it's like being in space. Nothing is up or down. Nothing is near or far. There's only darkness and the stars. Then you turn and the ship's there or the Earth or a station. You are able to orient yourself. But what if you turned and saw nothing? Only more darkness and stars?

"There are no more countries on Earth or anywhere in the solar system. They have—the messages told us—abandoned outmoded categories such as 'nation.' They have abandoned outmoded categories such as 'socialism.' The ideas of the nineteenth century have a historical interest, but are no longer relevant. It is no longer possible to use the constructs of Marxism. They simply don't work. That is what the messages said."

He picked up his bottle of beer and shook it. "As far as I can tell, these people have no interest in any kind of system: political or economic or intellectual." He stood up. "I need another beer. What about you?"

"What about Ivanova?" Derek asked.

He listened for a moment. "Still going strong. In any case I have given you the important information. Do you want anything to drink?"

"Beer," said Derek.

Agopian went into the cabin.

"Is he telling the truth?" I asked.

Derek made the gesture of uncertainty.

Agopian came back and handed a bottle to each of us. He sat down and made a noise between a groan and a sigh.

I drank beer. "You said that you began by changing the history."

He nodded.

"What else did you change?"

"You don't have to worry about the personal messages. We did very little to them. Most came from the first two or three decades of our journey. Do you ever think about the people who sent the messages? Our friends. Our families. They knew the people on the ship were frozen. They knew when we awoke, they would be dead.

"Obviously, in time, most of them gave up. Five years. Ten years. Only the fanatics sent much after that. We had moved out of their history and out of the space they knew. We became unreal to them.

"Those messages represented no danger at all. They were chatty and informal, disorganized, full of family news, exactly what you'd expect from Mother or Sister. We had to take out a few references to historical events. Otherwise nothing."

He paused. "Some of the factual material was okay. Such and such star has just gone nova. We have discovered a new kind of life on Titan.

"But the theories! I told you these people have no interest in any kind of framework. That is problem number one. Number two is—they don't seem to distinguish between fact and fiction—or between material that is relevant and everything else. Some of the messages sound like poetry. Others are stories with no point that I can find. Others sound like gossip or like a group of proverbs. And others are a string of unrelated facts that don't even belong to the same discipline.

"And intermixed with everything is *junk*: stupid jokes and ancient legends and holographic pictures of who knows what? The families of strangers. A vacation hotel on Mars.

"These are the messages from the scientists! Half the time they sound like some crazy old lady you meet in the park who has a theory about astrology and history. Or like the man who comes to fix the plumbing and explains the true cause of the latest viral plague. 'It all comes from Titan. They got things up there ya wouldn't believe. Doncha watch the holo?

Listen to me, someday a bug's coming down—make AIDS look like nothing. Hand me the wrench.'"

Derek grinned.

"It isn't funny!

"We tried to turn those messages into something that made sense. To give them a theoretical framework, to fit them into a system. It wasn't easy. We had to defrost a few scientists, people we thought would be reliable. Even they had trouble—especially the physicists. They said the physics theory is absolutely crazy." He smiled. "But interesting, they said, though they were not comfortable with the randomness or the requirement that various gods intervene, usually at the beginning or end of the universe, though gods are—I think—also required in order to explain the behavior of certain kinds of particles."

"Why are you telling us this?" asked Derek.

Agopian drank more beer. "I have been thinking about the men who worked for Stalin, taking the old Bolsheviks out of the photographs one by one as they were purged.

"The people who did these things had good reasons. Maybe not good to you or me, but convincing to them. The revolution was isolated and in danger. It had to be defended against its enemies, who took every setback, every quarrel and flaw, and made it monstrous.

"They were trying to protect the revolution when they clipped Leon Trotsky out of *Ten Days That Shook the World*.

"The trouble is—they were wrong, and they helped to destroy the expedition."

"What?" I said.

"I mean the revolution."

Derek made the gesture that meant "you are absolutely nuts."

"What does that mean?" asked Agopian.

"You people are crazy."

Agopian nodded. "That's right. And that is what I'm going to tell Ivanova. It has to stop. I'm not entirely certain what she will do. I want other people to know what is going on."

"You think she will harm you?"

"Accidents happen. There were people on the crew who refused to go along with the plan. We froze them."

"Forcibly?" I asked.

He nodded.

"There is a two percent chance of irreversible major damage," I said. "That's on the first time a person is frozen. Every time after, the damage rate goes up."

He nodded again. "It's possible that I'm a murderer. I think about that a lot. I'm not against killing per se. There are times when it is justified. But I don't think this is one of those times."

He took another swallow of beer, then set the bottle down and leaned forward. "I want to give Ivanova a chance to—what? Turn herself in, I guess. I don't like the idea of being a fink. But I don't want to give her the chance to eliminate me."

"Are you serious about this? Do you really think you're in danger?"

"I think there's a possibility. Not large. There's no way for her to freeze me here. And I don't think she's likely to kill me. But we have been playing a lot of stupid games." He paused and tilted his head. "They're done talking. I'd better get back." He stood.

"Is this a moral issue?" asked Derek. "Have you decided that lying is wrong?"

Agopian grinned. "That's an unusual question for you to ask."

Derek waited.

Agopian said, "I do not like to think that I'd fit into the era of Joseph Stalin. And I don't think we can get away with it. There has been too much lying, and it has involved too many people. It's only a matter of time before somebody talks—or somebody figures out what has been going on." He walked to the railing, then turned and looked back. "I kept the messages. When people see them, they are not going to want to go home." He went over the railing and onto shore. A minute or so later I heard his voice, greeting someone on the other boat.

Derek said, "This is not a situation that can be handled with beer. This calls for wine. Or maybe brandy." He got up and collected the bottles and went into the cabin.

I sat quietly, listening to Agopian speaking in Russian. His voice was light and quick and fluent. Ivanova's rich contralto answered him. They were not talking about anything serious. I could tell that by the tone.

Derek came back with two glasses of wine. He gave me one.

"He isn't a practical joker, is he?" I asked.

"No. And I can't imagine that a compulsive liar would have gotten on the ship. I think we can assume he's telling the truth."

"Amazing!"

"It certainly is that." He sat down and leaned his shoulders into the chair. "It explains some oddities in the information from home."

"What are we going to do?" I asked.

"Drink this wine, then go to bed."

I frowned.

"He isn't going to have his confrontation tonight. Eddie is there and Mr. Fang. He'll want to get Ivanova alone." He drank a little wine. A bug with scarlet wings drifted down into the light. It landed on the rim of his wine glass. He smiled. The bug remained for a minute or so, waving its wings. Then it took off again, floating over the railing into the darkness above the river.

"I think—tomorrow—we had better tell Eddie. We owe him that. If Mesrop is right, the messages are going to change how people think about this planet. It's possible that we may be looking for a new home."

"Here?" I asked.

"Maybe. The trip home is over a hundred years. We'll be two and a half centuries out-of-date. Maybe things will have swung back by then. I doubt it. History may be a helix. It is not a circle. We never return to the place where we began."

"You sound like a Marxist."

He stood up, grinning. "Those sad out-of-date people?" He set down his glass. It was still half-full of wine. "Poor stupid Agopian! Good night."

He entered the cabin. I finished my drink, then followed him, shutting off the lights.

I undressed in darkness, unfolded a bed, and lay down. How could I sleep? I listened to the breathing of my companions and thought about home. The Free State of Hawaii. The Great Lakes Confederation. Alta California. Nuevo Mexico. Gone. All gone. The nations and tribes of North America.

I woke and found the cabin empty, got dressed and went outside. Eddie and Derek sat drinking coffee. There was a pot on the table and an empty cup. I filled the cup, then sat down.

A lovely morning! Clouds floated over the valley, bright in the early sunlight. The river was in shadow. It gleamed dark brown, like bronze.

"Where is the oracle?" I asked.

"Up at the village," Derek said. "He's getting food. Tatiana went with him. She wanted another look at the natives in situ."

I glanced at Eddie. His expression was unusually somber. "Have you told him?"

Derek made the gesture of affirmation.

"What are we going to do?"

Eddie said, "I'd like to keep the story quiet, but I don't think it's possible."

"You would?" I drank a little coffee, then leaned back in my chair. Was there any pleasure equal to coffee on a cool summer morning?

Well, yes. But this wasn't the time to make a list.

"If I understand correctly, Mesrop says we won't fit in on Earth. I think we are going to hear arguments in favor of staying here and establishing a colony." He paused. "They must have been crazy. It doesn't make sense to me. There was no way they could keep a secret that big. There was no way they could succeed in rewriting that much history." He paused again. "I think I can understand what Agopian is doing now. He's pushing us toward intervention."

I made the gesture of disagreement. "I don't think he's plotting. I think he's trying to get out of a plot."

"Maybe."

"Don't underestimate him," Derek said. "And never think he does anything for simple reasons. He's a dangerous man. He thinks ideas are important."

"Don't you?" I asked.

"Ideas are fine to play with in a university. But they don't have a lot to do with life. I can't imagine killing for any kind of abstraction. And I certainly would not sacrifice myself. Agopian would. He has."

Eddie said, "What are you and Derek going to do? That's what I want to know." I looked at him.

"Are you going to tell this story to the people at the camp?"

"No."

Eddie looked surprised—and hopeful, if I was reading his expression right.

"That's up to Agopian. If he decides to keep quiet, or if anything happens to him, Derek and I will tell. Otherwise, no."

"Scratch plan A," said Derek. "Which is to shut up Agopian in one way or another. Lixia, you're closer to the coffee."

I refilled his cup.

"There's no escape, Eddie. Agopian's going to make his big confession. And we're going to start to think about staying on this planet. He made Earth sound really unpleasant."

"He might be wrong," said Eddie. "Or lying. There's no reason to believe him."

I leaned forward. "He kept copies of the messages. The original ones. The data is—are—there."

"He must have the biggest personal file on the ship," said Derek.

"He could have altered those messages. Maybe they're the fake ones."

Derek said, "You're suggesting that Agopian's story is a lie, and that he has been spending his spare time creating a fake history of Earth—which he'll now present as the real, suppressed history."

"Why not?" asked Eddie.

"It's a wonderful paranoid fantasy. But when we start looking, we're going to find his instructions to the comm system. We'll delete them and then we'll start to get messages that have not been changed. There's no way Agopian can fix the information that's still in transit. He may have been able to change the past. He can't change the future."

Eddie shook his head. "I still don't understand why they did it. If Agopian is telling the truth."

"Why did you ask us to change what Ivanova said when we translated for her?" I asked.

He looked angry. After a moment he said, "I will do what I have to, to keep the people here from suffering the way my people have suffered."

366

"They were trying to save the expedition," Derek said. "And—I think—
they were trying to save what they could from the past. They didn't want us
to lose what had been lost on Earth." He stood up. "I think it's time for
breakfast." He went into the cabin.

Eddie and I sat in silence, drinking coffee.

Derek came back out with muffins, butter, jam, and a fresh pot of coffee.
We ate. When we were done, Eddie stood. "I'm going to talk to Ivanova
and Mr. Fang. We have to decide when we're going to leave."

I gathered the dishes and took them to the galley, washed up and went
back on deck. Derek had gone off somewhere. My early morning happiness
had disappeared. Now I felt tense and a bit depressed. I wasn't looking forward to going back to camp. There was going to be a truly enormous fight. I
liked Agopian. Now he had turned into someone I didn't recognize. I had
thought I knew my planet's history. But it was changing and vanishing—like
what? Fog or mist. My past was burning off.

I decided to go up to the village.

It felt different today. There was an undercurrent of tension. Nothing I
could point to exactly. Something in the way that people moved, something
in the way they spoke or didn't speak.

It made me uncomfortable. I went to the edge of the village and wandered
there, avoiding people and watching the bugs in the vegetation. The day
grew hot. The air smelled of dung and the dry plain. Now and then the wind
blew the odor of wood smoke to me.

> So much beauty!
> So much beauty!
> Why do we waste our time?

I did my yoga, looking out at the plain, then turned and saw a dozen children. There were little ones like cubs—round and fat and naked except for
their fur—and lanky ones like colts—edgy, full of energy, ready to run. These
last wore clothes: faded tunics and ragged kilts. Play clothes.

One of the older children asked, "What are you doing?"

I didn't know the word for "exercise" or the word for "meditation."

"I am pulling out my body and pulling in my mind."

"Hu! You are strange!"

"That might be."

I asked them their names. They told me. They asked me when I was leaving. I said I didn't know.

"Tell us before you go," said one. "We want to go down to the river and
see your boats that move on their own."

367

Another one—a little one—said, "Like fishes! Like lizards!"

"All right."

I walked back through the village. The children accompanied me. They were silent most of the time. Now and then one would speak.

"That is my mother's tent."

"I shot a bird with my new bow."

"What is it like to have no hair?"

"Cool," I said. "I am able to feel the wind."

"But in the winter, you must be cold."

I made the gesture of agreement.

"I'd rather have fur."

We reached the far side of the village, and the children gestured farewell.

Agopian was on my boat, sitting on the deck. Derek and Eddie and Ivanova sat with him.

I climbed onboard.

"We were waiting for you," Derek said.

Agopian said, "It's done."

"I am not happy with Mesrop's precautions," Ivanova said. "He's acting as if I am some kind of criminal."

Agopian looked up. "Elizaveta, we have broken laws."

"For good reasons."

"That is something I'm having trouble understanding," I said. "What were the reasons? And where is the beer?"

"The usual place," said Derek. "Get one for me and Agopian."

When I came back out Ivanova said, "You will understand when you hear the messages. Socialism does not mean a reduction of everything to the lowest common denominator. It means giving people the freedom to achieve their full potential. It means a lifting of humanity. An ennobling." She paused. "How long did it take us? Four centuries? Two hundred years of struggle to end that horrible system and two hundred years of hard work to clean up the mess that it left behind. How many people died of hunger or were poisoned by all the different kinds of pollution? Have you ever looked at the statistics on starvation and disease?

"How many people were murdered because they wanted a union or a free election? Or something very simple. The right to decide whom they were going to love. The right to decide how many children they were going to bear.

"All that suffering—those generations of struggle." She had been looking down. Now she lifted her head. There were lines in her face that I didn't remember.

"We thought we had won. When we left Earth, when we began this journey, it seemed that humanity was about to achieve a golden age. A true socialist society.

"We woke at the edge of this system and found—I don't know how to describe it."

"Garbage," said Agopian. "It's as if the lowest and worst human thinking had become predominant. It really is awful, Lixia."

"You rewrote the messages because you didn't like them," I said. "History hadn't turned out the way you wanted it to. So you tried to remake it. Undo it."

"No," said Ivanova.

Agopian said, "Maybe."

Ivanova frowned at him, then looked at me. "What is going to happen next?"

"We'll go back to camp, and you and Agopian will tell your story."

She looked at Eddie. "Do you think this is a good idea?"

"No. But I can't see any way to shut up Lixia and Derek and Agopian."

"There isn't any way," I said. "I won't go along with a lie of this magnitude."

Agopian looked at me. He seemed a little drunk. "You are tougher than I am, Lixia, and more in love with abstractions. Truth. Beauty. Integrity. You'll destroy us all for those words."

"You are in no position to criticize," Ivanova said.

I looked at Eddie. "When are we leaving?"

"Tomorrow. Early. You and Derek ought to go up to the village and say good-bye formally."

Derek made the gesture of disagreement. "Angai said no more men. I think she's serious."

"The oracle is up there."

"He's holy. I'm not. I'm taking Angai at her word."

"I'll go up," I said. "After lunch and after a swim. Does anyone want to come with me?"

"Swimming?" asked Derek.

"To the village."

"I will," said Ivanova. "If Eddie thinks it's all right."

"I think we'll put off arresting anyone until we're back in camp. I don't know the procedure, and I don't really want to call and ask. It'd lead to a lot of questions." Eddie looked around. "Do the rest of you agree?"

Derek and I nodded.

Ivanova said, "I think I'll refrain from voting on this question."

Agopian nodded. "I'm abstaining, too."

"You might as well go," Eddie said to Ivanova.

"Thank you."

Derek and I made sandwiches. We ate, and I went for a swim. The water was cool. The river washed away a lot of my tension. I felt like floating down it, away from the village and the boats, away from all these people and their arguments. Of course, if I went far enough, I'd float into the middle of the lizard migration. I swam back and climbed onboard, grabbed a towel and tucked it around me.

Tatiana was back, sitting on the rear deck with Ivanova and Agopian. There was a bowl of fruit on the folding table next to her. Oranges, bananas, and bright green apples. A heap of orange peelings lay next to the bowl. The air was full of the aroma of orange.

Tatiana spoke in Russian, quickly and eagerly.

"What happened to the oracle?" I asked.

She glanced at me. "He stayed in the village. He was with someone. A large person with reddish fur in plain clothes."

Nia.

I went into the cabin and got dressed.

When I came out, Ivanova stood up. We climbed the bluff together.

There were children outside the village. They were standing facing the wind, holding their hands out, the palms forward.

"What are you doing?" I asked.

"You told us you could feel the wind. Our palms have no hair. We are feeling the wind and trying to understand what it would be like to feel that way all over."

I translated for Ivanova. She laughed. "They will have no trouble. It is the adults who'll be afraid and fight change."

The children stayed at the edge of the village, playing their game of pretending to be hairless. Ivanova and I walked to the main square. Angai was there, sitting under her awning. Nia and the oracle were with her.

I made the gesture of greeting.

Angai made the gesture that meant "sit down and stay awhile."

We seated ourselves in the shadow of the awning. The wind blew dust around the square.

"We are leaving in the morning," I said.

"Good," said Angai. "When you are gone, people will stop worrying. After a while this visit will seem like a dream to them or like a story told by an old woman about something that happened a long time ago. Then you will be able to return. They will be less frightened the second time. But remember—when you come, bring only women and make sure they are clever and sensible."

I translated for Ivanova.

She said, "Give Angai our thanks. Tell her, we will do as she asks. Tell her, when we come again we will bring many gifts and stories and no men."

I told Angai.

She made the gesture of acknowledgment. "I think this will turn out well, though I should not have gotten angry last night. Now I will have to find a way to make Anhar happy.

"Go now and take the oracle. I will ask the spirits to take care of you."

I made the gesture of gratitude. "That's it," I said to Ivanova. "She wants us out of the village."

We stood. So did the oracle. He had a big lumpy leather bag: his food.

I looked at Nia. "What about you?"

"I will stay here for another day or so. Then I plan to go north and visit Tanajin."

"After that?" I asked.

She made the gesture of uncertainty, stood up and hugged me. A tight hard hug that left me breathless.

"Come to our village," I said.

She made the gesture that meant "maybe."

"Go," said Angai.

The oracle started off. Ivanova and I followed.

When we reached the children again, they were playing with a ball. So much for the game of hairlessness.

I said, "We're leaving in the morning. Close to dawn, I think. Come down then if you want to see our boats."

"We will," one of the children said.

We walked to the edge of the bluff. Ivanova stopped and looked back at the village and the plain.

"Come on," the oracle said.

"The oracle is impatient," I said.

"I want to remember this."

She stood for another minute or two. The oracle fidgeted. I waved him on. Finally she looked at me. "I have not been especially clever in the last year. But I am not stupid. I have a good idea of what is going to happen to Mesrop and me."

She went down the bluff, following the oracle.

They would be tried for crimes against democracy and for endangering the lives of the people they had frozen. Maybe for murder. We had no provision for rehabilitation and no place to send people who had committed serious crimes. The only thing we could do was freeze them until we returned to Earth or until our colony had evolved far enough to have a really advanced psychotherapeutic facility or a prison.

This might be the last time that Ivanova saw a native village or a landscape like this one. I took another look at the windy plain and the children chasing their ball. Then I followed Ivanova down the bluff.

Nia

The hairless people left in the morning. The people of the village began packing in the afternoon. Nia helped Angai, but only with the things in the front room of the tent. The back room was the place where Angai kept her magic. Everything there was hidden by a curtain of red cloth embroidered with animals and spirits. The curtain went across the tent from top to bottom and side to side. Nothing came through it except the aroma of dry herbs and the feeling of magic. The feeling made Nia's skin itch and prickle.

She stayed as far from the curtain as possible, kneeling by the front door in the afternoon sunlight, folding clothing, and putting it in a chest made of leather.

On the other side of the room Hua knelt. She was right next to the curtain, below a picture of a spirit: an old man, naked, with his sexual member clearly visible. His back was hunched, and he leaned on a cane. The Dark One, thought Nia, in one of her many disguises.

Hua had laid out tools and was counting them before she packed them: knives of many sizes, needles, spoons made of polished wood and horn.

Angai was behind the curtain, packing up whatever she kept there, objects that Nia did not want to see.

"How can you bear to stay here?" Nia asked.

Hua looked up and made the gesture of inquiry.

"By the curtain. In this tent."

Hua repeated the gesture of inquiry.

"Nia has never liked magic," Angai said.

"It doesn't bother me," Hua said.

"A good thing," said Nia. "If you are going to be the next shamaness."

"Of course I am," said Hua. "Who else is there?" She was counting combs now. She laid them out, big ones and little ones, made of wood and horn and metal.

Nia realized her entire skin was itching. The feeling was especially bad between her shoulder blades and along her spine. "Keep some of those out. It's a long time since I've had a grooming done the proper way—by a friend or a female relative."

"All right," said Hua. She put two of the combs aside: one of ordinary size and a big one with wide gaps between the teeth.

Nia made a satisfied noise. "It will be something to remember when I am out on the plain."

"Aren't you coming with us?" asked Hua. Her voice sounded sharp and high.

"No."

"Why not? Has someone been giving you trouble? You aren't worried about Anhar, are you? Hasn't Angai told you that you can stay?"

Nia laid a tunic on the floor. It had long sleeves. She folded them in over the body of the tunic, smoothing the fabric. It was fine and soft, a gift from people living in the distant south.

"When I lived in the Iron Hills, I was with you and Anasu and Enshi. When I lived in the east, I was at the edge of the village, as far out as a man. I'm not used to being with a lot of people. I no longer know how to live in a village."

"You never really knew," said Angai through the curtain. "You always acted as if you were alone."

Nia felt surprised. She made the gesture that asked "is that really true?" But Angai couldn't see, of course.

Hua said, "My mother wants to know if you are certain."

"Yes." The curtain fluttered. Angai must have brushed against it. "I know you better than anyone, Nia. You are like a rock! You are like an arrow! You are what you are, and nothing can change you. You go where you go, and nothing can make you turn. You have never been an ordinary person."

"I didn't know that," said Nia.

Hua said, "I wanted you to stay with us. I wanted to hear your stories."

"I'm not going away forever. But I need time alone."

Angai said, "This is the right decision. I'd like Nia to stay. But I've seen the way the people of the village look at her. She makes them uneasy. If she goes, they will settle down after a while. Then—I think—she will be able to come back. But if she stays now, they will get angry. Too much has happened. They have seen too much that is new. If she stays now, they will drive her off."

Hua made the gesture of regret.

They kept working until the sky began to darken. Angai came out from behind the curtain. They ate dinner. Angai combed Nia's fur. Aiya! It felt good! Especially when Angai combed the thick fur on her back. She leaned against the comb—the big one—and groaned with pleasure.

When that was done, they talked for a while. Nothing important was said. Angai described the trail that she wanted to follow going south and the place she wanted to spend the winter. Nia asked a question now and then. Hua listened in silence.

At last they went to sleep. Nia kept waking. The tent door was open. But there was little wind. The air in the tent was motionless and warm. She looked out the door. There were stars above the tents of her former neighbors. So many! So thick and bright!

They got up at dawn and began to load the wagon. Anasu brought the wagon-pullers in: six fine bowhorn geldings. They hitched them up. The sky was clear. The day was going to be hot. Nia could feel it.

Angai said, "I'd like you to go back out and get an animal for Nia. White Spot or Sturdy or Broken Horn, whichever you find."

"Why does she need one?" asked Anasu. "I thought she was going to ride in the wagon."

"She is leaving us," Hua said.

"Why?"

"She wants to be alone."

"Aiya! What a family I have!" He turned his bowhorn and rode away.

Nia asked, "Is he angry?"

"Maybe a little," Hua said. "It has not been easy having you for a mother, even though Angai has protected us."

Nia made the gesture of apology.

"It could have been worse," Hua said. "We could have had Anhar for a mother. Or Ti-antai. A malicious woman. A woman who is a coward."

"Is that what you think about Ti-antai?"

"Maybe she isn't a coward," Hua said. "Maybe she has a little mind. She never thinks about anything except her children and their children and the neighbors."

"Isn't that enough?"

"Not for me," said Hua. "I am going to be a shamaness."

"Then you can help me now," said Angai. "I have many boxes full of magical objects, and they have to go into the wagon. Nia isn't going to touch them. I know that."

Hua grimaced and made the gesture of assent.

After the magic was loaded, they took down the tent. Nia helped. They loaded it into the wagon. By noon they were ready to go, and so was the rest of the village. Nia looked around. There wasn't a tent anywhere in sight. Instead there were wagons and bowhorns, women lifting boxes, children running. A few wagons had begun to move. A cloud of dust hung in midair to the west of the village.

Anasu came back, leading a bowhorn: a large young gelding. There was a large white mark in the middle of its chest. The mark was curved like a bow. The grip was at the bottom. The two arms of the bow rose up on either side. The mark reminded Nia of other things as well: the emblem for "pot," the emblem for "boat," and the Great Moon when it was thin. If Angai had the animal, it must be lucky—though it worried Nia to look at the mark and see so many things.

"It's five years old," said Angai. "There is no better traveler in the herd. Be careful, though. Sometimes, not often, it gets a little edgy."

"I have nothing to give in return," said Nia.

"You told me about the hairless people. You gave me good advice."

Nia made the gesture that meant "it was nothing."

"It is enough," said Angai.

Hua held out a pair of saddlebags. "This is for you. I've put in everything you ought to have. My mother—the friend of the shamaness—cannot go out onto the plain with nothing."

Nia took the bags and fastened them to her animal. There was a peculiar feeling in her chest.

Anasu twisted around and unfastened the cloak that lay behind his saddle. "This is for you also. A parting gift, though I have never heard of a boy giving one to his mother."

"The gift the boy gives is his life on the plain," said Angai. "He watches the herd. He guides it and guards it. That is enough. That balances the gifts his kinfolk give."

A true shamaness! thought Nia. She always had an answer. She was always ready to teach and explain.

She took the cloak. It was made of gray wool tufted on one side, so that it seemed like the pelt of an animal. Two brooches were fastened to it, large and made of silver. One was in the shape of a bowhorn lying down, its legs folded. The other was in the shape of a killer of the plain. A silver chain went between the brooches.

375

Anasu said, "It's a good cloak. You won't have to worry about rain as long as you have it. And you won't be cold even in the winter."

She fastened the cloak on top of the saddlebags, then mounted and looked at the three of them: the boy on his bowhorn, Angai and Hua standing in the middle of a patch of vegetation. Her hand felt numb. She could not move it. There were no words in her throat or mind.

"Always the same!" her friend told her. "There are things that you have never been able to say."

"I have never liked the moment of parting." She made the gesture of gratitude and the gesture of farewell, then turned her animal and rode away.

The entire village was in motion now, heading west. She guided her animal among the wagons, going in the opposite direction. The air was full of dust. Women shouted. Children yelled. Bowhorns made the grunting noise that meant they were working hard and not liking it.

> "Huh-nuh! Huh-nuh!
> Why are we doing this?
> We ought to be running
> free on the plain."

She reached the end of the village. There was nothing ahead except the rutted trail and the droppings of bowhorns. The droppings were fresh and shiny black. She reined White Spot for a moment. There was something else that she had not told Angai. When the parting was over, when the people were gone, she began—always—to feel happy. Aiya! To be traveling! Aiya! To be alone!

She was not sitting properly. Her back was curved, and her shoulder went down as if she carried a heavy load. Nia straightened herself and pushed her chest out. That was better. Now her lungs had room.

A voice said, "I have something to tell you, and I didn't want Angai to hear."

She looked back. It was Anasu. His animal breathed heavily through its open mouth.

She made the gesture of inquiry.

"I am planning to visit the hairless people—this winter, before I go through the change."

"Why?"

"Nothing like this has ever happened. There are no hairless people in any of the old stories and no boats like the one I rode on and certainly no men who live with women. This is utterly new. I want to see it, Nia! I want to understand.

"If I wait—who knows what will happen? Maybe I will turn into one of those men who can endure no one, not even women in the time for mating. Maybe I'll go crazy."

376

"That doesn't happen in our family," Nia said.

Anasu made the gesture of uncertainty. "And if everything goes well, if the change is perfectly ordinary, I will end up in the south. I've heard about that place! No women get down there. No one brings any information. The big men get everything, and the young men sit and wonder—what is going on in the rest of the world?"

Nia grunted and looked at her son. In the sunlight his dark fur gleamed, and there was—she could see now—a little red in it. Like copper, like his uncle Anasu.

"Be careful," she told him.

"Of course. I'm not a fool. I'll do nothing to get myself in trouble. I don't intend to end up like Enshi or like you."

"Be polite as well."

The boy made the gesture of assent. "If you come to the village of the hairless people—in the winter, not before—I'll be there."

"Most likely I will come," she said.

He made the gesture of satisfaction and the gesture of farewell and turned his animal away.

She rode north all day, following the trail of the village. In evening she made camp by a stream. A trickle of water ran down the middle of a wide sandy bed. It was enough. Nia watered her animal and then gathered wood from the bushes along the stream. She made a fire. There was food in the saddlebags: dried fruit and hard, dry travel-bread.

Hu! It was comfortable to sit and watch the flames dance red and yellow. White Spot was nearby. Nia heard the crunching of vegetation and the gurgle of the fluid in the bowhorn's stomach.

Out on the plain a *tulpa* cried, "Oop-oop. Oop-oop."

Nia listened for a while, then went to sleep.

She followed the trail of the village for two more days. On the morning of the third day she came to another trail, this one narrow and deep. Travelers had made it. They never used wagons. Instead they led strings of bowhorns loaded down with fine gifts from the Amber People and the People of Fur and Tin. Nia turned east, following the new trail. She traveled for another day. The weather stayed the same: hot and bright and clear. Hu! It was boring! She made up poems. She wondered what had happened to the oracle and Li-sa and Deragu. Were they back in their village? What about her children? Would they be all right? Would they be happy?

Angai had done a good job raising them. Why hadn't she praised her friend? Why hadn't she told Hua and Anasu, "You are good children"?

Toward evening there was a noise like thunder: loud and sharp. White Spot broke into a run.

377

Nia pulled on the reins. The animal did not stop. Instead it plunged off the trail into the vegetation. Nia kept pulling. The animal ran until they came to a stand of blade-leaf. It rose over both of them. The animal reared, then came down on all fours, shaking and snorting and sweating like one of the hairless people.

"This is no way to act," said Nia. "Be safe! Be happy! There is nothing to harm you." Nia stroked the animal's neck, then looked around. The sky was empty. "I've heard that before," she told the bowhorn. "It means that an island has fallen into Long Lake."

The animal shook its head, snorting again. Nia turned it back toward the trail.

At twilight she came to the river valley. She made camp on top of a bluff, and in the morning she rode down through a narrow ravine. Vines covered the walls, their leaves as red as copper. The air smelled of dust and dry vegetation.

At the bottom of the ravine the land was flat and covered with forest. She continued east. The trail was dry, but she could see that a lot of it would be underwater in the spring. Logs had been laid down in the low places and dirt piled over the logs, so the trail was raised. Aiya! What a construction! She had never seen anything like it before. Who had done it? Tanajin? Or some of the travelers? It was a good gift. Many people would praise it.

In the middle of the afternoon she came to the river. Brown water ran through a narrow channel. On the other side of the channel was an island. There was a raft pulled up on the shore of the island between the river and the trees.

Nia dismounted. The ground around her was covered with ashes and pieces of burnt wood. There were footprints in the dirt—people and bowhorns—and heaps of dung. All the dung was old.

She took care of her animal, then gathered wood and built a fire. Dead wood first. Not the rotten pieces that bugs had eaten. Good dry pieces, solid, with nothing on them except patches of the red scale plant. When the fire was burning really well, Nia added living wood. That made smoke. It rose up like the trunk of a tree, thick and dark.

Nothing happened for the rest of the day. She kept the fire burning. At night she slept close to it and woke several times to add wood. Anything could be in the forest: lizards as big as the *umazi*, killers with sharp claws, *osupai* or *tulpai*. The plain was better. She liked to see what was coming after her.

In the morning she gathered more wood. Her food was almost gone. She got the fire burning well, then sat down and waited. Her body was stiff. Her mind felt like an iron pot: heavy and empty.

In the middle of the day a person emerged from the forest on the island. She pushed the raft into the water and climbed onto it. A forked stick was fastened to the side of the raft. The person fitted a long paddle into the fork of the stick.

378

The raft drifted out into the river. The person began to move in a way that Nia did not understand at first: bending and straightening. The paddle rose and fell. Water dripped from the wide long blade.

Up and down. In and out of the water. After a while Nia could see what was happening. The paddle was driving the raft. Instead of going downstream with the current, it went across.

Slow work! And hard! Nia watched, feeling restless. It was never easy to sit with empty hands when other people were doing something useful. She got up and moved to the edge of the water.

The raft was close. The person on it was Tanajin. She glanced at Nia, but made no gesture of recognition. Instead she kept the paddle in motion. In spite of all her effort, the raft was drifting downstream. It would come to shore below Nia.

She walked along the bank, then took off her sandals and waded in. "What can I do?" she called.

Tanajin bent and grabbed something. "Here!" She tossed it.

A rope. It unwound in midair and fell into the water. Nia grabbed one end. The other end was fastened to the raft.

"Pull!" said Tanajin.

She wound the rope around her forearm till the slack was gone, then spread her feet and dug her toes into the muddy bottom, got a good grip on the rope and pulled.

Hunh!

The raft slowed.

Hunh!

The raft stopped.

Hunh!

The raft began to turn.

Tanajin swung the paddle out of the water. It stayed up, held by the forked stick, though Nia couldn't tell exactly how. Then she jumped in the river. Aiya! The splash! She was chest-deep in water, leaning against the raft and pushing hard. Nia kept pulling. The two of them grunted like bowhorns. The raft came to shore.

They climbed out of the water. Tanajin took the rope and fastened it around a tree. "Where is Ulzai?" she asked. "He didn't come back."

Nia made the gesture that meant "I don't know."

Tanajin made the gesture of inquiry.

"A lizard followed us into the rapids. Ulzai stood up to confront it. Something happened. I don't know what exactly. The boat went over. We all . . ." She closed her hand into a fist, then opened it. The gesture meant "scattered" or "gone."

379

"Ai!" said Tanajin.

"The lizard was not an *umazi*. Ulzai got a good look at the animal. He said it was nothing out of the ordinary. He told us about his dream. The *umazi* promised him they would be his death."

"What about the hairless people?" asked Tanajin. "And the crazy man? Did they drown?"

Nia made the gesture that meant "no." "There is a new village on the lake. Hairless people built it, and it looks like no other village I have ever seen. Lisa and Deragu are there. So is the oracle. I came to fix your pot."

Tanajin made the gesture that meant "let's get on with it."

They walked to Nia's camp. The fire was almost out. Tanajin kicked the branches apart. Was she crazy? Her feet were bare. She certainly looked angry. She was frowning, and the fur on her brow ridges came so far down that her eyes were hidden.

Nia saddled White Spot, moving carefully and making as little noise as possible. She led the animal to the raft and on. It wasn't easy. The animal shivered and snorted. "This is no way for a gelding to behave," said Nia. "Be calm! Don't act like a male!" The animal flicked its ears. Its tail quivered, but did not lift. That was a good sign. The animal was uneasy, but not really afraid. Not ready to show white and flee. Nia kept hold of the bridle and made soothing noises.

Tanajin untied the rope. She pushed off, using the paddle.

The raft moved gently. It was made of logs tied together. The rope wasn't the kind made on the plain, woven out of long narrow pieces of leather. This rope was made of a hairy fiber. Nia had seen its like in the east. The Copper People used it for making nets. It came from the distant south.

How many kinds of people were there? How many kinds of gifts?

They drifted toward the middle of the river. White Spot snorted and stamped a foot. Nia rubbed the furry neck. She looked back. There was a lizard in the river between them and the western shore. A big one, heading south.

Aiya! Nia tugged at the bridle, turning the head of the bowhorn, making certain that White Spot couldn't see. "Have there been many of those?" she asked.

Tanajin glanced up. "Lizards? Yes."

She went back to paddling. When they reached the island, she spoke again. "I see the lizards when I bring people across the river. They like to travel along this side. The water moves slowly, and there are marshes where they can hunt. The lizard that went after you was behaving very strangely."

"It was following blood," said Nia. "The oracle had an injury. He was bleeding into the water."

"He is the cause!"

Nia made the gesture of disagreement. "I think it goes further back. I think it was the spirits in the cave."

Tanajin made the gesture of inquiry.

Nia told her about the cave with pictures on the walls. "It was full of spirits, the oracle said. They were hungry. He fed them. But they were not satisfied. They wanted more blood. This is my opinion, anyway. I don't know for certain."

"It's too complicated for me," said Tanajin. "I need a shamaness. Maybe I ought to go and find one."

They pulled the raft out of the water and left it there, crossing the island on foot. Noisy birds filled the trees. The ground was covered with droppings: red and purple and white.

On the far side of the island was another raft. They used it to cross another channel.

The same thing happened. They pulled the raft onto the shore. They crossed the island. They found another raft.

"How much of this is there going to be?" asked Nia.

Tanajin made the gesture of ending or completion. "This is the last channel. There is no good way around the islands and if I try to cross the river all at once, the raft drifts too far down. I know. I have tried it."

Nia said, "The hairless people have a boat that moves by itself as if it had legs or fins."

"Is it magic?"

"No. It is driven by fire, though I don't understand how."

Tanajin made the gesture of amazement. But she didn't look amazed. Instead she looked tired.

They crossed the last channel. By this time the sun was gone, but the sky was still full of light. The air was almost motionless. It smelled of the river and of the bowhorn, which had dropped a heap of dung on the logs near Tanajin.

"Mind your animal," the woman said.

"I'm doing my best."

They reached the shore and pulled up the raft. The sky darkened. They walked north along the river till they came to Tanajin's house.

Nia took White Spot around back. She unsaddled the gelding and tied it, using a leather rope. The other two bowhorns were there, grazing on the short vegetation. She went around front. Tanajin had built a fire.

They ate without speaking. When they were done Tanajin went into her tent. She brought out a blanket. "I don't want you in my house, Nia. I am angry at the news you've brought. Why is Ulzai the only person who hasn't reappeared?"

Nia made the gesture of uncertainty.

Tanajin went inside.

Nia lay down. Bugs hummed around her. They bit her in the places where her fur was thin: at the edges of her hands, on the tops of her ears. She pulled the blanket up till it covered all of her and dreamed of being trapped in a dark place: a cave or a forest. There were people around her, moving and speaking. She couldn't see them and their language was not one she knew.

She woke at dawn. Tanajin came out and rebuilt the fire. They ate porridge.

Tanajin said, "I dreamed about Ulzai. His clothes were soaked. Water dripped off his fur. He spoke to me. I could not understand his words."

"I dreamed also," said Nia.

"About what?"

"Darkness. Being trapped. And people. I don't know which people. They spoke. I could not understand them."

"These are bad dreams. We need a ceremony of aversion." Tanajin frowned. "There are times I think this is no way to live. I have no female relatives. I have no shamaness. Now even Ulzai is gone."

Nia made the gesture of polite agreement. "You said you have tools. I am going to begin setting up a place to work."

Tanajin made the gesture of acknowledgment.

She built a forge downriver from the tent. It took nine days of hard work. The weather stayed the same. There were bugs every night. Tanajin gathered living wood and put it on the fire. The smoke drove away most of the bugs. Nia was too exhausted to mind the ones that remained.

Every morning she was stiff, but the stiffness wore off. The real problem was her hands. Blisters formed on the palms where the calluses had gotten thin. The blisters broke. The flesh beneath was red and tender. She wrapped pieces of fabric between her fingers and over the palms. Aiya! How clumsy that made her! She kept working.

"You don't have to hurry," said Tanajin.

"I like it. I understand what I am doing. It has been a long time since I've been able to say that." She paused, trying to think of a way to explain. "This is the thing I do. This is my gift."

Tanajin made the gesture of dubious comprehension.

The day that the forge was completed, something odd happened. A cloud appeared. No. A trail of smoke. It rose out of the south, going diagonally west, forming with amazing rapidity. Not like any smoke that Nia had ever seen. Up and up it went. Nia shaded her eyes. Was there something at the tip of the cloud? Something leaving the trail of smoke? That was hardly likely.

She listened. There was no sound of thunder and nothing in the sky except the trail, which had risen so high that she could no longer see the end of it.

382

"Huh!" She went back to work.

In the evening she went back to the house of Tanajin. The woman sat by her fire, cooking fish stew in a pot that hung from a tripod.

"What was that about?" she asked Nia.

"The cloud? I'm not certain. But the hairless people are south of here." Nia scratched her nose. "I wonder how many islands there are in the lake. I wish I had a talking box. I'd ask the oracle or Li-sa."

Tanajin made the gesture of inquiry.

Nia told her about the islands that fell out of the sky. "They come down with noise. Maybe they go up with smoke."

Tanajin made the gesture of doubt. "Many things fall out of the sky. Rain of different colors, snow, hail, pieces of iron and stone. I've never heard of anything going back up again. Only smoke rises."

Nia made the gesture that meant "you aren't thinking about what you are saying." "When the fire demons are active, the mountains throw up stones, and they can travel long distances. Ash rises at the same time, and fire."

"You think these people are a kind of demon?"

"No. I think they have tools that are nothing like our tools, and strange things happen around them."

Tanajin made the gesture of courteous doubt. "I am willing to believe that mountains cough up stones, though I have never seen one do it. I am not willing to believe that a lake can spit islands into the sky."

The next day Nia began to repair the tools that belonged to Tanajin. Travelers came from the east: eight women who belonged to the People of Fur and Tin.

Tanajin ferried them across the river. It took her two days. When she got back, she said, "They have come from visiting the Amber People. A bad visit! Everyone there is quarreling. A ceremony has been ruined. They have been accusing one another."

Nia shivered and made the gesture to avert bad consequences.

Tanajin went on. "They saw the cloud in the south. I told them about the hairless people. I said I knew the people existed. I had seen them. But I hadn't seen any islands fall out of the sky. That news came from Nia the Smith, I told them."

"You told them my name?"

Tanajin made the gesture that meant "don't worry." "I said you came from the east. They do not realize you are the woman who loved a man."

"That's good," said Nia.

She continued to work on Tanajin's belongings. The weather continued bright and hot. Late summer weather. The ground was dry, even close to the river. On the plain everything would be covered with dust. The village—traveling—would send up great dark clouds.

At night many arrows flashed out of the pattern of stars called the Great Wagon. That was ordinary. Those arrows came at the end of every summer. The Little Boys Who Never Grow Up were riding in their mother's wagon, shooting their bows. Aiya! When she caught them!

Nia finished with Tanajin's pots and began on her own gear: bridle bits, the rings on saddles, knives that needed sharpening, awls that would not punch through anything. Tanajin had a coil of iron wire. Nia made needles.

Now and then she saw clouds of the new kind: long and narrow. Usually they were in the south or southwest. They formed rapidly like the first cloud, and they were the same shape, but they didn't rise to the peak of the sky. Instead they were horizontal. It was easiest to see them in the evening. The sun lit them from below. They shone like colored banners: red, yellow, purple, orange, pink. Sometimes Nia thought she could make out the glint of metal. The thing that glinted was always at the front end of the cloud, at the place where the cloud began.

She worked and thought. After a while she got an idea. It seemed crazy to her. There was only one thing to do with a crazy idea. Tell it. Only men kept quiet when something was bothering them. Or women who were doing or thinking something that was shameful.

Nia spoke to Tanajin.

"The clouds are in the south, where the hairless people are. They are new, and the clouds are new. Therefore they are responsible."

"Maybe."

"I told you about their boats. The boats leave a trail in the water. The trail is white. It forms rapidly and then vanishes. Maybe the clouds are trails as well."

"In the sky?" said Tanajin. "Don't be ridiculous. First you said these people are able to fling stones around like demons. Now you say they can float in the sky like spirits. How likely is any of this?"

Nia made the gesture of concession. "Not very."

"You have spent too much time alone, Nia. You are getting crazy ideas."

Nia made the gesture that meant "yes."

Travelers came from the west and built a signal fire. Tanajin went to get them: five large morose women. Their tunics had brightly colored vertical stripes. Their saddlebags were different from anything Nia had ever seen before: large baskets made of some kind of plant fiber and striped horizontally.

The women spoke with thick accents. They belonged to the Finely Woven Basket People, they said. A boat had come to their village out of the sky.

"Huh!" said Tanajin.

"I say it was a boat because it carried people." The travel leader spoke. She was the largest of the women with a belly that made her look pregnant. But pregnant women did not usually travel. Maybe she was fat. Nia didn't know a polite way to ask.

"It didn't look like any boat I have seen. It looked like the birds that our neighbors make to hang on standards. The birds are gold. Their bodies are fat. Their wings are long and narrow. They have eyes made of various kinds of crystal."

Another woman said, "This thing—this boat—had two large eyes in front that shone like crystal. There were other eyes—little ones—that went along the sides. Hu! It was peculiar."

The travel leader frowned.

The other woman made the gesture that was an apology for interrupting.

The travel leader said, "The people in the boat had almost no fur. One of them spoke the language of gifts, though very badly. This person said they wanted to come and visit and exchange stories."

Tanajin looked at Nia. "You weren't crazy."

"What does that mean?" asked the travel leader.

"There have been clouds in the sky. This woman said they were caused by boats that belonged to the hairless people."

"How did you know?" asked a woman.

Nia said, "Finish your story. I will tell you later."

"We didn't know what to do," said the travel leader. "Our shamaness decided to ask for advice. She sent us to the Amber People to ask for their opinion. Another group has gone to the Iron People and another to the People of Fur and Tin.

"We have a quarrel going with the Gold People. They're our closest neighbors. They have tongues like knives and they like to make up satiric poetry. We aren't going to ask them for anything."

"Also," said another woman, "they live in the high mountains. We don't like going there. Hu! It is dark! The trail goes up and down!"

"We are people of the plain," said the leader. "We like to be able to see all the way to the horizon."

Nia made the gesture of agreement. "The Iron People have agreed to let the hairless people visit. I don't know what the Amber People have decided."

"That is how you know," said the travel leader. "You have seen these people."

"Yes," said Nia. "But I had not seen the kind of boat you describe."

The women asked questions. Nia said as little as possible. She didn't want to describe the long journey from the east. She didn't want to explain why she hadn't been living with her own people.

"It's obvious that you know more than you are telling," the travel leader said finally. "That's your decision and not our problem. We have been sent to the Amber People."

The next day the women continued on their journey. Nia finished working at the forge.

"I've been waiting for this," said Tanajin.

Nia made the gesture of inquiry.

"Ulzai keeps appearing in my dreams. He speaks urgently. I don't understand him. Usually he is wet. That ought to mean he has drowned, but I don't know for certain. What does he want? Why is he bothering me?"

Nia made the gesture of ignorance.

"I am going to make a new raft and float downriver. I'll ask about him in the village of the hairless people. Maybe they have found his body.

"After that I'll keep going. There is a village on the river below the lake. The people there never move. Their houses are wood. They are always in them." Tanajin paused.

"Their gift is a certain kind of very large fish. They smoke it and pickle it. They also preserve the eggs of the fish and the stuff that the male fish produce. Their shamaness is famous for her wisdom. I'm going to ask her to explain my dreams. Maybe I need a ceremony of propitiation."

"That could be," said Nia. "What about the crossing?"

"People can do what they used to do before I came."

"The crossing has been your gift."

"You will continue traveling. That's the kind of person you are. If I stay here alone, I'll go crazy. I'll find a new gift—maybe among the Fish Egg People, maybe farther south."

Nia helped Tanajin build the raft. It took five days. When they were finished she said, "Teach me how to paddle."

"Why?" asked Tanajin.

"I think I'll stay here for a while. When people come, I'll take them across. I'll explain that you have gone, and that I will be leaving soon. The news will get around. People will know to bring axes with them."

Tanajin made the gesture of agreement.

She stayed another fifteen days. They spent most of their waking time on the water. Nia learned how to swing the big heavy paddle and what lay under the surface of the river. There were islands that only appeared in the very worst dry years, but they were always there and the raft might get caught on one. There were logs—more than any person could count. Some floated on top of the water. Others floated underneath. Some had gotten caught in the mud of the river bottom and stood upright like living trees, their branches reaching toward the surface. Others were held less tightly by the mud and swung back and forth in the water.

"Like reeds in the wind," said Tanajin. "Or a tree that is starting to break."

"Aiya!" said Nia.

"Every kind of log is dangerous. If the raft gets caught, you may not be able to get free. Never let a rope trail. Always carry a knife. Always keep an eye on the surface. If there are swirls and eddies—avoid that place!"

"There is more to this than I realized," said Nia.

Tanajin barked. "You people in the north are so ignorant! You think the river is like the plain. You think that everything that matters is on the surface, where any fool can see it."

Nia kept her teeth clenched together. A teacher always had the right to at least a few insults. Everyone knew that. It was true among all peoples.

Finally Tanajin said, "You aren't skillful yet, and you don't know enough about the river, but I think you'll be able to manage. I'll leave you now."

Nia made the gesture of acknowledgment.

The next morning Tanajin piled her belongings on the new raft. Nia helped push the raft out into the river. Tanajin climbed on and made the gesture of farewell.

Nia waved in answer.

The raft floated out. Tanajin began to swing the paddle. Nia watched. The woman grew smaller and smaller. At last she was gone. The raft became a dot on the wide and shining river. Nia shaded her eyes. The raft was gone.

She moved her belongings into the empty tent, but she didn't sleep in it. It smelled of Tanajin, and the walls were braced with pieces of wood. They were too solid. A proper house ought to shift in the wind—not much, but enough so the people inside knew what was happening on the plain.

Every evening she took a blanket out front. She lay down by the fire and looked up. She began to notice things.

One was a light that moved like a moon, but was the wrong color: a silvery white. It followed a new trail, different from any of the old moons. Night after night it crossed above her. She had no idea what it was. Had one of the Two Lost Women come back?

There was a new star, too. It appeared in the same place every evening: at the center of the sky. The other stars moved around it. It did not move at all.

There were other lights: red and white and green. For the most part they were in the south, close to the horizon. They moved rapidly in all directions.

She became uneasy. It was one thing for the hairless people to make a new kind of cloud. There were a lot of different kinds of clouds, and they were always changing. One more kind wasn't likely to cause trouble. But a new star! A new moon! Lights that wandered like bugs! Here! There! Up! Down!

Smoke rose on the far side of the river. She went over. A man waited there. A big fellow with iron-gray fur.

"Who are you?" he asked. "Where is Tanajin?" He spoke with an accent she did not recognize.

387

"She left. I am taking care of the crossing."

"Huh!" the man said.

She took him across the river, along with two bowhorns. He gave her salt in a leather bag. The leather was thin and soft. She did not know what kind of animal it came from. The man did not explain who he was or why he was traveling through the land of the Iron People. Nia decided not to ask.

More days passed. The new moon kept traveling over. The new star remained at the center of the sky. Every few days she saw another one of the long clouds.

The Basket Women returned. Their leader said the Amber People had not been a lot of help. "They are busy performing ceremonies of aversion and propitiation. Something has gone wrong. They wouldn't tell us what, except to say the Trickster was behind it.

"This is a spirit we don't know about, though he sounds a bit like our Bird-faced Woman. A troublemaker! A sneak and liar! Though I have to say we owe a lot to the Bird-faced Woman. She gave us fire and taught us how to weave baskets."

Another woman said, "We shouldn't be too grateful. She convinced the First People that there was nothing wrong with incest. And she let the small black bug of death loose in the world."

The travel leader frowned. "The Amber People kept going on and on about this spirit. This Trickster. They told us the hairless people are not the problem. The Trickster is the problem. He is the one who is making changes in the sky."

"Have the hairless people paid a visit there?" asked Nia. She pointed east.

The travel leader made the gesture that meant "no." "I'm not certain they believed us when we told them about the hairless people and the boat that was able to fly. Maybe they thought we were liars, like the Trickster."

"Aiya!" said Nia. She took them across the river, then went back.

By this time the forest along the river had finished changing color. The trees were orange and yellow. The reeds in the marshes were red. Flocks of birds went overhead like clouds.

Nia began to worry about food. She was running out. Winter was coming. She made fish traps and set them in the river. Then she went into the forest, cut wood, and made a smoking rack. That was the safest way to preserve fish and meat. The smoke would hide the food aroma. The animals in the forest would not come looking for something to eat.

She made traps to set in the forest. Then she made a bow. It was the weak kind that people in the east used. But she did not have the materials to make a bow the right way out of layers of horn, and she wasn't a bow maker.

How could men survive alone? A woman needed an entire village full of people with different kinds of knowledge.

"Well," she told herself. "I know it is possible. I lived on my own before—except for Enshi, and he wasn't all that much help. I can do it again."

She gathered food. Clouds came out of the west, gray and solid-looking. They dropped rain on her. The rain was cold and heavy. Leaves came off the trees. They lay on the ground in the forest and floated past on the river. Red. Yellow. Orange. Pink. Purple.

The flocks of birds became less frequent. The bugs were almost gone.

Day and night she tended the smoking fire. Gray smoke twisted up into the gray sky. No animals came out of the forest to find out if she had anything edible. In this she was lucky. This was the time of year when every kind of thing looked for food—though not with desperation. Desperation would come later with the snow.

One afternoon Nia was in front of the tent, cleaning a groundbird. She cut the belly open and reached in, pulling out the guts. One of her bowhorns whistled: a sign of warning. She looked up. A rider was approaching, coming up the trail along the river. Nia stood up, holding the bloody guts. They were still attached to the bird, and when she stood she lifted the bird off the ground. For a moment it dangled at the end of a rope of guts. Then the rope broke. The bird fell. The rider reined his animal.

He was big and broad through the shoulders. His fur gleamed, even though the sky was dark and gray. His tunic was yellow, covered with embroidery. He wore gold bracelets and a gold fish-pendant that hung from a necklace of amber beads. "I heard the old crossing-woman was gone. The new one looks as if she belongs to the Iron People. She doesn't speak much and tells nothing about herself."

"Who can have told you this, Inzara?"

"The man whose gift is salt." Inzara dismounted. "Why don't you finish what you are doing, then wash your hands?"

He led his animal in back of the tent. She cleaned the bird and washed her hands in the river.

Inzara returned, carrying his saddlebags.

"What are you doing here? Shouldn't you be in the Winter Land, protecting your territory?"

"My brothers will take care of it for me. It doesn't matter this time of year, anyway."

She spitted the bird and set it up over the cooking fire. Inzara crouched down. Aiya! He was big, even resting on his heels.

"It's pretty obvious the world is changing. There is a new star in the sky and a new moon. A while back a young man came out of the village. I stopped him and spoke with him before I sent him on his way. He told me people had come from the far west, carrying their provisions in baskets and bringing a crazy story. Visitors came to them riding on a bird made out of metal. The visitors had no hair. The people from the west wanted advice. But my people were busy. They have been quarreling and performing ceremonies ever since they came to the Ropemaker's island. The guardian of the tower was dead. The tower itself was damaged."

"We did not touch the tower," said Nia.

"Birds or the wind," said Inzara. "In any case, the clans have been accusing one another of bad thoughts and magic. This is what the young man said. I could explain what really happened, but who listens to men about such things?" He paused. "I thought the world is changing, and it is obvious who is behind all the changes. The people without hair, the oracle, and Nia.

"The man who brings the salt came. He told me about the new woman at the river crossing. I thought, that is almost certainly Nia. How many strange women can there be, wandering around the plain?"

"That's good thinking, but why did you bother? I don't think I'm responsible for any of the changes, and if I am, there is nothing I can do about them now."

"Are the hairless people responsible?" asked Inzara.

"Maybe. I think so."

"And you are friends with them."

"Maybe."

"Tell me where you will be in the spring."

Nia looked up, surprised. "Why?"

"You have a lot of luck—more than any woman I've ever heard of. I'm not certain what kind of luck it is. At times it seems more bad than good. But it is certainly powerful, and there is no question about my luck. It is always good.

"If you had a child, and I was the father—or Ara—or Tzoon, think of the luck the child would have! Think of the power!"

Nia felt even more surprised. Her mouth hung open. Her hands stayed where they were, on her thighs.

He went on. "We have talked it over, the three of us. If you are interested, we will draw straws. The one who gets the long straw will go to meet you. This area would be good. There aren't likely to be any other men around. Or women. It's easy to get distracted in the time for mating, and this is something that ought to be done the right way. Carefully."

"No," said Nia.

Inzara made the gesture of inquiry.

"I have done too many strange things already, and I'm getting old. I don't think I want any more children."

"You have children already? Are there any daughters? How old are they?"

Nia made the gesture that meant "stop it" or "shut up."

"Why?" asked Inzara.

"This is crazy. Men don't pick the women they mate with. Men don't care who their children are or what the children are like."

"What do you know about men? What does any woman know? You sit in your villages! You chatter! You gossip! You tell one another what men are like. How can you possibly understand anything about us? Have you ever spent a winter alone on the plain?"

"Yes," said Nia.

He barked, then made the gesture of apology. "I was forgetting who you were." He paused and frowned. Then he spoke again. His voice was deep and even. He didn't sound the least bit crazy. "Tell me where you will be, Nia. Do you really want to mate with whatever man comes along? He might be a little man. He might be old or crazy. Who knows how the child will turn out?"

Nia looked at the bird cooking above the fire. The skin was turning brown. Liquid fat covered it and it shone. She turned the bird, then looked at Inzara. "I told you, I don't want any more children. Also, I am tired of doing things in new and unusual ways. I want to be ordinary for a while."

Inzara made the gesture that meant "that isn't likely to happen."

"Also, I don't like other people making plans for me. I do what I want."

"And you want to be ordinary," said Inzara. He stood up and stretched. Hu! He was enormous! His fur gleamed in the firelight. So did his jewelry. "Will you take me across the river?"

"Why do you want to go?"

"The hairless people have built a village south of here on the Long Lake. I want to see it."

"Why? You won't be able to go into it."

"Will the hairless people drive me out?"

Nia thought for a moment. "No."

"I can endure people. Look at me now. I've been sitting and talking with you, and it isn't the time for mating. If the village looks interesting, maybe I'll go in. Ara wants information. I am the one who gets along with people, so I am the one who came. But he's the one who's curious."

They ate the groundbird. Inzara took a blanket and went around the house. He slept on the ground next to his animal. Nia slept inside. She dreamt about the village of the hairless people. She was in it, wandering among the big round pale houses. Inzara was there, and other people she did not recognize. Some of them were real people, people with fur. Others were like Li-sa and Deragu.

In the morning she took Inzara across the river. "There is no good trail along the river. You will have to go west onto the plain and then south."

He made the gesture that meant he understood.

391

She went back to the house of Tanajin.

More days went by. There was a lot of rain. Leaves fell. The sun moved into the south. When it was visible, it had the pale look of winter. It was growing hungry, the old women used to say, though that made no sense to Nia. The sun was a buckle. Everyone knew that. The Mistress of the Forge had made it and given it to the Spirit of the Sky. He wore it on his belt. How could a buckle grow hungry?

There was no one to answer her question.

A group of travelers came out of the west: Amber Women, returning home. They were quiet and they looked perturbed. Nia did not ask why. She ferried them. They gave her a blanket made of spotted fur and a pot made of tin.

The weather kept getting colder. There was ice in the marshes now. It was thin and delicate, present in the early morning and gone by noon. If she touched it, it broke. Aiya! It was like the drinking cups of the hairless people or their strange square hollow pieces of ice.

The sun moved farther into the south. The sky was low and gray. One morning she heard thunder, but saw nothing.

Another island, she thought. Going up or coming down. How many were in the lake now? Where did they go when they left?

Inzara returned. He built a fire. She went and got him.

"I couldn't do it. I saw their boats and their wagons. I knew my brother would want to know more. But I wasn't able to force myself to go in. Even after the man without hair invited me."

Nia made the gesture of inquiry.

"The one I met before. Deragu. He found me on the bluff above the village. We talked. He said other people—real people—had come and looked at the village, but not come in. Not many. Three or maybe four. He asked me to give you a message."

"Yes?"

"Come to the village for the winter. You gave many gifts to the hairless people, he said, especially to him and Li-sa. They have given you little. This makes them uncomfortable, he said. A wagon will not move in a straight line if the bowhorns that pull it are not properly matched. A bow will not shoot in a straight line if the two arms are not of an equal length."

Nia frowned. "I don't remember that I gave them anything important."

Inzara made the gesture that meant "that may be." "An exchange is not completed until everyone agrees that it is completed. It's hard to say which kind of person causes more trouble—one who refuses to give or one who refuses to take."

Nia said nothing.

Inzara went on. "I mated one year with a woman who did not like taking. It almost drove me crazy. Everything I gave her was 'too much' or 'too lovely' or 'too good' for her. As for her gifts, which were just fine, she said, they were 'small' and 'ugly.' I wanted to hit her. I got away from her as quickly as possible."

Nia grunted.

Inzara said, "I knew the woman's mother. She had eyes like needles and a tongue like a knife. Nothing was ever good enough for her. I think the woman learned to apologize for everything she did. Hu! What an ugly habit!"

They reached the eastern shore of the river. Inzara helped her pull the raft up onto land. He took off his necklace of gold and amber and held it out. Nia thought of saying it was too much to give in exchange for a river crossing. But Inzara looked edgy, and she didn't want to argue with him. She took the necklace.

He mounted his animal and gathered the reins. He looked down at Nia. "I used to think that nothing frightened me except old age. But the village back there frightened me." He waved toward the west and south. "I'm angry with myself and restless. I'd better get going." He tugged on the reins. The animal turned. Inzara glanced back. "Maybe I will come again in the spring. Or maybe Ara will come. The village won't frighten him. And Tzoon is like a rock. Nothing ever bothers him."

He rode off. Nia put the necklace on. It was fine work. The amber was shaped into round beads, and the fish was made of tiny pieces of gold, fastened together. It wiggled like a real fish.

She walked back to camp.

The next day snow fell: large, soft flakes that melted as soon as they touched the ground. She packed her belongings and cleaned the house. She left a bag of dried food hanging from the roof pole. People might come. They might be hungry. She left a cooking pot, a jug for water, and a knife.

After that she took a good look at the bowhorns. Their hooves were healthy. There were no sores on their backs. They walked without favoring any foot or leg. Their eyes were clear. So were their nostrils. She found no evidence of worms or digging bugs.

Nia made the gesture of satisfaction.

Her hands were not entirely empty. She had three animals and food and the metal-working tools, which Tanajin had left. It was more than she had taken from the village of the Copper People. More than she had taken from her own village when she left the first time or the second time or the third.

The next day she crossed the river. She had to make two trips. The first one was easy. The air was still. The sky was low and gray, but nothing came out of it. She took two of the bowhorns and tied them on the western shore, then went back.

She loaded the rest of her belongings and led the third bowhorn onto the raft. It snorted and stamped a foot.

"Be patient! Be easy! The others gave me no trouble."

She pushed off. Snow began to fall. The flakes were big and soft. They drifted down slowly. By the time she reached the first island the eastern shore was gone, hidden by whiteness. She crossed the island and loaded everything onto the second raft.

The snow was staying this time, sticking to bare branches, sticking to the gear the bowhorn carried: the bags and blankets. There was snow on Nia's shoulders and snow on the rough bark of the logs that made up the raft. All around her flakes of snow touched the gray surface of the river and vanished.

Aiya! The whiteness! It hid the island she had just left, and she could not see the island that was her destination. Nia swung the paddle and grunted.

They landed at the far southern end of the island. Nia pulled the raft up on land, then looked at it. She ought to bring it upriver to the proper landing place. But that would take time, and the storm was getting worse.

"Let others deal with this problem," she said.

She led her animal across the island to the final raft.

That crossing was easier. The channel was narrow. But the snow kept getting thicker. It covered the raft and the bowhorn and Nia. Even the paddle was covered with snow. When she lifted it and swung it, pieces of snow fell off. They made noises when they hit the water.

A poem came to Nia. She didn't know if she'd learned it as a child or made it up right here in the middle of the river.

> Why do you come,
> oh, why do you come now,
> O people of the snow?
>
> People in white shoes,
> why do you bother me?

She reached the western shore and led the bowhorn off, praising it for good manners. It snorted and flicked its ears.

"I know. I know. You wanted to make trouble. But you held yourself in check. That's worth praising. It's over now." She looked at the river: the gray water and the falling snow. "We'll pull the raft up onto land, and then we will go and find your companions. And in the morning we'll go south."

Appendix A:
A Note on Pronunciation

I was raised on the Wade-Giles system of transliterating Chinese, but have
converted to Pinyin in this novel.

Lixia is pronounced *Lee-sha*.

Yunqi is pronounced *Yoon-chee*.

The word *zi*, which means "sage," is pronounced *zee*.

Zhuang Zi (*Chuang-tzu* in the old system) is pronounced *Juang-zee*.

The rest of the Chinese names are pronounced approximately the way they look.

The native *i*, like the Pinyin *i*, is long.

The native *a* is usually pronounced *ah* as in *father*.

Nia is pronounced *Nee-ah*.

In is pronounced *inn*.

Ar is pronounced as in *car* and *far*.

Inzara is pronounced *Innzarah*.

Ai is pronounced as in *hay*.

U is pronounced *oo*.

Nahusai is pronounced *Nahoosay*.

E is usually the vowel sound in *air* or *care*.

Gersu is pronounced *Gairsoo*.

O is the sound in *Oh* and *Oklahoma*.

Yohai is pronounced *Yohay*.

395

The sound spelled *kh* in the language of the Copper People is pronounced like the *ch* in *Bach*.

The natives all speak the language of gifts, but their pronunciation varies.

Nia can say *g* but not *k*. This is why her version of Derek's name is *Deragu*. There is no *sh* in her language. *Lixia* becomes *Li-sa*. The oracle can say *k* and *sh*, but not *p*. The native animal that Nia calls *osupa* is *osuba* to him.

All the native languages are accented. Usually the accent falls on the first syllable.

There are three native gestures that could be translated as "yes."

One is the gesture of affirmation, which means "yes, that is so."

Another is the gesture of agreement, which means "yes, I agree with you."

The third is the gesture of assent, which means "yes, that should, can, or will be done."

396

Appendix B:

Starship Design by Albert W. Kuhfeld, Ph.D.

For a reaction drive to push a ship near light-speed, the reaction mass itself must travel at relativistic velocities in a jet so hot no material substance can withstand it. Only a force field can handle the job.

Magnetic fields are the best-trained force fields we know: They're used in laboratories everywhere to control the paths of charged particles. Nuclear fusion is nature's way of making hot ions. A magnetic-mirror fusion reactor, with a leaky mirror to the aft, would create a rocketlike nuclear exhaust.

The reaction $Li^7 + H^1 = 2 He^4$ releases 17.3 MeV, with no neutral particles to carry off energy in random and uncontrollable directions. It's one of the more enthusiastic reactions of starbirth—any technology with fusion power should be able to handle it.[1]

Lithium hydride has a specific gravity of 0.78 and a melting point of 689 Celsius. Living quarters built inside a large chunk of this solid fuel are protected by sheer mass against most of the interstellar dust and gases. Hydrogen atoms make good shielding against neutrons, while magnetic fields steer away interstellar ions.

17.3 MeV_e, evenly divided between the two product nuclei, works out to about 22% of the speed of light. The (nonrelativistic) equation for ship velocity is $m \, dV + v_e \, dm = 0$, which integrates out to $V = v_e \ln(m_o/m)$.

[1] Harwit, Martin, *Astrophysical Concepts* (New York: John Wiley & Sons, 1973) pp. 335–43.

To reach 10% of light-speed, the ship would have to burn 37% of its mass; for 20% c, 61% of the mass. If you then slow back to zero, you will burn 61% and 85% of the mass respectively. 15% of light-speed would be a reasonable compromise. At 100% efficiency, accelerating to 15% of light-speed and then decelerating to rest, the ship would arrive with 25% of its starting mass, having used 75% as fuel and reaction mass. (Errors introduced by ignoring relativity are minor compared to those caused by assuming complete efficiency. Time dilation effects are only about 1%.) It takes less than two months at one gravity to reach 15% of light-speed. Even at a fraction of a g, the majority of the trip could be spent coasting.

(The rocket exhaust is powerful alpha radiation. This is an ideal vehicle for leaving your enemies behind, but be careful where you point the thing if you hope for a welcome upon your return.)

A ship traveling the 18.2 light-years to Sigma Draconis at 0.15 c would take 122 years, one way. It has to refuel (hope for a planet with a water ocean to supply lithium and hydrogen!) before returning. The round trip could barely be made in 250 years; with study time, more would be probable.

Most of the ship is fuel, a giant lithium-hydride cigar—white when pure, but who knows what impurities will creep in (or be found useful)? The long axis points in the direction of travel, to minimize cross-section and put as much mass as possible between the crew and anything they collide with. (At 0.15 c, cosmic gases become low-energy cosmic rays: grains of dust make large craters where they hit.)

Well ahead of the cigar is a repairable "umbrella" shield—very little mass, but enough to vaporize cosmic dust, spreading it out so it'll cause less damage to the main body of the ship. The living quarters are inside the "cigar," protected from the hazards of travel. Spiral tunnels wind forward and aft to the end caps; since radiation travels in straight lines, a spiral tunnel blocks it effectively.

A fusion rocket is behind the cigar, built of magnetic fields controlled and confined by superconducting magnets. There are many magnetic mirrors in series, so a particle leaking through one mirror finds itself confined in the next chamber. The fields move the ionized gases along in a manner similar to peristalsis with regions of high and low magnetic field sweeping aft. Ionized particles are held in the regions of low magnetic field by the stronger fields before and behind, compressed to greater and greater densities until they fuse. At this point the magnetic fields to the rear open up into a rocket nozzle of forces.

The rear-end cap slowly chews its way up the length of the ship, feeding fuel into the engine. The amount of lithium hydride before and behind the living quarters is chosen so the engine uses most of the rear fuel accelerating: then, as the ship nears its destination, the end caps are released and the ship reversed so the forward section (now needed more for fuel than shielding) docks into the engine. The umbrella shield is discarded as excess mass, and will be rebuilt during refueling.

Deceleration poses an interesting problem, since one can hardly put an umbrella shield behind the main engine. But the hot breath of an engine like this should sizzle nearly everything within a light-day of the nozzle into ionic vapors—and the engine's magnetic fields protect the ship from ions. An arriving ship appears as an enormous dim comet, with tail pointing along its path rather than away from the sun—and like comets of old, it can be an omen of change.

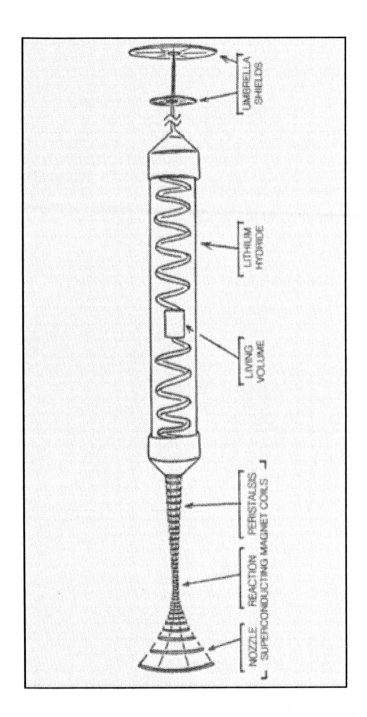

UMBRELLA SHIELDS

LITHIUM HYDRIDE

LIVING VOLUME

PERISTALSIS

REACTION

SUPERCONDUCTING MAGNET COILS

NOZZLE

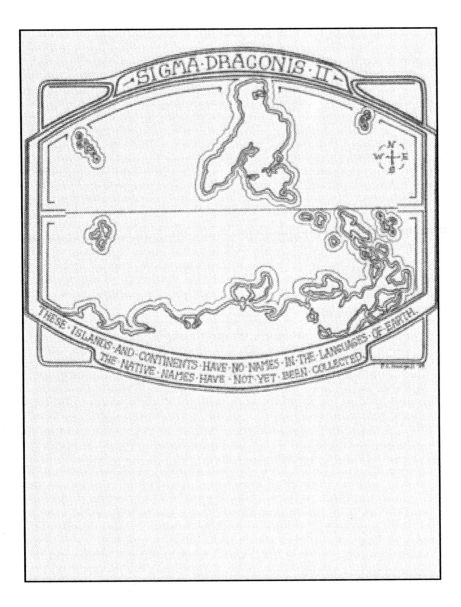

SIGMA·DRAGONIS·II

THESE·ISLANDS·AND·CONTINENTS·HAVE·NO·NAMES·IN·THE·LANGUAGES·OF·EARTH
THE·NATIVE·NAMES·HAVE·NOT·YET·BEEN·COLLECTED

About the Author

ELEANOR ARNASON is the author of five published novels and a number of poems and short stories. She has received the James Tiptree, Jr. award for "gender-bending SF," and the Mythopoeic Society's Fantasy Award for A Woman of the Iron People. She has also received the Minnesota Book Award for Ring of Swords. Her earlier novels include The Sword Smith, To the Resurrection Station, and Daughter of the Bear King. Her short stories include "The Warlord of Saturn," "The Lovers" (a preliminary nominee for awards in 1996), "Ace 167," "The Hound of Merin," and many others which have appeared in Orbit, New Improved Sun, Tales of the Unanticipated, Xanadu, A Room of One's Own, New Women of Wonder and The Norton Book of SF.

Printed in the United States
20111LVS00002B/375